THE
CHILDREN OF LYR
Book II

SISTER OF THE STARS

LINA C. AMAREGO

This book is a work of fiction. Names, characters, businesses, organizations, places, events, and incidents either are the product of the author's imagination or are used fictitiously. Any resemblance to actual persons, living or dead, events, or locales is entirely coincidental.

For information contact: LCamarego@gmail.com

Cover Design by COVERDUNGEONRABBIT

ISBN: 978-1-7348265-4-8

First Edition: APRIL 2021

CONTENT WARNING:
This book contains mature themes, including brief moments of violence, torture, suicidal ideation and actions, infanticide, and sexual content. This book is not suitable for readers under the age of 14. Reader discretion is advised.

Lina C. Amarego

Sister

of the

Stars

⚛

LINA C. AMAREGO

⚛

BOOK II
OF
THE CHILDREN OF LYR

SILVER WHEEL PRESS

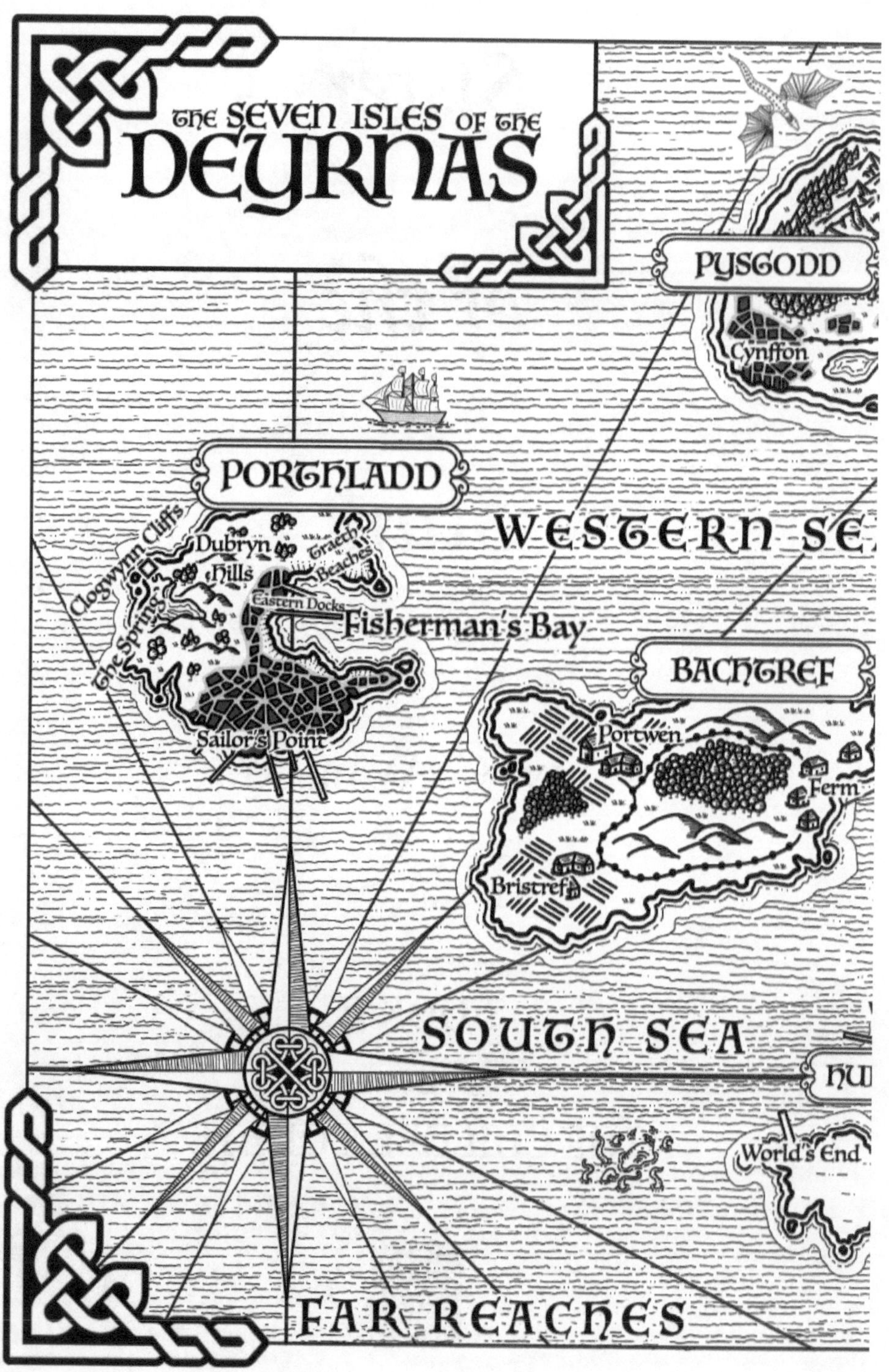

THE SEVEN ISLES OF THE
DEYRNAS
PYSGODD
Cynffon
PORTHLADD
WESTERN SE
Dubryn
Hills
Graeth
Beaches
Clogwynn Cliffs
Eastern Docks
Fisherman's Bay
The Spring
BACHTREF
Sailor's Point
Portwen
Ferm
Bristref
SOUTH SEA
HU
World's End
FAR REACHES

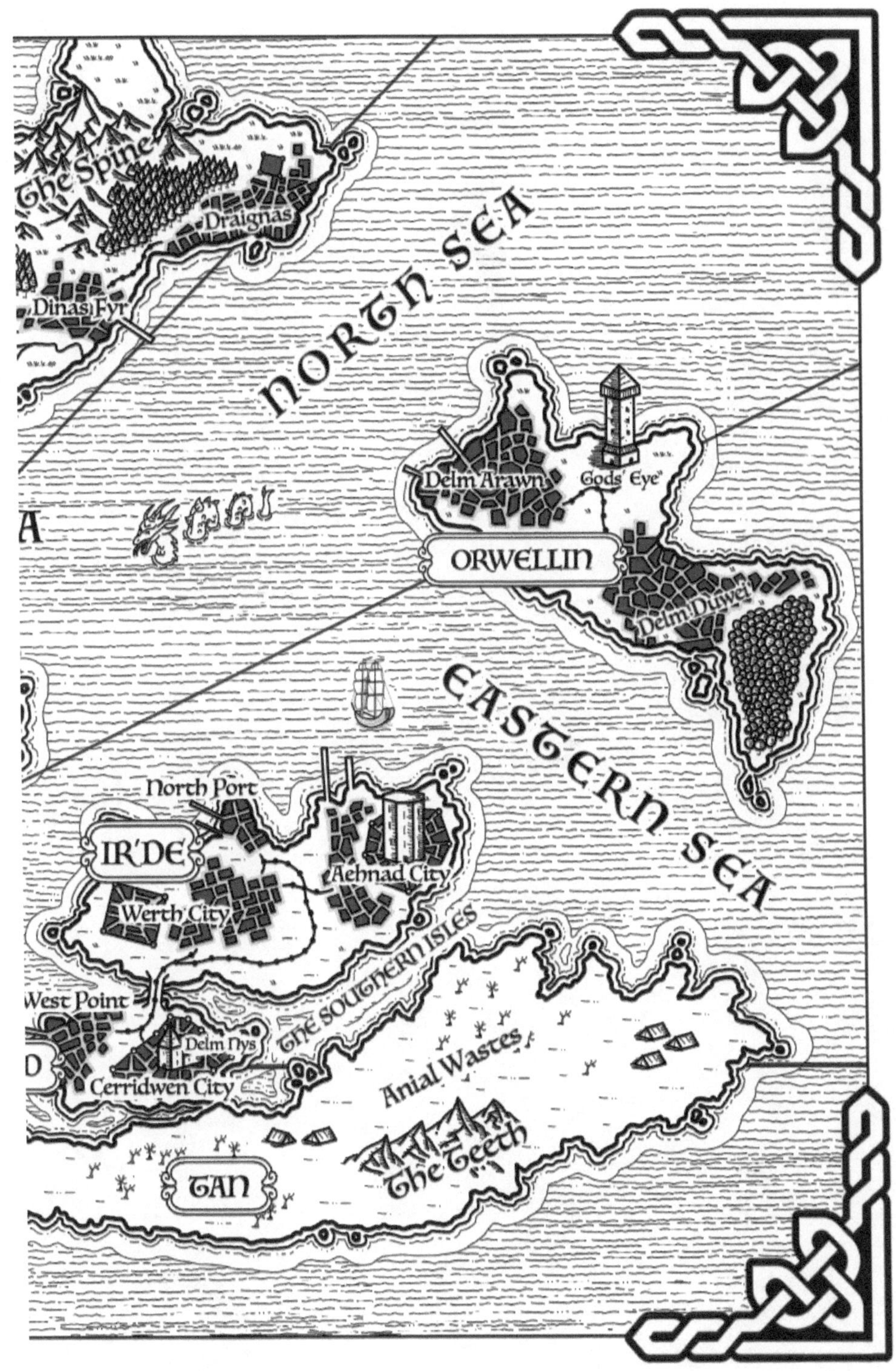
The Spine
Draignas
Dinas Fyr
NORTH SEA
Delm Arawn
Gods' Eye
ORWELLIN
Delm Duvel
A
EASTERN SEA
North Port
IR'DE
Aehnad City
Werth City
West Point
THE SOUTHERN ISLES
Delm Nys
Cerridwen City
Anial Wastes
TAN
The Teeth
D

To Jenny,

For reminding me that having a sister means never fighting the darkness alone.

And for those still fighting in need of a sisterhood.

PART

I

Curses and Cures

KEIRA

Death had a *smell.*

Not the smell of decomposition and rotting flesh, as I'd expected; instead, it smelled of fear and regret. Of opportunities missed and moments lost. Of the hateful words I couldn't take back and the ones left unsaid.

In the sweat-soaked nightmares that pulled me from rest every night, death smelled like citrus and metal as my husband bled out before me again and again. It smelled like cedar wood and burnt lavender, the memory of Aidan's funeral pyre. Death smelled like the wretched, festering black spot on my shoulder, a reminder of not only the souls I'd sent to the Dark God, but the promise that if I did not find an answer, I would soon be his, too.

I was drenched in the scent from dawn to dusk, its haunting odor inescapable no matter how I tried to rid myself of it.

It had been two months since my uncle died. Two months of banishment from the only home I'd ever known. Two months at sea, my only respite the warm taverns of whatever island we haunted. Two months of restless nights in dusty inns, of nightmares that had me screaming loud enough to wake up everyone on my floor. Two months of scouring half the Deyrnas for Weylin or any hint of something that could clear the spot on my shoulder and the darkness that made a home in my soul.

"I have a good feeling about this one, Keira." Ronan pressed a kiss into my hair, the setting sun haloing his in gold as we walked side-by-side through Hud's stone-laid streets. Wafts of poultices and potions assaulted my nostrils from the open windows of several sandstone shops, each busy with customers.

I doubted the one we sought would be so inviting.

"Ronan, we can't get our hopes up," I mumbled, but the knot in my stomach betrayed me. I *had* gotten my hopes up, despite the many times they were dashed.

Even though it was near night, the air was still uncomfortably warm, sticking to my sweat-licked skin. Two months in the heat of the South, and I still wasn't adapting. We'd spent the last month turning Ir'de upside down. There was nothing that money couldn't buy in the land of a thousand scents and silks, and our hearts were full of hope, blanketed in the extravagance. But the scent of death followed me through the winding streets despite the pungent spices in the air, each day growing stronger. And despite the island's abundant namesake, there were no answers in the marketplace, only dark glares and unfriendly responses.

They all said the same thing as they gazed on the growing black spot on my shoulder, fear spreading across their features like wildfire: Go home and take your filthy curse with you, *melthith*."

Melthith. Cursed one. The title weighed like shackles as my crew and I were turned away again and again, until Ir'de sent us back to the sea once more.

Ronan was quiet as we found the clinic we were looking for, the last building in this particular row. The outside needed upkeep even more than the shack back at the spring. Long arms of ivy clung to its side, masking the tan of the sandstone in deep greens. I supposed my face turned a similar color as we approached, the nerves in my gut rising to my throat. "This is it?"

"Aye." Ronan's voice was tighter than a sail in a windstorm. "Griffin's source was right. It's a dump, but perhaps that's exactly what we need."

I raised my hand to knock, swallowing down the lump of fear. I was Keira Mathonwy, Captain of the *Ceffyl Dwr*. I did not falter or yield.

A phantom pang in my shoulder warned me otherwise.

Before I could bring my fist to kiss the door, it swung open. A woman who could've been Esme's age stood in front of it, beady green eyes staring up at me from wrinkled sockets. A knife twisted in my gut as I remembered my fallen friend, another death that followed me wherever I went. I shook off the memory, focusing on all the ways this old woman was different. She wore a simple grey smock, painted with stains in every color, but the way her mouth quirked up made me shudder in my boots. The magick of the island armored this woman's very bones, ancient and angry as the sea itself.

"Can I help you?" Her voice sounded like ash and smoke, her Huddian accent thick with age.

Ronan laced his fingers through mine, his confidence seeping into my skin and awakening mine. "We were sent by a man named Jesper Vicaries." His other hand shook, so he stuffed it in his pocket. We didn't know how secure a source Griffin's newest gambling buddy was, but we'd prayed to Lyr all the same. The woman did not answer, but her brow furrowed in recognition as Ronan added, "He said you were the finest healer in Hud once...and the one most willing to take a risk."

The woman's emerald gaze narrowed on me as if she could smell the death scent too. "Come in, then, and be quick about it."

Another wave slammed through my gut as I crossed the threshold. The inside, much unlike the exterior, teemed with life. Plants of every variety dangled from baskets while sprigs of herbs dried from the rafters, the collection second only to the foliage of *Hiraeth* itself. On the shelves and counters were vials and pots filled with tinctures and mixtures like nothing I'd ever seen before, the entire room a testament to the work and dedication of the old crow. I inhaled deeply, the cacophony of smells almost enough to overpower the death scent, and spared a thought for those at home, for Vala and Reina who waited there. I imagined their eyes growing wide as they drank in the greenery, and the waves in my stomach ceased. For them, I could take whatever this woman had in store for me; for them, and for the rest of my family back on the ship, I could look death in the mouth and smile at it.

The old woman coughed, drawing me from my trance. "What risk are we talking about tonight, travelers?"

Ronan opened his mouth to answer, but I held up a hand to stop him. There were no words for this other than the odious title I'd been given. Instead of speaking it aloud, I unfastened my laces and lowered the collar of my deep blue tunic, allowing the full gore of my shoulder to blacken the room. The mark had spread—once a single spot just beneath my collarbone, now a splotch the size of a grown man's hand with spidery fingers reaching down my veins toward my bicep. I kept my expression tame, but even I was loath to look at it. "What do you have that can treat this?"

The woman's answering hiss knocked the wind from my sails again. When she looked away from the mark and back to me, her eyes were almost as black as the spot itself. "I take it you know what it is you are asking?"

I nodded once, my stomach turning to stone. Another dead end.

"Can you do anything for it?" Ronan's voice laced with worry as he gazed at the spot, the color blanching from his cheeks in perfect contrast.

"You know as well as I do, boy, this is not something one can heal." The woman chewed on her wrinkled lip. "You need someone who knows the ancient ways...or a miracle."

Ronan scoffed, denial scrunching his nose. "Doesn't half of Hud practice the old ways?"

The woman crossed her arms. "There is old, and then there is ancient." She pointed to my spot again, rigid with fear. "This is a *god's* spot. And no matter what any of the crackpots on this island might say to make a coin, only a handful of people in the world know the ways of the gods."

The shred of hope tore from my chest, but Ronan's Mathonwy mask slipped into place. "Mr. Vicaries said you might be that person exactly."

She shrugged and busied herself with watering a nearby fern, but I didn't miss the lie in the corner of her eye. "Jesper is an old barfly with loose lips and a wild imagination. You know how people talk. I am a simple healer, nothing more."

Papa always said nothing worth having came free. Our coffers were limited, our shredded trade agreements with Porthladd devastating most of our savings. But with some smuggling and Griffin's occasional gambling win, we'd saved a small purse for moments like this. I could smell the woman's power—and her greed—as clearly as the death scent. Emboldened, I plopped myself into the only chair in the room and exhaled. "He said you would say that." I nearly knocked over half a dozen of her precious plants as I placed my boots on the worktable and pulled the delicate coin purse from my pocket. I dangled it in front of her like a carrot in front of a horse, and her dark eyes sparkled. "He also said you might need something *extra* to remind you."

She swallowed hard, her eyes darting back and forth between the coin purse and my rancid shoulder. After a moment, she pinched the bridge of her nose. "I may have a vague idea of what you are talking about."

Ronan exhaled a breath of relief. The last morsel of hope rooted itself once more as I scowled at the woman. "So, what can I do about this?"

"There is nothing that can get rid of a *melthith*, not anymore. I knew a healer a long time ago who might have had the power, but she's been gone for half a century." The woman shoved my boots off the table and shot me a glare, but she came closer, studying the spot with needle-point scrutiny. "The only way to *clear* that spot is to pay the Dark God the soul he is owed."

I tried not to let the anchor that slammed through my gut show on my face as I tucked the coin purse back into my pocket. "This is a waste of our time, Ronan, let's go."

"Wait..." The woman grabbed my unaffected shoulder with surprising strength, anchoring me to the chair. "I can't get rid of it, but I know of ways to stop it from spreading."

Something unknotted within me. We needed answers, and yet again, there were none. But if there was anything to slow this process, to buy me time, I'd take it, if only to smooth the permanent wrinkles in my husband's worried brow. I'd pay prettily for it, too.

Ronan ran a hand through his hair, but his shoulders relaxed ever-so-slightly. "You should've led with that, woman. Whatever it is, tell us. We'll do it."

Evergreen eyes rolled with disdain. "You may call me Madame Hedd, not *woman*. And don't be so eager. You will not like what I have to say."

Rage bubbled beneath my skin. I came here for answers, not for tricks and riddles, and I was already short on time and coin. My hand flew instinctively to the dagger on my hip. "Spit it out, then, *Madame Hedd*."

She didn't flinch at my dagger, her gaze flitting instead to the pocket that held the purse. "Hand over the crowns, this information is not free."

I tossed her the bag, imagining Griffin's wince when he found out I wasted his precious winnings. She caught it with ease, snatching it from the air with more excitement than I thought possible from a woman of her age. The action reminded me again of Esme, the memory of her gunpowder-and-thunderstorm scent strong enough to bring tears to my eyes, but I would not open that basket of fish, not here. I focused instead on the sheen of greed in the woman's gaze as she weighed the bag in her hand.

Finally satisfied, she tucked it into her apron and looked back to me, appraising me with the same scrutiny as she had the bag. "The curse drains life force. You seem strong, it's not surprising you've lasted this long. But it will consume you too, eventually. Unless…"

"Unless?" Ronan prompted. I glanced up at the dark circles that were now permanent residents under his eyes. His patience had been wearing thin the last few days, and his skin paled in echo of it. We didn't have much time left until he'd need the spring again.

"Unless you give the curse another life force to drain." The woman carried on, grabbing a handful of leaves from what looked to be a peppermint plant and stuffing them into a vial of blue liquid. But before her next words, she stopped her fussing, eyeing my midsection with a sharp glint of mischief in her expression. "As a woman, you are lucky. There's a straightforward method for that."

A stone dropped through me at the repugnant insinuation spoken without weight. The echo of a cool voice brushed the back of my neck as if Connor Yorath himself was there to whisper in my ear. *A child, Ms. Mathonwy.*

"No." I swallowed the taste of bile on my tongue, grabbed Ronan's blue coat sleeve and dragged him toward the door, not waiting for his protest. "We're leaving."

"The man who owned the silver pistol." The woman's misty voice halted me before I could reach the threshold. I shot her a glare darker than my spot at the mention of the very pistol that put it there—Weylin's gun. My uncle had been in the wind since Aidan's death, not even showing his face for the funeral. My family assumed he was on one of his drunken benders, or that he had finally pissed off the wrong person at the wrong bar and gotten himself killed, but I had a hunch it had something to do with why Aidan wielded his most prized weapon that night at the docks.

With the mention of him still hanging between us, Madame Hedd studied me, catching how the hairs on my neck stood straight. A crooked smile crossed her features. "He is still missing, yes? I could help you track him."

A strange tingle travelled down my arm. Would Weylin have answers for us as the true master of the pistol? Or would finding him only bring on the troubles he was so intent on hiding from?

My words were bullets. "He is not our friend, and I don't want anything from you."

Madame Hedd patted the pocket of her apron where my precious coin rested. "Fine. Don't let me help you, I still got paid." She shrugged and tossed the vial of peppermint and blue liquid to Ronan. "But at least take this. For the fatigue and nausea."

"I'm not nauseous," I hissed, snatching the vial from Ronan.

She tore it right back from me, plopping it firmly in Ronan's hand again. "Not for you. For the walking corpse here."

Fire coated my veins as rage shot through me. "Go rot." I stormed from the greenhouse and into the equally warm night, the thick air closing around me as I struggled to breathe. My hands found my knees as the world spun. The death scent was thick in my nose again, burning me from the inside out. Everything was hot, my clothes sticking to my skin like a burial shroud.

There was no way out of this curse. Either I died, or something—no, *someone* else—did. And my husband was running out of time while I chased this fairytale. Had he been nauseous? Had I missed the signs? The pale skin, the bags under his eyes…

No, I hadn't missed them. I ignored them. Pretended it didn't mean anything, that it was just stress and exhaustion haunting his gaze.

For the walking corpse.

"Keira, wait." Ronan's hand on my back anchored me to my body. I turned to him, to the greying skin spread thinly across his high cheekbones, the eyes that lacked their usual sparkle. This was my fault, and still Ronan was concerned for me, when it should've been the other way around. His voice tightened, worry thick in his tone. "She was the last on the list. If she can help, we have to consider the option."

A wave of nausea rolled through me. Perhaps I needed the blue vial after all. "Did you hear what she was suggesting?" My voice quivered, just as weak and useless as I felt. "Ronan, a life force..."

A child, Mrs. Mathonwy. Connor's words were as clear in my head as Lyr's once were. But I hadn't heard the sea god's sage advice or sarcastic comments in months. He had abandoned me to the Dark God and whatever fate waited for me.

I would not let an innocent creature bear the burden instead.

Ronan must have read my thoughts on my face. He paled further. "I would never suggest that. But Lyr below, there has to be *something*. Maybe you can drain a different kind of life force, like an animal or plant."

I held up a hand to stop him. I knew in my soul there was no hope. But no matter what happened to me, I had to make sure my husband and my crew were safe, that this mark did not sink them when it took me. "There will be something." The smile I painted on my face was a lie, but my words felt true. "But not this. I'm not going to blacken my soul to save it."

The muscles in his jaw flickered as he saw right through my brave face. "Aye, Captain."

I wiped the sweat from the back of my neck, straightening my spine. "Don't you *'Aye, Captain'* me. You know I'm right." There was a flicker of my former authority in my voice, enough to almost convince myself. I grabbed my husband's hand, the coolness of his palm a respite against the southern heat. "I love you, Ronan."

A faint blush rose to his cheeks, fighting the edges of the shadows that rested there. "I love you too, Mrs. Mathonwy." He tucked me into his side, leading me down the road toward the northern docks. "Come on, we left Griffin in charge. If we don't get back soon, there won't be a ship left."

"Well, look what the Dark God dragged in." Griffin greeted us from his hammock on the main deck as we boarded the Ceffyl. He rolled from it, his ginger hair pointing in every direction, and stretched his limbs like he'd been sleeping most of the afternoon. So much for leaving him in charge. I scowled at him, but it only made him smile. "Still cursed?"

"Still a prick?" My eldest living male cousin was more like my brother or my best friend, but with a word and a wink, he knew exactly how to rile me. "Lyr below, I left you in charge."

I didn't see Rhett until he rolled from the hammock a moment later, blush coloring his cheeks. The two had grown inseparable during our time away, so I was less surprised than I was annoyed that they'd both been slacking. Rhett offered an apologetic smile and nudged Griffin's side. "Sorry, Keira, Griffin's affliction is incurable. If he doesn't cause some sort of mischief every ten minutes, he'll drop dead."

Forgetting his audience, Griffin smacked Rhett's ass with a gut-churning *thwack*, a low growl escaping his throat. "Watch it, Blondie, or I'll afflict *you*."

"Lyr below, get a room. You two make me sick." Saeth voiced my thoughts exactly as she climbed down from the crow's nest. I said a silent prayer of gratitude for my razor-edged cousin. At least *one* of them was working. She dropped down to the deck with ease, a budding sailor now. She'd recently chopped her copper hair, the sharp cut following the even sharper line of her jaw. In the last months, she'd become one of the crew's most valuable assets, and it struck me how well she *looked* the part now. The memory of a silk-wrapped little girl running down a dock in her corset and heels filled my chest with pride. She had chosen this fate that day, and a part of me knew she'd never look back.

Another part of me knew she'd be the one to keep it all together if I failed to find an answer.

"Any luck, Captain?" She watched me with her hawk eyes, expectant and hopeful. Shame washed over me, the air too hot again, even with the sea breeze playing with my long braid.

"We're still exploring options." Ronan squeezed my hand, the simple gesture threatening to break me.

"That's a no." Saeth voiced my thoughts again, and to her credit, she did not let her shoulders slump like mine did.

"Aye, that's a no." I lifted my chin, my only defense against the growing pool of worry in my core.

"We'll find something." Stony resolve replaced the mischief in Griffin's expression. He folded his arms and jerked his chin to where his twin swords rested against the mizzenmast. "Truth knows. You'll be just fine."

I wished that alone was enough to soothe the rawness in my nerves.

"Where's Reagan?" I scanned the deck for her, not ready to tell the little dragon the bad news.

Rhett winced. "Terrorizing Tarran, trying to get him to teach her to shoot."

"Unacceptable." Ronan ran a hand through his hair. "That little girl will turn me grey before I'm thirty, Lyr willing I live that rutting long."

On cue, Reagan sauntered up the steps from below deck, nearly as graceful as her mother now. The two months at sea had done her as well as Saeth. Her deep purple tunic and tightly cinched sword belt hugged the faint outline of muscle along her form, her newfound womanliness only accentuating it further. But behind her eyes, the familiar dragon's fire still burned, fierce as ever. She directed the blast toward Ronan. "Stop calling me a little girl, I'm thirteen now." She narrowed her chestnut eyes and flipped her braid over her shoulder to emphasize her point. "I'm old enough to learn."

Tarran shuffled up the steps behind her, his usually sunny disposition dark, as if he'd just been punched in the gut. Knowing Reagan, she probably did just that.

"Do you prefer little demon, then?" I raised an eyebrow at my kindred spirit in a mixture of admonishment and approval. She winked back at me, and I couldn't help the shadow of a laugh that warmed my chest. "Tarran, you look worse for wear."

"I didn't teach her, I promise," my cousin sighed, plopping down on a crate, his entire frame sinking. A glimmer of hope breathed life back into his deflated chest as he eyed the blue vial strapped to Ronan's belt. "Any news?"

Another knife twisted in my chest, but Griffin saved me from answering again. "She found a cure, but she's going to need your liver, Tarran." He clasped the freckled boy's shoulders with put-on gentleness. "Sorry, buddy."

"What?" Tarran's eyes widened as he turned to me, panic clear on his sun-kissed face. "That's—"

Saeth's shrill laughter interrupted her twin before he could perjure himself any further. "Don't tease him, Griffin, you'll kill the last three thoughts he has swimming in the scummy pond he calls his head."

Tarran shot her a surly look. "Shut up, Saeth, go write another letter to your fleabag."

"You know what? I will."

Their banter and the responding laughter from the rest of my crew, *my family*, was almost enough to make me whole again. Maybe there would be a way. Maybe this wasn't the last option. Lyr below, stranger miracles had happened. If someone told me a year ago that I'd be banished on a ship full of Mathonwys and Branwens after sailing to a mythical lost island and then fighting my uncle to the death, I'd have slapped them.

No, this wasn't the end. I would find a way, no matter what it took. And in the meantime, my family was looking to me to lead them. I was a Captain. It was about damned time I started acting like one.

I straightened my sleeves. "What news from Ellian?"

Saeth snapped her attention back to me at the mention of her favorite topic, abandoning her brutal assault on Tarran like an old sock. "Aye, I just picked up the letter in town. Seems Connor has appointed the new councilman." She produced said letter from her tunic, and I didn't miss the twitch of her lip as she reread the contents. "Greyson Leary is his name."

I scoured my memory for any details of the man. "I know the name. Son of a smaller shipping family...I think he sails the *Madyn*."

"Aye, that's the one. She's a pretty ship," Ronan offered, settling onto the crate next to Tarran.

"He cheats at cards, too." Griffin sank back into his hammock with a pout.

All that aside, I didn't know enough about the man to make a decision on him one way or another. But one thing was clear: if Connor was appointing him, then he was not on our side.

Saeth folded the letter with care before tucking it back into its place, throat bobbing. When her eyes met mine, there was something dark and dangerous in them. "Keira, Porthladd is getting restless. Connor is still pulling strings, passing tariffs and sanctions left and right. Ellian's getting worried, and frankly, so am I."

I sighed, pinching the bridge of my nose. My banishment had cost me more dearly than I expected, but I hadn't thought about what it cost the people I left behind. I couldn't set foot on Porthladdian soil, but my crew could. The people there needed them more than I did right now. And if Connor Yorath tried to sink me for it, I'd drag him down with me.

"I think it's time to go back anyway." I squared my shoulders. "It's been a month, and Ronan is starting to look sickly."

My husband rolled his eyes, his brave mask perfectly in place. "I'm fine, Keira, I'm more worried about you."

"I know, but you should check in with the aunts, see how all of Connor's shit is affecting them. And at least we know how to make *you* feel better." I stroked his cheek, admiring his fine blond stubble. "I won't risk us both."

Ronan tucked an errant strand of hair behind my ear, letting his mask slip just for me. Fear rested there, but so did hope—and love, brighter than ever, despite the darkness that hunted us. "To Porthladd, then?"

I smiled at my husband, hope stirring in my core again. "Aye, my love. To Porthladd."

Porthladd's form stretched across the horizon was enough to bring me to my knees. The sun was high, noontide lapping her edges with gentle kisses, the late fall air giving me a proper use for my coat for the first time in two months. We were anchored half a league from the shore, as per the terms of my banishment, but I could still make out little details from my perch on the bow. The green and white of *Dubryn* Hill. The yellow sand of the *Traeth* beaches. Smoke and steam rising from chimneys in the town square.

I missed it all terribly.

Ronan stood behind me, tentative. This was not our first trip back. We had made a stop after our first month at sea to bring what limited supplies we were allowed to carry to Reina, while Ronan took a soak in the spring. Last time, I stowed myself below deck for the duration of the visit. I hadn't wanted to see it, to be tempted by the quaint charm and the easy waters. Like a coward, I hid from it, unable to face the reality. Today, I needed whatever little morsel of my past I could get.

Ronan wrapped his arms around me, nuzzling his face into the crook of my neck. "How does it feel to be home?"

I tore my eyes off the shoreline, shifting in his grasp so I faced him instead. "You're my home."

"It'll be a short bath, I promise." He kissed my cheek, lips cold. I hoped it was the weather, not his affliction, that chilled him.

I slid my arms around his broad back so he couldn't see my worry. "No, take your time. You need it."

"I love you, Keira girl," he whispered into my hair, the only words that could truly make me feel at home.

I'd never miss an opportunity to say them back. Never again. "I love you more, Ronan."

Boots on wood and a chuckle broke us apart. "And I love you both the most." Griffin was already dressed and armed. His Branwen blue coat, sleeves still missing, covered a deep red tunic I could only assume was Rhett's, intended to give his poor father a heart attack. His swords, Truth and Triumph, sat at their proper place on his back, completing the look. "Let's go, pretty boy, my Ma's berry bread is waiting."

A wistful wind tugged at my heartstrings, but I covered it with a scowl as I smacked my cousin's arm. "Save some for me, you cad."

"Captain, which sword do you think will make Vala cry harder?" Saeth said by way of hello, admiring two of my favorite blades, balancing them in her delicate hands.

I rubbed my temples. I was happy to miss whatever trouble she was planning. "Leave the swords, Saeth."

She quirked her head to the side, just as she did whenever the details of a bad idea were falling into place. "You're right, I'll spend the day at Ellian's and avoid home altogether."

Ronan laughed, and I nudged his side. Poor Ellian was in for a rough night.

The rest of the crew said their goodbyes with little fanfare, Reagan especially excited to see her mama. I kept a brave face as I waved off the longboat, until they were nothing more than a tiny dot against Porthladd's mass. Until I was truly alone.

It was almost noon already, and they'd all be back by sundown, but time seemed to crawl by as I counted the seconds. The sea slapped against the boat in time with my counting, a siren song calling for me. For a moment, it was as if I could feel it again—the tingle in my fingertips, the purring in my core. I closed my eyes, reaching into that hidden part of myself, the part that could command seas and call forth storms; but as it had been since my uncle shot me, it was empty. There was nothing left to answer my call, nothing to conjure or conquer or control. Nothing of Lyr's gift left, only the vacant shadow of what once was.

I was alone. Powerless.

After ten minutes in solitude, I decided to stop feeling sorry for myself and do something with my time. I grabbed the swords Saeth left behind and started my routine, the dance as familiar as my own name. Jab, swipe, parry, dodge, over and over until sweat streaked down my back even amidst the cool breeze. Jab, dodge, swing. Until my shoulder ached, deep within my bones.

I gritted my teeth against it. The Dark God would not have me. This body was mine to command, now and to the end of time.

Strike, swing, jab.

After an hour or two of swinging blindly at my invisible opponent, I threw my swords to the deck. It was too quiet. I missed my crew's laughter, Ronan's working hum, Griffin sharpening his weapons. Lyr below, I even missed Saeth and Tarran's bickering.

I hated this. The waiting. The *wanting*. I imagined Reagan, tucked into Reina's kitchen, swapping stories while her delicious chicken roasted over the fire. Or Griffin and Rhett, sitting uncomfortably at Vala's table while she roasted *them* about their relationship, Tarran watching and laughing at them for once.

A glutton for punishment, I let myself imagine Ronan lowering himself into the spring, the closest place to a home I'd ever had, wishing desperately that I was there too, soaking and swimming and whatever else came next.

I needed to stop thinking about him. Lyr's ass, I needed to stop thinking, period.

I did so the only way I knew how; I dragged the hammock from its hold and pitched it in record time, grateful for something to do with my hands. The sun was still high, so I had to squint at the sky when I finally laid back. But I pulled my coat around me, breathing in the familiar salty air. The sun in the south was my enemy, harsh, incessant, burning. But here it was my dearest friend, caressing my cheeks with gentle warmth as I let my body sink further into the hammock.

This was home too. This ship. This sunshine. I could miss a few meals and laughs if it meant I could keep this.

As I laid there, alone and finally content to wait, the whispers started.

Keiraaa.

I jolted upright, searching for the source of the voice.

No, not voice. *Voices.* Hundreds or thousands of them, whispering my name from the ship's shadows.

Keeeiraaaa. Ariannad. Duweeeeeni.

Same.

Same.

I drew my sword instinctively, whipping around for the source of the mysterious chorus, but I knew in my core that there was no one there. The voices were inside me, in the deepest parts of my soul, much like Lyr's once was.

But this was not my sunken friend. These voices held no warmth or familiarity. They were cold, a dissonant symphony of ghosts calling from a dark beyond I could not see and could not run from.

One voice, a man's, darker than midnight and colder than ice, cut through the noise.

We're all the same when we're dead, Keira girl.

Baths and Burdens

RONAN

The turquoise spring was once a daydream. Now, it was a nightmare.

Moonlight bathed the water silver, the spiraling tendrils of steam like ghostly fingers ready to drag me under. The bone-white willows were even paler than I remembered, their bark as bleached and brittle as skeletons. Still, I all but hobbled toward the garish scene, my breath coming in ragged gasps, my body aching for it far more than I'd ever admit.

I didn't wait to strip, not caring to look if there was a couple in the shack already. Though I supposed there were worse ways to ruin a honeymoon. Mine certainly had its fair share of awkwardness. Seeing a random naked man having a magical bath wasn't nearly as traumatizing as having your new wife press a knife to your throat.

My clothes discarded, I lowered into the spring, biting my lip to stifle a moan. On impact, the water glowed a soft gold, glimmering as it rippled around me. I shuddered where we met, a jolt of lightning buzzing through me.

It was ecstasy. Pure, unadulterated euphoria.

And I hated it.

I hated every rutting second of it. I hated that I needed this, that my body was weak and useless without it. I barely had the energy the last few days to act like myself, but every breath and every step had been a labor. Otherworld be damned, it was torture.

But what I hated most was how much I wanted this.

I was an addict. After the first time, I felt new. Lyr's ass, better than new. I felt like I could move mountains with my bare hands and change the stars with a look if I wanted to. Like a god made flesh, the world mine to command. I had been starving for the feeling ever since. Day one back on the ship, and it filled my dreams. Day twelve, it was all I could think about. And as my energy drained and my body failed...Lyr below, if I had to wait another day, I might have killed for it.

I let myself sink further into the odious water. The glow burned brighter as it remade me, the buzz turning into a full-on simmer. It was all I could do not to lose myself to the sensation, to just float in this bliss until it consumed me whole.

It was no wonder that the sharp silver of Keira's gaze had turned grey with pity. She could smell it on me, the pathetic desire, the weakness of will and body. And she still smiled at me and gave me sweet kisses, but not the way she used to. It was always laced with worry.

I prayed that the spring could ease the cold weight of my self-loathing as it stitched my body back together. Tonight, I'd be whole again. Tonight, she'd look at me like I was a man and not a burden.

Willing my mind to rutting shut up, I dipped my head under the water.

My regret was instantaneous.

Welcome back, boy.

His voice replaced my own thoughts as it slithered into my consciousness. A chill ran down my spine despite the warm water. This was not the first time hearing Lyr's call. He'd spoken to me during my first unaccompanied visit, scaring the metaphorical pants off me with his gurgled whisper. I hadn't told Keira for fear of what it meant or what she might say. But tonight, I was not surprised or afraid. I was irritated.

"No." I kept my voice detached, slipping into the comfortable old role as I sneered at my invisible interrupter. "This is not my problem."

A dark chuckle bubbled in my mind like a stone skipping across water. *Whose problem am I, then?*

"Go talk to my wife." I dismissed the mischievous god and pushed myself onto the bank, the action ridiculously easy with the lightning running through my veins. I had no desire to bathe with a god today.

The late fall breeze licked at my bare, wet skin, but I was still radiating warmth as I pulled on my trousers. I hated that, too. Hated that it didn't matter if it was a winter wind or a summer scorcher. I didn't feel it. I only felt the water coating my insides with its warmth and power. Or, in the worst moments, I only felt its absence.

Lyr, inconsiderate that I ignored him, sighed as another gust swayed the willows' white branches. *I can't. She's no longer my charge.*

I stopped in my tracks, my hands fisted in the shirt over my head. "Well, whose charge is she, then?"

When Lyr didn't answer, my rage ignited, an oiled wick meeting a flame. I imagined my wife, alone on the *Ceffyl*, her midnight hair probably a crow's nest in this wind. I imagined her silver eyes like steel on fire in this late afternoon sun, the light reflecting in their metallic hue. And then I remembered the obsidian spot that scarred her ivory flesh, not like the deep brown constellation of freckles that dotted her delicate nose and other shoulder. It was a parasite, eating her alive from the inside out.

"One bullet, and you abandon her completely, is that it?" I scoffed, nearly ripping my shirt. "Some god you are."

Finally, my fury met with another as his voice crashed back into me like a tidal wave. *Not one bullet. Two. Hers and* yours. *And she chose yours.*

And that was what I hated most. That this lifeforce, this endless pool of energy pulsing through my very essence, remaking me whole again and again...it could've been hers instead. My anger extinguished like a candle in the wind. The same empty, helpless feeling crawled into my core in its place. "I didn't have a choice."

Only fate decides.

Fate didn't choose for me. Keira did. Fate wanted me dead. And I was. I remembered nothing of the Otherside, only the *vacant* feeling that still haunted my nightmares. But Keira found another way for me; Keira pulled me back from the depths, rescuing me from my black fate, only to secure her own.

Darkness crept along my spine, but I shook it off. I would not let it consume me. I would take this power, and I would make it mine. It would no longer control me, I would be its master. And with it, I would find a way to save my wife, even if it cost me everything.

My familiar mask fell back into place. I hoped the sea god couldn't hear my thoughts in return. "Do you mind? Can't you let a man get dressed in peace?"

Not when you spend so much time away. It's not good for you.

If Lyr had a body and a face instead of spring water and sea foam, I would have punched him. "*This* is no good for me." I finally managed to pull my rutting clothes back on as I spat at my disembodied opponent, "This has made me pathetic. And I've had enough."

I would not waste another moment of my physical fortitude bickering with a deity. My wife waited for me. Without any further hesitation, I stepped into my boots and headed down the side of the hill.

But I did not miss the drowned god's final warning, or the sadness in his tone.

Don't be a stranger, boy. She'll need you strong for what's to come. They both will.

3

Feasts and Fables

KEIRA

After the voices came and went, I was on high alert, every creak of the ship sending shivers down my spine. The whispers replayed in my head over and over, my only comfort the steady sound of the water hitting the hull.

Four long hours later, my crew clamored back onto the ship, their laughter a welcome break from the uncomfortable silence. I nearly choked on a sob as Ronan appeared first over the rail, his cheeks flushed pink and his eyes sparkling in the setting sunlight. I was on him in less than a second, wrapping my arms tightly around his slim waist, content to never let him go again. My husband laughed as he pressed a kiss into my hair and pulled me closer.

"You look better," I mumbled into his chest, the sound of his strong heartbeat enough to chase away the lingering ghosts.

"Good as new." He tucked an errant strand of my hair behind my ear, and I marveled at how bright his skin looked in the misty gold sunset. A blue-eyed wink filled my core with heat. "I missed you very much, Mrs. Mathonwy. Especially in the spring."

"Insufferable cad," I breathed, painfully aware of how my pulse quickened and the knot deep within my center tightened. If the rest of the crew wasn't filing onto the deck, I'd have taken him right then and there.

"Miss us?" Griffin teased as he hoisted himself onto the deck.

"Like I miss a thorn in my boot." I begrudgingly let go of my husband to shoot my cousin a dark look, but there was no bite behind my bark and I couldn't help the grin that tugged at the corner of my mouth. Griffin was trouble's puppet, but he had a way of clearing even the darkest clouds from the sky. Mischief danced in the corner of his eye, a question in our unspoken language. *You alright, Shrimpy?*

I flicked him once, his fire and fortitude warming even the coldest parts of my heart. *I am now.*

I had missed them like a decked fish misses water. But seeing all six members of my crew, healthy and jovial and very *real*, my thundering heart quieted, ease washing over me like the sea kissing the sandy shore. What I wasn't prepared for was the seventh person Rhett helped over the rail, her wispy blonde hair luminous in the sunset, her impossibly white smile warmer than a southern wind.

"How about me?" Reina fixed her skirt, bracing herself on the rail as she found her sea legs. The White Snake was a vision, her plain red dress and deep brown cloak nothing to marvel at; but paired with her ethereal grace, she was as regal as a silk-and-diamond-clad queen—one that certainly did not belong on a ship. Only a few seconds on deck, and her pale skin tinted green.

"Reina!" I almost knocked her overboard as I bombarded her with a tight hug. "What are you—?"

She steadied herself against my frame, a knowing look in her eye. "Figured I would say hello to ye, and see what kind of condition my daughter has been livin' in." Cocking her head, a snake about to strike, she addressed the crew. "Which one of ye taught her to curse?"

We all answered together: "Griffin."

"Guilty as charged." He bowed, proud of his corruption, sending Reagan into a frenzy of giggles. "Sorry, Madame Reina."

"Aye, ye will be." She smacked the back of his bowed head, and the whole crew roared with laughter, Saeth going as far as snorting sharply through her angular nose.

I swear I could've kissed her. Perhaps she did belong on the ship, with her practiced scowl and the straight back of a captain. Had we traded places, she would have this ship in tip-top shape in no time.

Griffin rubbed the back of his head but knew to keep quiet as he helped Tarran and Rhett heave the last of the supply crates back onto the ship. With the final basket, the familiar scent of orange and ginger coaxed drool to the corner of my mouth. "What's that smell?"

"Mama cooked." Reagan smirked, her swagger giving way to her girlish joy. Even her dragon-like temper could be swayed with the promise of a full belly and a mother's love.

Reina spread blankets on the deck, the crate's smell too enticing to resist. Each revealed parcel was more alluring than the last: fresh-made biscuits with some sort of citrus jam, roasted potatoes and sweet pumpkin from the fall harvest, and four whole chickens each with Reina's signature citrus-spiced glaze. It must have cost her a fortune to put together, but our hungry eyes would've given her an arm and a leg for just a taste. Reina stuck her hands to her hips and raised a groomed brow. "Come eat before it all gets cold."

She didn't have to tell any of us twice. Within moments, all eight of us were seated around the delicious fare, our grubby hands digging in with fervent intensity. With a bite of citrus chicken, I was transported to the first night I'd spent in Reina's kitchen—the night she forgave me for what I'd done to Reagan's father. The night they both welcomed me into their lives with open arms and hearts and I gave them mine in return, even if I didn't realize it then.

My throat thick with emotion, it was a labor to swallow down the rest of my meal. I deserved none of this. Reagan's song-bird laughter, Tarran's sunshine smile, Griffin's cat-like grin, Rhett's stoic pout, Saeth's dagger sharp wit, Reina's elysian grace—Ronan's unconditional love—this patchwork family around me, their loyalty, their trust, their forgiveness for all the wrongs I had done. I had earned none of it. The only thing I'd truly earned was the dark reminder on my shoulder, and the sure demise it would one day bring.

But until then, I would savor every stolen moment of beauty this life afforded me. Reaching for an extra biscuit, I nestled into Ronan's side, memorizing the perfect fit of him. I didn't know how long I had left, but I would not deny myself this simple pleasure any longer.

Tarran broke my trance as he shoved a whole chicken leg in his freckled cheeks, moaning, "So good, Reina."

"Lyr's ass." Griffin ruffled the boy's mop of ginger curls. "Get a room before you give that chicken the business, Tarran." Tarran's face went redder than Reina's dress, sending a fresh round of laughter washing through the crew.

Everyone ate until their bellies were about to burst and laughed until their eyes shone with silver tears. And just like that first night, Reagan did not waste any time before she donned her puppy eyes and begged Ronan for a story.

"Just one before bed?" she pleaded, resting her head on her mother's lap for added effect. For someone who insisted on being seen as a grown up, she had no qualms about using her sheer adorableness to her advantage.

In her defense, it absolutely worked.

"Aye, only one, then you're headed below deck and I'm headed inland to take your Mama home." Ronan stood, and I whined in the absence of his heat against me.

Saeth was less amused, wielding her butter knife like a cutlass and stabbing herself another biscuit. "Lyr help me, if it's the one with Airid again, I'll make you stay with Griffin tonight," she threatened her cabinmate, waving the skewered bread in Reagan's face.

"I don't care if she's cute, she'll have to fight me for it," Rhett growled playfully, the mug of ale emboldening him as he scooted closer to his redheaded bedfellow. Reagan rolled her eyes, but I didn't miss the way Griffin's nose scrunched up, a real smile breaking across his features. I shot him a look, a clear signal in our unspoken language. *You're in deep.*

He only offered a curt nod in response, but the blush that colored his cheeks was enough. My own cheeks warmed. Griffin deserved to love and be loved more than anyone.

"I've got a better idea." Ronan rolled back the sleeves of his blue coat, accentuating the corded muscles of his forearms. It made my heart flutter to see him in my family's colors. With a grand flourish to the sky, he began his performance before we could stop him. "Ever wonder how the stars were created, little one?"

"We're listening." Reagan relaxed further into her mother's embrace, eyes brighter than those stars peeking out in the dusky night. I sat straighter, pulling my coat tight around me. As much as I missed Ronan's warmth, his stories always managed to nourish the small, vulnerable part of me that still believed in happy endings.

Ronan waited for silence, until he knew all eyes were on him, breath held in anticipation of his tale. Finally, with a crooked grin, the story began. "In the beginning, before the gods lived among us, before their gifts were watered down, there was only darkness and light. And on the horizon, where the dark crashed against the light, the first gods were born." His voice was barely above a whisper, but it carried across the deck, enveloping us. "The first was Donn, the keeper of the light. She was the ruler of the heavens, the realm of the gods, and by her power, life came to be…both the gods and men."

"I bet she's as pretty as Mama." Reagan beamed up at her mother, and Reina melted, tucking her close.

"Kiss ass," Saeth teased, earning a laugh from the little dragon.

Not to be outdone, my showboat husband cleared his throat, dragging our attention back to the picture he painted. "Next was her husband, Arawn, the keeper of the dark. He ruled over the Otherworld, where he was charged to keep all terror, war, sickness, and death at bay so that life could run free."

At the mention of the Dark God, a chill ran up my spine, the hair on my neck springing to attention. My hand flew to my shoulder instinctively, and Ronan's keen eyes didn't miss the action. He offered an apologetic smile before continuing on, gesturing broadly to the open horizon behind him. "And the third was Donn's brother, Lyr, the god of the sea, who was charged to keep the balance between light and dark."

"Lyr keep us." Rhett raised a glass, his cheeks rosy with drink, and the rest of the crew echoed the cheer. I stayed silent, the sick feeling in my gut only growing.

Lyr would keep them. But he'd already left me behind.

Ronan raised a hand to quiet the chorus, a conductor at work. "For millennia, the three gods ruled over the universe, and they were loved by both the new gods they created and by man. Their children lived together in harmony, the young gods helping their human brothers and sisters with the gifts Donn gave them. But none were loved more than Donn, the mother who had created all. Over time, Arawn grew jealous of his wife, the darkness eating away at his mind. He unleashed terror and death among the land of men, wreaking havoc wherever he went."

"Sounds like Griffin when he's hungry," Tarran snorted. Griffin rolled his eyes, and Reagan giggled, hiding her face in her mother's skirt.

The wholesomeness of their banter quieted my nerves. This was just another story. No matter the parallels to my own, it did not change my fate for better or for worse. I hugged my knees to my chest to keep out the cold, focusing instead on how bright my husband's eyes glimmered as he weaved his tapestry, an artist in motion.

"When Donn heard of her husband's betrayal, she banished him to the Otherworld for eternity and cursed the land to only hold the souls of the wicked and damned. But Arawn's jealousy knew no bounds. In a fit of rage, he took his spear and drove it through his wife's heart." Ronan drew his sword, pantomiming the action, falling dramatically to his knees as he tucked his blade beneath his arm.

Reagan and Saeth clapped, encouraging a fake, sputtering cough from Ronan.

I sucked my bottom lip to keep from smiling. *Insufferable cad.*

Ronan was not done, his hand dramatically on his forehead as he continued, "Weakened by the blow, she could not resist as he took her power and scattered it across the sky, trapping the light in thousands of fragments called stars, too vast for her to ever collect them all. And when she was powerless at last, he banished her to the island of the lost and struck her name from all the world so no one would remember her."

Reagan bolted upright, brows knit in confusion and defiance. "Wait, this one is so sad. I wanted a happier story."

Papa used to say happy endings were won through painful middle parts. Whenever I'd run to him crying with knee-scrape or heartache, he'd scoop me into his embrace and remind me the pain was temporary. *"If it still hurts, it's not the end,"* he'd say with a grin and a peck on the cheek, his words the only bandage I'd ever need.

I looked at my youngest cousin by marriage, at the hurt and brimstone in her stare. If anyone would fight for a happy ending, it was her. And I'd fight by her side, with a smile and a warm word ready to conquer the painful middle.

"I promise it gets better, little dragon." Ronan broke character, petting his cousin's hair. Then he stood again, radiating power as he prepared for the grand finale. "The other gods wept for their mother, but none were powerful enough to stand against Arawn's rule. But Lyr, the cleverest god of them all, would not let his sister's legacy be destroyed. With his seas, he split the realm of men, dividing it into many islands, so Arawn's path of destruction could no longer reach them all. His control weakened, Lyr and the other gods vowed to live among us and protect those islands and keep Donn's creations alive. And that is how the Seven Isles of the Deyrnas came to be, with Lyr protecting us all from Arawn's clutches."

My stomach clenched around itself as the same dark chorus of voices echoed in the back of my head.

All but one.

I tried to school my features, hoping none of my crew could see how the blood ran from my face.

If it still hurts, it's not the end.

This was not the end of our story. The voices, my mark...this was the painful middle.

Ronan let his words hang in the air a moment longer before falling into a deep bow, cheers and shouts erupting from his audience. I shook away the lingering chill, forcing myself to clap with my family.

"How am I supposed to sleep with that story in my mind?" Reagan whined, folding her arms across herself.

"You'll manage." Ronan winked, his storytelling persona falling away to reveal the tenderhearted boy I knew and loved. "Bedtime, Reagan."

"I'm too old for a bedtime."

"And I'm too young to have a daughter that talks back." Reina's stern tone left no room for argument. "Now give yer ma a hug and get gone."

"Come on, Reagan. I'm beat too." Saeth stretched as she stood up, ushering her roommate below deck.

Reagan gave her mother a lingering hug and a quick peck before trailing after her chosen sister. I noted how Reina's gaze trailed after the girl, an edge of melancholy in her tawny stare. Pride and grief tangled together, the trademarks of a parent's love so clear, it had me missing my own.

For the briefest flicker of a moment, I let myself mourn the mother I never knew. Had her embrace been as warm and unconditional? Would she be proud of the woman I was?

I waved the thought off before it could break me. I had no business craving hugs from phantoms. Lyr below, I was an emotional wreck tonight. I needed some rest, if only to steady the tide in my chest. In the morning, I'd have myself in order.

"I think I'll head down too." I squeezed Reina's hand, so grateful for even a few captured moments of her charm. I cleared my throat before coughing up my best attempt at a captain's command. "Tarran, you have first watch. Rhett and Griffin, row Reina ashore."

Rhett and Griffin made haste, packing up Reina's things and readying the lifeboat, Tarran climbing sleepily up the mast to the crow's nest. But Reina bit her delicate bottom lip, hesitant. "Actually, I... Well, as much as I wanted to see Reagan and spend some time with ye, my visit had another purpose."

"What's wrong?" I stuffed my hands in my pockets, a bad habit I'd picked up from Ronan whenever I was nervous. Reina's light was inexhaustible, but the shadow that crept along her features made her look older. Unsure.

"I'm sorry t' bring ye bad news..." She swallowed hard, fidgeting with the folds of her skirt, the action so foreign from the queen of poise herself. "But things are getting tight at home. People are struggling, Keira. Connor's sanctions...well, ye have to be rich or kiss his slimy arse to get by nowadays. Ellian and Madame Agatha are outvoted, but the Raven is at least serving as a front for yer Auntie Vala and I to smuggle whatever Reese can get his hands on."

"Bastards," I cursed under my breath, pinching the bridge of my nose. Anger bubbled in my core, the feast we just devoured churning in my core like regret. What had Reina traded for such a luxury? What had we stolen from hungry Porthladdian families tonight?

Connor was the king of worms, a parasite born only to feed off the hard work and sweat of others, and I knew in my bones that this fresh wave of greed was personal. Banishment was not enough. He wanted me to see my people starve from afar, just close enough to feel their pain but too distant to do anything about it.

I wanted to scream, to punch something, to draw my sword and cut down every son of a bitch between myself and that scum until it was his blood coating my sword. But I bit back my rage, swallowing down before it could push past my lips. Papa used to say the mark of a true captain was not someone who sought to gain power over others, but someone who had power over themselves. If I let my anger and fear show, I was only hurting an already worried Reina. If I let Connor get a rise out of me, I was letting him win again, playing right into his trap.

No, I needed to show her my strength. My steadiness. Even if it was a lie.

If it still hurts, it's not the end.

I loosed a quiet breath. "The *Ceffyl* can't be seen frequenting Porthladd's shores, but I can see what I can do to help Reese increase his hauls. Griffin has been making new friends in Ir'de, maybe some of them are willing to trade." I willed a smile to my face, a mere shadow of the one my father used to wear. He was so much better at this than I was, but I had to try. I pulled Reina into a hug before she could see my mask slip. "It'll be alright, Reina. Now go home and get some rest."

Reina pushed back to meet my gaze. Worry still rested on her brow. Worry...and the distinct tint of pity. "There's something else. Something worse."

My blood froze. "What could be worse than starving?"

Reina shut her eyes as the words came tumbling out of her. "Yer auntie was against it, so don't be cross with her...but ye know how yer cousin can be..."

"Finna?" My heart stuttered. Finna was a bitch and a half, but if something happened to her, especially after I'd taken the crew and left her to fend for herself, I'd never forgive myself. I grabbed Reina's shoulders as gently as I could, forcing her to look at me. "What's wrong, Reina?"

Reina steeled herself, the White Snake turned stone. "Finna is engaged."

I dropped my hands, another prickle of anger rolling up my back. I didn't mind a joke now and again, but coming from Reina, it stung. I saw no reason why my cousin settling down could ever be worse than starving. "Well, congrats to her, then," I scoffed.

Reina did not blink, that same flicker of pity in her gaze. No, this was not a prank. Something was terribly wrong. Finally, she spoke, her sweet voice heavy with emotion. "She's engaged to Councilman Yorath."

Betrothals and Black Spots

KEIRA

Any and all of my attempts to remain calm were dashed at the mention of Connor's name. Red flooded my vision, and before I could hurt anyone, my husband led me below deck to the Captain's quarters.

Finna was getting married. To Connor Yorath, of all people.

I imagined my cousin, the picture of beauty, next to Connor's gaunt, sunken form. I wanted to vomit. I wanted to scream or set something on fire.

"I'll kill him, Ronan," I seethed, twisting my favorite dagger in my hand. I didn't remember unsheathing it, but it didn't matter. I would gut that bottom-feeding prick like a fish, and for once in my Lyr-forsaken life, I wouldn't feel guilty about it. Not for a second.

"And what does that do?" Ronan moved to lace his fingers through mine, but I flicked him away. I didn't want to be coddled. I wanted to be unchained, to be free to unleash my wild rage directly on the man who deserved it most, who had taken everything and was still out for more. When would it be enough? Did my entire family, or worse, all of Porthladd, have to suffer to satisfy Connor's endless greed?

And my vapid cousin. Had he tricked her? Or did she willingly agree, the cruel, vain streak in her grasping for power the only way she knew how?

Papa used to say Finna was made of the same dark magic as sirens. She had fangs and claws underneath those glittering scales of hers, ready to drown and devour anyone that underestimated her. I could only hope that Connor was her intended prey, not my family.

I punched the nearest wall, not caring that my knuckles split open, only wishing that I had cracked them over someone's jaw. "I'm going to strangle Finna with her own stupid, curly hair. It's been a long time coming, and I think it's finally time to smack sense into her giant head."

"Steady, Mrs. Mathonwy, come back to me." Ronan's grip was firm against my shoulders, his stare penetrating. I sighed, the edge of my acidic anger dulling as his wide hands cradled me. "Your cousin has always had a mind of her own and going after Connor will only make things worse for the people we love. If Finna wants to marry that slime ball and have her happy ending, let her. We already have ours."

His words stilled my internal storm, and I let him envelop me in a warm hug. I breathed in his scent, citrus and spring water, and let it quell the last edges of my fury. Part of me knew he was right. Beneath her full-lipped smile, Finna always had a vicious set of teeth. For years, she'd been brewing in her jealousy, waiting for the opportunity to bite. Her opinion of me was always poor, growing only darker when Aidan died with my knife pressed into his skull. But the fact that Ronan was right didn't soften the sting of her betrayal.

"I'm still angry."

"I know," my husband said, rubbing small circles over my back.

I pressed myself further into his broad chest. Ronan had seen my worst, my grief and jealousy and rage, and still hadn't run from it. He was still here, holding me close, until the rest of it faded away and it was just us. "I'm happy, too."

"Why is that?"

"You look much better." I pulled back to admire his post-spring glow, a different part of me filled with joy. What a selfish sea-cow I was for letting anything upset me when the spring's miracle had just given more of what mattered most. "Our happy ending just got a little longer."

The smile that broke across his face was enough to stop my heart. "I don't just look better, I *am* better. I feel so energized. Like I've got lightning in my veins."

My heart restarted, fluttering in my chest with new vigor. I could almost see it, the fire burning in his core, the starlight sparkling in his devastating eyes. Finna could make her wedding bed with Yorath if that's what she wanted. She could curse my name and Connor could banish me until the end of time. I had already won my prize. He was standing before me looking like a god, the Lyr-blessed spring water remaking him.

Finna used to say the best remedy for an aching heart was a warm body. If my cousin was intent on causing me heartache, my husband and his virility would be my cure.

"Maybe you do have magic in your blood," I teased, caressing his chest and letting my hand wander to the belt that rested on his slim hips. "Tell me, any other parts feeling particularly *vital* tonight?"

Ronan's breath shallowed, his eyes settling on my lips. I purposefully sucked my bottom lip into my teeth, guiding my husband to our bed with a gentle shove to his hip bones.

He raised a brow at me, but sat on the mattress, patting his lap with a certain authority that made me shudder. "A minute ago, you were set on throttling Connor and Finna, and now you want to make love?"

"Let me be perfectly clear, Mr. Mathonwy." I mounted his powerful thighs so our chests pressed together, our faces only an inch apart. "I always want to make love to you. But please don't mention Finna or Connor or anyone else while I'm straddling you, alright?"

Strong hands gripped my hips, digging into the soft flesh with a pleasant pain. Ronan looked up at me through his thick lashes, licking his full lips, his velvet voice vibrating through me. "You're the only one on my mind, Mrs. Mathonwy."

The hold on my civility snapped. My mouth crashed against his, needing to taste him, to claim him. He met my need, his lips battling for dominance, his tongue tracing my mouth with equal fervor. A small moan escaped my throat, and he stiffened beneath me, his control dissolving. His hands were everywhere, roving up my back, my sides, every pass increasing my heated need.

When his lips moved from mine and travelled down my neck in lazy, messy strokes, I rocked against him, my fingers finding anchor in his soft curls. In the months since our first time, this thrill never lessened. This man could undo me with a less than kiss and a look, but his expert mouth against my collarbone was enough to make me want to scream his name.

Knowing my growing need, he stripped my coat off with little resistance, working with deft fingers on the laces of my tunic before brushing it from my shoulders.

Then he stopped.

"Why are you stopping?" I whined, grinding my hips against his thickening center, but he steadied me with a firm grip.

His eyes were fixed on my shoulder, where the spidery black veins marred my creme-colored skin. Pain crossed his face, dropping an icy ball of shame through me. "Is it—does it hurt?"

I cupped his face in my hands, redirecting his gaze to meet mine. "No, Ronan, I barely feel it. I promise I'm alright," I lied with as much conviction as I could. Right now, I wanted to be felt. I wanted to be touched and kissed and loved into blissful oblivion. I palmed his length through his leather trousers, making my desire clear. "Now *this,* I feel."

His teeth grazed the side of my neck. "I'm yours. Every last bit of me."

We both shrugged out of our trousers, ungraceful but fast in our aching haste, until finally I lowered myself onto him, his silken steel filling my slick heat perfectly.

"You feel so good," I moaned against him as I let myself adjust to the pleasurable pain of his intrusion, until slowly I began to rock back and forth, needing *more*.

Ronan groaned beneath me, matching my pace with thrusts of his own. I pushed him back on the bed, the position making for a deeper fit, my breath hitching in my throat. Ronan's expert hands cupped my breasts, the calloused pads of his fingers brushing over my budding desire. This was what I needed. Much like sparring, fucking gave me my body back. With every thrust, Ronan anchored me to this world, until I no longer belonged to the Dark God and wholly to the man deep inside of my sweetest parts.

"Please, I'm—" I whined as the tight pleasure rose through me, a wave begging to crash. In a swift, graceful hold, Ronan had me on my back, his chiseled frame hovering over me as he pushed me over the edge of my passion.

"Sing for me, Keira," he growled in my ear, his breath caressing the sensitive shell, and I broke apart beneath him, singing his name to the heavens until I became a mewling, panting mess of rolling pleasure. As I tightened around him, his release billowed inside me and he collapsed into my arms.

"I love you," he gasped, kissing the hollow of my neck with reverence.

"I love *you*." I held him closer for a moment, relishing in the heat and sweat and scent of our togetherness.

We cleaned and clothed ourselves slowly, neither of us rushing to leave the moment of bliss. But the world waited, and no matter how many times Ronan filled me with his love and light, the shadows still crept back in.

"What are we supposed to do now?" He laid down and pulled me to him, his arms the only cage I welcomed.

"Ready for round two?" I teased, but it was shallow. We had plans to make and people who counted on us. Counted on *me*.

"And you say I'm insufferable." Ronan's deep laugh vibrated through his chest, but I could hear the worry in his velvet timbre. "I meant about Connor's sanctions. Reina is never worried, not like that. Things aren't pretty."

I breathed in his scent again—our scent—letting it clear my head and quiet my nerves. As usual, he was right. I hadn't known Reina long, but she would not have come tonight if she weren't desperate. And even if Finna deserved to choose whichever fresh hell suited her best, she was still a Branwen. I didn't have enough family left to let pride get in my way. I traced the outline of my husband's chest tattoo, the mark that had saved both of us once before. We'd run out of dumb luck and divine favors. Now, we had to act on our own. Now it was our turn to make things right.

"Tomorrow, we sail to Bachtref. See what we can bargain for with what we have left, or if we can offer our services in exchange for surplus from the harvest. I don't think anyone would mind a few days' work in the fields or in an inn for some grain. Then we can transfer it all to Reese, let him and Ellian distribute it where Porthladd needs it most." The plan wasn't perfect, but it was honest. We didn't have much to offer besides our strength and our ship, and every one of us would give that and more if we could. I sighed, letting the rest of the pieces fall into place as I spoke. "Lyr help her, I hope Finna knows what she's doing. Maybe she thinks marrying Connor will give her some influence, help her fix things at home. I'll have Griffin send her a letter. She has a soft spot for her brother." I prayed to all the gods wandering the earth and heavens that my Siren Queen of a cousin would not sink her fangs into our exposed throats.

"You're brilliant." Ronan kissed the top of my head, making me feel like I was ten feet tall and stronger than an ox with two simple words.

"Turns out I think much clearer with you next to me." I closed my eyes, listening to the sound of his heartbeat, strong and sure—my own personal lullaby.

He stroked my hair with his free hand, coaxing me further into that deep, warm place of rest that only he could give me. "I'm right here, Keira girl. Always."

I was up on the deck. A cold Northern wind tousled my hair, too cold for fall in Porthladd. I scanned the night for my crew, but no one was there. I opened my mouth to call for them, for anyone, but no sound came out.

Fear shot through me, colder than the wind. Where was everyone? I tried to call out again, but again, I met with silence. Panic clawed its way up my throat until I was choking on it. I spun around, dizzying myself, looking for anything, anyone to save me.

Then I saw him.

He stood just beyond my reach, his ginger beard peppered with gray, his hazel eyes bright in the moonlight.

"Papa," I somehow choked out, stumbling him and falling into his cold embrace. But his hold was too tight, squeezing against my ribs until the air rushed from my lungs. "Ow, Papa—" I gasped, my lungs burning and screaming for air.

The viper's hold crushed me further, until blinding, piercing pain lit through me as my bones shattered. "Try again," he whispered in my ear, his voice low and frigid. Then he let me go, let me fall to the ground in a crumpled, defeated heap. But when I looked up, my stomach dropped.

It wasn't Papa. It was Aidan. They had always been so similar. But now his skin was pale and sickly against his beard, his hazel eyes turning black. And on his forehead, a black, oozing spot, right where Ronan's bullet belonged.

And when he smiled, more of the same black pus spilled from his swollen lips. "We're all the same when we're dead, Keira girl."

When I woke screaming, Ronan was already holding me, stroking my hair. "Shh, it's alright. I'm here. I'm here."

"It was Aidan, he was going to—"

"He can't hurt you Keira. They can't hurt us anymore." He rocked me and held me until my sobs quieted and my breath steadied. But no matter how many kisses he showered me with, or how tightly he held me, Aidan's words remained.

We were the same, him and I. Murderers plotting and planning on borrowed time. And mine was almost up.

5

Gifts and Guards

KEIRA

The sail to Bachtref was only a half a day downwind from Porthladd's shores, so we docked before noontide. But none of us were prepared for what we'd find there.

Bachtref felt like Porthladd's little sister, the island made up of mostly lush farmland and kind, simple people who worshiped the harvest god Bris; in turn, he blessed them with booming crops and healthy livestock. My family and I loved the warm, hearty feel of the island and sailed every fall to join the revelry of the harvest festival. Most years, it was my favorite adventure. The whole clan would pile onto the *Ceffyl,* ready to dive into the sweetly spiced pumpkin-and-nut dishes and carve faces into gourds to ward off wandering spirits and fair-folk. When we were little, Griffin, Finna, and I would have contests to see who could create the best face in our vegetable canvases. Somehow, despite Griffin's mastery of the sword and my unparalleled knife skills, Finna always won. Still, we'd all laugh and feast and drink together, any lingering animosity and sourness falling away with the browning leaves. It was a celebration of the cycle of life, of the sacrificial harvest that would keep us all warm and alive through winter.

We'd missed the celebration this year, with me banished and so many of us missing or dead, but perhaps it was for the best. As it stood, the island looked like it could barely feed its own people, never mind half a dozen Porthladdian sailors. The grassy shore, which usually stayed green well into the winter season, was already brown and patchy. Portwen Market, the northernmost trading post, which usually bustled with the noise of people buying and selling, was quiet. Only a few supply stalls remained open, their shelves as empty as the streets. The people seemed just as dull and faded, skin tight to their thin bodies, eyes decorated with dark bags.

The Land of Plenty was starving.

"Lyr below, what happened here?" Griffin cursed under his breath as we scanned the empty streets. His hand kept twitching, itching to grab the swords at his back.

"Are we sure we're in the right place, Captain?" Tarran asked, the sun running from his smile. The last time he'd been here, he and Saeth had gotten into an argument over who could eat more pie; now it looked like we'd all be fighting over scraps, if there were any left at all.

I stuck my hands in my pockets and didn't answer. I wasn't sure of anything anymore.

We stopped at the nearest open trading stall where an old man with a sour face stood sentinel over the single bushel of wheat and three small birds that made up his wares.

"Good morning, sir," I said softly, keeping my tone as kind as possible. He wouldn't part with his meager treasure easily. "Can I—?"

"Fuck off."

Papa was right— hunger made people mean.

I opened my mouth to argue, but Ronan tugged my coat sleeve, motioning toward a young woman and her small son right next to us. He was no more than eight, with a large white birthmark that decorated the left cheek of his clay-colored skin, like the gods forgot to paint that spot when they sculpted him. His mother's hair was dark and curly, made darker still by the mud that coated it. But her brown eyes were kind, and the boy wore a bright smile despite the rags he dressed in.

My face emptied of blood. These people were desperate, they didn't need uppity Northern sailors picking a fight. I offered the woman a sympathetic smile, signaling the crew to move on and find the next stall before I started a scene.

The woman followed, her son bobbing quietly behind. "Don't mind Mr. Dynna, he's...well, we all are a little sore. He lost his wife to sickness."

I stopped in my tracks, my own grief flickering in response. I spared a glance back to the old man in the stall, offering a silent prayer to Lyr on his behalf. "We're sorry to intrude."

"No apology necessary, madame." The boy beamed up at me, a slight lisp decorating his speech.

"What's your name, little bear?" Reagan giggled, and his smile doubled in size at the sound.

"I'm Toivo, what's yours?" He puffed out his little chest and bowed, sending another wave of laughter through us. His mother grinned as well, but it didn't reach her eyes or clear the exhaustion on her brow.

"What happened here?" I asked as Reagan and Ronan started entertaining the young boy, making silly faces at him.

The woman swallowed hard, her warm skin ashen. "Bad harvest. A plague of...well, we don't really know, but it killed over half the crops, then had its way with the livestock."

My breath rushed from my lungs. Toivo was already hanging off Griffin and Rhett's arms, his gap-toothed grin bright as Tarran made a face at him this time. How long until he was too weak to play? How long until he starved to death?

"How long has it been?" I said out loud, barely a whisper.

The woman's lips made a tight line. "Two months? Things turned fast. Fate is a bitch like that." Her eyes were still kind, glistening with either hope for the future or acceptance of her cruel fate. "The rich have managed to do some extra business with Ir'de. The Southern Isles haven't been hit yet, Bris bless them. Ya might wanna pack up and sail south while the wind is still warm."

Acceptance, then. She knew she didn't have much time left. Still, she was willing to offer a gentle word to some strangers for nothing in return.

My heart sank to my boots, but the sea-salt in my veins sang with fury. No one could stop famine, but where was their council? Or the High Council? Our system was flawed—snakes with money and ambition like Connor wormed their way into positions on every island, Bachtref no exception—but there were still good counselors like Ellian out there who spoke for the people. Where were the other islands and their charity?

Worse, was this darkness spreading?

I cleared the ball of fury from my throat. "Have you had any assistance? People must know about this."

"Some Orwellin missionaries from *Delm Arawn* were poking around here, offering their prayers to the Dark God on our behalf," she scoffed. "For some people, that's enough. They'll pray to whatever empty promise helps them sleep better at night. They think Bris abandoned them, so they whisper to whoever will listen. But if ye ask me, rations would be a lot nicer than prayers right now."

My shoulder throbbed with a faraway pain. I knew all too well how useless prayers to absent gods could be, but I steeled myself before I could mock this woman's suffering with my own warped sense of injustice. I couldn't change the tides of fate. I couldn't wish away famine, or think away corruption, or control the Councils. Lyr below, I couldn't even manage to save my own life, the dark spot an ever-present symbol of my repeated defeat. But maybe I could save one woman and a boy. Maybe I could give them a fighting chance.

Small victories, Keira girl.

"Thank you for your time," I choked out, unstrapping my sapphire dagger from my hip. It was a reminder of all that I had lost, and its weight was too heavy for me to bear anymore. But in this woman's care, it could be used for good. I shoved it into her hands. "Here."

I could feel my crew's eyes all shift to me, could feel them still in unison, breaths held. But I didn't care. I closed her fingers around its hilt.

The woman blinked, moving to hand it back to me. "I've nothin' to trade, girl."

I held up my hand. "Not a trade. A gift."

"It's a pretty trinket, but it won't feed Toivo."

"No, it won't." I felt lighter already as I admired how lovely it looked in her work-worn hands. "But it's made of Pysgoddian steel. And those stones in the hilt are real, too. Take that to Ir'de, and you can buy enough oranges to feed the boy for a year."

Her eyes flashed to mine, something unrecognizable swimming in the silver tears that lined them. "I—thank you." She clutched the dagger to her chest, a death sentence turned lifeline. Her smile now was free of worry. "If ya need to feed yerselves and have a drink before ya ship off, head down to the Golden Sickle pub. It's my brother's place. Tell him Amilee sent ya, and you and yer crew drink free tonight."

Gratitude and guilt fought for purchase in my chest, stealing my voice. It was one thing for me to free myself of a dagger knowing I had twenty others on board my father's ship. But to feed a crew of foreign sailors when she was barely more than skin and bones...that was true generosity.

"Then we should be thanking you." Ronan, Lyr bless him, chimed in, placing a warm hand on Amilee's shoulder. "We'll be on our way, but we wish you the best."

Reagan slid her arm through mine, gently tugging me away from the small family before I could hand them the rest of my wardrobe.

"Not that I needed a reminder," she whispered, nuzzling closer to my side. "But you're one hell of a captain."

I sighed, guilt's long fingers still clutching my chest. "I know we aren't in a position to be giving things away. But they reminded me of you and your mama. I had to do something."

"We'll manage with what we have left." Confidence and surety laced Ronan's tone as he joined us, always the perfect counter for my insecurity. Whenever I felt small, he was there, his back straight and jaw set. "They were on their last legs. You did the right thing."

I didn't realize there were tears in my eyes until one slid down my cheek. Ronan wiped it away with a tender thumb across my face. Warmth filled my core, steady and sure as the evening sun.

As usual, Griffin shattered the moment with a sinister glint in his expression. "Now, who needs a drink?"

Papa used to say every problem was made smaller with a full belly and a cup of ale. However, after my fourth, I was still waiting for better.

The hole-in-the-wall tavern was rickety at best, hurting as sorely as the rest of the island, but it would do for the evening. The ale was old, but Amilee was true to her word, and the barkeep didn't charge us a single coin…though I made sure to slip a sack of silver into one of the barmaid's pockets, if only to assuage my own guilt. I refused to take handouts from beggars.

Despite the disrepair, the small hunks of bread were surprisingly fresh, and the benches didn't leave splinters in our asses. In the warm lowlight, it reminded me of *the Dancing Raven*, knotting a pang of longing in my stomach. I missed drinking in the *Raven*. I missed card nights, watching Griffin lose hand after hand while I bluffed my way to victory. Missed Agatha's knowing stare and air of mystery. Missed the stench of debauchery and seawater that seeped into the very floorboards. Lyr below, I even missed the drunken fights and backwater deals.

Then again, if Reina's warning was true, home wasn't in its best shape either. I didn't know if I could bear to see it crumbling. The very thought was enough to make a woman drink.

Luckily, my crew was on the exact same page. The tavern was near empty, only a few loners at nearby tables nursing their drinks and suppers, so we spread ourselves across the longest table, kicking our feet up and keeping our glasses—and the oblivious barmaid's pockets—full.

"*Lechyd Da!*" Griffin hoisted his ninth mug of ale high, his words slurred. I'd have to add a few more silvers to the tab at this rate.

"*Lechyd Da.*" All but Reagan responded, lifting our own glasses. I tossed my head back and downed mine in a few sloppy gulps, not caring if I was a mess. Lyr's ass, I'd earned a night of drunken revelry, and so had my crew. Griffin surpassed drunk three mugs ago even with the watered down ones we'd been handing him, Rhett not far behind. Even Ronan was six drinks in, he and Tarran playing a hysterical game where they tried to bounce coins into each other's cups. Turns out, Tarran was a natural at it, and my poor husband would have a hangover in the morning to prove it. A ping, and Tarran sank another coin into Ronan's mug. I winked at my husband as he shot me a pitiful look, his golden skin flushing green.

Reagan clapped, bouncing up and down in her seat, stars in her doe eyes turned to my cousin. "Do it again!"

Tarran puffed out his chest like a blowfish, Reagan's girlish encouragement awakening the man in him. Ronan caught my eye and raised his brow, a moment passing between us—the memory of a different deckhand trying to impress a young girl.

Falling in love with Ronan the first time was so easy. Sneaking Papa's ale from below deck when no one was watching… holding hands underneath the starlight… sharing sweet, unbelievably awkward kisses in the moon's embrace.

It felt like a lifetime ago, that young love, with all the darkness we had walked through since. I knew Tarran and Reagan would have their share of darkness, too. But for now, they deserved to float in that easy spring.

Apparently, after a few drinks, I was a hopeless romantic. As Reagan's giggle filled the dim inn with new light, I couldn't help but smile.

Saeth, however, was not full of the same sentimentality, and made a motion to gag. "Reagan, please stop encouraging him. He'll start to think he's funny."

Emboldened by the stale ale and Reagan's starry stare, Tarran offered his twin a vulgar gesture I could only assume he picked up from Griffin. "Oh shut up, you bitter hag."

Saeth's eyes went wide, but no amount of ale could dull her dagger-tipped tongue. "Bite me, you overgrown weed."

But something had changed in her twin, whether it was the ale's doing or the curly-haired dragon sitting to his left. And for once in his Lyr-forsaken life, he didn't bat an eye. "Does Ellian know you like it rough?"

I had to hold my nose to stop myself from snorting my ale all over the table. "Tarran, dear boy," I sputtered, coughing on a laugh, "I think you might actually be funny."

This was all I'd ever need. A few hunks of warm bread and several mugs of old booze. My family, healthy and whole, laughing loudly in a tavern. A ship and the vast sea, ready to take me on the next adventure with them.

Small victories.

Griffin, a few laughs behind, caught wind of the situation, and clapped a large hand on Tarran's back with a devilish grin. "Barkeep! Another of your best for my idiot cousin."

Before the barkeep could acknowledge his loud request, another man stepped up to the table, his height darkening our view. "Can I buy you a drink instead, sir?" He addressed Griffin directly in a thick accent, but I would be a liar if I said I didn't turn to look at him. And I mean *really* look at him.

Dressed in a smart black uniform with brass buttons down the front, he was out of place in the rundown tavern. If I had to guess by the longsword securely on his hip, he was a guard for some councilmember. But with a face like that, he was perhaps out of place everywhere. His dark beard was perfectly groomed, accentuating the sharp line of his strong jaw before carrying into the perfect waves of his hairline. A perfect bun smoothed and captured his mane of coiled hair in a knot so fine it could make any true sailor swoon. But what captivated me most was his easy smile, teeth like stars against the night sky of his deep skin. I didn't miss how Saeth licked her lips, or how Tarran scooted closer to Reagan instinctually.

I must have been staring too, because my husband nudged my side, an eyebrow raised. I rolled my eyes. I was married, not blind.

Griffin's eyesight was just as keen.

"Who am I to say no to such a gentleman?" He stared at the man, his mouth open and fiery eyes burning. But his expression shifted, recognition settling despite the cloud of ale. "Wait—I know you."

In one swift motion, the man tossed three silver pieces at the barkeep and pulled a chair up to our table. "We met in Ir'de. Madame Katrin's."

Tarran nearly spat out his drink at the mention of Ir'de's most famous and exclusive brothel, but Griffin's grin only widened. "Ahh, that's right. Drystan, yes?" My cousin leaned back in his chair, legs spread uncomfortably wide. The action might have earned a laugh, if not for Rhett's darkening expression. His entire frame went rigid, clenching his mug in a white-knuckled chokehold.

Drystan, however, leaned toward my masochist cousin. "And you're Griffin, if I recall correctly. I never forget a handsome face."

Rhett's face went white, and the rest of us sucked in a collective breath, waiting for the powder keg to explode. And whether it was the stress of Finna's impending nuptials, or the hungry bellies we couldn't feed, or the sheer fact that his middle name was trouble, Griffin sabotaged himself with a wink. "And *I'd* never forget such a fantastic ass."

I was waiting for it, but I still flinched when Rhett stood, shoved his chair back, and tossed the contents of his drink into Griffin's face. "Go ahead, man bun. He's all yours."

He didn't wait before stalking out the door.

Griffin went pale as he wiped the ale from his eyes, then stumbled after the fuming blond. "Rhett—Rhett, wait, I was only teasing—"

The rest of us sat at the table in a pregnant silence, exchanging furtive glances, daring each other to speak first. Drystan, Lyr bless him, took the bait. "I seem to have missed an important cue." He brought his mug to his full lips, sitting uncomfortably upright in the tavern chair. After a long swig of his drink, he stood, offering a slight bow. "I apologize if my actions caused you any discomfort."

I opened my mouth to bid him farewell, but my husband interjected first, saving me before I stuck my boot in my mouth. "No please, sit." He leaned back in his own chair for emphasis. "Let us buy you a drink on behalf of those two sorry asses. My name is Ronan, and this is my wife, Captain Keira Mathonwy." He looped his arm around the back of my chair, but I noted the edge of possessiveness in the way he angled himself toward me.

I leaned into him, a small part of me enjoying this jealous side of Ronan. But I gestured to Drystan's still empty chair with a warm smile on my face, Vala's favorite 'honey before vinegar' lesson swimming in my ear. There was no use offending a guard of his apparent stature over a little lovers' spat and some ale.

Drystan studied us both, weighing that same decision. After what seemed like forever, he finally exhaled sharply and sat back down, an uncertain grin playing at the edge of his full lips.

My crew did not need any further invitation.

"I'm Saeth." The half-inebriated redhead leaned forward in a very Finna-like fashion, accentuating what little bosom she had.

She was all sharp lines and angles, and if this man wanted Griffin, she was barking up the wrong tree.

To my surprise, Drystan took her hand and placed a chaste kiss on her knuckles. "The pleasure is mine."

"I'm Tarran." The boy offered a halfhearted wave as his sister blushed, whatever bold streak he'd felt a moment before dissipating like sunshine during twilight.

"And I'm Reagan." The youngest's hand shot out faster than a viper strike until she remembered herself, pulling it back with reddening ears. She gestured instead to her benchmate, a shoddy attempt to downplay her awkwardness. "And this is Tarran."

Drystan laughed, eyes the same copper as his buttons crinkling at the corners. "So he mentioned, but thank you for the reminder. My memory isn't what it used to be."

I swallowed a chuckle and cleared my throat. "Drystan, you said? That's interesting, are you from these parts?" The answer was clearly *no*, but Reagan's appreciative glance was worth sounding like an idiot.

Drystan, the perfect gentleman, answered without sarcasm. "Not quite. From Orwellin originally, I work as a High Council guard there." He swirled the contents of his mug, a memory hardening his brass stare. "But I've been on leave for a few weeks, ever since…"

"Since what?" Saeth pressed, catching the melancholy in his tone.

Drystan shrugged and sat straighter. "You know how it is. Things are bad everywhere."

The hair on my neck rose at the vagueness of his answer, watching his throat bob uncomfortably. He wasn't lying, but he was hiding something. A man in his position probably hid *many* things— things that could frighten and astound. Things that could probably end a High Councilmember's career, if the right pressure was applied.

I thought of Connor's gaunt haughtiness, the way he would stare down the bridge of his sharp nose at me like I was nothing. A man like that had to have dark secrets, even if he hid them well. But this beautiful man before me, this *gift* from Griffin...he might know where to look.

"Aye, things are bad everywhere." I painted on my best Mathonwy snake smile, pushing the pitcher of ale toward my newest companion with a sympathetic tilt of my head. "But I would imagine a man of your position has certain protections. Working for the High Council has to have its perks." I leaned closer, ignoring the burning sensation of Ronan's eyes on my back.

But again, Drystan surprised me. Instead of smiling back or brushing it off with another vague remark, he stiffened. "Aye, we have perks. Paid leave every three months, three square meals a day, a room and a bed to sleep in. That's a lot more than many have. But the High Council meets in Orwellin. We have our serving of horseshit handed to us first. And by the gods, when the people you're guarding are the real monsters..."

Dark skin paled around the knuckles with how tightly he gripped his draft of ale. I studied him a moment longer, unsure of how to respond. He knew secrets, alright. Maybe ones even blacker than I could imagine. The weight of them sat heavy on his proud shoulders.

Before I could find the words, Drystan cleared his throat. "Anyway, Bachtref has been nice, but I sail back tomorrow, whether I like it or not."

"I'll drink to that." Ronan looked at Drystan with an unnamed respect glistening in his pools of blue and raised his glass. "*Lechyd Da*, my friend."

"*Lechyd Da.*" Drystan forced another starry smile, the heaviness of his truths still hanging in the air. But intent on brushing it away, he nudged Saeth's arm playfully. "So, big red is taken then? How about you, young miss?"

Saeth was deprived of the opportunity to respond when an entangled Griffin and Rhett crashed back through the tavern doors with a loud thud. And as we cursed their names for being so damn loud and clumsy, our voices were drowned out by the booming tirade of a very large, very angry Bachtreffian farmer.

"By Bris's sickle, I'll run ya perverts through!" The dark-skinned man bellowed, swinging his own sickle above his head like a madman.

"Ahhh, Keira, a hand!" my cousin called over his shoulder to me, tripping again over Rhett as he struggled to his feet.

"Right on cue," I muttered to myself, Ronan flanking me as I rushed to Griffin's aid. I motioned for Tarran to stay back with Reagan; I had a feeling things were about to get ugly.

Ronan moved first, jumping in front of the enraged farmer before he could land another kick to Rhett's abdomen, his hands raised in surrender. "Sir, let's settle this like men."

He answered by punching my husband square in the jaw, knocking him onto the pile of idiots.

Red flashed in my vision. I was sure Griffin and Rhett had both earned their lumps, but Ronan was innocent. My hand instinctively flew to my hip, only to remember I'd given my dagger away earlier that morning, Lyr damn my good intentions.

I was unarmed, but I was not about to let anyone hit my husband without paying for it. It'd been a while since I'd been in a good fistfight, anyway.

The farmer wasn't expecting me as I lunged for him, colliding with his midsection and tackling him to the floor. Papa always said the big ones fell the hardest. The farmer hit the hardwood with a satisfying smack, but he had far more reach than I did, and before I could regain my footing, he ensnared my wrist in his long, coarse fingers and yanked me back down. My elbow cracked against the floor, a hiss escaping my lips as my vision blurred.

"By the gods," Drystan cursed in his deep velvet voice. "Is it always like this?"

"You dodged a bullet," Saeth answered flatly.

My vision clearing, I shuffled to my feet, whirling around to face the farmer's counter. Sure enough, the big oaf was already standing, his sickle raised once more, his murderous intent focused solely on me.

"Drop your sword, sir," Drystan commanded, his longsword drawn and ready. The weapon was superior to the tool in the large man's hand, but anyone with eyes knew Drystan was the real weapon. One wrong move, and his expert training would have this man bleeding out on the floor.

The farmer's eyes welled with rage, darting back and forth between me, the three fools shuffling to their feet behind me, and Drystan's sword. Finally, the sickle clattered to the ground.

"This pervert 'ad is cock out, takin' a piss on my property!" The man pointed a giant finger at Rhett, but his furious look was trained on Griffin alone. "An' this one. Ye should've heard the things he was sayin' to my wife when she came out to shoo them off! He should hang for it, the foul little shit."

"We know." I cast a glare toward Griffin as I brushed myself off, careful of my elbow. "Let us buy you a drink, sir."

The man opened his mouth to protest, but Saeth's needle-point tongue cut him off. "Or perhaps a trinket for your lovely wife?" She fiddled with her ring on her hand—her mother's ring, a simple gold piece with a tiny emerald stone in the center—and popped it off. "Here, take this. Make all this filth go away with something that sparkles."

It was my turn to flounder around with my mouth hanging open as I thought for the command to stop her, but a knowing look from Ronan quieted me.

The ring was her mother's last gift to her. We still had no clue who lit the fire that killed poor Alina, and Saeth was particularly protective of her mother's memory.

But perhaps Saeth didn't need answers or justice for her mother's death. Perhaps I wasn't the only one who needed unburdening.

The farmer's gaze flicked between Saeth and the ring, searching for the trick. When he found none, he snatched it from her grasp, albeit with a little more gentleness than he afforded the rest of us. "Fine, seems fair enough," he grumbled, then snapped back to Drystan, who he assumed was in charge at this point. "Keep a leash on yer dog, will ye?"

"Aye, sir," I answered instead, trying to stitch together the shreds of my Captain's confidence.

The man lumbered out with a final nod, and I let myself deflate just a little as I surveyed my crew. Ronan was up, holding his face where the man hit him, but otherwise unhurt. Reagan and Tarran slowly approached, Tarran's brow knit and Reagan practically oozing excitement to be so close to the action this time. Rhett and Griffin were conscious, but still groaning on the floor, half-drunk and bruised all over.

Drystan, however, was still rigid, staring at Saeth with an intense mix of curiosity and something else I couldn't name.

"Where did you get that ring?" he asked, his voice low and urgent.

Saeth shrugged, unreadable as ever while she stared at the open door. "Was my mother's. It didn't suit me much anymore, so it was time to be rid of it."

Urgency turned to excitement as Drystan stroked his trimmed beard. "Does it have a companion?"

"Our father's, why?" Tarran's answered for her as he helped a moaning Griffin stand.

Drystan scanned the twins' faces, recognition slowly dawning in his expression. "The sailor taking me back to Orwellin in the morning wears one just like that. His name is Weylin, I believe."

6

Reunions and Regrets

KEIRA

It was cold on the northern docks as we stalked our prey. A pack of hungry wolves ready to hunt, we crouched low behind a few crates next to an old schooner called the *Redwhyr*—the ship Drystan was supposed to board in a few hours. The early morning haze was enough to search by as we stared down our prodigal uncle, finally returned to us. He slumped over a barrel, passed out with an empty bottle in his hand, ginger-and-silver beard glistening with drink. His coat was black and threadbare, devoid of any coat of arms or ornamentation.

A traitor's crest.

I thought of the rescued portrait I still carried in my coat pocket of Papa and his brothers. I couldn't bear to part with it, the only likeness of my father I had left. But I wondered how the man in front of me went from the young, devoted sailor depicted there to the treacherous pirate he was now.

I wondered how Papa would feel to see another brother abandoning the Branwen colors.

My instincts warred within me. Half of me wanted to throttle the old drunk before he could even get a word in and tie him to the bow of the *Ceffyl* as a trophy. The other half knew we needed him alive—and conscious, unfortunately—for what came next.

A hand tugged at my coat sleeve, pulling me back to my pack before my feral half could bite. "Are you sure it's him, Captain?" Reagan whispered, her eyes narrowed. She'd only known the stories of Weylin, and perhaps we'd embellished his ugliness in our portrayal.

Saeth's eyesight, however, was keen as ever. Her voice was as low as the morning tide, barely more than a growl as she regarded her father for the first time in months. "That's Weylin, alright."

I could hear the mischievous grin in Griffin's tone without turning to look at him. "Thank you, Drys. This means more than you know."

Drystan, crouched on my left, smiled brilliantly. "I'm just happy to help reunite a family."

He had a knight's heart alright, but he perhaps wasn't as sharp as I had pegged him to be. "Mhmm. It's going to be one happy reunion. Stay here with Reagan, will you?" I clapped him on the back, hoping he would understand the underlying apology for what I was about to do.

No more hunting. No more hiding, skulking around the seven isles without direction. It was time to strike.

I stood first, flattening my coat against me. I still smelled of cheap ale and blood, but perhaps that was appropriate for the role I was about to play. With a sharp inhale, I donned my favorite mask and lifted my chin. "Deckhand Branwen?"

The old man stirred at the name, snorting and stumbling awake. "What do ye want—" He stopped short as he eyed my Branwen crest. "Oh, Lyr's ass."

Dropping his bottle, he turned to run. But my husband and Rhett were already in place behind him, catching him in his tracks.

"Miss us?" Ronan's voice was low as he steadied Weylin, the devil dancing in his eyes.

Rhett flexed next to him, the action visible even through the thick material of his coat. "Stay right where you are, old man."

"We just want to talk." I stuffed my hands in my pockets as I cornered my uncle, my snake smile on my face. "We don't want to hurt you."

"Speak for yourself," Saeth hissed as she emerged from the shadows, a blade sharpened for battle. I couldn't say I blamed her. I needed Weylin for answers, but Saeth had a whole childhood of miserable memories to unload. She stood with her hands planted to her hips as she waited for a response, accentuating the billowing blue tunic and skin-tight leather trousers she wore.

Weylin's eyes went wide, then narrowed in recognition. "Saeth?"

"Father." She unsheathed her dagger, turning it over in her hands. "Long time since we've seen your ugly mug. Tell me, what have you been up to?"

I wasn't expecting a warm welcome from the old man, but the outright hatred simmering in his beady eyes as he regarded his daughter made me shudder. "If yer mother were alive to see ye like this, she'd wish she were dead all over." He accentuated the cruel insult by spitting at her feet.

Saeth was made of iron and forged in fire, but even steel sings when struck. Shock splayed across her features, silver tears lining the green of her eyes. Alina's name was too precious to be hurled like a weapon. Weylin's filthy mouth had no business taking it in vain. I might have punched him straight across his pitiful face if Griffin didn't beat me to it.

With a crack, his fist connected with Weylin's jaw, sending him staggering into Ronan and Rhett. He cursed under his breath, standing back up and squaring off to my impossibly large cousin, teeth bared like a trapped rat. Griffin towered over him, fists clenched at his sides. "Apologize to her, you sad old fu—"

"Whoa." Tarran gripped Griffin's shoulder tightly, clouds of pity darkening his eyes as he reached to help his father back up. His soft spot for the old man would always be his weakness…not that I could blame him. Lyr knew I was even more protective of my Papa's reputation now that he was no longer alive to defend it himself. But Tarran's tight jaw signaled that even his vast-as-the-sky patience wavered. He dropped his voice low, offering a glance to the other sailors readying their ships in the early light. "Steady, Griff. There are other people on this pier."

I looked to where Reagan waited with Drystan, and the little dragon met my gaze, concern painting her pretty face. I passed her a silent signal to keep the guard safe—and close. If this escalated, we might need his intervention. Hoping it didn't come to that, I rallied my resolve and put aside the part of me that wanted to skewer my uncle like a fish. "Tarran is right. No more bickering. This is a parlay, Weylin. We just want to talk."

His lips pulled back over his teeth. "I'm not talking to some feral Mathonwy bitch and her pack of wild dogs!"

Life on the dock stirred as his vicious insult pierced the morning quiet. Judgmental eyes followed the sound, farmers and sailors with jobs to do who had no time for family squabbles. My nails bit into flesh as I fisted my hands, embarrassment flooding my cheeks and anger flashing through my core. I could withstand his insults— Lyr knew I'd faced worse—if it meant a shot at righting some wrongs. "Please, just come talk to us on the ship. We're making a scene here."

Darkness clouded my uncle's eyes. "Aye, better on the ship where yer husband can slit my throat like he did yer father's. Or will it be ye, Keira? Like ye stabbed Aidan?"

The two corpses that haunted my sleep swam to the surface of my mind, bloated and bloody, lifeless eyes staring into nothing. My breath came short. I wanted to snap back, to claim my innocence, but bile surged up my throat, choking me.

Saeth came to my rescue, emotion thick in her voice. "Aidan killed Cedric, you half-wit. And he shot Keira with *your* rutting guns."

I thought again of the portrait in my coat pocket. Of the brothers turned betrayers. Of the bullets and blades that ended them both and the Branwen brothers they left behind. One, chained to his grief and a barstool. The other in front of me.

Surprise lifted his eyebrows, and for a flicker of a moment, he had nothing to say. Neither did my crew. It had been months since any of us confronted the truth so plainly. True as her words were, something still felt wrong inside of me, a piece of my core dissonant with the reality of it. Somehow, it felt wrong to blame it all on Aidan, when I had done nothing to stop it from happening.

The chasm in my chest grew as my crew averted their gazes. The only person with the courage to meet my stare was Weylin, his confusion and pain mirroring mine. A strange pair we were, both guilty by association, both accessories to Aidan's scheme. Both trying to run from our part in it before it could catch us.

Rhett's baritone broke the uncomfortable quiet, dragging me back to myself. "Captain, we have company." He nodded east to a man making a beeline for us, his tall silhouette dark against the rising sun.

I squinted into the light, hand instinctively flying to my empty dagger holster. My crew shifted with me as naturally as ripples in a pond. Ronan and Griffin flanked me, Rhett and Tarran still holding Weylin while Saeth smartly moved to block him from view. The six of us breathed in unison, waiting with anticipation. I shot another look at Reagan, a warning to stay back. We did not need a guard to bear witness to whatever trouble waltzed our way. Clever as she was, she tugged Drystan's coat sleeve, pulling him out of sight behind the docked silhouette of a nearby cutter.

Ronan's hand found the small of my back, a gentle reassurance that he was with me, that I was *safe*. I inhaled deeply, letting the warmth of his fingertips ignite the forge of my strength.

The form took shape, dipped and baked in trouble: a tall man with deep amber skin in a grey coat and shiny new boots that clicked against the dock. I'd seen him a handful of times, but there was no mistaking the black wolverine crest on either lapel of his expensive threads.

Greyson Leary. Captain of the *Madyn*, councilman, and Connor's newly appointed guard dog.

My crew closed ranks, preparing for an unfriendly encounter. Weylin glared at the man, but stayed quiet, realizing the only thing worse for him than being with us was answering to the Council.

Leary didn't seem to notice our hostility, greeting me with a grin and open arms like an old friend. "Ahh, Captain Branwen, just the woman I was after!"

The hair at the nape of my neck prickled as my maiden name struck me, his honey-dipped insult subtle but well-placed. Smoothing out my coat, I painted on an uninterested facade, looking him over once before responding coolly, "It's Captain Mathonwy. And you are…?"

Leary winced, but quickly recovered, his smile widening to expose his teeth. "Captain Greyson Leary, at your service."

Saeth stepped forward, tilting her head to the side. "I don't recall any of us asking for it."

Pride roared through me. In a sea of swords, she was queen of needles—small but razor sharp, and precise enough to get under anyone's skin.

Enemy or not, something resembling respect flashed through Leary's expression as he regarded Saeth. "Well, if I'm being truthful with you, I'm here on an errand for a friend." He winked at her before turning his attention back to me. "High Councilman Yorath sends his regards."

Not to be outdone, Griffin slinked closer, a cat stalking a canary. "Ah yes, I did hear about you. You're Yorath's new puppet." Mischief twinkled in the red of his eye as he rose to his full height and flicked an invisible speck of dust from Leary's coat. "Tell me, how does his hand feel up your—?"

"Just tell us why you're here and be on your way, Councilman." I interrupted my cousin, a warning hand on his shoulder before this went from trading insults to trading blows. "Our crew is tired and you're cutting into our breakfast."

Leary paused, assessing Griffin with keen eyes, before acknowledging me again. "I'll be brief then." His leer returned as he produced a small, cream-colored envelope from his breast pocket. "For you, Captain *Branwen*."

"Captain *Mathonwy*." Ronan plucked the letter from Leary's fingers and wiped it on his coat, inspecting it closely before handing it to me. A sneer tugged at the corner of my mouth at my husband's subtle mockery; I'd forgotten how wicked his mask could be and how much I *liked* that part of him.

Carefully, I took the letter and opened it. Every ounce of the control I'd mustered in the moment before was washed away in the tidal wave of rage that consumed me as I read the contents.

You are cordially invited
to the wedding of
High Councilman Connor Yorath and Mistress Finna Branwen
On the seventh of November.

The beautiful calligraphy did nothing to make the words any less ugly, the physical evidence of my cousin's betrayal now resting in my hands. Then, along the bottom, in Finna's hasty handwriting, a personalized note addressed to me:

Can't wait to see you there, Keira girl.

"What is this?"

Leary shrugged, gold eyes simmering. They were the same hue as Drystan's, but without the warmth, only the same metallic harshness. "Straight from the puppet master himself." He'd had the advantage all along, but now he pressed it, stepping in until he was close enough to whisper. "There's going to be a wedding, Captain Branwen, and your sweet cousin wants you there in your best rags. And lucky for you, the Council and I have agreed to temporarily suspend your banishment for the happy nuptials."

"What?" Ronan's mask fell away completely as outrage and joy fought for dominance in his expression.

Leary ignored him entirely, tapping the edge of the invitation before retreating, victorious. "You'll have three days. That should be just long enough for you to screw it all up again. See you in two weeks."

"Go rot," I spat as he disappeared into the sunlight. But my stomach flipped twice, a fish frying on a skillet, as I reread the invitation again.

Three days in Porthladd.

"Well, this is a trap," Rhett sighed.

Three days. Three *whole* days. Lyr below, if this was a trap, it was tempting enough to get caught for. But to have to sit through the ceremony as my eldest living cousin shackled herself to the man hell-bent on ruining my life, to watch as he confined her to a life of misery…

Vicious and venomous as she was, no one deserved that fate. And I certainly didn't want to watch.

"This could be Finna's way of telling us it's safe," Griffin countered, taking the invitation from me with surprising care. Finna was his sister after all, and no matter the hurts that passed between them, they had a strange bond the rest of us couldn't share. He hadn't said anything after Reina told us about the wedding, but he'd been searching for answers at the bottom of every bottle from Porthladd to Bachtref. He pressed further, holding the invitation to his chest, "You know how she is, the manipulation she's capable of…what if Connor is *her* puppet?"

For a moment, I shared his hope, a wistfulness for the cousin who had taught me to braid my hair and flirt with boys. She was vain and stubborn and cruel, but she was not foolish. Papa used to say Branwens were born of the sea and stars. A siren queen, Finna had both the fury of the sea and the heat of the stars in her veins, and I wanted to believe with all my heart that the blackness of Connor's soul could never darken that.

"She was always the cleverest out of ye lot," Weylin grumbled, a foreign softness in his tone.

I looked at my uncle as I silently agreed with him for the first time in a decade. He met my gaze, both a challenge and a resignation in his tired eyes. Not an agreement, but an *understanding*. A reminder that despite our deep-seated differences, we were made of the same star-stuff. We were kin, whether we liked it or not, and that used to mean something to the Branwen Clan.

"It would be nice to have someone on the inside." I finally spoke aloud, a dangerous commitment to the wish in my chest.

I glanced at my husband, the only person I'd ever truly trust with my hopes and fears. He nodded once, blue eyes sparkling with the unwavering resolve I needed from him. "Only one way to find out."

The sheer weight of my love for the man in front of me was enough to crush me, yet I felt lighter than air. We would go to Porthladd. We would go home. And maybe, just maybe, Finna would surprise us all and hand us the key to our redemption.

A cough shook me from my trance. I turned to meet Drystan's apologetic grin. Reagan flanked him, curiosity burning in her eyes, but she didn't voice it.

"Sorry to ruin your plans, Drys." I smiled at my new ally, the handsome man who had given me nothing but deliverance even when all I offered in return was grief.

He waved my apology away, kindness in his metallic stare. "I can tell that this is a bad time, and I hate to intrude again...but I take it my passage back to Orwellin has been cancelled?"

Weylin interjected before I could. "No, we're still going."

I whipped around to my uncle, ignoring Drystan completely as the fire burned through me. *So much for understanding.* "No, we are not. We'll make another run to Ir'de for supplies, then we are back to Porthladd, and you're coming with us. Vala has been worried sick and you have a lot to answer for."

Weylin rolled his eyes, his frustration clashing with mine. "If ye want answers, we sail to Orwellin."

"What is there for you in Orwellin, old man?" Griffin groaned, as tired of this game as I was.

The look my uncle gave him could boil a lobster, but he kept his voice even. "If my hunch is right, my guns are there." With a curled, wrinkled grin, he nodded to my shoulder. "And so is yer cure."

7

Marks and Mutiny

KEIRA

The crew was on the ship by the morning tide, our course set for the very last place in the Deyrnas I'd ever want to go.

Orwellin.

The island of temples was beautiful in its own haunting way. The towers of each tributary reached toward the gods, looming over the rest of us mortals with keen judgement. It was where the most pious Deyrnasians made their stay, the sanctuaries and shrines filled with devotees of every god from every island. Some even worshiped the Dark God himself, unfearing and unflinching as they embraced the Otherworld. I'd been a few times with Papa, ferrying goods to *Delm Duwei*, the Holy City, from all over, awe filling my young heart each time I caught glimpses of the black-robed worshipers.

It was also where the High Council met.

The islands worked independently, but a representative from each made pilgrimages to the marbled city to oversee the peace between us and create trade agreements to share resources. And, in rare cases, to wage war.

I shuddered at the thought of running into Connor or another unfavorable High Councilman. I doubted I'd be welcomed, especially with the mark on my shoulder. A cursed *Melthith* had no place in the Holy City.

Yet our course was set, the wind in our favor. We'd brought Drystan along, the only kindness we could offer the poor guard after causing so much trouble. Now, as noon approached, he sat straight-backed at the bow of the ship, unbound curls flowing like a flag in the wind, learning sailor's knots with Saeth and Reagan.

"Like this?" He presented a near-perfect reef knot to Reagan with a coy smile.

She examined it with vicious scrutiny, chestnut eyes narrowed. "It's getting there. Good thing you're pretty."

The guard's mouth fell open, light dancing against the copper of his eyes, but Saeth beat him to the punchline. "Good thing you're too young for him, little dragon." She snatched the knot from Reagan's clutches, handing it back to a beaming Drystan with a wink. "If you want, later I can teach you other applications for that knot, Drys."

I mumbled a prayer to Lyr on Drystan's behalf. I doubted his training covered how to deal with whatever my cousin had in store for him.

Tarran and Griffin watched absentmindedly from their posts, Griffin watching Drys, and Tarran, Reagan. Both sported jealous scowls. I had to bite back a laugh. I wanted to join them, to tie knots and feel the sea spray my face and let my cousins stitch my soul back together. But I had a far more unpleasant conversation waiting for me belowdecks.

Ronan flanked me as I crawled into the bowels of the ship where my uncle waited in the brig. The light filtered through the cracks of the floorboards above us, casting his form in shadows. He was slumped against a wall, hugging a pillow to his chest as he snored. Griffin had thrown a few old blankets in there with him since he'd come willingly but I doubted he was anything close to comfortable.

He was about to be decidedly less so as I unlocked the barred door and nudged him awake with my boot.

He woke with a start, eyes scanning the unfamiliar surroundings. I crouched down to meet his height, glad for my husband's steady presence in the doorway. My unbothered mask slipped easily over my face, hiding the fear and uncertainty that bubbled within me. "How did you know about my mark?"

"I could smell it on ye." Weylin's voice was gruff, unfeeling. "Death."

My blood turned to ice. I knew the scent well, the rot and regret that seeped into my skin. No scrubbing could erase it. I never realized others could smell it on me, too. I tried to stay calm, but my hands shook. Did this mean my time was running short? The ship swayed, or maybe I did.

Weylin offered me a look that resembled pity. Before I could slap it off him, he raised a chained wrist and lifted the hem of his grubby, dirt-stained shirt to reveal his abdomen. My throat went dry, and Ronan sucked in a sharp breath behind me.

Just above his navel, a spot dark enough to consume shadows marked his oily skin. Even in the dim lighting, it was unmistakable.

My eyes shot to his. His lips tightened into a thin line of distaste. "Stench never goes away. Though I find it's harder to tell when it's covered with booze."

Surprise and sorrow fought for dominance as my tongue fumbled to find words. "You're a—"

"*Melthith*." My uncle finished for me, the word dripping with disdain. "How did ye think I got those guns? They came with a price. That's why I need them back."

I studied him for a moment. His rage dissipated with mine, and all that was left was age and sorrow. He wore it in every wrinkle and line that sagged his face. He looked exhausted to the very core, like existence itself was burdensome. I wondered how much of that heaviness rested in my own gaze. The cold, empty feeling of death crept along my spine again, and though I couldn't hear the creatures this time, I knew they were listening. Knew they sat just at the edge of oblivion, waiting for me to give in.

Weylin looked like he was close to the precipice. But underneath the weight of sorrow, there was something smoldering, like the molten lava hidden under the ash.

He still had hope.

If it still hurt, it wasn't the end.

There was still a way.

"I was told there is no cure." My voice found its footing in that small pocket of hope. I did not care much for my uncle, but I didn't want either of us to suffer this fate. If saving us from it meant becoming his ally once more, I could do it.

Weylin rolled his eyes. "If ye were in Hud, ye just didn't like the answer."

I shuddered at the thought of the one option I'd been presented with. *Yer lucky, as a woman, it's quite easy...*

"I'm not that much of a monster," I snarled.

"Aye, yer not," he conceded, rubbing at his wrists. Red, angry welts started to form. "Not yet, anyway. Give it twenty years."

His words stung like a slap across the face, but deep down, I feared he was right. I was already desperate enough to hunt down and chain up my own kin for answers. If I even made it twenty years, I didn't know how long my strong morals would keep me alive. And I didn't trust myself enough to choose righteousness over survival.

My husband, however, still only saw my gilded parts.

"Watch your tongue, or it will be my distinct pleasure to remove it." He loomed over Weylin and me like a statue, eyes just as cold. Maybe it was the spring water freshly flowing through his veins, but he looked like he could snap my poor uncle in half without a second thought.

I held my hand up, a signal to stand down, but Weylin cut in. "Ye can't threaten me, boy, I have nothing left to lose." He laughed, harsh and lifeless, his eyes echoing the emptiness of that sound.

Ronan's throat bobbed as he stepped back. No matter how angry he was, there was no reason to kick a man who was already dead inside.

I pinched the bridge of my nose. The scent between us both was suffocating, especially in the cramped brig. I just prayed to Lyr that Ronan couldn't smell it.

Looking to my uncle, I discarded my facade, laying bare my weakness and weariness. "You said you had answers. How have you survived this long?"

"Ye can't erase a debt, but ye can pay it in different ways. I chose to work fer the Dark God to buy myself time, and I've sent him plenty of souls to compensate. Each one buys time, but never enough. And since I used the gun, whenever my time comes, my soul is his, no questions asked." No remorse on his face, only truth. Perhaps a younger, idealistic Weylin regretted his path, but the man before me had long since given up on any hope of true salvation. He only sought survival.

Ronan's voice rumbled through his chest, a dragon getting ready to spew fire. "So there is no cure, only a treatment."

"Not quite." Weylin's soulless stare shot to my husband. "Some souls carry more weight. The soul of an innocent is priceless."

"Then why are you still cursed?" I tried to erase the judgment from my voice, my disgust coating my lips.

"Innocence is hard to come by. We're all monsters underneath."

His words clanged through me like steel striking iron. I didn't know if I was far gone enough to make that choice. I'd killed before, and I was already guaranteed my spot in the Dark God's council. But taking the life of an innocent?

Part of me still hoped that I was better. Or that I could be.

I'd rather be dead than be a liar or a cheat. My father's words flowed through my head, renewing my strength. I straightened my spine. "I'm not making a deal with the devil himself to shoot innocent people to avoid the consequences."

Weylin waved off my moral sensibilities. "Fine, no guns, but ye can still pass it on to someone else."

I stood, ignoring how my knees protested as I rose from my crouch. I would be better. I *had* to be better. For Papa. For the only Branwen that ever truly deserved the name. "I'm done with this." I turned and brushed through the door, no closer to any answers, but feeling so much lighter than when I first descended the steps.

"There are devotees in Orwellin," Weylin called after me, chains clattering as he yanked on them. The edge to his voice halted me in my tracks, and he continued, knowing I was a fish on the hook. "Ones that spend all their time in the *Delm Arawn*, praying to the Dark God, waitin' fer him to take them and honor them."

Heat flickered through me, and I spun on my heel to face him. "You want me to *give* my curse to an innocent person?" I snapped. My husband put a steadying hand on the small of my back, but I could feel the anticipation in his touch.

Weylin shook his head, something blackening his already hollow expression. "They're not all innocent, only a good way to buy time. But even if they were..." he scoffed to himself— "you'd be fulfilling their wildest dreams. They take vows of silence, devote their whole lives to prayin' for that fucker to snatch them."

I let his words sink in, rooted to my spot. I could walk away now. I *should* walk away. Devoted or not, they were still people, and what kind of person was I if I simply passed on my curse to another?

But I couldn't leave. Despite my best intentions, all I could do was stand there, gaping at my uncle, hope and duty warring in my chest.

"How does it happen?" Ronan asked for me, his voice thick with an emotion I couldn't name.

Weylin looked at me, nothing masking the truth in his words now. "There's a ritual. I've never seen it done, but I've heard of it. It's not pretty fer either party, but ye'll survive."

My husband winced. "How did no one in Hud or Ir'de know about this?"

Weylin shrugged. "Ye and I both know southerners avoid Orwellin like the plague. Most people do. No one wants the High

Council's attention. And the devotees are..." His face scrunched. "Unsavory."

"Which leaves us with a predicament as well," Ronan barreled on. He talked of barriers, but his eyes still burned with excitement. I knew that face. My husband was already plotting, paces ahead of me, leaving me in the dust with a sinking feeling in my gut. "I doubt the High Council would be very receptive to an outlaw banished for murder and her uncle who's charged with half a dozen other petty crimes across the Deyrnas."

To my surprise, Weylin joined him in his scheming, a crooked grin twisting his face. "They might be kinder if we enter with a strapping young guard."

"So this is a *we* now?" I spat, silencing them both. My cheeks heated, my hands knotted at my sides. I deserved a say in my own destiny, and I didn't need Weylin corrupting my husband. Even if Ronan easily forgot what Weylin had done to us, I didn't. "Thought I was a feral Mathonwy bitch."

"Ye are." My uncle's gaze held no trace of malice, only that desperate emptiness. "And I'm a drunk *melthith* that can't get his guns back and save his own arse without yer guard and yer ship."

"So we have an understanding." Ronan jumped in before I could process his words. A hurricane of rage and sorrow burst through my chest, aching at my husband's eagerness. Ronan never spoke for me, never assumed he knew my mind before asking. But he stood there, so thirsty for any solution he'd drink sand if Weylin told him it was water.

I did not recognize that man. Then again, I barely recognized myself anymore.

"I haven't agreed to anything yet." I swallowed back my anger, shooting a dark look at the creature possessing my husband's body. My throat constricted, I forced myself to address my uncle. "Rest up, old man. You look like crap."

I didn't wait for his response this time as I stormed out of the brig.

Footsteps behind me signaled Ronan's pursuit, but I didn't slow. I didn't want to talk to him, to see that hunger in his expression, to know how deeply my own wild need ran. But in a few long strides, he caught up to me, large hand taking my wrist. Steeling myself, I turned to face him, glad that we were still belowdecks. I wasn't ready to face him in full daylight. I could still see the burning beneath the blue of his eyes, like the ocean set ablaze by sunset.

"It's a good deal, Keira."

"No, Ronan. It isn't." I shrugged him off me. Hurt pooled in his expression, and my whole chest tightened in response, but I couldn't spare his feelings. Not when his honor, his *soul* was at stake. I pulled in a steadying breath. "There is no good in any of this. Either I die, or I pass my curse on to some other poor bastard so enchanted by those crazy devotees he thinks death is better."

I was expecting his disappointment, or gentle resistance. I was not expecting his sheer rage. He looked at me as if I spat on his mother's corpse.

"Lyr's ass, Keira, it *is* better!" He slammed his fist against the nearest wooden beam, shaking it as his voice echoed through the small cabin. "Anything is better than you dying! I don't care about the cost."

"My life isn't worth my soul. Or yours, for that matter," I thundered back, anger sputtering in my core.

Ronan laughed dryly, his mask cracking. "And what about me? What is *my* life worth?"

"What?"

He pointed roughly to my shoulder, tears budding in his eyes. "You only have that mark because you chose to save my life before your own. So now I get to live with the guilt while you get to be the righteous one?"

I gaped at him, my eyes prickling at his accusation. The ghost of his corpse floated through my mind, and sick burned the lining of my throat. "Ronan, you were *dead.* I had no time, no choice—"

"You absolutely had a choice, and you made it without looking back. It was quick and foolish, but you made it," he hissed, cutting me off. His jaw muscle flickered as he struggled to contain his temper. It was a full ten seconds before his breathing was even again. Then his hands found mine, the soft calluses of his fingers tracing circles over my skin. "I can't do this without you. Reagan, Griffin, the crew...we're all lost if you aren't leading us. I need you—we *all* need you, especially with everything going on back home. So this time, *I'm choosing*. I'm choosing you."

I stared up at him, struggling to find my voice. I wanted to comfort him, to hold him until the hurt in his eyes faded away. But I couldn't. I couldn't regret the choices that brought me this far. As much as I didn't want to abandon my crew, *my family*...I would not take someone else from theirs. Hysterical devotee or not. I opened my mouth to say just that, but Ronan pressed a finger to my lips.

"We are sailing to Orwellin." Determination laced his voice. "We go, we make a crazy devotee's day, and get you healed. That's it."

He stepped back, and I instantly missed the heat of him. "Ronan..." I pleaded, reaching for him, but he sidestepped my advance.

"That wasn't a question." His mask slipped back in place, the cold, unfeeling one he saved for his toughest adversaries. He pushed past me, climbing the stairs to the deck. "And if you have a problem with it, Captain Mathonwy, I will mutiny."

Drinks and Drowned Gods

RONAN

Captain Keira Branwen-Mathonwy had a keen talent for making my blood boil. I regretted my whole existence instantly when the pain swam in her eyes, the word 'mutiny' a dagger directly through her fourth and fifth ribs. My tongue was a wicked master with a mind of its own, and the curse hurtled out of me before I could calculate the cost.

I regretted that I hurt her. I didn't regret saving her.

But when she refused to see me later that night after the crew agreed to my rotten plan, my own wound was just as fresh. To my chagrin, the salve I needed for it was not at the bottom of a mug of ale, nor in the deck of cards Griffin shuffled.

The galley was cramped, the smell of smoke and liquor assaulting my senses as he took another puff of his lavender-and-hemp pipe, turning the deck in his deft hands. Rhett sat to his right, long hair pulled back from his face in a set of braids from Reagan that diminished the effectiveness of the dagger-point look he shot at Drystan. The guard seemed unfazed, picking his teeth and smirking at Saeth, whose boots rested casually on the table, accentuating the length of her legs. The only person actually paying attention to the game was Tarran, his young face screwed up in concentration as he studied his hand, his demise still inevitable.

The scene would've usually been all I needed to clear the dark clouds of my mood. But the itch for the spring gnawed at the already-frayed edges of my patience, and without Keira at my right, everything felt empty. The thought of her cursing my name in her cabin was not something I was unfamiliar with, but it never failed to knock me from my center.

I slammed my mug down, empty again.

"Whoa, easy there." Griffin huffed another puff of smoke at my face, a slap-happy grin swirling on his.

I waved the cloud away, irritation prickling underneath my skin. "Be a dear and just deal the cards, Griffin."

Drystan's too-bright stare bored holes into my threadbare facade. His strong hand clapped my shoulder. "You did the right thing. She'll come round."

The wick lit, rage engulfing me, all witty retorts turning to ash on my tongue. I had no quarrel with Drys, but I would not hesitate to skewer him with my words if he spoke so casually about my wife again.

Rhett beat me to it, tilting his head at the handsome guard. "You know this from your long and intimate friendship with her?"

Saeth knocked the table with her boot, nudging Rhett with a scowl. "Leave him be, he's the only one she isn't mad at. We all voted against her, remember?"

"Can we please just play?" Tarran's shoulders slumped as he fiddled with his hand, his bluff clear to everyone within seven leagues.

I ran a hand over my face. For every moment this little band of misfits cleared the darkness and filled my life with light, there were moments like these where every quip and jab made me want to run my fist through a wall.

"Deal the cards, Griffin." My voice was tighter than the need pulling at my gut. "Before Tarran has a conniption."

Despite the hazy warmth of his high, Griffin's keen eyes narrowed at me. He leaned across the table, sunset gaze reddening in the lanternlight. "Feeling sorry for yourself, hmm?" A baiting smirk crawled over his face, intended to rattle me. "Poor, innocent Ronan. Have you thought about her stake in this? Her choice?"

My grip on my mug went white. "I thought you were on my side."

Griffin rolled his eyes, smoke making him bold. "Daft prick. If you think there are sides, you're wrong." He flipped the cards in his hands with a scoff. "This is survival, and she's doing her best. You have no idea the weight that's on her shoulders right now. I agree that Orwellin is worth a look, and Keira needs a cure. But she's allowed to be pissed off about it."

There was a tense moment of silence, the only sound Griffin dealing the next hand. He was right, of course. What had I done to lessen the burden on her shoulders? She held the lives of her crew and her family in her hands every day, despite her own pain and exhaustion. What had I done to help other than put my own fear and worry in her hands, asking her to fix it for me?

Perhaps Orwellin would hold the answer to that question, too.

"When did you get so...considerate?" Saeth broke the awkward silence, examining Griffin like a winning hand and leaning further back in her chair, draping an arm around Drystan's wide shoulders.

"When you were still in diapers, Saeth." Griffin eyed the spot where Saeth touched Drys, his mouth a tight line, before he picked up his cards a little too forcefully. "Now, let's play."

"Finally," Tarran sighed with an eye roll.

The fact that Griffin and Rhett were both as aggravated as I was did wonders to soothe the edges of my annoyance. Misery loved company, and if I wasn't going to have my wife to warm my bed tonight, it seemed only fair that my coconspirators would be lonely, too.

My hand was shit—a fitting portrayal of my current luck—and the first few rounds went to Drystan, the rest of the crew groaning every time he swept the pool of chips closer to him.

"It's the mark, if you ask me," he commented out of the blue as he gathered his winnings again. I froze, his casual comment an arrow through my chest.

"We didn't ask you," Rhett snapped, counting his last four chips with a dark glare at the guard.

I smacked the back of my cousin's head before pressing Drystan. "What does that mean?"

The guard looked up, a mask slipping back to place as he realized his blunder. Jaw tight, he calculated his next step precisely; then, toying with a chip, he sighed, shoulders tense. "I've seen it before...seen people coming to the temples looking for answers. It doesn't just drain them physically, but emotionally, too. Plays tricks. Half of them are mad by the time they get to us. The fact that she's still so in command of her senses is a testament to how hard she's fighting it."

"That, or she's already mad." Saeth shrugged, nuzzling closer to Drystan's side.

My stomach knotted, sick and whiskey mixing. The image of the odious mark scarring my wife's pretty skin swirled with the contents of my gut, guilt rising to my throat and choking my next words. Lyr below, what in the Deyrnas was this woman bearing alone? I saw the ghosts in her eyes every night when she woke up screaming, saw the dark circles that rested underneath. But I had ignored too much of it, consoling my own guilt instead of her pain.

I found my voice hiding beneath the mountain of shame. "Do they ever get answers? The ones who come to the temples?"

Drystan regarded me with a kind smile, but it stopped short of his eyes. "Sometimes, just not always the ones they are looking for." Tearing his gaze from me, he counted his winnings and threw his hand down onto the table. "If you will excuse me, friends, it's time to turn in for the night. I haven't quite gotten my sea legs yet, and the drinks aren't helping."

"Lyr's ass," Tarran groaned as Drystan stood, tossing in his cards and counting the silver pieces he owed.

"I'll be off too," I excused myself, standing without bothering to collect my cards. I needed space to collect my thoughts instead. "Saeth, don't be too harsh on poor Tarran."

My boots carried me to the main deck, the sea air refreshing after the smoke and tension of the galley. I closed my eyes and let the crisp wind work against my cheeks, still hot from drinking. It was a small, external relief, nothing like the spring or my wife's arms, but still, I relished it.

I would save her, whatever it took. Orwellin would have the answers, and if Drystan was right, and they weren't the ones we were looking for, I'd scour the whole Deyrnas until we found something worthwhile. If there were no other alternatives, we'd find a life to sacrifice instead. My wife was a goddess, a gift to mankind from the heavens, carried on the sea's back and delivered as a light in the darkness. To save her, I'd cut down a thousand lives and sacrifice my own soul. She was worth more than the whole world…if it took setting it all ablaze to save her, so be it. I'd strike the first match.

She needs you tonight.

I swore under my breath as his voice echoed through me, nearly knocking me on my ass with shock. I'd heard him in the spring, but this was the first time he'd dared speak to me off-island.

I straightened my sleeves, subduing my fear and letting my mask slip back into place. "She doesn't seem to want me right now, if you haven't noticed."

Needing and wanting are very different.

Something dark flashed through me, a dormant dragon baring its fangs. Like Griffin, the sunken god was right, and the reminder of how neglectful I'd been carved another piece of my heart out. But I didn't want to hear it, not from a god that was as useless as me.

I looked out at the black horizon, the moon reflecting on the water the only indication of where the sky and sea met. "If I recall correctly, she needed you, too. Where were you then?" I didn't wait for an answer before I stuffed my hands in my pockets and descended below to my cousin's quarters.

You need to come back soon.

A final warning, one I didn't need. I already knew too well.

9

Temples and Tyrany

KEIRA

My husband made good on his word. The cunning snake he was, he told Griffin and Saeth the whole truth. Within ten minutes, they echoed his threats of mutiny, and our course was set without my consent.

I spent the five-day trip in my cabin, alone, coming out only to grab food or a moment of fresh air. If I was barred from making my own choices, the rest of them could run this gods-forsaken ship on their own. Ronan tried to come to bed the first night, but I told him he could go make his 'own choices' in Rhett's cabin. I regretted it almost instantly.

Without the distraction of my family, it was hard to keep the voices at bay. They became a steady presence, a soft buzzing in my ear that played on repeat from sunup to sundown. The closer we came to the Dark God's temple, the louder they grew, whispers spiraling into full shrieks of pain and torment. By day three, I was ready to rip my hair out and shove it in my ears like cotton; anything to stop the noise.

By day five, I was used to it.

I knew I was being petty and selfish and childish. Knew that my crew deserved a Captain and my husband deserved a wife who loved him, even when she was angry. But I couldn't bring myself to apologize, to make it right. Not when a part of me thought that maybe I deserved it. Maybe I deserved the taunting voices, their incessant cries that had even found a way into my nightmares. Maybe I deserved my crew's resentment, their anger and hurt that grew every day I stayed quiet.

Maybe it would make it easier for them to let me go when the time came.

A knock on my door the morning of the sixth day signaled our arrival. Griffin poked his head in, not waiting for permission. He wore civilian clothes instead of his colors, a dull brown coat with brass buttons replacing his normal blue one. He still wore Truth and Triumph proudly on his back, but a hat covered his signature red hair. If it weren't for the smirk that crossed his freckled features, I might not have recognized him. "Captain, we're here."

"Oh, am I still Captain?" I narrowed my eyes at him. Part of me was glad he came, the voices subsiding the second his soothing presence entered the door, but another part was hurt. Griffin had always been my best friend. My first mate. Since we were little, we made all our bad decisions together, come hell or high water. "Thought you all mutinied."

"You're still Captain." He folded his arms across his chest, giving me a look he usually saved for Finna when she was being a vain cow. "But you're acting like a child. Grow up, Keira. If not for your own sake, for mine. For the crew." He paused, his expression softening. "Now, when we get off this ship, you better say something nice to that poor husband of yours so he stops sulking, and then you better lead us like you were born to."

His words struck an exposed wound, but I knew he was right. Griffin, true to his swords, was made of honesty and grit. He was a blunt weapon with no need to hide who he was or how he felt—and he wouldn't let me hide from myself, either. If our roles were reversed, I'd have said the same thing to him.

I was acting like a child. Ronan would not have called mutiny if he wasn't desperate, and I had made him so, holding onto ideals that got me nowhere instead of standing beside the man who'd follow me everywhere. A real Captain listened to their crew. They didn't abandon them to go cry about it belowdecks.

The mark of a true Captain was not someone who sought to gain power over others, but someone who had power over themselves.

I couldn't help the hitch in my voice. "You sound like Papa."

"Good, maybe you'll listen to me, then." He shrugged, his full grin returning. "Let's go, Shrimpy, we're wasting daylight. We only have two days on this island before we high-tail it home for the wedding of the century."

"Aye, Deckhand Branwen." I placed a hand on his arm, a silent *thank you* in the gesture. "Let's go."

In the light of early morning, the black marble streets of *Delm Arawn* glistened like stars.

The city was covered in the obsidian stone, the greatest man-made feat in all the Deyrnas. The tribute to the Dark God himself both took my breath away and made me sick, the blackness matching my decorated skin. The buildings were just as gaudy, gemstone and ebony mosaics painting their faces, statues and trimmed hedges cluttering the lawns. Tall, sharp spires pointed skyward, many supporting the Dark God's black flag as if his cold curse was a gift.

None stood taller than the Gods' Eye tower. Legend had it that the obsidian monstrosity was built before the Deyrnas was even founded, perhaps crafted by the Dark God himself. Its mass stood out against the powdery clouds, triumphant and menacing, the sunlight glinting off the thousands of windows like jewels. Its shadow loomed over us, a reminder that the gods were always watching—that they still lived among us, hidden in plain sight.

I prayed that Lyr was with them. I would need his guidance for what we were about to do.

"This place is incredible!" Saeth practically vibrated with excitement, sharp eyes soaking in every detail. Only a weapon like her could find solace in the city of stone. She spun, her plain, olive-colored dress catching the wind like a fall leaf floating from a tree. The townsfolk milling about shot her bleak glares, our drab grey-and-green rags sunny in contrast with their stiff black frocks. The city was built as a temple, not a tourist destination, and they didn't have a reputation for being friendly.

But I couldn't blame Saeth for her enthusiasm, not entirely. I remembered the first time I visited, remembered asking Papa the name of every statue and artwork we passed with the same fleeting innocence. Part of me felt guilty for leaving Tarran and Reagan on the ship, knowing how desperate the girl was to see the Nightless City, but I could not guarantee her safety. Beautiful as it was, it was still a potential trap.

"This place really is amazing." Even Rhett's form melted as he marveled it all, somehow soft and warm against the harsh rock.

"Don't be too impressed," Drystan warned, his uniform blending into the blackness. He smiled at Saeth, but his expression was drawn as he smoothed back his curls into another tight bun. For someone so desperate to be back, he didn't seem happy to be home. "It's only beautiful on the outside."

"Stay close," Ronan muttered, hand drifting to the pistol at his hip. His eyes found mine as I watched him, and he nodded, the corner of his mouth quirking up. I smiled in return. It wasn't the apology that either of us deserved, but it was a promise that it was coming.

The knot in my stomach unraveled. Despite my boorish behavior, my husband still loved me. That was enough to get me through whatever today held.

We walked through the city, the winding streets narrowing as we approached the apex. A temple with at least two dozen sharp spires stood tall in front of us, a black heart at the center of the island. Deep dread sloshed through me at the sight, my shoulder whispering with glee.

Drystan cleared his throat. "This is where I must leave you. The main building of *Delm Arawn* is over there." He motioned toward the temple, as if we could miss it. His brass-button eyes were full of warmth as he patted my hand, a gentleman through and through. "I hope you find your answers, Captain."

For once, I was truly grateful for Griffin's insatiable flirtatiousness. I smiled at my newfound friend. "Thank you, Drystan. For everything. Best of luck to you."

The warmth faded from his gaze, replaced with something I couldn't name. His voice dipped. "Stay safe, but don't stay too long. I meant what I said. There are some rotten things happening beneath the surface here."

My head swam at the warning, and I narrowed my eyes. But he pulled away before I could ask the questions churning in my chest. With a polite nod to the rest of the crew, he made his exit.

"Goodbye now!" Rhett waved sarcastically in his general direction, a smirk tugging at his normally flat expression.

Griffin rolled his eyes. "You didn't have to be so rude."

"It's instinct now, since I've been spending all my time with you." Rhett's Mathonwy mask fell back into place, but I had to stifle a laugh when he winked at my cousin.

"Let's move," I said. "We don't want to attract any attention."

The entrance to the temple of *Delm Arawn* was just as intricate and ominous as the rest of the black city, its marble columns towering over us like giants. Gargoyles and statues topped each one, dark-eyed sentries watching our every move. Our boots clicked across the charcoal marble floor as we passed the rows of masked guards standing at silent attention, all wearing the same uniform as Drystan.

Think tall, you'll be tall.

My father's advice fortified me. I rolled my shoulders back and stood straighter.

The temple foyer was small despite its ostentatiousness, with only a deep-stained wooden desk in front of the door into the sanctuary. A receptionist perched on a stool, dull robes consuming his small frame, his nose so deep in a stack of papers we were greeted only by the bald spot on the top of his head.

There was only one way in, and I wasn't about to be deterred by a secretary and his feathered pen. I rapped my fingers across the deep mahogany mantle, grabbing the petite man's attention. He looked up at me in annoyance over his thin wire glasses. "State your business."

I fixed my coat. It wasn't my normal Branwen blue, replaced instead with a plain grey thing, but Papa always said a coat didn't make a Captain. It was my job to fill it. "We are here to inquire about a meeting with a devotee."

The man sighed and tapped the sheet before him with his quill. "Name here."

I swallowed hard, my confidence faltering. I did not want the Council or anyone else to know my business here. My heart thundered, half of me ready to sprint from this place and never look back, but Ronan intervened before I could run, with a steady hand on the small of my back and a smile painted on his face. "Any devotee will do, we didn't have a specific one in mind."

The receptionist's jaw flexed in irritation. He shoved the quill closer to me, ignoring Ronan entirely. "No, *your* name."

"You can call me whatever you feel like moaning later." Griffin rested his elbow on my shoulder, waggling his eyebrows at the small man, the action dripping with condescension. I cursed my cousin under my breath.

The man shot from his seat, ready to show Griffin the door. But he stopped, mouth gaping, as his eyes flicked back and forth between the both of us. The anchor in my gut threatened to pull me to my knees when clear recognition lit his features and he pointed a shaking finger at me. "Wait, I know you."

I fought to keep the sinking feeling in my core from mirroring itself in my face. "I'm sorry, I don't—"

"Mathonwy. Keira Mathonwy." His lips pulled back in a smug leer as he pointed instead to a poster on the announcement board behind him. Sure enough, there was my face, expertly drawn and staring back at me. They had nearly every detail: my freckles, the sharp tilt of my nose, my dark mane of hair. Only the eye color was wrong, a smudged charcoal instead of piercing silver. The faces of the rest of my crew peeked from behind my portrait, save Tarran and Reagan. Griffin's unmistakable head of red curls, Saeth's angular chin, Ronan's sapphire eyes and crooked nose...

They had been waiting for us.

The man's smile grew sinister. "Wait here." He sauntered behind the door to the left.

"This isn't good." Griffin's arm fell to his side as he voiced my thoughts, the other hand twitching toward Truth and Triumph.

I smacked his shoulder, heat flaring inside me as I nervously eyed the guards still positioned at the door. "No thanks to you and your mouth."

"It's your face on the warning poster too." Saeth's razor-edged bluntness cut through the churning in my chest. She pushed Griffin out of the way and seized my shoulder. "This entire thing was a bad idea. We should make a run—"

"Ahh, Madame Mathonwy." A woman's voice cut through the air like a blade, shrill and demanding as she approached. She was not beautiful, but she was captivating. Dark eyes sharper than knife-tips bore into me, and it looked like the life had been sucked from the very marrow of her slender frame. She dressed from collar to boot in a billowy black frock, only her pale, skeletal fingers visible as they reached out to shake my hand. Still, frightening as she was, it was hard to look away from her. She was danger and darkness embodied in a dress.

Griffin's hand twitched again as Ronan and Rhett instinctively stepped in front of Saeth. I was immediately grateful we left Tarran and Reagan behind as I lifted my chin and grasped the woman's hand firmly. I met with surprising cold, but I schooled my features into submission. "*Captain* Mathonwy, actually. And you are?"

Her painted red lips quirked to the side. "Councilwoman Morwyn Locasta, at your service."

My stomach knotted. I thrust my hands into my pockets, if only so she couldn't see them shake. Locasta was the High Councilwoman to Orwellin itself. As chairperson of the entire Council, she was the most powerful woman in the entire Deyrnas. And as fate would have it, she had my wanted poster on her front door.

But I would not run. I needed answers, and my crew needed me alive. We had come too far to be turned away. So I would lie and cheat and steal and fight the Dark God himself if that's what it took. "My pleasure," I managed through gritted teeth, the hair on the back of my neck standing at full mast.

Locasta walked around the desk with eerie grace, sunken eyes raking over each one of my crew members with careful consideration until she was only inches from my face. "What brings you to our capitol, *Madame* Mathonwy?"

The first rule of negotiating was to act like it already belonged to you. I stood straighter to meet her height, until we were two wolves eye to eye, snarling behind our smiles. "We seek a meeting with a devotee."

Locasta clicked her tongue with disdain, a fake pout on her thin lips. "Ah, well I'm afraid you'll be disappointed."

I tilted my head, irritation prickling under my skin. "We were told anyone can meet with them. It's our right as citizens of the Deyrnas."

Her eyebrows flew up, a mixture of surprise and smug amusement dancing across the pale planes on her face. "Yes, well, rights are reserved for those who haven't been banished from their homes after murdering their uncles."

Her words were a gunshot through the gut. "What?"

Locasta brushed an invisible speck of dust from my coat, close enough that I could smell her. The scent of rose bath soap covered the faint odor of rot. Her grin became a grimace as she tucked a strand of my hair behind my ear. "Councilman Yorath is a very dear friend of mine, you see, and he informed me of your plight. I'm afraid that I cannot put any of the devotees in harm's way, no matter how beguiling you are."

Rage seared through me and I smacked her hand away. I wanted to vomit or run or stab something—which first, I couldn't decide. We should never have come to this island. I knew it was a mistake before we even set sail, but I let hope cloud my judgement and desire taint my instincts. Now I had walked my entire crew into the wolves' den and shoved my head in her maw.

"Then I'll go." Ronan stepped forward, his best serpent's smile plastered on his face. A viper circling a guard dog, he towered over Locasta, stance casual but eyes full of menace. "I haven't been convicted of anything. Surely my rights as a citizen mean something to a leader like you. Keira will just wait here under your watchful gaze while I go have a chat."

Locasta's throat bobbed as she narrowed her eyes at my husband. She smoothed her dress, though it wasn't ruffled. "I'm sorry, sir, but I must admit, my friend warned me thoroughly, and as High Councilwoman of this fair island, I have to pass my judgement accordingly. Guards, please see these young friends out."

Without hesitation, two of the hooded guards swooped upon us. The first snatched my arm, yanking me back from Locasta.

"Let go of my wife if you value your meaningless existence." My husband's voice was cold enough to freeze the sun as his hand flew to the pistol at his hip. The rest of my crew fell into ready stances, Griffin drawing Truth from its sheath, Rhett at his side in less than a wink.

I shoved the guard off me, signaling my crew to stand down. This was not a gun fight, and I knew we were outmatched. I glanced back at the row of guards at the door, all ready to come to their superior's aid at a single call. "I'm fine, Ronan. We'll leave." I choked down my fear, taking a careful step back toward Locasta. I kept my chin high, but she merely grinned, inhaling my scent like a bloodhound.

I would not be afraid. I was a *blaidd* with fangs and claws and cunning. And I knew how to hold a grudge. "Now this is personal, Councilwoman."

Something dark and *familiar* flashed in her ebony gaze, and a chill ran up my spine. "Connor did have a message, I recall, if I did ever make your acquaintance." She leaned in, her breath hot in my face as she whispered so only I could hear, "He said that as long as you're miserable, he wins."

IO

Councils and Cages

KEIRA

Like last week's trash, the two guards escorted us not through the front door, but through a service hallway that led under the building. One led, a regulation pistol drawn, and the other followed behind with his sword at our backs. They'd disarmed us, and our swords and daggers and pistols clanked in the canvas sack the second guard carried, a clamorous song to signal our surrender. There was very little chance we could get away without taking a hit. So we followed, against our better judgement, into the bowels of *Delm Arawn*.

The further we went, the stronger the smell of death and rot grew, mimicking the mark on my shoulder. At some point, the sunlight stopped pouring through the windows, our only light the lanterns that lined the walls. I caught my husband's gaze in the dimness, and he nodded, concern knotting his brow. I hoped to Lyr that this particular path was just a scare tactic, not some indication that we would be buried alive in this hellscape.

Griffin scrunched his nose up, thick arms folded in a pout. "This is horseshit. If I ever see that woman again, I'm going to—"

"Stay quiet," the guard in front commanded, his voice strangely familiar. He stopped moving, holding up a hand to Griffin.

"I'm going to get you out of here before they send more of us after you."

Before Griffin could protest, the guard tore off his mask, revealing an unmistakable tight bun and copper stare.

"Drystan?" My heart thundered in my chest, this time with hope.

Our friend was here to save us. But from what, we didn't know.

Griffin's pout flushed into a full-fledged smile as he beheld our savior. "See Rhett? I told you it was good to make friends with a man in uniform."

"I said *quiet*." Drystan peered around, stance ready, fully alert. He wore his authority like a cape resting on his broad shoulders. "Leith, leave the weapons and go secure the doors," he ordered the guard behind us before ushering us forward.

The second guard pulled off his mask. He was a young boy, no older than Tarran, but he had a strong jaw and kind eyes. It was clear he did not really belong yet, a boy playing grown-up in a soldier's uniform. But his loyalty to Drystan was also written boldly across his boyish face and quick salute. "Aye, Colonel Farchos." The boy let the sack of our armaments clatter to the floor as he disappeared into the shadows from whence we came, not looking back.

"*Colonel* Farchos?" I narrowed my eyes at Drystan as I palmed my spare dagger. "Someone failed to mention that."

Sadness laced his smile. "Would you have still sailed with me if I told you?"

He was right. I would never have let him on my ship or near my crew had I known his status. It was one thing to harbor a random guard, but a highly ranked official? Lyr's ass, I'd have to be crazy. But he had been kind to us from the first moment in the bar, despite his position. As I studied him, his expression held no trace of malice or dishonesty, the secrets that previously rested there imperceptible. If what he said was true, my crew needed him.

I sighed, letting my walls fall. "Want to tell us what's going on now?"

Something akin to relief washed over him. "I didn't know you were a wanted woman until I saw the posters...but there are no answers for your mark. None that would be in your best interest." His throat bobbed, the truth heavy on his tongue. But then he squared his shoulders, donning his authority once more. "Now I'm taking you out through the back way so maybe you can make it back to your ship before the Councilwoman sets it on fire."

I looked to my crew, their faces set. They trusted him too. I nodded once to our unexpected savior. "Lead the way, Colonel."

Weapons drawn, we followed him deeper, darkness creeping along the walls—and that's when the voices returned. Moaning and whining, they echoed through the stone, desperate and tortured. I squeezed my dagger tighter, trying to shut them out, but they grew louder as we descended, groans turning into pleas and whispers melting into shrieks of pain. Next to me, Ronan soured.

"Do I want to know where those sounds are coming from, Colonel?

I stopped in my tracks, glancing quickly at my husband, my limbs locking. *He heard them, too?*

"What in Lyr's name is that?" Saeth covered her ears with the heels of her hand.

So this wasn't in my head. This was real.

"Your god can't hear you here," Drystan chuckled humorlessly. "Eyes forward, keep moving. I'm so sorry."

As we moved forward, the voices swelled, until finally the narrow hallway emptied into a larger room. The smell of death hit me first, then piss and rot and worse, tinged with fear and mixed with agony. I covered my nose with my sleeve, gagging once as my eyes adjusted. When the shapes defined themselves in the dark, my stomach truly rose to my mouth. It was a room full of cages, rows and rows of them, some stacked on top of each other, filling the cavernous room to the brim.

Cages full of people.

Or, what was left of them. Their forms were skeletal, eyes dull and lifeless as they moaned into the nothingness. Gasps and hisses sounded through my crew, and Saeth emptied her breakfast onto the cold ground.

My voice was thick as I rounded on Drystan. "What is this?"

"Reality." His voice cracked with ache and horror deeper than mine. "We have to keep moving."

He strode forward, his head down as he passed the aisles of prisoners. I rushed after him, yanking his arm, forcing him to meet my gaze. "We can't just...we have to do something."

Brass turned to stone, determination masking pain. "No, you have to leave. Now let's go, before my colleagues arrest you and throw you into the cells with the rest of them."

I bit my lip, looking back at my crew. Their horror was apparent in the slump of their shoulders and the tears forming in the corners of their eyes. This was wrong. A part of me—the part that was my father's daughter, the part that stood for something— screamed for justice.

But a louder part, selfish and calculating, knew the cost of taking action. We didn't have time to play hero today, and my crew always came first.

So I swallowed down my bleeding heart and trudged after Drystan, head down and heart broken. My crew, true and loyal as they were, followed.

I kept my eyes on the dirty floor as we passed, ignoring the scent that assaulted my nose, the hands that reached out to us, the voices that called for help and mercy. I hated every shaky step, but I pushed forward, each cry and desperate plea echoing through me.

I would remember every one. And when my crew was safe and sound, I would find a way to make it right. I would make every monster on this island pay.

"*Ariannad!*" A quiet male voice somehow broke through the rest, as if he'd whispered directly in my ear. I stilled as the name sank through me. It was the same name I'd heard on *Hiraeth* so many months ago, the one that haunted my nightmares every night since.

But his words were not of fear or pain or sorrow. His was a victory cry.

"*Ariannad*, please! Please!" he cried again, somehow farther away this time.

I followed the voice to a cage on the bottom row to my left, to a boy no older than Saeth, with hair as black as mine and sharp eyes that shone even in the darkness of the room. I moved to him, not entirely of my own volition, as he said the name over and over again like a prayer.

"Stop!" Drystan gripped my shoulder tightly. "Some of them are dangerous."

"Let go," I hissed, half-wild and fully enraged. He obeyed, shock plain on his features, but I didn't care. I knelt before the boy in the cage until my eyes could meet his. Something locked and unlocked in my chest as I stared at his dirt-covered face, an answer and a question in one. "Who are you, and how do you know that name?"

His hand shot through the bars, gripping mine firmly but gently. "Take me with you, *Ariannad*."

I tried to shake him off, but he held tighter—not out of malice, but a reminder. A reminder that he was real and tangible. I could hide my face and avert my gaze but matter how many times I bowed my head and looked away, he was still there.

I did not shake him off again. Instead I covered his hand with mine, my voice softer this time. "I asked you how you knew that name."

"*Duweni*." A smile broke across his features, eyes crinkling. He spoke reverently, like a priest singing a hymn, not a prisoner trapped in a cage. "We are the same. My name is Vian, and the winds have told me about the woman with the moon in her eyes and raven hair. I was told you are the redemption."

His words should have alarmed me, should have confused me. But for the first time in two and a half months, something stirred in my chest, a flicker of the power I'd known before.

Truth, it sang through my veins, filling me with warmth. It was not Lyr's voice, or the dark whispers I'd come to know, but something deeper. Stronger. Brighter. And *mine*.

"Vian," I whispered his name back to him, every instinct in my body telling me not to let go of his hand.

A hand on my shoulder pulled me from the moment. Drystan looked down at us, concern and urgency twisting his jaw. "There will be more guards, I can't protect you forever…"

I stood again, but Vian held on, desperation finding its way in his tone. "No, please, I cannot stay here. You need me, too."

I looked between him and the guard. Drystan's throat bobbed. I knew he was right; we didn't have much time, and there was very little a crew of five and a single guard could do if the full weight of the Orwellin military bore down on us. But my mind was made up the second I heard the boy's call, a forgotten part of me roaring back to life. I was meant to walk through these dungeons today. I was meant to meet this boy, and I was meant to deliver him to safety. It was an irrefutable fact as true to my soul as my own name.

I squeezed Vian's hand before steeling my gaze and turning to Drystan. "We're taking him."

The guard's face fell, panic setting in. "Captain, I can't let you do that."

I pursed my lips. I didn't want to hurt him, not after all he'd done for us. But I was left with no choice. This wasn't about morals or ideals anymore. This was fate. I could not leave this boy behind.

I turned to my crew. "Rhett?"

"My pleasure, Captain." He grinned. Drystan's realization came too late as he fumbled to draw his sword. Faster than a hurricane, Rhett brought the hilt of his blade down over the Colonel's head. The man collapsed on impact, eyes rolling in the back of his skull. Rhett patted his face. "Sorry pretty boy, but we'll find our way from here."

I knelt beside the guard, inspecting for blood, making sure Rhett hadn't hit him too hard. He'd have a headache from the Otherworld, but he'd be alright. I signaled Griffin, and he helped me prop him against the nearest wall. "Sorry, friend, but this is best for you, too. Now you have an excuse for why we got away." I ripped the hem of my tunic, using the length of fabric to tie his hands together. I stood, feeling more certain than I had in months, and looked to my crew, their faces expectant. "I'm sorry if I just screwed us all to the Otherworld."

"Even so." Saeth's jaw was tight, her hazel eyes like steel right out of the forge. "We're all glad you did, Captain."

My heart swelled with pride, but we didn't have time for sentimentality. "Anyone see a key?"

"We don't need keys." Saeth pulled a few hair pins from her coat pocket. Wasting no time, she knelt before Vian's cage, focus falling over her.

My youngest cousin never ceased to surprise me. The Queen of Needles always came prepared. "Where on earth did you learn that?"

"Believe it or not, Finna." She shrugged as the lock popped with a satisfying click. "How do you think she snuck out to meet her beaus?"

My heart stalled at the mention of my eldest cousin, but I shook it off. There was work to be done. I would worry about our next destination after we survived this trip. "Ronan, help Saeth pick as many as you can. We won't be able to reach them all, but if we set a few loose, it might buy us time." I pointed to the nearest cages whose weakened inhabitants still moaned and called to us. We wouldn't be able to take them with us, not without alerting the guards and putting us in danger, but we could at least give them a head start. "Griffin, Rhett, guard the entrance."

"Already on it." Griffin drew his swords with a grin, Rhett hot on his heels as they moved to block the door.

"Thank you," Vian croaked as he crawled from his cage, standing on shaky limbs.

"Are you alright?" I rushed to his side, pulling his arm around my shoulders to support his weight. He was taller than he seemed, almost Ronan's height, but desperately thin ribs poked me from underneath his rags.

"I am now." He sagged into me, but his smile was brighter than the sun on water.

I grinned back, not daring to question the instant kinship with the boy. Fate was a tricky mistress that had all the answers and never needed a reason. "You don't have any clues on how we get out of here, do you?"

"I've been planning a way out since I was seven." His laughter was dark and hoarse. "I can lead you out."

Something growled in my chest. *Seven? How long had this boy suffered?* I swore again that one day, I'd make the monsters who put him here pay for every moment of pain he'd endured.

Chaos erupted around us as Ronan and Saeth picked the locks and the prisoners crawled out, some crying with joy, others stunned silent. But they all had the same word on their lips as they passed me, and it echoed through the chamber like an anthem.

Rydha. Liberator.

We managed to open a dozen cages, some with three or four people inside, before I signaled our retreat. We had no more time. Drystan already stirred, and his colleagues would hear the ruckus we made and be down to investigate soon enough.

We handed our lockpicks to a woman a little older than us who seemed to be in the best shape physically.

"Thank you, *Rydha*," she whispered through chapped lips, clutching the small pins like they were life itself.

Something in my core sputtered to life, proud and victorious. We had come for answers and failed, but we had gained something far more valuable.

Saeth took Vian's other side, but the boy was so thin I could've managed on my own. We made our way to the exit, a small passage that Vian insisted we could follow all the way to the docks.

"The guards use it when they want to go get drunk with the sailors and don't want to get caught," he explained, rolling his impossibly dark eyes. "They forget we can hear."

"They'll know it was us," Ronan whispered, concern on his brow as we followed Vian's instructions through the tight corridor.

"Good." I grinned, victory still burning through my veins like starlight. "Connor isn't the only one who can send messages."

Songbirds and Saviors

KEIRA

Vian, true to his word, led us through the dark tunnels to the docks, where Tarran and Reagan waited on the *Ceffyl*. They were both safe, but shocked when we returned with Vian, bruised and scarred and filthy as he was.

And without Weylin.

The old man was nowhere to be found, as Tarran and Reagan had discovered first, a note in his cell in lieu of the man himself.

Went to get me guns. Don't wait fer me. Best of luck.

-W

I cursed under my breath, shaking with rage. "Old bastard."

"I'm sorry Keira, I didn't think to check on him." Tarran ran his hands through his mop of ginger curls, brow wrinkled.

"We got bored, so we were playing cards in the galley—" Reagan gnawed her lower lip, eyes lining with tears.

"It's not your fault." I fought back the frustration rising up my throat with a shallow smile and looked at the meager note again, wishing it would catch on fire and burn all of *Delm Arawn* down with it. "Rhett, Griffin, how long would it take you two to search the docks?"

Rhett cast a piteous glance toward Tarran and Reagan. "Too long."

Saeth stole the note from my hands, crumpling it up and crushing it under her boot. Her eyes flicked up to mine, filled with riotous tears that did not match the ice in her voice, colder and harder than the streets of the Nightless City. "Dark God damn him. Keira, we should move. We don't have time to wait for the bastard."

I stared at her a moment. Steel sang when struck, but Saeth was made of something stronger. I let her diamond exterior sharpen mine.

Papa used to say no Branwen was left behind, but Weylin shed the name the day he sold it to the Dark God. If he wanted to stay on this gods-forsaken island with his guns, he could do just that. He'd lied to me about a cure. He'd used me and then abandoned us, just as he had time and time again. He didn't deserve a ride home.

We had bigger fish to fry.

"Hoist the anchor." My command left no room for protest, not that any of my crew dared. "Ronan, go help the boy clean himself up."

Ronan's left hand hovered over the pistol at his hip as he held onto Vian, but he didn't say a word when he ushered our guest belowdecks.

We wasted no more time hoisting our sails to full mast, our eyes on the horizon. It was only a matter of time before the High Council figured out what we had done, and we didn't want to be within ten leagues of the place when they put it all together.

As Orwellin's form shrank behind us, the ache in my shoulder subsided but the deeper chasm in my chest grew. There would never be a remedy that could erase the memory of what we'd seen in the dungeons. I said a silent prayer for the lost souls we left behind; my ship was not large enough to carry them all, but I'd carry the weight on my shoulders for the rest of my life.

We were only six or seven leagues from shore when Vian found his way back to the main deck. Without the dirt caking his face, he was undeniably handsome. Dressed in a pair of Ronan's black trousers and a white tunic left untucked, he seemed taller, but all the more innocent. Delicate. Pretty pale skin stretched across high cheekbones, accentuated by the tousled black hair that danced in the wind as he leaned against the starboard rail.

But in the peculiar slant of his ebony eyes, something smoldered and burned. A man who'd been caged his whole life feeling the sea wind on his face for the first time. He closed his eyes, lost in the sensation, holding his fingers out as if he was trying to catch it as he murmured quiet prayers.

Drystan's words repeated in a faint corner of my mind. *Be careful. Some of them are dangerous.*

Perhaps I should've been more cautious before inviting him aboard my ship. Perhaps I should've weighed the risk like a good Captain or had Griffin and his swords keep an eye on the wraith. But every time I looked at him, his form elegant against the horizon, the mistrustful, cautious part of me scattered in the wind. The same tug in my chest carried me forward, questions blazing through my mind.

"Vian…" I said softly as I approached. "That's an interesting name."

"Vian Imari." He did not open his eyes as he responded, a grin on his slim features. "I chose it for myself."

"Where are you from?"

Dark eyes opened, shadows dancing across his features. "The pit."

"Look, kid, you have to be more specific," I tried to keep my tone light, but a chord struck within me, a dozen more questions rushing to the surface. "I don't do well with riddles."

Vian turned to face me fully, the sharp angle of his chin tilted. "The pit. Where you found me. That is where I am from."

My jaw dropped as shock and rage raced through me. "You were raised there?"

He scoffed humorlessly, staring out again at the open ocean. "Born."

The wind picked up around us and a chill ran down my spine. I had no words, nothing to describe the deep ache that filled my chest. This boy was *born* in that hellhole. Born to the darkness and death, a black swan with clipped wings that never got a chance to fly.

Tears sprang to my eyes, but I would not taint his suffering with my reaction to it. Instead, I made a silent vow. I didn't know why the gods put me in this boy's path, nor how he knew what he knew. I didn't know why I was so drawn to him, like a mother bird called back to its nest. But I would never cage the sparrow before me; I would do everything in my power to see him free.

"Lyr's left ass cheek." A tiny voice behind us pulled me from my thoughts. I turned to see Reagan staring open-mouthed at Vian. "You're prettier than a girl."

"Reagan, language," I scolded, embarrassment flushing my cheeks. We didn't just rescue this boy to gape at him, even if she *was* right.

Vian didn't seem to notice the crude comment, pricking up like a songbird on a branch. "You worship Lyr?" His head tilted dramatically, confusion on his features. "Not the Dark God?"

Reagan snorted. "Why in the seven isles would we ever worship him?" She stuck her fists to her hips, narrowing her eyes at him. "We aren't crazy."

"The temple men say all should worship the darkness," Vian recited coolly, stepping closer to the young dragon. "It is why we exist. So we can be closer to him."

"You're a devotee?" I eyed him skeptically. As badly as I felt for him, I was not comfortable with the idea of someone who worshipped the Dark God on my ship. My hand flew instinctively to rub my shoulder.

"No." Vian looked at me with a small grin, and the air rushed back into my lungs. "I speak only to Nef, the sky goddess. That is why they kept me below. I was not ready to be made whole."

Reagan snickered, arms folded across her tiny chest. "You are very strange."

Vian's obsidian eyes flicked to her, the dark clouds disappearing. "You are very short."

Shock lifted her eyebrows, but she schooled her expression, her Mathonwy mask almost as complete as her cousins'. She studied the boy a moment, then another, weighing his worth. Vian stood tall, unflinching beneath the dragon's glare. Finally, she exhaled, extending a small hand. "I'm Reagan. I'm thirteen."

Vian took her hand and shook, long fingers dwarfing hers. "I am Vian. I'm sixteen…I think."

"Well, you might be older than me, but I have been on the ship longer, so I have seniority." She lifted her chin, glancing at me with the authority of a sailor twice her age. "Right, Captain?"

I did my best to fight the smile that threatened to diminish the stern look I shot her. "Reagan, do me a favor and go terrorize someone else for a bit."

"Fine, Tarran probably hasn't been bullied enough yet today anyway." Reagan shrugged, tossing her long braid over her shoulder. "Welcome aboard, Vian."

She sauntered away, taking her warmth and fire with her, leaving us in the cold. Vian's eyes followed her, amusement swimming in their depths, but I couldn't seem to shake the darkness resting on my shoulders as I regarded the boy carefully, my mark aching.

I voiced my next question as carefully as I could. "So you all were kept there to die for the Dark God?"

"We are slaves. For people like you." I tensed as he pointed directly to where my mark was hidden. "But I was unworthy." A boxy smile graced his features, as if he was proud of his status, and my stomach knotted. A smarter version of me might have questioned how he could sense my mark, but guilt gnawed at my gut instead.

For people like you.

People like me, who were cursed and desperate and willing to pass it off on some poor 'devotee' who didn't know better.

But there were no devotees. They were slaves, trapped and manipulated and used for selfish gain. For *my gain*, had I gone through with it. Had I not been thwarted by Locasta and unwittingly saved by Drystan.

"Well, you're safe now," I choked out, the guilt churning in my stomach. I wanted it to be true. I wanted to keep him safe, if only in atonement for the part I played in his terror.

"No, I am not safe." Vian regarded me with sympathy, like I was the victim, not him. He smiled with his whole face again. "But I am free. And that is more important."

"Get some rest, kid," I mumbled, turning away before the gnawing feeling in my chest could consume all of me. "We have a long sail ahead of us."

"You are a prisoner too."

"What?" I spun to face him again.

He did not look at me, only at the horizon, and what lay beyond it. "The mark. I can hear it. It has you trapped."

My heart stopped, then started again. As if summoned, the ache on my shoulder worsened, voices whispering in the recesses of my mind. Could he hear them, too?

I knew he was waiting for a response. A large part of me wanted to tell him he was crazy, that I had no clue what he meant. To deny the black truth.

"Aye. And it scares me," I said instead, shocking myself with the admission.

Vian turned to me, his expression filled with the same reverence in which he regarded the horizon, dark eyes sparkling. "We are all prisoners, *Ariannad*. One way or another." There was no judgement or malice in his tone, only hope. "But you are strong enough to break us all free."

The trip home was far smoother than the trip to Orwellin. A warm southern wind was in our favor, making the six-day trip almost pleasurable. Vian made his mark on the ship and the crew just as easily, his breezy smile and lofty way of speaking charming my family. He had a captivating way of seeing the world, as if he were seeing it for the first time, and it warmed something in me I couldn't name.

Though I supposed he truly *was* seeing it for the first time. But for someone who spent his entire life in a dark cage, he made friends rather naturally.

"So your swords tell you secrets." Vian stared in awe at *Truth* as he sat precariously on the bow one afternoon, curiosity lighting his eyes.

Griffin perked up, unsheathing his blade and handing it straight to the boy as if it were an extra pair of socks and not his most prized possession. "Aye. She's a fine blade."

I eyed my cousin suspiciously. He never let anyone he didn't trust touch that sword. Griffin caught my glance and shrugged once, a smirk at the corner of his mouth while Vian examined the blade. I didn't know what the sword had whispered to him, but if Vian could earn Truth's approval, there was little anyone could do to protest.

"Spectacular." The boy ran a thin finger over the sharp edge, wincing as it drew a few drops of blood from his fingertip. His smile was feral as he looked back to Griffin. "Would you teach me to use it?"

"Careful, kid." Rhett plopped onto the rail next to him, nudging him in the ribs. "Most lessons from Griffin will get you in major trouble."

Vian's smile widened. "Sounds like fun."

I didn't know if Rhett or Griffin laughed louder. The two spent the rest of the afternoon teaching the newcomer the ins and outs of swordfighting and sailing, as well as life lessons I prayed to Lyr he wouldn't listen to. Reagan and Saeth were equally captivated, often staring at him and giggling to themselves whenever he'd flip his chin length black hair, much to poor Tarran's dismay.

The only person who seemed wary was Ronan. Whenever Vian was above deck—which was often, since he had a well-deserved aversion to the tight, dark quarters below—Ronan would watch him, his jaw tight and brow furrowed.

I decided not to push it, not after our last fight. I knew he was hurt, and harboring a former slave that we freed from the capitol was probably not his idea of a fun afternoon outing. Especially since it meant we didn't get what he was desperate enough to mutiny for.

He'd come to me when he was ready. Or so I hoped.

It took him until the fourth night of our journey home. It was late, the moon already nearing her midnight apex. I watched her from my hammock, the warm wind playing with my hair. The night was cool, but the crisp air and salt spray was heavenly. It was perfect, really…except for my husband's absence at my side.

He must have felt it too, the growing schism between us that felt like a missing limb, because he nuzzled into the hammock with me moments later. We were silent for a while, letting all the things that had gone said and unsaid sit between us. We waited until our breathing synchronized, my head on his chest and his arm tucked around my side.

He broke the silence first, pressing a kiss into my hair. "Are you alright, Keira girl?"

I was quiet for another moment, listening to his heartbeat as I weighed the question. Truthfully, I was not alright. I was still scarred and broken and cursed. But something had reignited inside me in the bowels of *Delm Arawn*, something I had thought to be dead. It was fragile and dim, only a mirror image of what it had once been, but it still burned deep down, a spark ready to be fanned into a flame.

"Believe it or not, yes," I answered, rubbing tender circles across my husband's chest, tracing the spot where his tattoo lay hidden. "Better than I've been in a long time. I don't know what it is, but the boy gives me hope. I'm sorry you're not fond of him."

It was Ronan's turn to carefully contemplate his response, his throat bobbing. "I like the boy, I do..." he hedged as he searched for the words, holding me tighter, as if I were going to crumble and drift away like a sandstatue if he let go. "I'm just...sorry that I pushed you to go. That island was a mistake. I should never have believed your uncle, and I was cruel and too assertive. The boy...he's just a reminder of my mistake. A reminder that I was willing to kill an innocent, tortured soul for my own selfish gain."

I couldn't see his face, but something wet hit my hair as his tears flowed. My heart ached for him, for the pain I'd put him through myself. He deserved so much more than a life of fear and futility. He deserved happiness and surety. I could not fault him for wanting that so badly he'd do anything for it.

I would too.

"No, you were right." I peppered kisses along his chest and neck, hoping they could somehow patch the holes in this sinking ship. Then I sat up so I was facing him. The glassiness of his sapphire gaze threatened to break me, but I owed it to him to be strong. "We have to fight this. I need to be here for my family. For *you*, Ronan. And if we hadn't gone to the island, we wouldn't have seen the truth. People have to know what is going on. I mean, *slaves* in the Deyrnas? This is bigger than all of us." I paused, stroking his cheek, wiping away the last bit of wetness from his tan skin. "Vian is not a reminder of your failure or selfishness, he's a reminder of your victory. We saved that boy. And we'll save everyone else like him, including ourselves."

Ronan looked at me with clear eyes, silver-teared sorrow replaced with the warm glow of something much more potent. "I love you."

"I love you too." I placed a chaste kiss on his lips, hoping the action could convey just how deeply I meant it. "And we'll figure this out. All of it."

I prayed to Lyr it was not a lie.

We laid there for a few more hours that felt like moments, gazing up at the moon. I wondered if she could see us, could feel the love we shared most deeply in her presence. Wondered if maybe she was staring back down at us, pity and mercy aching in her chest, as she counted our numbered nights like this.

Ronan cleared his voice, dragging me back to the earth. "So, are you ready for the wedding?"

I sighed, remembering that the trouble at our backs was not the only battle we'd be fighting this week. "I'm ready to be home. To see Reina and Vala and Ellian…"

"But not Finna and Connor," Ronan finished for me.

I burrowed deeper into his side, breathing in the sea salt and sweat of him. It was enough to chase away the worry sitting in my chest. "No. But I will be by the time we dock." With Ronan at my side, I could face a thousand Connors and Finnas.

He chuckled into my hair, a glimmer of the sarcastic sea-snake I knew and loved slithering back into his tone. "Is there anything you can't do, Mrs. Mathonwy?"

"I can't resist you." I sat up again so I could wiggle my eyebrows at him. He took the bait, leaning down to finally kiss me. It was warm and soft, just like the sun that peeked over the horizon line.

There were many things I couldn't do yet. I couldn't stop the famine wreaking havoc in Bachtref or the poverty in Porthladd. I couldn't free the slaves in Orwellin or even free my cousin from a loveless marriage. Lyr below, I couldn't even save myself.

But for the man with the sea in his eyes and poetry on his lips, the man with the wit of a snake and the heart of a dragon…the man who kissed me now like I was a goddess to be worshiped and adored…

I would try. With all my might, I would try.

12

Homecomings and Heartbreak

KEIRA

It took every ounce of strength I had not to burst into tears the moment we made landfall.

Porthladd was the most beautiful thing I'd ever laid eyes on, glittering in the midday sun, the tide lapping lovingly against her frame. My hands shook as I secured the mooring and anchored, the *Ceffyl Dwr* finally home in the docks of Sailor's Point. When my boots hit the wooden planks, when I was officially standing in Porthladd once more, I nearly fell to my knees just to kiss the ground.

I was here. *I was home.*

To my surprise, there were no guards or councilmembers waiting to drag me away in chains, only disgruntled sailors tending their ships and townsfolk milling about in the nearby market.

Every scent and scene and sound hit me with a wave of nostalgia. I couldn't decide where to look first as we made our way through the town, the cobblestone beneath my boots more precious than any marble-laid street. So much of it was exactly as it had been months before, like it had frozen in time while it waited to greet me with open arms.

"Welcome home, Keira girl." My husband slipped an arm around my waist as we entered town square. I leaned into him, glad to be back not just for my sake, but for his. It'd been nearly three weeks since his last visit, and some time in the spring might ease the edges of his nerves. And mine.

The hustle and bustle of the midday market pooled around us as my crew and I moved through. Some offered us strange, even dirty looks, but I didn't care. People could think what they wanted about me. I was too busy ogling my hometown like I'd never seen it before. Like I might never see it again.

But something *was* different.

The faces that stared back at us were thinner. Tired. The scent of fresh-cooked fish that usually wafted down from the Eastern Docks was noticeably absent. The market stalls, while still busy, had much less to sell, people haggling over the last few loaves of bread or sacks of potatoes. It wasn't the same desolation as Bachtref, but the signs of famine and ruin lurked around every corner, waiting eagerly to sink their teeth into my home next.

Papa once taught me the best way to boil a frog was to heat the water slowly so it wouldn't jump out. By the look of things, it wouldn't be long before Porthladd was in the same frog stew as its little sister.

Homesickness turned into a mix of guilt and rage in my gut. I'd have to warn Ellian and Agatha when I saw them before this mess boiled them alive, too.

It was Tarran who pointed out the even-grimmer change to Porthladd's landscape, the final ingredient in the shit soup. Frowning, he dipped closer to me to murmur in my ear. "Captain, stay alert. We have company."

Sure enough, black uniforms stood out against the simple civilian wear of the crowd, some hooded and masked. There weren't many, but there were enough of them, ominous sentries watching over the crowd with hawk eyes. My stomach sank to my toes as I recognized the uniforms.

Guards from Orwellin.

Griffin noticed the same time I did, muscles flexing as he crossed his arms and glared at one of them. "Seems like someone did some redecorating. Since when are there guards around Porthladd?"

"For the wedding?" Saeth mused, her fingers twitching by her dagger as she scanned the crowd, noting the guards' positions. "Connor is a High Councilman, he might have some distinguished guests that need protecting."

"Makes sense, but doesn't make me feel any more at home," Rhett said under his breath, instinctively stepping closer to Reagan and Vian, every inch of his chiseled frame tense.

I glanced at Vian, whose cloak luckily covered most of his face. Had it been a mistake to bring him here? Would our efforts to free him be wasted by a sham of a wedding and a few guards-for-hire?

"If they knew about this..." Ronan, reading my mind, gestured noncommittally toward Vian— "they would've stopped us at the docks. My guess is these guards got here far before we made a scene in Orwellin."

"Even if word catches up with us..." Saeth followed his train of thinking, a detached smirk on her face. "They'd have to admit they have slaves to acknowledge we set them free. I doubt that would help their case."

"We can only hope," I hedged, still eyeing a nearby soldier with a wary glare. "Let's get to the Manor before someone notices our little stowaway."

Vian shrugged and removed his hood. The rest of the crew sucked in a communal breath, but the boy chuckled. "Don't worry, they will not look. They are used to averting their eyes." An eye-wrinkling smile devastated his features. "I could stand in front of them and ask to shake their hands, and they would not recognize me."

His actions were reckless, but he was right. I saw nothing of the dirt-covered slave in the young man before me. And regrettably,

I could not remember any of the other faces we passed that day. I instead remembered the way Drystan kept his head down, as if not seeing them meant they weren't there.

"Hope you're right, kid." Ronan clapped him on the shoulder, ushering him forward before we could test his theory. We climbed the northern district toward Mathonwy Manor—toward *home*—eager to put the black-hooded guards behind us.

The sight of the Manor, which had once filled me with immeasurable dread, now made my heart skip a beat. The white marble columns were pillars of sanctuary, the tall turrets reaching victoriously toward the sky. I had to swallow down the thick emotion that coated my throat.

"A castle the color of clouds," Vian mumbled, his pitch-dark eyes rounder than the full moon.

We climbed the steps and pushed in the front door. From the foyer, I could already smell Reina's cooking, coaxing up a deep wave of hunger not just for the food, but for the woman preparing it. I didn't wait for my crew as I barreled through the sitting room and into the small kitchen.

I was surprised to find I was not the only visitor.

A woman sat on a stool, back straight as she stirred her afternoon tea, her honey-brown curls piled in a bun on her head. Her warm eyes filled with tears as she took me in. "Keira?"

I didn't have time to react before she stood and crushed me in a hug. "Hello, Auntie Vala," I chuckled into her hair as I hugged her back. I raised an eyebrow at Reina, confused to see Vala *here* of all places, but the blonde simply shrugged.

My aunt stepped back, arms on my shoulders as she appraised me properly. "Oh my word, Keira girl, yer a sight for sore eyes." She gripped my face, studying me like a prized horse. "Ye look like hell, though."

"I know, I know." I swatted her away playfully. "How are you?"

"Oh, it's all this awful business with the wedding." She swayed dramatically, plopping back onto her stool with a huff. "Finna's always been a hard-headed girl, but I don't trust that weasel of a man one bit. And the sanctions have been terrible. Yer Auntie Reina and I have been hosting a little soup kitchen out the back here for weeks just to get people fed." She droned on like she was reading her grocery list, but the gravity of her words weighed heavy on me. The letters Saeth received had given us a hint, but the scale of this madness was more than I could bear.

Vala must have noticed my look of concern, because she offered a compromised smile before continuing. "Yer friend Ellian has been a gods-send; he's been looking the other way and even helping us get supplies. But to plan a wedding in all this? Finna better have something up that tailored sleeve of hers."

"I'm sure she does, Auntie Vala." Ronan sauntered into the room, the rest of the crew hot on his heels. He swooped down to peck Reina's cheek before the woman pushed past him to tackle Reagan in an embrace.

"Mama, you're embarrassing me," Reagan whined, but the light in her eyes told a different story. Griffin and Tarran scooped Vala into bone-crushing hugs before stealing the stools beside her. Rhett plopped down in front of Reina's workstation with an uncharacteristic smile, and Saeth leaned against the counter between them in an unladylike fashion that earned her a stern look from Vala. My chest full of warmth, I pulled a stool up next to my husband, folding into his side. It was Reina's keen eyes that caught the only person still standing in the doorway like a lost puppy.

"He's new," she said gently as she regarded Vian kindly, play-whispering to Reagan. "Who is yer friend, little dragon?"

Vian cleared his throat, bowing at the waist. "I'm Vian."

"Well, Vian!" Reina loosed a surprise laugh at the gesture. "I'm Reina. Why don't ye settle in, I'll fix ye something to eat, hm?"

"Fix him a lot, Rei, he's too skinny to be sailin'," Vala echoed, the insult sharp but the accompanying expression full of affection.

Reagan latched onto Vian's wrist and dragged him toward the nearest seat, and Vian smiled sheepishly, earning another giggle from the young dragon. After a few moments of laughter and banter, he relaxed into his stool.

It warmed my heart to see him sitting here, a part of not just the crew, but the *family*. He belonged here, with us. Not in some dark cage on that wretched island.

The feeling struck something deep in my chest. He'd always somehow been a part of this, a part I didn't know was missing until he was seated at Reina's kitchen table laughing with us.

"Where'd ye pick this runt up?" Vala passed him the plate of cheeses and fruits she'd been snacking on. It seemed the Mathonwy's fruit trade from Ir'de was still strong enough to keep us fed, at least for now.

Reagan intercepted, popping a grape into her mouth. "We found him in a cage in Orwe—"

Ronan clamped a hand over her mouth before she could say more. "Don't talk with food in your mouth, little dragon."

Reina eyed them suspiciously but went back to work fixing Vian a plate. "I'll pretend I didn't hear that." She shook her head, a grin curling her lips as she set a giant, steaming pastry in front of the boy. "Eat up, Vian."

"Yes, ma'am. Nef bless you." His eyes went wide at the golden mountain before him, and I suppressed a laugh. Reina raised a brow at the subtle mention of the sky goddess, but didn't press, passing plates around to the rest of the crew. The familiar, comfortable silence of mouths being occupied fell over the room, broken only by chewing and the occasional appreciative hum as we savored the homecooked fare.

"How's Papa?" Griffin eventually sighed, patting his full stomach and leaning back.

A pang of guilt seared through me. I'd been avoiding all mention of my uncle Donnall since the day of Aidan's funeral. The hurt in his eyes when he accused me of murder had cut me to the quick. I stared at my now empty plate, both desperate and afraid of Vala's answer.

"Don't get me started." She sounded sore, rolling another round of guilt through me. "A sailor without a ship is a useless thing. He's been loafing around like a wounded animal, and instead of helping me plan, he's been drinking and gambling at the Raven every night."

My chest constricted. If I was landlocked without a ship to sail on and without my crew behind me, I'd be in far worse shape. We'd left him behind to grieve alone, and this was our fault.

My fault.

"I'll go see him later," Griffin grumbled, lines forming across his brow. He was worried too, though he would never admit it. Instead, he reached across the table to the pitcher of cheap cooking wine Reina had put out and poured himself a full goblet. I frowned, remembering his last drunken night in Bachtref. If this particular way of distracting himself continued, I'd have to say something. I opened my mouth to warn my cousin but was silenced by a question that made me wish I had my own drink in my hands.

"Any sight of Weylin?" Vala asked.

I winced. I frankly didn't care if the old man croaked after everything he'd put us through, but Vala cared for her brother-in-law. He was the only one she and Donnall had left.

Clouds covered Tarran's face, dark and stormy. "Papa is—"

"Still in the wind," Saeth answered sharply, giving him a look that could skin a cat. "We haven't seen him."

I nodded once. I hated keeping Vala in the dark, but this was Saeth's choice. Her relationship with her father was bitter at best, and she deserved the chance to process things without Vala's grief erasing the truth of her hurt.

Vala simply smiled, buying Saeth's pretty lie without inspection. "Oh well. He'll turn up when he's ready."

I swear to Lyr, Reina looked at Saeth like she could smell the lie fresh on her breath but said nothing.

"Enough of all this sad business," she commanded with all the authority of a councilwoman and the steel of a sailor, waving her dishrag at us like a cutlass. "Keira only has three days here, and I'm determined to put some color back into those cheeks before ye go again. So sit down, drink up, and someone tell me what ye've been up to with my daughter."

She pushed a goblet of wine my way. I gripped it with eager fingers, ready to join my cousin in drowning my woes. Reina was right. I had three days before my reality came crashing down around me and I was exiled to my ship once more, and two of them would be spent at a wedding straight out of my darkest nightmares.

I let the warm liquid burn down my throat, wishing it were stronger. Every bite and sip still tasted like guilt as I imagined the starving masses in Bachtref, but I couldn't help them with Reina's cheap wine and cheese anyway.

The night continued, the drinks soothing any lingering tension, jokes and jabs bubbling up in its absence. Saeth and Tarran traded insults that landed like blows, the rest of us chuckling at their expense, while Griffin taught a doe-eyed Vian the intricate nuances of his favorite drinking games. Ronan launched into a story at some point, a nonsense tale about an orphaned girl who freed a blind raven from its cage and then sirens led them to the realm of the gods. We all contributed, fanning his ego with *oohs* and *ahhs*, laughing when the story bade us to.

It was then that a cough behind us ruptured the delicate peace. I spun to the sound, a little quicker than my current sobriety level would allow.

It wasn't the liquor that made my stomach coil.

"Am I interrupting something?" Finna smirked as she stood in the doorway with her hand on her hip, wrapped in a deep purple dress that dipped dangerously into her bust. I was not ready for the wave of envy that rocked me from my stool at the sight of my eldest cousin. I was angry at the wedding, and part of me wanted to smack the smirk on her face into next week. And I was surprised as well by the small, tender part that wanted to hug her, to throw my arms around her shoulders and pretend we were little girls again.

But I also wasn't prepared for the jealousy. She looked so *healthy*, a luxury I lacked as of late. Her skin glowed, even in the dim lanternlight, her crimson curls silken and in perfect order. And with the expensive, form-hugging dress that accentuated every full curve…

It was the uniform of a sellout. She'd once called me the council's whore, an insult that still sat with me months later. While I'd resented the comment then…Lyr below, what I'd give to have something come easy. To feel healthy and to not worry about the mouths I had to feed and the people I had to protect.

"Lyr's ass," Tarran muttered, reminding the rest of us to scrape our jaws off the floor.

I plastered on my own smile, one I knew did nothing to hide the sea of mixed emotions swirling across my face. "Hello, Finna."

Vala stood, folding her arms across her chest with the same reproach she used to save for when she caught Finna sneaking in after a rendezvous. "Well, look who decided to grace us with her presence. If it isn't the Queen of the Deyrnas."

"I'm not here for you, Mother." Finna rolled her eyes, brushing into the kitchen with the grace of a queen and the bitter smirk of a witch. Vala opened her mouth to protest, but Finna silenced her with a hand, jade eyes locking on me with an intensity that made me squirm. "I'm here for Keira. Let's chat, shall we?"

The heat raced from my face, likely the color too, but I stood anyway, squaring my shoulders. I instinctively smoothed out my braid, suddenly self-conscious about my ragtag, sea-worn appearance. I'd known this talk was coming. We'd left too much unsaid the last time we parted, and if there was any chance of stopping this wildfire of a wedding, I had to take it. Sure, I didn't imagine this standoff with me half-drunk and fully exhausted, but I would stand my ground.

Think tall, you'll be tall.

"After you, Cousin." I grinned, gesturing toward the sitting room. Finna sashayed ahead, not sparing me a glance over her shoulder to assure I was following. She knew I would.

"Don't kill her," Ronan whispered with a reassuring squeeze to my fingers.

No promises, I thought, stepping over the threshold.

Finna was already seated on the red velvet chaise of the Mathonwy drawing room, feigned indifference masking the impatience that only showed in the way she tapped the armrest with her fingers. I lowered myself onto a golden chair, kicking my feet up. This was my husband's sitting room, and that was his favorite seat she perched in. This was not her negotiation, it was *mine.* I would not balk just because she strolled in with a ring on her finger and a new dress accentuating her figure.

But I couldn't help the softness in my tone as I appraised her. "You look well, Finna. Healthy."

"Aye, I'm happy, too." She tilted her head, a saccharine grin on her full lips. "You, on the other hand…"

I waved her off, my cheeks heating. "Spare me the insult, I know what I look like."

To my surprise, she quieted, saving whatever clever quip she'd concocted. This was new. Finna never passed an opportunity to flaunt her wit, and she was even less likely to spare my feelings.

I studied her, trying to peel back the layers of nonchalance she wore like jewelry. Maybe Griffin was right after all. Maybe she had a plan in that pretty head of hers.

I sighed, discarding my facade. I didn't want a negotiation, I wanted a truce that would not happen unless I was willing to show some vulnerability. I sat up and leaned forward, elbows resting on my knees. "Really, Finna, Connor? You know you can do better than that arse. He's a monster, and you could have any man in the whole Deyrnas."

Finna's brows flew up in the surprise, but it quickly changed to a grimace. "Connor isn't a monster. He's a gentleman. He's intelligent and cunning and well-mannered. And he's a High Councilman, the most powerful man in Porthladd." She sat back in her chair, staring off into the distance with a victorious grin. "It doesn't come much better than that."

The unexpected warmth to her tone sent a chill down my spine. I could not imagine the slimy, underhanded bully of a man treating a woman with anything other than disdain and bitterness. But Finna, the same girl who'd written the book on wooing men, seemed genuinely *charmed*.

"So you really are marrying him then." All the envy and anger I felt toward her moments before was replaced with nothing but pity. Finna could've been a queen, but she'd settle instead as Connor's footstool. "Griffin will be disappointed. We'd hoped…"

"Hoped what?" she spat, green gaze burning like a forest fire. "That I was just getting in his good graces to get you back? After you killed Aidan and tore this family apart? After all of you *abandoned* me here to go play pirates on that little ship of yours?" She shot to her feet, silver tears lining her eyes. "You're just jealous because you went from the golden child with all the power to the castaway, and I'm about to be the most powerful woman in the Deyrnas. And *you hate it.*"

The insult stung like a fresh slap, but not as much as the fact she thought I'd abandoned her. Never once did she express interest in following us, and after our last fight, I assumed she'd be content to never see me again.

But I did abandon her. I left her behind and took everyone who'd ever given a damn about her with me.

I did my best to keep my voice soft as I approached her. "Finna, I'm not jealous or angry. I'm sorry." I placed a hand on her delicate shoulder, but she slapped it away. I took a deep breath, laying bare the ache in my chest. "I'm so sorry I didn't clean up my mess here before leaving, and I'm sorry you couldn't come with us. But Connor didn't leave me a choice. He *ruined* my life. He took everything from me, from *us*, Finna. And if you go through with this, he'll ruin yours, too, for the fun of it."

For a moment, she just stared at me, my truth hanging in the air between us. I held my breath, afraid to startle her, waiting for my cousin to come back to me, to come *home*. But instead, I watched as she donned her familiar role again, hiding behind her layers of steeled silk and skepticism. "You'll be your own ruination. I want no part in it."

"Finna." My voice cracked over her name, my stomach sinking.

"Enough of this." She flipped her hair over her shoulder, unbothered and bored once more as she shot me a look. "I only came because Connor wanted me to remind you to be on your best behavior. This probation is temporary."

I swallowed hard, trying to collect the broken pieces of my shattered heart. "Aye, well, thank you for the message."

She shrugged, heading for the exit with a swish of her skirts. But she paused at the doorway, a real smile breaking across her face as she rested one hand on her abdomen. "But if you're good, Keira, maybe we'll even let you come back when my baby is born."

13

Babies and Betrothals

KEIRA

The news of the pregnancy spread through my family like wildfire, devastating us all with equal ferocity.

Finna was pregnant, presumably with that monster's baby.

My dreams that night were haunted by redheaded, black-eyed demon children with Connor's gaunt cheeks and Finna's smirk. They crawled out from the shadows, pointed teeth exposed as they chased me across the world, ready to sink their fangs into me and drag me to the Dark God's keep. I tossed and turned, grabbing the pillows beside me for comfort that did not come. Ronan took the night to soak in the spring, and as much as he needed it, I wished I didn't need *him* to get me through the night.

We were all quiet the next day as we prepared for the wedding, milling about Mathonwy Manor like ghost ships searching for shore. We barely picked at the delicious orange and cranberry scones Reina made from scratch, none of us able to stomach anything substantial. Griffin chose mead instead, and I honestly couldn't blame him—Finna was his sister, after all. Even Tarran, who never missed a single meal and could probably eat a whole roast pig for a light snack, pushed his plate away with a frown. Reina would have to distribute the scraps to those who needed it more.

It didn't feel like we were headed to a wedding. It felt like a funeral.

After breakfast, I made my way to the bedroom Ronan and I shared to sulk in private before donning my attire. The room was plush, so much warmer in its decor than the rest of the mansion. I wondered if that was Ronan's doing. Instead of marble and gold, everything was painted in warm beiges and deep burgundies, like the inside of a wine bottle. Fluffy white pillows covered the soft, impossibly large four-poster bed that took up much of the room. I plopped onto it with a sigh, drifting deep into its cloudy softness as I stared at the ceiling.

I thought of my own wedding night—dressing in the bare, dusty room in Branwen Townhouse, wearing Finna's old blue dress while Vala and Saeth did their best to make me feel less alone. I might have jumped off the side of Clogwyn Cliffs that night had it not been for Saeth's blunt humor and Vala's tough love. Finna too, had done her part, her subtle teasing a welcome relief from my anguish.

I wondered if Finna had someone to tease her and make her laugh today. At least Vala would be by her side, angry for sure, but not enough to miss the chance to pamper her only daughter. Even if she was only leading a lamb to its slaughter.

A knock on the door had me sitting upright. I couldn't put aside reality any longer, it seemed.

"Come in," I muttered, taking out the dress Reina had picked for me from the mahogany wardrobe. Reina herself flitted through the door, somehow already prepared in an A-line gown the color of rose petals that hung loosely off her shoulders. Green vines crawled up the pink tulle in intricate swirls, like someone had plucked her from her own rose garden. Her silken blonde curls were piled on the top of her head in a complex weave that made her look even more like a queen from a storybook. A gentle smile graced her features.

"You alright?" she asked.

"Aye, I will be."

Reina said nothing for a moment, gesturing to the dress on the bed. After her deft fingers tied my hair up in a slick knot, she helped me into the gown in silence, smoothing the soft fabric so it sat comfortably. Her hands still resting on my hips, she turned me toward the floor length mirror.

I gasped when I saw my reflection. I did not have the same unfiltered softness of Reina, or the buxom seductiveness Finna possessed, but I was striking. Reina's taste was exquisite, the dress fitting like it was designed for me alone. The crimson gown's high neck and long sleeves covered the mark on my shoulder and lengthened my features in an almost regal way. The color was harsh against my pale skin and in stark contrast to my silver eyes and raven hair, but the corseted bodice cinched my waist before billowing out around my hips, softening the look slightly.

I was beautiful. Powerful.

Reina grinned over my shoulder, taking pride in her handiwork. "No one can take that power away from ye, Keira. Not even Connor Yorath."

"Thank you, Reina." I faced her, patting her hand softly. "But I'm not worried for me, I'm worried for Finna."

Reina nodded. "You'll understand when you have wee ones of your own...but we can't always protect the people we love, even if we want to. It kills me every time I let Reagan walk out that door, but if I stopped her...it might protect her from some things, but it would break her spirit. Trust me, I tried." She looked away for a moment, emotion evident in the bob of her throat before she cleared it again. "Finna will be alright. Your Auntie raised her smart, and she'll find a way to make this right."

I let her words cradle me as I painted on a collected mask, my last accessory of the afternoon. "Aye, I hope."

She patted my cheek, then motioned for me to turn around. "Here, let me lace you up."

A voice in the doorway halted her from doing just that. "Mind if I cut in?"

I spun to see my husband standing there, looking like a painter's visage of a god. He was already dressed in a fitted blue suit that brought out his sapphire eyes and hugged every sculpted muscle of his powerful thighs, the buttoned jacket accentuating the perfect V of his torso. My mouth went dry, and my heart did somersaults in my chest.

Nothing else mattered as long as he was alright. Nothing.

He sauntered in, the grin on his face an indication that he knew exactly how good he looked. I'd be lying if I said I didn't miss this cocky, arrogant side of him, so often cloaked in layers of fear and worry that clung to us both like a wet blanket.

"I'll do the laces, Reina." Ronan's lip twitched as he raked his eyes over me. "Go get the little dragon ready."

I licked my lips, but Reina was having none of her nephew's antics. She placed a stern hand on her hip. "And what do you know about lacing corsets, Ronan Mathowny?"

He tucked his hands in his pockets, teasing her with a wink. "I've unlaced enough to understand the general mechanics."

Reina's cheeks flushed scarlet. "That's my cue to leave." She hurried out the door, mumbling something under her breath about 'feral youngins.'

I frowned at my husband with fake irritation. "Insufferable cad. That's no way to speak to your wife." I smacked his arm as he pulled me closer by the hips.

A deep chuckle radiated through him as he tucked his face into the crook of my neck, pressing a suggestive kiss over the silk at the base of my throat. "Hmm, and how should I address you, Mrs. Mathonwy?"

"Such a tease." I wiggled my eyebrows and pushed him away slightly, my hand resting on his chest. I scanned his face, admiring how bright his skin was, his eyes sparkling. "You're in a good mood."

He flashed me my favorite uninhibited smile. "Can't help it. The spring does wonders, but seeing you looking like this, wearing my colors?" he growled, shamelessly staring at the way the dress hugged my curves, one hand aimlessly roving over my backside. "How could I resist?"

I wanted nothing more than to melt into his touch, to let him rip off this stupid dress and ravage me on the soft bed. But I inhaled, sobering myself before his very scent intoxicated me, and took a definitive step back. "Well, you'll have to. I need help getting this contraption *on*, not taking it off." Ronan pouted, but I held a finger to his lips before he could voice his counterattack. "But later, perhaps you wouldn't mind helping with that, hmm?"

"Now who is teasing who?" My husband scowled playfully but took a respectful step back before either of us got carried away. He looked me over once more, this time with a twinge of reverence softening the intensity of his gaze. "I mean it. The red suits you. But I expected you in Branwen blue."

I took another moment in the mirror, drinking in my reflection, hoping I could feel as brave as I looked. "I'll always be a Branwen, but I'm also a Mathonwy. I need to borrow some of that sea-snake charm to make it through today." I shot him a grin that could rival his well-practiced smirk. "Plus, if I'm in red, it'll be harder to see bloodstains."

His eyebrows lifted in amusement. "Who are you planning to make bleed tonight?"

I shrugged, smoothing out my skirt. "Whoever deserves it."

Ronan made quick work of the laces at my back with surprisingly deft fingers, pulling them tight but leaving room in my ribcage so it didn't feel like I was drowning. I smiled broadly, but his brow furrowed. "By the way, when was the last time?"

"Last time what?"

"Last time you bled."

I frowned at the odd question, but racked my brain for the answer, the unfortunate memory rising to the surface. "When I was shot."

Ronan's expression clouded, but he shook his head. "No, I mean your cycle." His tone was gentle, but I didn't miss the worry.

My stomach sank as I tried to think back. The last time, I was in Ir'de, grateful for how soft the bedding was in the land of silk...but that was almost six weeks ago now.

Panic threatened to seize my throat, but I took a shuddering breath to try and think clearly. The one before that had been late too, I reminded myself, and light, like my body could barely spare the resources. My eyes met my husband's, who watched on with concern. "It's a little late...but my body has been so strange with this spot, I don't know."

He ran his palm over his face, then sighed, forcing a smile. "We'll have Vala check you out later, before we set sail again." He took my hands in his like I was something fragile. "With Finna being pregnant, it just got me thinking..."

I froze, thinking of the woman in Hud who suggested I use *that* as a weapon against my curse. The color drained from my face, the world spinning as all the blood pooled into the knot in my stomach. That was not a pathway I needed to go down today.

I squeezed his fingers tightly, trying to reassure both him and myself. "No, you're right. I'm sure I'm just a little late, but we should be cautious...a child right now would not be good for either of us."

Something skittered across his features as he looked to where our fingers interlocked. He rubbed the back of my hand with his thumb, a tender brightness shimmering in his gemstone irises. "How about one day?"

My heart shuddered at his words, at how softly they fell from his lips. I swallowed, doing my best to erase the nightmarish image of the woman in Hud from my mind.

Instead, I let myself really imagine the possibility for the first time. A little blonde-haired girl with silver eyes and Ronan's heart-stopping smile danced across my mind, her laughter like the sound of wind on the water; or a midnight-haired boy with eyes like the sea and his papa's heart of gold, beaming as he learned to tie knots…

They were perfect, and my heart ached for them in a way I'd never felt.

But a filthy *melthith* like me didn't deserve that kind of happiness. I was not in the position to make them a reality right now, maybe not ever. As long as this curse burned through my shoulder, I was a walking plague, ruining any chance at a family.

No, I would not bring anyone else into my personal hell. I would not damn my child to this fate.

I didn't realize I had tears in my eyes until Ronan wiped them away. "Hey, hey, shhh. Forget it, we don't have to talk about this now, I—"

I silenced him with a chaste kiss, pouring all my love and hope and sorrow and pain into the space where our lips met. I cupped his face in my hands when I pulled away, holding him tenderly like I had the whole world in between my hands. And I did. He *was* my whole world. He was the wind in my sails and my guiding star, my sun, my moon, my everything.

But maybe one day, 'just us' wouldn't be enough anymore. Even if I didn't deserve that pure, unconditional joy, Ronan did. So I would do anything I could to give it to him.

For the first time in days, my smile was not forced. "One day, Mr. Mathonwy, we'll have a whole crew of our own."

We were running late to my cousin's wedding. Somehow, it was not mine and Ronan's fault, though we did dawdle after our talk, spending some time to communicate in a much more *physical* way just how much we meant to each other. Instead, it was Saeth that held back our departure by nearly half an hour, claiming it was impossible to find something 'life-ruining' enough to wear in the many closets of

Mathonwy Manor. After what seemed like forever, she settled on something silver, and we finally loaded ourselves into the carriages and were on our way. I shared one with Ronan, Griffin, and Rhett, with Reagan, Saeth, Tarran, Vian, and Reina following in the one behind us.

As the streets of Porthladd blurred outside the carriage window, I couldn't help the nausea rising to my throat. It was dizzying, mirroring my inner turmoil. Ronan's gentle hand on my knee was the only thing mooring me to my body.

Needing desperately to look anywhere but outside, I watched my cousin instead. Griffin fiddled with the high neck of his green embroidered tunic, his curls tamed but his expression still wild. He was dreading this as much as I was. I smiled when Rhett nudged his side, the gesture small yet so full of comfort. It was strange to see them so dressed up, Rhett's hair washed, sweeping the shoulders of his deep maroon jacket. They were a handsome couple. I hoped one day, if we survived tonight, we'd be celebrating their union under fairer skies.

I thought I'd be relieved when we finally stopped in front of the Yorath Estate. I was not. Connor's family home was just as drab and morose as the man himself, nearly as large as the Mathonwy Manor, made of dull grey stone and framed by an intimidating iron gate. Guards stood at attention at the entrance while guests filed in, dressed in colorful livery that stood stark against the estate's dark visage. All of Porthladd had received the invitation, and it seemed not a single person wanted to miss the chance to get a peek inside the elusive councilman's private quarters. Or perhaps, they were simply drawn to the promise of a hot, free meal.

Dread knotted in my gut as we stepped out of the carriage. I linked my arm through Ronan's, letting him anchor me as we patiently waited in line.

The closer we got to the entrance, the more I wanted to hurl. We passed the guards without anyone stopping us, but my heart still threatened to beat out of my chest. As we approached the door, I looked back at the gate.

Perhaps it wasn't meant to keep us out today. Perhaps it was designed to keep the horrors of this place in.

The interior of Connor's home was even more morbid. Clean tile floors and bare walls made it look more like a tomb than a homestead; there were meager decorations scattered about, candles leading the guests to the main event, accompanied by stiff white flowers in plain clay pots. I wondered how long it would take for Finna to breathe life into these halls.

My heart sank as we entered the ballroom. The tall windows were shuttered, casting the room in shadows. Neat rows of chairs filled the space, but aside from a small, black marble altar, the room was devoid of all signs of life.

"This place gives me the creeps," Griffin whined, twitching toward swords that weren't there. I hated that none of us were armed, but it was part of my probationary terms, and I wasn't leaving my family to suffer this alone. Even if we all felt naked without our extended limbs.

But every instinct prickled within me. I didn't need Griffin's magic swords to know how fundamentally *wrong* this place was.

"It's like the dungeons," Ronan murmured. "The same sinking feeling."

I swallowed, trying not to dwell on how right he was.

"Well, look what the tide dragged in," a familiar voice said behind us, washing my panic away for the moment.

"Ellian!" I forgot where I was when I wrapped my friend in a hug, relishing in his leather-and-pine scent.

"Lyr below, it is good to see you back on land!" He lifted me up in a bear hug before setting me down to look me over. "I've missed you."

I felt nothing more than pure kinship toward the man in front of me, but it made me so happy to see how dapper he looked. His chocolate curls hung lower now, grown out in the months we'd spent apart, and he somehow looked even taller, his strong frame accentuated by his forest-green suit. As usual, expensive fur lined the lapels of his jacket, a homage to his wealth and a hint at his truth. "I missed you too, friend."

Ronan found my side again, nodding stiffly to the councilman. "It's good to see you well, Ellian."

Ellian clapped him on the shoulder, energetic as ever. "You too, Mathonwy. Though things aren't well, not really." He scowled, lowering his voice so none of the other guests milling about could hear. "I take it Saeth's been sharing my letters?"

Ronan rolled his eyes. "Minus the intimate parts, yes."

"It's worse now, Captain." He shook his head, checking over his shoulder to make sure none of the partygoers were eavesdropping. "I'll fill you in later, but nothing good is coming."

"Oh, joy." Sarcasm dripped from my tone, earning an eye roll from my friend. "I have...news for you too. It's bad out there."

"Bad how?" His brow furrowed.

I thought for a moment, studying Ellian. I could still see the *blaidd* in his eyes, their piercing green hue the same as his inner wolf's. He had trusted me with his greatest secret, had sacrificed his own privacy to warn me and protect me time and time again. It was my turn to warn him.

"There are slaves on Orwellin." My voice was dangerously low. "You might want to check that out."

Every muscle in his frame tensed, eyes brimming as he snarled, "Leeches. I bet Connor knows, too." He exhaled sharply, pinching the bridge of his nose. "Never a dull moment, is there, Captain?"

I nodded, but the moment was interrupted as the rest of my crew made their way into the ballroom. Saeth entered first, catching the eyes of many onlookers, and Ellian's jaw went slack. Griffin whistled lewdly, earning a smack from Rhett across the back of the head.

"Hey, puppy." She sauntered toward Ellian first, the metallic hue of her dress glistening in the lowlight, the plunging neckline accentuating every sharp angle of her frame.

"Saeth." Ellian swallowed, taking a long look at the dagger in a dress. "You look…"

She flashed him a devastating smile. "Scandalous enough to make my father shit himself if he decides to show up?"

"No." Ellian's throat bobbed, the tension in his shoulders melting. "You look wonderful."

Saeth blushed, tucking a strand of her chin-length hair behind her ear, just as Tarran and the rest of my family joined us.

"Let's go, lovebirds." Tarran threw a protective arm around his twin's shoulder. "The ceremony is about to start. We should find our seats."

"Who's the new kid?" Ellian leaned down to whisper, nodding to where Vian trailed behind us, Reagan on his arm and a goofy grin on his face. They looked effervescent, Reagan in a soft golden-yellow and Vian in a deep blue that accompanied it perfectly, like the sun hanging in the early morning sky.

I shrugged, the nausea in my middle subsiding as I admired my newfound friend's apparent happiness. "A slave from Orwellin."

Ellian's eyebrows flew up. "Oh good, and you brought him to the wedding."

"Never a dull moment, Ellian," I echoed with a smirk.

"Is this what all weddings are like?" Reagan said by way of hello, her scowl contrasting the romance of her attire. "No wonder Mama never wanted to come to them."

"Would you have preferred to stay home?" Ronan folded his arms, the Sea Snake rearing his head for a fight. "I'm sure Vian would accompany you back to the manor, it's probably safer for you both there anyway."

The little dragon snorted, but a smile cut across her face. "Over my dead body."

"Don't worry, little one, your wedding will be a much happier occasion." Ellian beamed, patting the top of her head with his massive hand.

Reagan swatted the shifter away, mischief brimming in her chestnut stare. "Who says I'm ever getting married? You're the one that needs a leash, fleabag, not me."

My laugh was unfiltered and real, joined by Ronan and Ellian's. Reagan was supposed to look up to me, not the other way around, but there were moments I wished I could tear a page from her lesson book on life. If I could have even an ounce of her spitfire, I'd manage to survive the day.

Papa once said I was the fiercest thing on two legs. I would've lost the title if he ever met Reagan.

My moment of joy was doused by a sudden gust of Orwellin-black darkness.

"Lyr's bollocks," Griffin cursed under his breath, nudging my side as his eyes locked onto a target a few paces ahead of us. "Is that who I think it is?"

I followed his gaze, and my stomach dropped.

Her black hair and sunken cheeks were unmistakable, her wraithlike form even more ghostly in the stale light of the ballroom. She was speaking to a few other stiff-backed, high-collared individuals I didn't recognize, but could only assume were other councilmembers.

"Locasta," I hissed, halting in my tracks before the desire to rush her and ring her neck to take over. How she got here so swiftly, when the *Ceffyl* was one of the fastest ships in the Deyrnas, I had no idea. But my skin prickled with fear at the sight of her. "Vian, maybe you should go back to the Manor."

The boy shook his head, fists clenched at his sides. "No. I need to be here." He bit the side of his cheek, inhaling deeply. "The wind demands it."

I nodded but didn't let my guard down. If she was here and we weren't already in chains, she must not know it was us who freed the slaves. Or Saeth's estimation was right…she couldn't call us out without exposing her own dark scheme. Either way, I was not about to underestimate her cruelty again. If she was Connor's accomplice, she was just as capable of tyranny and trickery as he was.

"So ye did come." I jumped as a deep voice behind us pulled me from inspecting Locasta's dark form.

Bleary, bloodshot eyes met mine as I spun around. Vala had stuffed him in a fresh blue tunic and vest, but Donnall's silver-and-red hair was untamed, and I could already smell the liquor on his breath from where he stood an arm's length away.

"Papa." Griffin's face fell as he reached out to the drunken ghost of his father.

"Don't touch me, ye traitor." Donnall stumbled as he brushed his son's hand away, voice too loud for indoors. Eyes followed the sound, but Donnall didn't pay them any heed, turning his contemptuous gaze to Ronan and me. "Bold of ye to show up here with the kin-killers."

The words were like a dagger to my skull. When I was little, Donnall used to put me on his shoulders so I could reach the rigging. He'd always felt so strong, so sure beneath me. But this man was an empty husk, hollowed out by my dagger, filled instead with whiskey and hatred—hatred for me and my husband. For what we did to his brother.

Ronan seemed unfazed as he picked an errant strand off Donnall's azure waistcoat. "If I'm not mistaken, we were explicitly invited."

Donnall scowled at him, reddening with rage. "Yer lucky my daughter is kinder than I am, or you'd be rotting in a cell."

"You're lucky Ronan and Keira are here, Papa." Griffin straightened his shoulders as he looked down at his father, pity and pride sharing space in his gaze. "Otherwise we'd all be rotting at the bottom of the sea."

Donnall scoffed and walked away, mumbling curses under his breath as he approached Captain Leary near the altar.

Griffin slumped beside me as he watched his father get ready to sacrifice his sister. They hadn't been close for years, not since Owen died. Vala could look past the hurt, could see her living son as clearly as the one she lost. But Donnall never fully forgave the Swordsinger or his blond bedfellow.

I squeezed my cousin's hand, one kin-killer to another, a signal in our unspoken language. *He'll come around.*

Griffin's smile didn't meet his eyes. "Let's sit before people start lining up to insult us." He didn't need to tell me twice.

My eyes stayed fixed forward as we filed into the third row of seats on the bride's side, ignoring the stares boring into our backs. People muttered around us, hushed whispers with acerbic edges flying as we settled into the hard-backed chairs. I only sat taller, letting their hateful glares and speculative murmurs glance off me. Ronan's fingers laced through mine, a gentle reminder I was not alone today.

"You ready for this?" His sapphire eyes searched mine.

"You mean am I ready to sit in a room that's made up almost entirely of people who want me dead while I watch my cousin marry my mortal enemy?" I raised my eyebrow.

His lips quirked up. "Aye, that."

"No," I breathed, grateful for the warmth of his palm against mine. "But her mind is made up. And I'll be here for my family no matter how hard it is."

Griffin leaned into my other side, making no secret that he'd been listening in. "Maybe Finna's right. When you married Ronan, I thought you were batshit crazy, but now look at us."

My lips pursed, the idea sour on my tongue. "Perhaps."

Tarran, who sat in the row directly behind me, leaned forward, determination clear in the set of his jaw. "And if not, she has all of us to protect her when this goes south."

My gaze softened at my youngest cousin and the dreamy ideals that still puffed out his chest. I remembered my own wedding again, the way he had the same starlit look in his eyes when he came to my defense. He was unafraid and unashamed of his loyalty, a trait many people in the room would do well to emulate.

"You're right, sunshine," I murmured, using his mother's favorite nickname for him. He blushed, settling back into his seat with a proud glow.

Maybe I was a kin-killer. Maybe we all deserved the Dark God's wrath for all that we'd done, or worse, the things we hadn't. But maybe there was hope, too. Maybe, if we all held onto each other a little tighter, the special magic that wove my crew together would be enough to stitch the frayed pieces of the rest of our family back together.

The warmth that spread through my chest at the thought extinguished as Captain Leary made his way to the altar, holding up his hands to silence the crowd. "Ladies and gentlemen, please welcome the bride and groom."

14

Vows and Villainy

KEIRA

"Welcome, all, to this monumental occasion," Leary boomed, surveying the crowd with a wrinkled brow and a scowl. "As Captain of the *Madyn* and Councilman to this fair island, it is my honor to join these two lovers in matrimony."

My stomach lurched, and I had to bite my lip to keep from hurling.

Finna and Connor stood before Leary, my cousin ethereal in her sparkling ivory gown made of moonstone and gossamer with intricate beading across the front. It rested just off her shoulders before sliding down her frame and cascading behind her like a waterfall. Purple foxglove wove in her auburn hair, contrasting with the warm porcelain of her skin; she was like the moon itself, full and bright against the blackness of night.

The blackness of Connor Yorath.

He was clad in a dark suit, his cheeks hollow and his deep brown hair slicked to his head. He looked sickly next to the goddess that was my cousin, but power radiated from his slender frame. Finna stared at him with starry eyes, a woman enchanted, her soft fingers clutching his spidery hands like they were her liferope.

It made me sick. I gripped Ronan's hand tighter, shifting in my seat uncomfortably. I wished Papa were here. Somehow, he'd put a stop to this. Or perhaps, had Aidan not killed him, this would not have happened in the first place. He always had a plan, a direction, like a compass steadily pointing north. Without him, I was floundering, a wheel without someone to steer it.

Let me be the compass, Keira girl, and you can be my little silver wheel, he used to say, his eyes fixed on the horizon.

I kept my eyes forward as the ritual tied my cousin to her fate; as they repeated the terms, hands clasped together, Leary tying the knot with a symbolic silk thread. It was an old practice, favored when the gods still walked among us, that usually only the most pious couples practiced.

My wedding had been rushed and forced, skipping straight to the end. I barely remembered my vows, only Esme's hurried voice and Ronan's imposing heat next to me. But like all effective torture, Connor took his time as he nailed Finna's coffin before the congregation and the gods themselves.

"May Bris keep our table full, may Nef keep our skies clear, may Cerridwen keep the fires of passion stoked, may Brigid line our path in gold, may Gwynn guide us when the night gets dark." Finna thanked each and every god for their blessing, her voice strong and sure. "And may Lyr keep us in his embrace."

Part of me wished Lyr would drown me now.

"Keira," a voice two seats down whispered loudly. I snapped toward the sound to see Vian hunched over, distress written across his features. I held a finger to my lips; if we interrupted this service, we'd have a whole other beast to contend with.

Leary cleared his throat, silencing the room as he drove toward the climax of the ceremony. "Do you, High Councilman Connor Yorath, take Finna Branwen to be your wife?"

My entire body went numb, praying to any and every god that would listen to end this now. Wherever they were hiding, I needed their intervention more than ever. My breath held, I prayed to Cerridwen that my cousin would break through whatever enchantment held her in place. To Nef, that a swift wind would carry her away into fairer skies. To Bris, that his mighty sickle would sever Connor's head from his shoulders. To Gwynn, that his dogs would devour the slimy, manipulative man and gnaw on his bones.

To Lyr, that he'd keep us all from the darkness threatening to consume us from within.

A sly, smug smile broke across Connor's sunken face, and I swear to the gods, he glared my way before he said, "I do, darling, I do."

My heart dropped, and the world swayed. People around us clapped, a few even cheering for Connor's vow.

"*Ariannad,*" Vian hissed, the word somehow finding its way directly to me despite the cheers around us. "Something is not right."

"Do not use that name in public." Guilt instantly stabbed at my side; I knew how overwhelmed the poor boy must be, but I was barely hanging on for dear life. I did not have the space or time to soothe him. "Save it for after," I said as gently as I could.

Leary's tirade against my sanity continued. "And do you, Finna Branwen, take Connor Yorath to be your husband?"

My cousin hesitated, and for a fraction of a moment, my heart stopped. She looked over her shoulder, casting a wistful glance to where we sat, and I held my breath. Maybe she'd realized the truth. She didn't need that man, or any for that matter, even if she was carrying his baby. We would help her, all of us, a whole village ready to raise that child in love and light, far away from the wake of Connor's shadow.

But instead, after a deep, steadying breath, she turned back to Connor. "Yes." She smiled, but this time it didn't meet her eyes. "Of course."

At that, my whole chest collapsed. I clenched my fists, wishing I could drive one through a wall. I hated this. I hated being a bystander to my own cousin's sure demise.

Seas and storms had once yielded my command. Now I didn't even have the power to stop the tears streaking freely down my cheeks.

Leary, on the other hand, let out what looked to be a sigh of relief. I wondered how much of his own fate rested in the success of this union. Connor must've had his balls in a tight vise to make him do this song and dance. "Does anyone object to this marriage?"

Yes, I wanted to scream until my throat burned. *Stop it. Stop this.*

But the room stayed silent. Against every instinct in my body, so did I.

Leary held out a moment longer, the painful quiet suspended as he waited for it to break. But the only sound was Connor clearing his throat, a clear reminder for Leary to get on with it. Leary stuffed his hands in his coat pockets, dark eyes saddened. "Then I pronounce thee husband and wife. Kiss your bride, Councilman."

When Connor's thin lips greedily pressed to Finna's plump ones, the crowd erupted into cheers.

"I'm going to yack up my breakfast." Griffin's face was stony, his tongue poking the inside of his cheek, a telltale sign that he was half ready to punch someone's lights out. I wanted to empty my guts on the floor too. I wanted to cry and scream and beg Finna to run away and never look back.

But I couldn't. None of us could. We had as little control over Finna as we had over the southern winds. They would evade us no matter how quickly we chased after them. But I had other people I could protect. I couldn't predict the outcome, but I could control my reaction to it. The mark of a true captain was not someone who sought to gain power over others, but someone who had power over themselves. My crew still needed their Captain, and even if Finna didn't need me, I needed her to know I was always there, waiting.

I squared my shoulders, giving Griffin's arm a squeeze. "Vian looks worse for wear too. Maybe go for a stroll?" I suggested, knowing damn well that Griffin needed some space before he caused a scene.

Griffin tore his gaze away from the altar and turned to me with a grateful smile. "Aye, Captain." He smiled at Vian, who honestly looked worse than I felt. In the few moments since the ceremony had started, he had gone from handsome to haggard, his hair disheveled from pulling on it, his eyes darting around the room.

"Keira, we have to go away from here." His voice was frantic, fear splayed across his features for the first time since I met him. Even in the darkness of the dungeon, he had seemed composed, but the way he chewed his bottom lip frightened me. "I don't know what's wrong...but the wind is worried."

Panic threatened to grip my chest, but I pushed it down. The boy had been through hell, and I could only imagine the sheer trauma of seeing Locasta here today. He was overwhelmed, and he didn't need me to exacerbate that with my own anxiety. He needed me calm, a buoy still afloat amidst the storm.

I grabbed his shoulders tightly, locking eyes. "Vian, I can't leave, but I understand. Griffin is going to take you for a walk."

He swallowed, throat bobbing. "Yes. Maybe...maybe I need more air."

Griffin and Rhett took either side of him, leading him away from the ballroom. I mouthed a *thank you* to my cousin, who only responded with a mute, *No, thank you,* before they disappeared beyond the door. Reagan watched after them, concern misplaced on her delicate features. But Tarran was quicker than I was, and when he dropped his arm across her shoulder and pulled her to his side, she relaxed.

As my crew and I reattached our pretend smiles and hid away our broken hearts, the guards made quick work of removing the chairs, turning the space into a proper ballroom once more. The altar was replaced by a small bandstand, and soon a quartet started playing. Their tune was stiff, nothing like the merriment of one of Ellian's jigs, but people flooded the dancefloor anyway, twirling and stumbling together. Tarran led Reagan among them, her golden-yellow dress shimmering as she spun, like sunlight on the horizon.

Saeth cut a path to Ellian, the blacksmith the only one brave enough to wield that dagger of a girl. A wolfish grin splayed across his features as she dragged him into the dance. Ronan found Reina and caught her in his arms despite the blush that flooded her cheeks, the White Snake long overdue for a dance.

Much like the night of my own wedding, I didn't feel like dancing. Instead, I perched along a wall, content to watch, grateful for the flute of sparkling wine a servant handed me. Sipping the bubbly liquid, I let my gaze drift to Finna as she floated among her guests, radiant as ever, greeting each of them like a queen would her subjects. She was born to be the center of attention, her happiness contagious, lighting the faces of every man, woman, and child in attendance.

In so many ways, this was the Finna of my childhood. The girl who could make me laugh and would tell me love stories with stars in her eyes. The girl who would braid my hair until I was smiling ear to ear, just so she could tell me how pretty I was.

I wondered if she remembered the part of me that would always admire her.

Downing the rest of my drink for some much-needed liquid courage, I walked up to where old Howell Wynne, the burly leader of the fisherman's guild, trapped her as he droned on.

"Do you mind if I steal the beautiful bride for a moment, Councilman Wynne?" I asked with a sharp grin, relishing only slightly how the Councilman's eyes widened in fear, like I was a sea-witch come to steal away the princess. After a quick grunt and a nod, he departed, leaving Finna and me momentarily alone.

"Keira." Finna stared at me, astonishment and suspicion battling for victory in her expression.

"I meant it." I let out my first easy smile of the night, hoping it conveyed my sincerity. "You look incredible."

She blinked twice but did not let her confusion show beyond that as she straightened her skirt. "Thank you."

I didn't know if it was the alcohol that made me both bold and sentimental, but I couldn't help the truth tumbling out of me. "Listen, I know we don't...well, we haven't been on the best of terms, and a lot of that is on me," I stammered, rubbing the back of my neck as I tried to string my words into something coherent. "You don't have to like me or trust me. I get it."

"I—" Finna started, but quieted when I grabbed her hands.

"Please know, if you or the baby ever need anything..." I squeezed tightly, speaking from the part of me that was her kin before anything else, "I'll be here for you. Banishment or not."

Finna stared at me in silence as she pulled her hands away. A part of me deflated, and I turned to go, but a delicate grip on my arm stopped me.

"I'm going to name him Owen." Her mask dissolved as a smile brighter than the sun overtook her whole face. She dropped her hand from my arm to rest across her stomach. "My son."

My chest constricted in a tight ache, but one I relished in at the memory of Owen, the brother she'd lost to the blood feud. He was one of the kindest men I'd ever met, smart and gentle in a way not many men were willing to be. He would've been one hell of an uncle to the little boy waiting to meet us.

Gingerly, I placed my hand over hers for a moment, hoping to let the baby know his Auntie Keira was here, too. "How did you know? You're barely showing."

Finna smiled broadly again, the sight so rare it drew out a smile from me, too. "Agatha Amos," she chuckled like she was thinking about a secret only she knew. "She has..."

"The cards?" I gasped, remembering the ornate card box that sang to my power and the unheeded warning the councilwoman had given me.

Finna's eyebrow quirked up. "Aye."

I laughed. "Then I hope she's right. Owen would be so proud of you."

At that, her eyes softened. "Be careful," she said, with a fondness not directed at me in the better part of five years. "Take care of the crew."

"You be careful, too. You'll have a little one to take care of soon."

There was so much more I wanted to say. So much more she deserved to hear. But a dark presence at my back froze the unspoken words on my tongue, an icy voice sending a chill up my spine.

"Hello, ladies." Locasta floated between us, the scent of rose and rot assaulting my nostrils. My stomach turned, and it took all my energy not to puke on the witch. Finna squirmed a bit, too, her fake smile even less convincing than usual, a protective hand on her belly.

"Councilwoman, it's a pleasure," she lied, stepping toward me and wrapping her arm through mine. "My cousin and I were just about to—"

"I won't trouble you for long, Mrs. Yorath." Locasta cut her off with vicious precision, dark eyes fixed on my cousin's womb. Her lips pulled back over her teeth in a hungry smile. "I just wanted to extend my congratulations. Your new husband just informed me we should be expecting a little miracle very soon."

I held Finna tighter to me, the hair on the back of my neck standing to attention. "We?" I snarled, no longer hiding my fangs. "Didn't realize you had any part in this."

Locasta tore her eyes from Finna, turning her darkness on me. "As a High Councilwoman, I find that I have a part in everything that happens in the Deyrnas. *Everything.*"

My nails dug into my palms. "Funny, that's how I feel about my family. Anyone who touches them will have me to answer to."

Finna squeezed my arm before letting go, her fake laugh breaking the tension like glass. "How nice it will be for me to have both of you in my corner!"

Locasta's long fingers reached out, brushing against Finna's midsection with sickening tenderness. "Oh, yes, my dear. I'll be right by your side. This child will usher in a new era of greatness for the Deyrnas. It's in his blood, his soul."

I couldn't stop myself from snatching her thin wrist away. Locasta's eyes flew wide with shock, but I squeezed her sandpaper skin tighter. Starlight clashed against the night sky in the place we touched, an ancient battle raging on with my wrath inside me.

Wrong. Everything about her was wrong, like peeking through the veil to the Otherworld.

Finna's hand on my shoulder pulled me back to the land of the living, a vulpine smirk on her lips. "Sorry, Councilwoman, we're still training my cousin. She's never been very civil, and parties bring out the worst in her."

I released Locasta's arm, the insult rattling through me, but Locasta simply grimaced. "No matter. Your son will one day bring out the best in us all." The corner of her lip twitched, then she stalked off into the crowd, my relief instantaneous. Finna sighed, haughtiness melting from her frame.

"Witch of a woman. Gives me the creeps." She spat the words out like she was trying to rid the taste of something bitter from her mouth. Something rotten.

My chest swelled with pride, erasing the sting of her insult. In her own way, Finna had saved me, too, her weapons a smile and a snarky comment. Perhaps we were family after all, two warriors using the only tools we knew.

Someone cleared their throat behind me, and I turned to find my husband with his hand extended. "Can I have this dance, Mrs. Mathonwy?"

I slipped my palm eagerly into his, and he tugged me closer, leading my hand to his broad shoulder before he slipped his around my waist. Like sun after a rainstorm, he was exactly what I needed to clear away the lingering darkness of Locasta's presence. I turned to bid Finna farewell, but she'd already moved on, chatting with the next guest, and I was forgotten in her wake. Part of me wanted to follow her, to finish tying the strings of our fates back together, but perhaps I didn't need to. Perhaps knowing we'd protect each other from afar was enough.

I looked back to my husband as we swayed to the stiff melody. "Finna looks...happy," Ronan murmured, pressing his cheek to mine and leading me around the dancefloor in lazy turns.

I melted further into his touch, savoring the hard-muscled frame that held me upright. "We're in a room full of people who can't take their eyes off her," I joked, though my usual bite was gone after the moment we'd shared. "Of course she's happy."

"Really?" my husband growled in my ear. Heat pooled between my legs as his breath tickled the sensitive lobe. "I only have eyes for you."

"Insufferable." I breathed in his scent as I pressed closer. Perhaps a more sober version of myself would be scandalized dancing so intimately and unguarded in a room full of enemies, but my thoughts were solely focused on the tingling in my pit and the heat of the man before me.

His velvet voice only ignited my desire further, the hand at my waist pressing into the soft flesh of my hips. "It's a shame we never got to do this at our own wedding. You're a lovely dancer."

Lyr below, I would never tire of this man's wicked tongue.

"You're a smooth talker," I muttered breathlessly, letting my imagination drift to other uses for my favorite parts of him.

We could have a thousand years together, and it would still never be enough. Ronan Mathonwy was rotten and wicked, but never boring. Never dull. Centuries would not be enough to uncover all the mysteries of him I wanted to explore, like the uncharted waters of the far reaches.

We didn't have centuries. Sometimes it felt like we only had days or minutes left, our luck hanging on by a single careworn thread. But I would spend every moment I had left cherishing the enigma of my husband.

My daydream was cut short by a light tap at my shoulder. "May I cut in?"

I didn't need to turn around to identify the voice. The shudder that ran down my spine was enough. But equal parts brave and stupid, and perhaps a little tipsy, I turned around to meet Connor's expectant gaze anyway. He stood with his hands crossed in front of him, a smug, entitled glimmer in his eyes.

"Like hell you can." Ronan's voice was colder than ice as he tightened his grip on me. "Go dance with your new bride."

Connor picked a speck of grime from his nail, unfazed by Ronan's territorial glare. "Humor me." His lips curled into a smirk. "It's in your best interest."

My heart thundered in my ears as I recounted every cruel trick this man had pulled, but part of me knew he was right. Knew that if I didn't play his game tonight, I might never see Porthladd or my family again. So I would dance when he beckoned, like a marionette on a string.

I shot Connor a look that could fillet a fish, but I let go of my husband. Ronan's jaw clenched, but he stepped aside. I instantly missed his warmth, the safety of his arms, but I could play this round if only to keep him safe.

Connor's grin widened as I stepped into his embrace, putting as much distance between our bodies as my armspan would allow. His clammy palm possessed mine, and I had to bite my cheek to stifle the string of curses that fought to empty themselves all over him.

"What do you want?" I growled, looking anywhere but his face. Still, I could feel his breath against my cheek as we began to spin in time with the music.

"If you make a scene, you'll never see your family again," he whispered in my ear as his hand snaked around my waist, pulling me tighter to him. "Clear?"

I was ready to throw a punch, but I restrained myself, channeling all my rage to the heel of my shoe as I crushed his toes underneath. He hissed when I made contact, stumbling for a moment before he shot me a dark glare.

"Sorry." I feigned innocence as he cursed under his breath. "I must be clumsy."

"No matter." He straightened again, though a grimace still hung on his face. He licked his lips as he looked me over, a wolf ready to devour its prey. "You look stunning in red."

"My cousin, *your wife*, would not be happy to hear you talking to another woman like that."

"I only mean to compliment you. We are family now, after all." He leaned in closer, the smell of his liquor-sweetened breath assaulting my nostrils. His voice dipped half an octave lower, husky and menacing. "It's a shame your poor uncle couldn't see you all dressed up. Lyr rest his soul."

I swear my heart stopped. I shoved away from him, hot tears stinging my eyes. I could withstand his creepy compliments and below-the-belt insults, but the mention of Aidan was enough to reopen a deep, festering wound in the pit of my stomach. "How dare you. Leave Aidan out of this."

Connor tilted his head to the side in mock confusion. "Oh no, dear girl." His lecherous smile widened, a snake showing its fangs before it struck. "I meant your other uncle. Weylin, was it?"

Everything stopped moving. I could no longer hear the music over my heartbeat. "What about Weylin?"

Connor stepped closer, and somehow, despite the ringing in my ears, I heard every rutting word that dropped from his lips. "Someone had to take the fall for the stunt you pulled in Orwellin." Spindly fingers reached out to tuck an errant strand of hair behind my ear. "Shouldn't have left him behind. Don't worry, his death was quick. Locasta made sure of it."

I find that I have a part in everything that happens in the Deyrnas. Everything.

His words hit harder than a punch to the stomach. The world swayed beneath me, and it took every muscle in my body to fight to stay upright.

Weylin was dead?

No. No, he couldn't be. He'd been on my ship last week, complaining and scheming like he always did. He was probably drunk somewhere, polishing his guns and lighting a smoke. He was a cockroach, a *survivor,* and it would take more than the likes of Connor Yorath to finally end him.

But Connor was still beaming, a man victorious. A man that had no reason to lie—only a reason to gloat.

Something snapped inside me, and before I could think it through, my hand was clenched around his skinny rutting neck.

Terror flashed through his eyes as his hands flew to my wrist, but I squeezed tighter. Gasps echoed around us, but I didn't care. Someone might have called my name, but it didn't fully register. Red colored my vision. "Connor, what did you do?" I demanded, pressing my fingers into the vulnerable, quivering flesh of his neck.

Before he could answer, hands grabbed me from behind, dragging me away. He dropped to his knees when my grip went lax, gasping for air. Strong arms yanked my hands behind me, and I screamed as blinding pain shot through my bad shoulder.

"Let me go!" I tried to pull my hands free, kicking and fighting for leverage, but the guard holding me steady was twice my size, and my shoulder throbbed relentlessly.

Angry, screaming voices erupted around me, Ronan barreling toward me with fire in his eyes. "Touch her and I will find a thousand ways to end your pathetic life." His voice was low and lethal, the quiet threat entirely real, but two more guards swooped in on him, caging him in their grasp before he could reach me.

"Are you alright, Councilman?" the mountain holding my wrists asked, fingers tightening as he increased the pressure. I hissed as the pain seared again.

"Yes, thank you, Lieutenant Quinton," Connor finally croaked as he stood, brushing himself off in feigned nonchalance. But even though I was incapacitated, he still stood five paces away. "Please take the suspect away for further questioning."

Ellian pushed through the crowd, his emerald eyes blazing. "What is she being charged with? I'm a Councilman. I deserve to know."

Connor straightened his coat, shooting Ellian a dark glare for the challenge.

This was his trap. He'd laid it well, and like a true fool, I had walked right into it. Somehow I knew deep in my gut that I wouldn't be getting out of this one. No matter who came to my defense, Connor had delivered his final strike.

He knew it as well as I did.

"Keira Mathonwy, you are under arrest for the murder of Weylin Branwen," he announced for the crowd. As the collective gasp echoed through the room, he leaned in with a satisfied smirk and said just for me, "Someone had to take the fall for that, too, kin-killer."

15

Chains and Changelings

KEIRA

The dungeons beneath Porthladd's council building were colder than a Pysgoddian winter. The chill crept into my bones, my wet, torn dress a meager barrier between against the elements. It might have been three hours or three days, I didn't know. All I knew was the guard's strong hands at the back of my hair, shoving my head deep into the freezing cold barrel of water over and over again until my lungs burned and my vision went black.

It was a cruel torture. This water didn't speak to me, it didn't bend to my will. Insult to injury, it only stole the air from my lungs and the heat from my body. It defied me, reminding me just how weak and useless I was.

He told me it would end if I confessed. If I claimed responsibility for murdering yet another uncle.

Kin-killer.

I stayed silent.

"If ye won't use yer air to talk, ye don't get any," the guard barked, then thrust my head beneath the icy surface once more.

He held me down longer this time, so long I thought my lungs would collapse as I fought against the chains at my wrists and my ankles. I coughed and sputtered when the guard finally pulled my head back, blackness swimming in the corners of my vision. I sucked the air greedily, vowing to never take it for granted again.

"Well, hello, Mrs. Mathonwy." A shadow approached in the darkness, my exhausted eyes struggling to make out the form. But I knew the voice. Knew the hatred and contempt it saved only for me.

"Piss off." My voice was hoarse, but the venom was there.

The guard yanked my hair so hard I saw stars. "Aye, no disrespecting the Councilman like that. Unless ye like it rough, hmm sweetheart?" His body blocked the single torchlight, his face inches from mine, stale breath hot on my face.

"I don't know, do you, big boy?" I sneered back, his laughter only adding fuel to my fire. I jerked my knee up as high as the chains would allow, hitting his sensitive manhood dead-on despite my restraints.

The man hit the ground, groaning and cursing as he tended his bruised ego. I ignored him, my focus turning to the real enemy.

Connor watched, faint amusement in the tilt of his head. "Such a shame to see you like this. Too bad you couldn't behave. My bride is beside herself right now. Seems she was fond of you, after all." He stepped closer to the bars, rapping his long fingers against them in a disinterested rhythm. "But don't worry, Captain Mathonwy. I'll beat that out of her before the baby comes."

I surged against my chains, rage reanimating my exhausted limbs. "If you touch her or that baby, I will slit your throat."

I swear I saw Connor flinch before the guard, regaining his composure, thrust me back into the cold, metallic chair against the wall. My back smacked into it, fresh pain rattling through me. I bit my lip to stifle a cry.

Connor laughed, the sound dry and mocking. "Dear girl, I would worry more about your own fate right now."

"You can spin your lies all you want. I'm innocent, and you have no proof." My mouth was ash and my muscles were on fire, but I poured every ounce of energy I had left into my threat. "I'll be out of this little cell before you know it, and this time, I'm coming for your blood."

Connor didn't flinch this time. He only shrugged. "But we do have proof."

My laugh was humorless in a shallow attempt to hide the fear prickling at the back of my neck. "Sure, and Lyr's my uncle."

Connor rested his arms fully over the bars. He was taunting me, so close, but so untouchable. "We have your dagger, the one half this island has seen you carry for years, stuck in his chest."

My gut clenched involuntarily. I hadn't eaten in days, my stomach completely empty, but the instinct to hurl still rose through my chest.

Connor was lying. He had to be. I'd given my dagger to the kind family in Bachtref, to the boy with the birthmark and bright eyes, to his poor mother...

But the sinking feeling in my core reminded me they had been desperate. Perhaps desperate enough to sell that dagger and my secrets to whichever devil offered the most coin or food.

I tried to keep the quiver from reaching my voice. "I lost my dagger weeks ago, you idiot."

Connor's beady eyes narrowed. "Not lost, was it?" Slowly, he reached into his coat. "What a distinct mark that boy had on his face, I'd never seen a birthmark like that before. What were their names again... Amilee, was it? And the boy...Tomas, Tobias..."

"Toivo." I would not forget his name or his sweet smile. And I would not let Connor taint it with his odious tongue.

But then as he produced the dagger, *my dagger*, all the resistance turned to ash in my mouth, my throat going dry and my heart shuddering to a stop. Connor flipped the blade over in his hands with an irreverent grimace. "Aye. They weren't very willing to part with this silly trinket at first, but Leary made them an offer they couldn't turn down. Poor things." He tapped the dagger against the cell, fake sincerity dripping from his tone. "Don't worry, they didn't suffer long."

No.

This wasn't real. It couldn't be. It couldn't bear the color of their blood on my hands.

Something stirred in my chest, the shadows of a storm that once would've raged and howled against Yorath's tyranny. I jumped to my feet again, blood pounding in my ears. "You monster."

"And then we have Councilman Leary's testimony," Connor continued, absolutely numb to the insult.

Everything tilted, the blood rushing from my face. "What?"

"Keep up, Keira, I'm telling you just how guilty you are." Connor clicked his tongue, rapping the dagger against my cage once more, like an Ir'desian carnival master baiting an animal. "Leary saw you that day in Bachtref arguing with dear Uncle Weylin. Said he looked worse for wear, that your crew had him cornered, and he even watched one of your lackeys punch him so you could kidnap him on that silly ship of yours."

Everything stopped for a moment. It was like I was under water again, struggling to breathe. The air rushed from my lungs, the world spinning as I fought to catch my breath. "That's not—" But my lips couldn't form an explanation or excuse.

There was none.

Connor was right. That is *exactly* what that day on the docks looked like to an outsider. Leary and half a dozen other sailors would swear by it. Lyr below, we did take him against his will, even kept him in the brig…and now he was dead. Body found on the last island I visited, with my rutting dagger in his chest. With Councilman Leary's direct testimony…

There was no escape this time.

The walls closed in on me, the air vanishing from the room. My legs were lead beneath me.

I was going to be convicted of murder.

Like a novice, every single move I made in the last two months had played directly into Connor's plan. Every act of defiance, every counterstrike and parry...they were all premeditated. Everything I did meant nothing.

He won.

"I'll be keeping you close this time." Connor's voice cut through the panic, crawling into my very soul and taking root. He stepped away from the cage, arms folded, the picture of victory as he delivered his killing blow. "No banishment where you can run off and make a mess wherever you please. No, you won't be leaving Porthladd ever again. This time, I'll make sure you rot where I can see you."

I waited for him to leave before I fell to my knees, sobs overtaking me.

The guard stopped his assault after Connor left, knowing my self-inflicted torture would be worse than anything he could think up. Instead, he and two others stood outside my cage, spectators enjoying my unravelling from a comfortable distance.

I laid on the dungeon floor, every part of me aching in the cold, but I didn't care. The ache in my chest was far deeper, a chill that no warmth or sunlight would ever chase away.

I failed. I failed myself and everyone around me. I was not just a *Melthith*, a cursed one. I *was* the curse. The plague. Everything I touched turned to shite, and everyone that got caught in my wake ended up broken or dead.

Just like Amilee and Toivo, two more innocents caught in my path of destruction. My act of charity was their death sentence. They were nothing but kind, and I had inadvertently killed them for their good nature.

And Weylin...Weylin was dead. Another Branwen cut down and left to rot. Another of my father's brothers joining him at the Dark God's throne. And I was going to prison for it.

I hadn't actually held the dagger, but I might as well have. I had dragged him to Orwellin and left him behind to pay the price for my mess. Left him to be slaughtered like an animal by the true monsters. His death was my fault, as were Amilee and Toivo's, and Roland and Lochlan and…

And Aidan.

Because I was nothing but chaos made flesh, destruction veiled by good intentions and bad decisions. Because I was not strong enough to stop any of it. Now, I would finally pay the price.

At some point, my eyes closed, the voices creeping back into my mind my only company.

Ariannad. Melthith. Failure.

Murderer. Kin-killer. Cursed one.

I didn't know how long I lay there, numb and empty while the voices harassed me, trapped somewhere between sleep and awake. It continued until a strange, whistled melody drowned out the horrid singing, the tune so haunting and melancholy I was sure I imagined it.

"*Ariannad?* Wake up," a voice muttered, somehow closer and louder than all the rest. My eyes fluttered open, searching for the sound.

A familiar form crouched over me as my eyes adjusted, black hair falling into his face. Something stirred within me, pushing me to sitting, even as every muscle in my body screamed against it. "Vian?" I croaked through cracked, dry lips.

He didn't answer, fiddling with the chains on my aching wrists, a small silver object in his hands.

"What are you—?"

"Quiet," he commanded, the shackles coming undone with a satisfying click as he moved to my ankles.

Confusion clouded my brain, everything foggy from exhaustion and despair. "Why, what is this?"

The boy paused, dark eyes flicking up to me, burning with determination. "You saved me first. Now it's my turn."

"Where are the guards?" Panic surged in uneven waves as the haziness cleared. I scanned the darkness for the black uniforms of my captors, but the room was as bare as it was cold.

A warning bell clanged within me. There had been three guards earlier. How had Vian slipped past them? Where did they go, and how much time did we have?

Vian flashed a square grin that illuminated the darkness. "Don't worry, they won't come back. They are very busy chasing a *blaidd*."

All the blood in my body pooled into my toes. "Ellian?"

"No, he is safe and sound in the council building. But the wind has some very convincing tricks up her sleeve." Vian shook his head, and equal parts relief and terror reanimated my frozen heart. "But let's not stick around for when they finally figure it out, hm?"

Something akin to hope flared in my chest, bursting through my veins despite the heaviness of my limbs. Vian came to rescue me. He came to help me escape.

I deserved to pay for my crimes, but I couldn't make anything right if I was trapped in a cell for the rest of my life. My crew still needed me.

My crew. Lyr below, were they alright? Was Ronan? Did Connor have them too, or did he save his vengeance just for me?

Instincts took over, and I adjusted to help Vian. After another second, my ankles were free, and he pulled me to my feet. "How did you find me?"

Vian shrugged. "I don't know much, I only know dungeons. Yours isn't very hard to figure out." With a small grin, he pocketed the silver pick and drew a dagger that I instantly recognized as Reagan's. The dragon-headed hilt still sparkled even in the darkness, and the confidence of his hold suggested this was not his first time wielding it. Slave turned master, he pushed open my cell door, beckoning me to follow.

I followed up the stone steps that were, again, miraculously unguarded. The wind's wicked trick was foolhardy.

My legs were rubber beneath me, but I dragged myself forward, only tripping on the tattered remnants of my dress twice. Vian, on the other hand, stepped quietly in and out of the shadows, like he was made of one himself.

"We have to get to the rest of the crew," I whispered, trying to keep pace.

Vian shook his head. "No time. Come, a friend is going to take us away."

I halted in my tracks. I didn't have a plan, but I needed to get to them. I needed to make sure they were safe, to lead them away from this hellhole as soon as possible. Maybe this time we could take Finna and Vala and Reina too, and finally put Connor and his reign of terror behind us for good.

Vian stopped, running a palm over his face, despair resting on his delicate features. "No, *Ariannad*, not today. The crew is safer here. Ronan has been upstairs in the council building for a full day fighting to see you, the rest of your crew, too. Everyone will know he didn't do this, so he is safe there." His tone was gentle, but every word cracked my already-fragile heart. "Ronan needs to stay here, safe by the spring."

Everything within me shattered at his words. The dam holding back my tears broke, and the sobs silently raked through me again. I wanted to protest, to demand that he take me to my husband and my family. I wanted to run straight to Mathonwy Manor, to hold Ronan until everything felt safe and right and whole again.

But I couldn't. Because Vian was right. There was no outrunning Connor, not together, and if my crew fled, he'd hunt them, too, and we'd all hang. And Ronan...

Ronan needed the spring to survive. If he ran away with me, if I asked him to come, it would kill him. *I* would kill him.

So I threw my shoulders back and nodded. I would not be the cause of my husband's demise, even if it meant breaking my own heart.

I didn't say anything else as Vian guided me out of the jailhouse. The chill night air hit my skin like a thousand needles, but I didn't care. It felt good to feel anything but numb, and it was better than the pain that threatened to carve my heart from my chest.

There were no guards at the door, either. On cue, a ghostly howl cried out from the south, by Sailor's Point, followed by chaotic shouts. Vian's trap was carefully set, a songbird hawklike in his deadly precision. For the first moment since we found him in the dungeon, I thought that perhaps I should be *afraid* of him. But then again, Papa used to say fear was a luxury for those with options. Vian was my only hope.

I tried not to think about it, only the task ahead. Keep my feet underneath me. Keep breathing. Keep moving. Don't think of them. Don't think of *him*.

I followed Vian's near-silent form through the streets of Porthladd. He was surefooted as we crawled through the shadows of the Eastern Docks, like he was the one who lived here his whole life, not me. The town seemed foreign as I passed through it, like I was an outsider looking in. A few stragglers mulled about, but we passed them without even a glance in our direction, like we were invisible. Or perhaps they were enchanted, strolling about in a dreamlike stupor, blind to our existence.

Before I could ask, we were suddenly in front of the last building in Porthladd I'd ever think of coming to for aid.

Madame Neirida's Odds and Ends.

I opened my mouth to question Vian, but abruptly shut it when the woman herself emerged from the doorway like she was expecting us, a dark cloak hugging her shoulders and a scowl on her otherwise-beautiful face.

"Yer late," she hissed, ushering us inside the overstuffed, lantern-lit store. Its crowded shelves sparkled with objects of every shape and size, and it was surprisingly warm despite the chill outside. Yet I couldn't help the shudder that ran down my spine. Something was off, *different*. Vian and Neirida's eyes were locked, a silent conversation happening between them.

"What is going on?" I stared between them, trying to make sense of what was happening.

Vian bit his lip, tearing his gaze from Neirida. The woman rolled her eyes, then dipped behind the counter of the store, disappearing altogether. My instincts prickled, but Vian's hands gripped my shoulders, pulling my focus back to him. "I promise I will explain later," he whispered, midnight eyes boring holes into mine. His gaze was reassuring, something deep within me ringing true as I met his stare, but urgency coated his voice. "You have to trust me. This is why we were brought together."

I had no clue what was going on, and there was a part of me that wanted to turn around and crawl back to the dungeon, to let myself rot for my sins. Or to gather my skirts and run to Ronan, hoping he had a better plan to get us out of this mess.

But I couldn't do either. So I nodded, and Vian loosed a sigh of relief.

Right on cue, Neirida popped her head above the counter. "Here, Vian, the boat is ready."

Vian nodded, trapping my wrist and pulling me with him. "Thank you, Miss."

As we turned the corner, surprise crashed over me like a wave. Neirida descended down a trapdoor, and I followed, fumbling down the wooden ladder beneath the store and into what looked like a stockroom.

We wove through piles and piles of boxes and crates teeming with treasures of all varieties. Lanternlight refracted from the glittering jewels, scattering the shadows, but it was like looking at the water on a sunny afternoon, my eyes fighting the adjustment. I swore under my breath as my legs smacked against something sharp, but Vian did not slow, dragging me through the maze.

Finally, we hit a wall, and Neirida stopped. With a final nod to her co-conspirator, she pressed a seam in the wall, opening a secret back door. My eyes adjusted again to the moonlight pouring through the opening, and sea air hit my face instantly.

We were at what looked like the very edge of the Eastern Docks, and in front of us, sure enough, a little sailboat waited. It had a single sail, and the oars looked like they'd been chewed on by something with very large teeth. The hull was dented, her seaworthiness questionable.

In black ink, a name graced her side. *Tysor.* Treasure.

Reality slammed into me like a ton of bricks. I was leaving. I was *escaping*, a convict on the run, aided by a foreign former slave and the town con-artist.

Vian didn't seem to notice my distress, hopping into the boat and untying the mooring knot like I'd taught him.

"Where are we going?" I tried to hide the panic in my voice, but failed, the air thinning around me.

Vian looked up, extending a hand to help me into the shoddy seacraft. "Far away, where no one can find us."

I stepped back out of his reach, turning on Neirida. "Why are *you* helping me?"

Something that looked like guilt flickered across her features for a moment as she pursed her lips. "I didn't need a reason last time."

"You do now." I clenched my fists at my sides, remembering the last time she'd come to my aid: Ronan's coat. An unexpected gift from this witch of a woman, but a gift indeed. Had I not been wearing it that night on my ship, I'd be serving my sentence in the Otherworld. The ache in my shoulder flared as if it remembered, too.

Papa once said Madame Neirida was a siren in maiden's clothes. I wondered if her song of pity was meant to lure me to her watery keep.

My hands relaxed at my sides, knowing how much I owed Neirida already. But that wasn't enough reassurance to leave my life behind and sail off into the night on a sad excuse for a raft. I lifted my chin, silently begging for some glimmer of an explanation before I dove into the dark waters headfirst.

The woman sighed heavily, staring at the moon as it hung in the sky above us, a watchful sentry. "A very important person wants to see you safe. I owe that person everything."

My confusion only grew, a thunderstorm of doubt raging within me. But Neirida rolled her eyes, shoving me toward the *Tysor.* "Enough stalling, girl, now go."

I stumbled into it, Vian catching me and helping me over the shallow rail. Quicker than a whip, the boy set to securing the sail, a strong gust rocking the craft as if the wind itself was hurrying us along.

But I couldn't go, not yet. I grabbed the mooring rope, holding the ship close to the dock for just a moment longer. "Wait, Neirida," I called after her, scoundrel tears streaming down my face. "I need you to give my husband a message."

She folded her arms around her ample chest, but her tone was soft. "What is it?"

A hurricane of emotions whirled through my chest, the wind picking up around us, echoing my inner turmoil. What could I say to convey everything I felt? Leaving him behind felt like tearing my own heart, still beating, from my chest. Everything hurt. My whole body shook, the very thought of being without him turning my legs to lead. The air thinned even further, my breathing shallow.

How could I survive without him by my side? How could I even breathe without him there?

I didn't know. But I had to keep him safe. Even if it meant I had to leave.

"Tell him I'm safe, and that I love him, and..." I choked out between sobs, hating myself more and more with every word that tumbled from my lips. "Tell him not to come for me."

As the words broke me from the inside out, I let go of the rope and let the *Tysor* carry us into the unforgiving sea.

PART

2

◇ 16

Waves and Winds

KEIRA

The farther from home the winds and the waves carried us, the emptier I felt. Days bled into nights as we floated along, drifters without a course. The *Tysor* was not built for long journeys, yet she managed to stay afloat as the days crept along, our path never straying into rough waters.

I wished it would. I wished the sea would just take me now before my misery could do the trick. So I laid there, not bothering to try, content to fry under the hot sun and shrivel up until I couldn't feel anything anymore. I knew I wasn't being fair to Vian—the poor boy was a fish out of water as he scrambled to secure ropes and adjust the sails—but I couldn't bring myself to do anything to help. Food tasted like ash in my mouth. Sleep evaded me, the shrieks and whispers waking me with throat burning from screams of my own. I could barely stand and stare out toward the horizon without wanting to throw myself into the deep blue and swim all the way home to Porthladd.

To Ronan.

Lyr below, the very thought of his name was enough to start another wave of back-breaking sobs. They wracked through my whole body until I was gasping for air, hugging my knees to my chest to keep myself from falling apart entirely.

When my tears ran dry and my lips were too cracked for screaming, I let the silence envelop me and tried to forget who I was.

Vian was the perfect company. We barely spoke, but we didn't need to. He seemed content to just exist, occasionally muttering to himself about the wind, and he never asked me why I woke up choking on my own sobs. He only held me to his side until I quieted, humming a bittersweet melody that made me feel less alone.

Not once did he look at me like I was something broken or useless. His eyes held no trace of pity as he handed me a hunk of bread to eat, nor did they judge me when I nibbled without tasting.

But I was a broken, useless *Melthith*. And I was dragging him along with me.

I didn't know how many days or weeks we'd been sailing, but I could tell by the furrowing of Vian's brow that it was longer than he'd intended. The hunks of bread he forced me to swallow got smaller and smaller, the sips of water few and far between.

Our supplies were running low.

I didn't care if I starved or drowned or shriveled away beneath the beating sun, but I didn't want to condemn my friend to the same fate. He'd sacrificed everything to save me, and even if I wasn't worth saving, I would not let his efforts go to waste.

It was a little after noon one day, the sun high in a vast expanse of blue, when I decided we had to see this course through. Not for me, but for him. Wherever we were going, I'd make sure he'd find a safe passage back to Porthladd, or wherever he wanted to go. Then I could crawl into a hole somewhere and rot.

"Will you tell me where we are going yet, Vian?" I croaked, and he jumped from where he was sitting on the rail.

He assessed me for a moment, as if he were worried I'd start speaking in tongues next, then shook his head. "I can't."

I frowned. He'd gotten us this far, and insane as it was, I trusted him implicitly. There was something about the bird-eyed boy that sang the song of my soul, a bond running deeper than I was capable of exploring. But I wasn't so confident he could get us to port anymore, glancing at the dwindling supply pile. "Why not?"

Vian shrugged, an easy smile breaking across his face like a wave against the shore. "Because I don't know."

I froze, my jaw dropping. "You mean to tell me you have no idea where we're going?"

"Not a clue," he giggled, sitting back and resting his head on his hands. "I'm letting the wind take us where we are meant to go."

For the first time in days, something akin to irritation bubbled underneath my skin. All this time, I'd let him captain, thinking the firm determination resting on his shoulders was the indication of a well-thought out plan.

But I was a fool. This boy spent his whole life in a cell. He had no concept of the world outside the stories he claimed the wind shared.

"You're insane." He flinched at my harsh tone, but I didn't have time to feel bad about it. I stood, pacing the small deck with frantic strides. Why had I been so complacent? Lyr below, I didn't care if I ended up at the bottom of a reef, but Vian was too young for that fate.

My fingers flew to my neck, and my panic rose when I realized nothing was there.

I didn't have Papa's compass.

I cursed under my breath. I should've never gone to the wedding without it. It was probably still resting on the night table next to Ronan's bed.

For the first time in four years, I felt truly alone.

I tried to keep the fresh wave of panic and sorrow at bay, glancing back to the dark-haired boy stretched out under the sun like a housecat, grinning like a fool. Papa would've liked Vian; he would've laughed at his colorful way of speaking, would've ruffled his messy mop of hair with a warm smile. He would've insisted on keeping him safe and taking him under his wing.

I had to protect this idiot, to get him to safety.

I stared up at the sun, gauging our direction. We were heading southeast, but there was nothing but sea around us, and the stars wouldn't be out for hours.

Where in Lyr's name were we? Why hadn't I paid closer attention? I hissed under my breath, and Vian sat up again, confusion painted on his young features.

"It's all right, Keira. The wind knows the way."

I rolled my eyes, crossing to the ship's small wheel, shifting our course due north. We'd been sailing for so long and the sun was hot enough that I assumed we'd already passed the Southern Islands. If we kept course, we'd be venturing into the far reaches, and we'd be dead in the water. But if we turned north, we'd hit something, depending on how far east or west we already were. It wasn't sublime, but it was an educated guess I was willing to make for Vian's sake.

But Vian bolted from his seat. "No, that's the wrong way!" he cried, yanking the wheel so hard we nearly capsized as the vessel turned sharply.

I tumbled into the single mast, smacking my elbow hard. Rubbing the tender spot, I righted myself. "What in Lyr's name, Vian?"

"South." Vian gripped the wheel with white-knuckled fingers, staring at the horizon. "The wind says the place we are looking for is south."

Frustration prickled across my skin as I stuck my hand on my hip. "Does the wind want to let me know where we're going, then?"

Vian shook his head again. "She says you've been there before."

"Oh, the wind is a *she* now?" I laughed humorlessly, plopping onto the small bench on the starboard side. I could already feel myself deflating again, the urge to curl up into a ball and cry swimming right beneath the surface of my control. "Tell *her majesty* she'll have to be more specific. I've been to a lot of places." But my bite was gone. I didn't have the energy to bicker.

Vian let go of the wheel and sat beside me. "She says we are close."

I pinched the bridge of my nose, sinking further into my seat. Vian looked so assured. He trusted the voice guiding him, perhaps more than he trusted himself.

I remembered the inner voice that had once guided me. I had defied him just as many times as I listened, but I'd never doubted what he said was true. Without his wisdom, my husband would be dead. I might be as well. Even though he'd abandoned me, I trusted him. So I'd have to trust Vian's companion, too.

"Are they all this vague?" I muttered to myself, but Vian perked up.

"Who?"

"The wind, the sea...the gods…whoever it is whispering in our ears." I listened closely to the sound of the ocean around us. The waves lapped against the hull like the beat to a song without a melody. It was soothing, like the memory of a lullaby. I couldn't hear Lyr's song anymore, but somehow I knew he was still singing it...perhaps to another lonely girl who deserved it more. "The sea used to tell me things too," I admitted aloud, hoping that saying it would make it true again.

"I know, *Ariannad,*" Vian hummed, eyes closing as he leaned back. I wondered if he heard the music. What songs did the wind sing?

"Is that how you know that name?" I asked instead, ignoring the strange tingling in the depths of my core as I said it aloud. "*Ariannad?*"

Vian was quiet for a moment before he opened his eyes again, head tilting up to face me. "Yes."

I looked down at my lap, the intensity of his stare too demanding. "What does it mean?"

I could feel his eyes on my face, and a blush heated my cheeks. With a sigh, he stood, shoving his hands in his pockets. But I didn't miss the way the corner of his lip twitched upward. "You'd know if you listened."

His words struck a chord in a part of me I didn't know was there. It simmered just beneath my skin, teasing me and testing me. It begged me to remember something long forgotten, something both far away and deep within.

Come and listen, Ariannad, the new voice whispered, so quiet I might have imagined it. It was warm and bright, like starlight on a cloudless night. *We're all waiting.*

I clenched my fists in an effort not to shudder. I didn't want to think about who or what waited beyond. Instead, I turned to the boy standing next to me. "What should I call you, then?"

He cocked his head. "My name is Vian."

I had to bite my lip not to laugh at him. "And my name is Keira, yet you insist on calling me *Ariannad,* a name I've only heard under unfortunate circumstances." I narrowed my eyes. "So, if I let you call me that, I need a nickname for you."

Vian scrunched up his nose as he thought, fidgeting with his hands. "*Tyawell?* It's what the other devotees in Orwellin called me. It means *wind whisperer.*"

Something dark clattered through my empty shell at the mention of Orwellin and the devotees, the people I left behind. I couldn't help the tinge of guilt coloring my voice. "Is that a name you like?"

His dark eyes filled with sadness. "No."

"Then pick one you do."

A grin crossed his face like a shooting star at midnight. "I like Vian."

Lyr below, this frustrating, delightful boy. Had he grown up with us in Porthladd instead of in the bowels of *Delm Arawn,* I could only imagine the havoc he might have wreaked with that knowing grin.

That long-forgotten otherness sloshed around in my pit, begging to be addressed. I crossed my arms. "Yes, I know. But all sailors get a nickname. Griffin is the Swordsinger, Reagan is the Little Dragon, I'm the NightMare of the Four seas, Ronan is—" I stopped before I could plunge that dagger into my heart, afraid that even saying his name might shatter me entirely. I cleared my throat, dislodging the emotion that choked me. "Anyway. Maybe something badass, like the Obsidian Hawk, or the Black Phoenix—"

"*Wynnaid.*" He cut me off, flashing another toothy smile that could chase away even the darkest shadows.

"*Wynnaid.*" I repeated it, warmth spreading through the marrow of my bones. "What does it mean?"

A faint breeze tousled his hair, brushing it off his forehead like a gentle caress. "Soul wind."

Soul Wind. It fit. Off-center as he was, he'd breezed his way right into my heart, my soul knowing his the moment he muttered my name from his dark cell. "*Wynnaid.* I like it."

Vian reached out, flicking my matted hair from my face with as much tenderness as the wind danced in his. "I like you. I'm very glad you're not dying right now."

A 'me too' died on my tongue before I could give the lie life. But the fractured, jagged shards of my heart all ached at once. In many ways, I was already halfway to the Otherworld. A cursed *Melthith*. A fugitive. A murderer. I didn't care what happened to me, not without my family and my husband by my side.

But I wasn't alone. Not with Vian steering my ship, the Soul Wind strong in my sails.

Come and listen, Ariannad. We're all waiting.

The rest of the day went by smoothly. I managed to make myself a little less useless, cleaning the deck with Vian under the setting sun, taking stock of our rations. The most pressing concern was the half-empty barrel of water, but we still had time. If we were careful, we could last another week on what we still had.

I knew it was absurd, but for the first time since Finna's wedding, I wasn't angry or scared. Since the moment she married Yorath, everything felt upside down. But there was a strange relief that embraced me as I accepted my fate. We were already fugitives on the run, lost at sea, with nothing more than a breeze and a few loaves of stale bread to see us through. At least things really couldn't get much worse from there.

Naturally, I was wrong. Things could get worse. And they did.

The sun had fully set when the weather changed. It was the breeze that picked up first, gentle licks turning into vicious, bone-chilling gusts. Then came the rain, the dark clouds blotting out the stars, leaving us fully lost.

What started as a drizzle soon became a full-blown typhoon. Rain came at us sideways, blurring our vision and soaking us to the core. Waves rocked the tiny seacraft so hard, it was a struggle to stay standing as we fervently prayed she wouldn't flip. My legs felt like ice, every muscle aching. I hadn't eaten properly in who knew how long, and my body was sore and out of practice. But panic and adrenaline fortified my nerves as I tied back the sails and secured the lines. I was a sailor before anything else. I could weather the storm if it meant keeping Vian safe.

"Can you tell the wind to settle down? This boat is not built for this!" I yelled over the roaring wind, holding onto Vian and the mast as we rode another surge.

He grimaced, clinging to the shoddy mast for dear life. "She...isn't listening."

"Ask again!" I shouted back. I had to be a raving lunatic, but there was no other solution. If we didn't receive some divine intervention, we'd capsize.

Vian shook his head, his face twisted in fear. I cursed under my breath, tying us together while the waves assaulted the hull.

Ropes burned my palms as I struggled to keep them in place, every muscle straining.

If the gods abandoned us again, I would not. I did not need their Otherworldly strength to keep this hunk of shit afloat. I would do it myself, with my own mortal strength and will and fire.

A wave crested against the horizon, taller than a Pysgoddian mountain, and an anchor dropped through my gut.

This was it. We were going under.

But we wouldn't drown. Not on my watch.

I scrambled for a barrel, securing our rope to it as I braced for impact. Vian stared up at the towering mass, face ashen.

"Vian!" I grabbed his face, turning him to look at me and not our impending doom. "Hold on to me no matter what, *Wynnaid*."

Panic washed over his face when the ship groaned, tilting as the undertow dragged us up toward the apex of the watery colossus. Long fingers dug into my shoulders. "Help! Keira, I—"

I pulled him close, hugging him and the barrel as tightly as I could. "Hold on to me."

And we held onto each other as the wave crashed into us and dragged us into the deep blue.

Brothers and Blame

RONAN

People leave.

My mother used to say that leaving was one of the few guarantees in life. It happens in different ways, but no matter if they choose to or not, eventually, everyone leaves.

Sometimes, they'd leave on a funeral pyre of rose petals, pushed into the waiting sea. Sometimes they'd vanish in the middle of the night without telling you where they're going, their only parting message a warning not to follow.

A goodbye.

I was foolish to think Keira was any different. Foolish and proud, pretending that the laws of men and gods didn't apply to us. It was childish to believe that our marriage alone could conquer death and misery. Maybe I had read too many books, sweet stories that tricked me into believing a strong will and a true love could defy fate.

It would have been a lie if I said I didn't blame her. I did.

My love was strong enough. My love was not easily challenged. Standing in Connor Yorath's office, I was prepared to shout and yell and defy the verdict over and over again until they dragged me to the Otherworld. I was prepared to cut down all of

Porthladd and Orwellin, the entire *Deymas*, for Lyr's sake, if that's what it took to free her.

I didn't blame her for running. I would have too. I would do anything to keep her from the gallows, so if my ranting and raving wasn't enough, I would have run with her all the way to the Otherworld and back. Lyr's ass, I was angry more at myself for not thinking of the idea first.

I blamed her for leaving me behind.

More than anything, I missed her. I missed the silver glint of her eye, like a dagger in the moonlight. I missed her lavender and cedar scent, warm and fresh as she embraced me with her whole heart. I missed being useful by her side. I missed having a purpose on her ship, her steady guidance a beacon on a black horizon.

It had been two weeks. I'd been away longer before, but now every second felt like a lifetime.

Maybe because I knew this time, she wasn't coming back.

I decided to wait out the rest of my pitiful existence in Mathonwy Manor; my ornate, personal prison. I stared up at the ceiling, tracing the knots in the wood like she always did, wishing she were with me as I wasted away.

This was how I mourned. Just like when I'd been shipwrecked in *Hiraeth*, like when the Council signed my divorce papers, I would drink and pout until I felt numb enough to breathe again. Reina brought me food every day, accompanied by her pity-steeped stare, and I would stumble to the bathroom to wash my face every few days or so.

Otherwise, I was content to rot.

A knock on my door interrupted my drink-sleep-piss-sob cycle. I didn't know what time it was, and frankly, I didn't care. "Go away," I growled, but my aggression was a mask crafted from habit and not from fire.

"Griffin, he's not seeing anyone right now," Reina whispered outside my door, her voice coated in a thick layer of sympathy that made my skin crawl. I didn't want her pity, I wanted to be left alone.

Griffin's deep voice was void of compassion. "All due respect, Madame Reina, but move yourself, or I'll move you."

My ears pricked up, an old instinct flickering inside me before I shoved it back down and sank further into my very empty mattress. I pulled a pillow over my ears to tune out the rising conflict in front of my door. I knew Reina would have him tamed and out of my hair in no time.

"Griff—"

"Shut it, Rhett, you know I'm right."

"He needs space."

"He's had enough." The door banged open as Griffin barged past a concerned Reina and surly Rhett. My kin exchanged a wary look before leaving me to Griffin's fury. He stomped toward me, cheeks as red as his flaming hair, arms crossed. "Get up."

For a moment, I was tempted to spar with him, to get under his freckled skin and see how far I could push. To see if he was hurting, too. But the spark was doused faster than it came, the emptiness in my chest swallowing it whole. I turned over, burrowing myself further into the pillow. "Go away."

"No." He ripped the blanket from me, throwing it on the ground for emphasis, and smacked my ass like a prized horse's flank. "Get up."

Something small shifted, a match flickering in an endless night, but I extinguished it. "Don't you have a card game to lose somewhere or a relationship to ruin?" I grabbed the blanket from the floor. "I said go."

Griffin stepped on the fabric before I could return to my cave of despair. He quirked an eyebrow, his stare equal parts challenging and mocking. "Make me."

Something rumbled deep in my chest, a single strike of lightning in an otherwise-empty sky. Two weeks ago, I'd have put him in a headlock until he yelled uncle, or until Keira split us up, whichever came first.

Keira.

I shut the thought out before it could eat me from the inside out. "Fine. Stand there and stare at me, then. Make sure you get my good side." I rolled over to face the opposite wall, no energy left for Griffin and his knowing glare. "I don't care."

"Right, enough of this sad sack bullshit," my cousin-in-law exhaled once before planting a hard shove into my side. I toppled out of the bed, hitting the floor with a loud *thud* that sounded as bad as it hurt.

"What in Lyr's name?" I rubbed the tender spot already forming at my elbow.

Griffin crouched down next to me, determination blazing in his eye. "You're getting up, you're going to go take a bath because you smell like arse, and then we are setting sail."

I sat up, the emptiness echoing through me. I wished I could bottle his rage, his drive, like lightning against dry wood, and drink it. But even Griffin's steel couldn't bring her back. Nothing could.

"There's no point."

"No point?" Griffin's laugh was harsh as he ran a hand over his face. Before I could react, he shot to his feet, a shaking finger pointed out my window. "Ronan, look out there. Look at Porthladd. People are starving. Dying. What the hell would Keira say if she could hear you say there is no point?"

His words were like ice running down my spine. "She left, Griffin." My fingernails dug into my hands as I choked on the words. My tone was venomous, but I didn't feel like a snake—only the discarded skin after a shedding. I hated the way my voice shook. "She *left*. She doesn't get a say."

Griffin's expression softened for less than a moment before he hauled me back to my feet. "Well, then let's go find her."

I pushed him away, the emptiness inside turning tumultuous, a black hole devouring itself. "She doesn't want to be found."

"For now. It's not safe for her here. So let's go do something productive to try and make it safe."

My jaw clenched as I struggled to swallow his words. I didn't want to be productive. I wanted to pout and whine and rot until I was nothing. I wasn't cut from the same cloth as him and Keira. I didn't know how to create gold from shit with my will and steel alone. I was a coward, a secondary character in my own story, content to follow the true heroes around until they discarded me. "If she wanted my help, she would've asked. I'm better off staying out of the way. I'm not a leader, Griffin. Keira was the leader—I'm a drifter."

"Screw that, Ronan!" Griffin shoved me with surprising force. I stumbled back, legs lead and heart pounding as Griffin unleashed himself on me. "She might not have asked for your help, but *I* am. Reagan, Saeth, Tarran, Rhett...we need you. This island needs you. *I need you*, brother. Keira left us to save us, because she *trusted* us to do the damn job."

We stared at each other, and for the first time in weeks, something other than misery flickered through me. Griffin wasn't built to be Captain, either, and yet here he was, still standing strong for his crew and family. His sagging frame shouted the evidence of his exhaustion despite the mask he wore to hide it. But steady as a mountain, he still stood by me, even at my most rotten, and called me brother.

Sensing my wavering resolve, he clapped me on the shoulder. His grin was not out of pity, but respect, something I didn't deserve but desperately craved. "Go wash your arse in that silly spring, Ro, and let's get going. There's work to do."

The very mention of the spring sent a wave of nausea rolling through me. It hadn't been long, but the cravings were strong, like a lodestone pulling me to the source. Like with Keira absent, the pit in my gut was even emptier, a husk missing its most essential piece.

Still, a moment alone in the spring didn't sound so terrible. Maybe I'd get lucky and Lyr would drown me.

"Can I come in?" a voice called from just outside the door, pulling me back.

I ran my hand through my mess of matted curls. "Is there a sign on my door that says 'open for business' that I am unaware of? Lyr below, can't a man have some privacy?"

"You've had plenty." Griffin rolled his eyes. "Come in, Ellian."

I whipped my head around to where Ellian's massive frame darkened the doorway. Finally, after weeks of lying dormant, the dragon in my chest stirred, huffing smoke from its snout as my anger awakened.

"I know I'm never your favorite person, but we have bigger issues to deal with." Ellian entered with his hands up in surrender, a puppy with his tail between his legs, but it did nothing to quell the heat burning through my veins.

I stuffed my hands in my pockets, my mask slipping back on like I'd never taken it off. "You're bold for showing up here, *Councilman*." I emphasized his esteemed title, though I meant it entirely as an insult. I knew I wasn't being entirely fair, but I didn't care. What good was the position of Councilman if again and again he was useless against Connor's tyranny?

The pain that broke across his expression was a punch to the gut. "I tried to get her out, Ronan. I know she didn't do it. But Connor's frame job was tightly woven...it was out of my hands."

"What useless appendages, then," I scoffed, staring him down. My voice was calm, but the beast stirred inside, gnashing its teeth together, desperate to be freed. "They're always conveniently tied."

"You're no better, you asshat," Griffin commented as he wedged his way between us, dwarfing us both. I shot him a dirty look, but the fire in my core sputtered out, the beast tamed once more. He was right. Ellian didn't deserve my reproach, and I didn't have the energy to start a fight. I just didn't want to shoulder the blame for my wife's absence alone.

I bit my lip, schooling my features into submission once more. I looked to Ellian, to the pain and urgency in his gaze, and nodded. "The point, fleabag. Get to it."

Ellian sighed, tired and heavy. "Keira was right. About everything. About the slaves, about what they are hiding in Orwellin..." He sagged against my doorframe, the weight of that message enough to burden anyone.

Griffin's fingers twitched at his sides. "We know, we were there."

Ellian shook his head. "But it's bigger than that, boys." He rubbed tired eyes. "The famine, the crops...they are behind it all. Connor, too."

The dragon roared with new purpose. "*What?*"

"I—I don't know why. But it's true. I was listening in—perk of the wolf ears, I don't need to be close to be accurate—and I overheard Morwyn Locasta talking to Connor..." Deep sadness and vicious rage mixed in the young wolf's expression as he met my gaze, a desperate plea for help swimming in his. "Ronan, we need you and the crew. They are trying to start a war."

18

Hostages and Hideaways

KEIRA

I woke to sand in every crevice.

As expected, my head felt like an anchor had been dropped over it, every muscle in my body aching and sore. What I wasn't expecting was the rope tied securely around my wrists and ankles, biting into my flesh with a sharp burn.

I groaned as I struggled to open my eyes, straining against my restraints. Vian's blurred form lay next to me, still unconscious against the pink sand, but from he seemed to have made it in one piece.

We had survived. By some miracle, we escaped Porthladd, escaped *Connor*, without dying.

Somehow, I had still ended up with my wrists bound.

I reached for Vian in panic, but a bare foot stopped my hand before I could comfort him. I looked up, blinking against the blinding sunlight as the form of my captor swam into view. Tall, her dark skin stark against the morning sun, she glowered down at me with piercing orange eyes. A long staff pressed against my chin before I could jolt upright.

"Nelle, wake the boy up," she commanded a smaller woman flitting behind her.

Adrenaline sang through me, chasing away the aches and leaving me only with instinct as I surveyed my assailants and surroundings. The tall woman was clearly a warrior, by blood and profession. She wore linen pants that only hit her knees and a simple white band around her breasts, but by the lean cut of her muscular frame, it was obvious she didn't need armor to protect herself. A ribbon tamed her wild brown curls, the same sunset-orange as her eyes. She was feline and feral in appearance, a lioness poised to attack.

My stomach rolled, fear prickling the back of my neck. If I had to guess by her looks and the way she handled her weapon like she was born with it, she was Tannian.

The smaller woman was not. Her dark waves were longer, framing her slim build and porcelain skin. Large, distinguishable violet eyes marked her as Psygoddian. She wore the same simple linens as the other woman, but the deep purple belt at her waist emphasized the feminine curve of her hips as she bent down next to Vian.

"Good morning, sunshine," she hummed, stroking his cheek. I flinched against the staff at my neck, panic surging through me, but Vian groaned, floating back to consciousness once more. "Good to see you awake." The woman smiled, flashing brilliant white teeth.

My brain struggled to process the conflicting pair, the lion and dove working in tandem. "Who are you?" My voice was hoarse, my mouth dry as the sand beneath me.

The smaller woman—Nelle—opened her mouth to answer with that same maternal smile, but the taller woman cut her off with a sharp glare. "I will be asking the questions here." She pressed her staff deeper into my chest, pinning me to the hot sand. "Who are *you?*"

Part of me wanted to spit in her face and call her mother a whore as a thank you for her unfriendly greeting, but the smarter part of me overruled. I was unarmed, restrained, and weakened by the shipwreck. I didn't have a leg to stand on if it came to blows, especially not against this formidable fighter. I had to be compliant and clever if I was going to get us out of this alive.

When I was younger, Papa used to tell me I was the fiercest thing on two legs. But ferocity without cunning was a recipe for a bruise and a bad day.

Instincts finally orienting themselves, I searched my surroundings. Green, vine-covered trees decorated the shoreline, so this was not the Tannian desert, luckily. But that still didn't answer the very important question of where we'd landed. If we were somewhere else in the Deyrnas, it could spell trouble.

"Where are we?" I voiced the thought aloud before I could catch myself. When was the last time I had something to drink? I couldn't remember, but the headache pounding against my skull suggested it had been too long.

The warrior woman planted a sharp kick to my side that stole the air from my chest.

"Siobhan!" Nelle shrieked.

The name struck a familiar chord in me as Siobhan crouched down, growling in my face, "I said, *I* am asking the questions. And I don't like to ask twice."

"Keira," I coughed, my ribs screaming. But I hesitated, my last name catching in my throat. I remembered the posters with my name on them in Orwellin, and until I could discern who these women worked for, I had to be extra cautious. "Keira Branwen. This is my friend, Vian." I gestured to him, still gently groaning as Nelle petted his hair.

Violet eyes shot to me, curiosity and concern fighting for dominance. "Branwen?"

"Aye." I looked at the smaller woman, her kind expression reminding me so much of Reina. My heart broke at the thought of another goodbye I'd never get to say, but I swallowed the sadness that rose to my throat. I could be sentimental later. Now, I just needed to survive. If there was an appeal to be made, it was with this woman. "We were shipwrecked. We don't even know where we are, and we mean you no harm."

"I thought…" Nelle's mouth pressed into a tight line, then softened again. "Never mind."

Before I could pursue that, another woman made her way from the treeline. She wore the same linens, distinguished only by the crimson sash draped around her waist. It must have been some kind of uniform, but one I'd never seen before. I tensed as I waited to see which woman's disposition she'd share.

"Nelle? Siobhan?" she called, practically floating toward us. She was just as tall as Siobhan, but lithe instead of muscular, like a dancer from Ir'de. "Everything alright?"

She appraised me with a hand stuck to the generous curve of her hip. The action oozed pure sensuality, and I gulped, blush coloring my cheeks. In many ways, she reminded me of Finna—the intensity, the effortlessness, the glimmer of something sharper beneath the silk. Her deep auburn hair fanned her heart-shaped face in a way that even Finna couldn't replicate with all of the product and curlers in the world. The nymph of a woman looked at me with a hungry, ruby stare that could make a grown man sweat.

"Trespassers," Siobhan snarled, her staff still uncomfortably at my throat.

"Oh hush, Sho." Nelle helped Vian into a sitting position, pushing his hair from his eyes to further inspect him. "The poor kids are scared."

I locked gazes with Vian in a silent, burning question. *Are you alright?*

His nod was the only confirmation I needed, my breath rushing out with relief. Siobhan, however, prickled further, grimacing at Vian like he was a threat. "Marina, do it."

I shifted, tensing to roll or stumble or fight if I needed to, even in my compromised position. The graceful woman fiddled with a long auburn lock as she watched us. "Siobhan, I don't—"

"Now."

Marina sighed, sharing a long look with Nelle I couldn't quite name before approaching me cautiously, like I was a wounded animal. Wordless, she sat at my side, and Siobhan moved her staff from my neck. Closing her vermillion eyes, Marina reached for my hands.

I froze as she touched me, an icy sensation running down my spine. Perhaps it was the dehydration, but something rolled through my stomach, demanding to be released.

I lurched, expecting sick to rise up my throat, but instead I started speaking, no control over my own tongue. "Please, I mean no harm." It was my voice and my words, but I was not the captain of my own body. The word vomit continued, spilling from me like a waterfall over a cliff. "We fled my home island to escape. I was framed for murder, and they were going to hang me. My friend was a slave, we rescued him from Orwellin."

Marina dropped my hands, an apology swimming in her gemstone stare, and the tidal wave of truth stopped. I clamped my hands over my traitorous mouth, horror and panic fighting for purchase in my chest.

"What did you do to her?" Vian found his voice, shoving Nelle off him as he fought to crawl to me, but a sharp jab to the shoulder from Siobhan's staff stopped him. Red colored my vision, anger surging through me like lightning as I twisted to my knees. Still bound and awkward, I threw myself at the back of Siobhan's calves, knocking her to the sand. Shock hung her jaw wide as she toppled over, and before she could get her bearings, I looped the rope that trapped my hands around her neck and rolled on top of her.

"Don't you dare touch him," I snarled, leaning into my weight.

Hooking her leg behind mine, Siobhan bucked her hips and flipped us back over faster than I could think, pinning me with her elbow against my windpipe. "Not so mouthy now, are we?"

"Stop it *now*, Siobhan." Nelle's voice was quiet but firm, cutting through our struggle with the efficiency of a sharpened dagger. "They've been through enough, the poor creatures."

"You heard her yourself," Siobhan spat, but much to my surprise, shoved off me with a grimace. "She's an escaped convict!"

I rubbed the tender spot forming on my neck, but the look I gave the lioness could set a fire to a wet log. "I told you, I was framed. And that boy is innocent."

Siobhan spun at me, rage clear in her citrine stare, but then she blanched, looking past me.

"That's enough, ladies," another female voice said, ethereal and weighty. "Stand down, Siobhan."

If the first three women were beautiful, the one who uttered the last command was Otherworldly. She looked no older than Vala, but her face held none of my aunt's wear or wrinkles. Moon-white hair fell to her waist in ringlets, not a strand out of place, and constellations of freckles covered every exposed inch of cream-colored skin.

She belonged in a storybook. With a gossamer white dress clinging to her supple form, she was an enchantress, gliding across the pink sands of some distant fairytale. But the look in her silver eyes as she stared at me sent a chill up my spine. I'd been cautious and nervous since I woke, uncertain and out of my element, but the feeling of sheer dread that pooled in my already-turning stomach was of another caliber entirely.

"Danura." Siobhan fell into a deep bow, Marina and Nelle mimicking the motion.

The name triggered the reflection of a memory, but its origin evaded me. I shifted closer to Vian, putting his thin frame behind me. I had no leverage, no real chance at protecting us, but I would not abandon my charge.

Danura ignored her bowing subjects, gaze locked on me and me alone. "It's Keira, yes?"

"How did you—?"

She crossed to me, iridescent dress swishing around her, a smile breaking across her face like a wave. "Marina, if you would?"

The sensuous woman knelt before me, untying my hands with deft fingers, somehow avoiding touching my skin directly. "Vian Imari, six feet tall, one hundred and fifty pounds, threat level eight of ten, and he's a *Tyawell*. A wind whisperer. Keira Mathonwy. Five foot seven inches tall, one hundred and forty-three pounds," she muttered as she worked, like she was reading my life story from a book in front of her. I gasped, pulling my hands away, but Marina continued, unfazed, "Threat level nine of ten, but currently not exhibiting any signs of aggression."

Danura waved the analysis off before I could raise my voice to protest, stepping closer to me and offering a porcelain hand. "We've been expecting you, darling."

The hair on my neck stood upright, the sand against my skin suddenly coarse and grating. I looked around again at the too-green foliage just beyond the sand, to the peppering of brightly colored flowers woven through it. Birdsong sweeter than any flute floated in the distance, enchanting and symphonic. Mist wrapped itself around the tall, thick tree branches, ghostly soldiers draped in mystery. Realization settled in my bones, heavy as an anchor.

Danura…Nelle…Marina…Siobhan. I'd heard those names before, their praises sung by my favorite voice in the entire world.

I asked the question again, hoping desperately to be wrong. "Where are we?"

"You don't recognize it?" Danura's delicate brow furrowed as Marina freed me from my restraints. "Darling girl, let me officially welcome you back to *Hiraeth*."

Against every instinct in my body, I let the women lead Vian and me through the dense jungle of *Hiraeth*.

We were in *Hiraeth*. The island of lost things, where the flowers were as fragrant as they were poisonous, where snakes spoke in riddles and daggers kept their secrets. Where time slowed and beasts roamed and ships wrecked, never to sail home again. And I was letting the same strangers who had tied me up like a roast pig lead me deeper into the island's maw.

Blindfolded.

"This would be easier if we could see," Vian whined somewhere behind me, and a root snapped underfoot as one or both of us tripped over it.

It was disorienting, stumbling blindly, my only guide Nelle's steady hand on my back. But there was a part of me that cherished the feeling of fear and discomfort prickling in my core. It was proof that I was still alive, my heartbeat still thundering in my ears, even if I had very little to live for.

"I hope you both know this is only precautionary." Danura sounded a few paces ahead, her voice still carrying like a song in the wind. "My island is a bit tricky. But I promise, you two are guests."

"This island gives me the spooks and I've been here for years," Marina sang. "It really is for your own good that you can't see it."

"I've heard that before." Vian's voice was tight, unleashing a renewed wave of fear down my spine. "It's rarely true."

His words thickened the air, Marina and the other women falling silent. A part of me agreed with Vian—it was hard to trust those who obviously didn't trust us enough to see their hiding spot. The part of me that was my father's daughter might have fought harder. A more reckless part didn't care if we were being led to our deaths, the last fight left in me exhausted from the tussle with Siobhan.

Another quieter part remembered Ronan's stories, his fondness for these women who had given him a home and called him a friend.

The thought of Ronan elicited a deep ache in my gut. I had cursed him to this island the first time, and now I was stuck here to save him. Destiny had a horrendous sense of irony.

The urge to crumple into the dirt and cry was overwhelming, but I could not. I had to keep pushing for Vian's sake, until I knew if I could trust these women, until he was safe and sound.

A surly grunt from Siobhan broke the silence and pulled me back to reality. "We're almost there."

After a few more clumsy steps, Nelle caught my arm to halt me. I stiffened as quick fingers untied the cloth covering my eyes, blinking a few times against the harsh sunlight.

"Welcome to Annwyn." Nelle's smile was full of warmth and light as she stepped aside to reveal our destination. "Our home."

The view stole the breath from my chest.

Anwynn was paradise. Small, evenly built straw-roofed huts decorated a wide, circular clearing, each framed with strong bamboo. Seashell wind chimes and woven dream charms made of every colored feather imaginable decorated the doors. Under the windows, planters of bioluminescent flowers chased away the shadows the tall palms cast. A lazy river, bluer than Lyr's spring, curved through the center, feeding the neat rows of wide-petaled lotus flowers that dappled the river pink, their scent sweetening the air. That river babbled in perfect harmony with the birds, and a deep, forgotten part of me wanted to join in the song.

Unmarred by the outside world, it was a sanctuary in the middle of this nightmare of an island. It was so easy to see why this had been Ronan's home. How he had the strength to leave it, I had no idea.

Then again, I had found the strength to leave him.

"Nef's breath," Vian swore as he took it all in, bringing me back from the precipice of my thoughts, earning a laugh from both Marina and Nelle. His boyish grin was infectious, warming even my broken heart. Siobhan, somehow immune, stalked off into a nearby hut without another word.

I relaxed considerably in her absence. As much as I wanted to take a crack at her now that my hands were untied, I knew it was best we put as much distance between us as possible. I looked instead at the huts, counting nearly a dozen, imagining what brand of islander each might hold.

"This is beautiful," I said, trying not to imagine Ronan hiding in one of those same huts, waiting for me.

Nelle gave my shoulder a reassuring squeeze as if she were an old friend, not someone I'd just met. "Your husband said the same thing."

The words were intended to soothe, but they gutted me. This was all wrong. He should've been here with me, by my side as he had been since we were ten. Or I should've been home, fighting for myself and my family, not surrounded by suspicious strangers on the island of the lost and damned.

The impact of what I'd done finally hit me, the urge to vomit all over the colorful sand rising up like a volcano ready to explode.

I left him. I left him alone to fight my battles and feed my family. I left the one person who made me feel whole and real, running off to a fantasy land where none of my problems could find me.

But I couldn't go back, not now, maybe not ever. If I went back now, I'd be hung. By fleeing, I had all but certified my guilt. Though I cared very little for my life, I would not put Ronan through the pain of watching me meet my death at the end of a rope. Even if I did evade the gallows, by miracle or trickery, the black spot on my shoulder still grew day by day, evidence that mine were numbered.

How long did I have until it consumed me? I'd been so distracted with the wedding and the fallout, I hadn't thought that forsaking my home also meant forsaking the search for a cure. I shuddered as I imagined that grisly finale.

No. Leaving had been the right choice, if only to spare Ronan from the inevitable.

"So you did know Ronan." I choked out his name. It felt like swallowing nails, but I needed to feel this pain, to face what I'd done in front of these women and whoever else would bear witness to my transgressions.

Nelle offered a sad smile, understanding laced in the furrow of her brow, like she could see how bone-deep his name cut me. Strange validation settled in my stomach; I had only known her for a matter of hours, yet in her amethyst stare, I felt seen, like she'd known me all my life and I'd known her just as dearly. "I knew him very well."

"Ronan Francis Mathonwy." Marina fiddled with her ruby sash, the faint traces of a smirk playing on her full lips. "Twenty-one years old, six foot two, one hundred and eighty-three pounds of muscle and sex appeal. Threat level five out of ten, entertainment level ten of ten. If you ask me, we knew him *too* well," she laughed, smacking Vian on the shoulder. I froze, my lungs seizing in my chest, but Marina didn't notice and carried on, toying with a lock of hair as she recounted the memory. "I was born into a performing troupe, and even I had never met someone so fond of hearing himself speak."

Nelle stared at her friend. "Marina, that was—"

"Absolutely accurate." I silenced Nelle's protest and shot the women a smile. They *knew* him. The perfect picture they painted of my husband carved my heart from my chest, but it also fortified me, turning the same heart to stone. It hurt worse than death, but I would endure it. It was my sentence for leaving, one I'd gladly bear it if guaranteed my husband's safety. To hear them speak of him like a friend was just as healing as it was hurtful. They had harbored him, sheltered him from the storm; but more than that, they had gotten to know him, to cherish his whims and chide his shortcomings. They had become his people when I refused him. Tears stung my eyes, gratitude and agony battling in my chest.

"I—thank you for taking him in. He told me about you, about what you did for him—I can't—" The sobs took over as the whirlwind escalated, stealing the air from my lungs. The world spun, the dizzying colors of the island dancing around me in a frenzied jig. I barely felt Nelle pull me in a hug, pressing me into her hair. Her scent was both floral and earthy, like jasmine and spice, and it grounded me like one of Vala's fainting vapors.

When I was four or five, Papa lost me in the markets of the Eastern Docks. He was distracted that day, negotiating something with old man Llewellyn. Something must have caught my eye, and I wandered off, the pull of wonder heavier than the chains of safety. I didn't remember what had called me away from my father's side, I only remembered the fear afterwards. The market spinning around me, faster than a hurricane, faces and voices I didn't know all blurring together in the typhoon. When Papa finally found me, four streets away, I was wrapped around a kind fish vendor's leg, sobbing into the woman's skirt, calling his name over and over.

Today, I felt just as small, even in Nelle's slender embrace. Her arms weren't Ronan's or Papa's. Like the woman in the market, she was only one step sideways of a stranger. Yet I melted effortlessly into the contact, desperate for anything that could stop the storm.

"Shh, deary, it's alright," she repeated over and over until I could breathe again, stroking my hair. After a moment, another set of hands gently rubbed my back, a warm tingle lighter than air running down my spine and mooring me to my body. I greedily sucked in my first steady breath, wishing Papa were here to be the one to remind me how.

Instead, it was Danura's glowing face behind me, her expression painted with a strange sort of regret I couldn't place. She dropped her hand from my back, awkwardness apparent even in the grace of her limbs, and cleared her throat. "It was a pleasure to have Ronan as our guest. Just as it is a pleasure to host you both until you can get back on your feet." Politeness hardened her silver stare as she gestured to the quaint settlement behind her. "Nelle, why don't you take Keira and Vian to their huts for the day? It seems it's been a long journey."

Nelle nodded, but it was Vian stepped closer to me, lanky form shaking. "We aren't staying together?"

Danura blinked twice. "I assumed you'd want space—"

I shoved the lost little girl back into the recesses of my mind, forgetting the warmth of Danura's hands as I reminded myself where I was. This was not the Eastern Market, Danura was not a fish-peddler, and I was not a useless girl, not anymore. I was a Captain now, and I had a crew of one to take care of.

"He's staying with me." It was a command, not a question, and I gripped Vian's hand in silent promise. I'd been terrible and useless, but my *Wynnaid* still saw me safely to shore. He deserved the same in return. I rolled my shoulders back as I stared down Danura, determination renewed. "If that's alright."

Danura appraised me with pursed lips. She wasn't used to being given orders, nor did she like it, that much was clear; but whatever obligation she had to maintain a sense of peace won out. She nodded once to Nelle, who squealed in delight. Vian relaxed at my side—my first small victory in weeks.

"Right this way!" Giddily, Nelle linked arms with Vian and me, pulling us away from Danura's watchful stare and further into the compound. We passed a few rows of uniform huts, but just like their garb, each with a slight personal flare. One had twinkling parchment lanterns hung in front, painted with silhouettes of sirens swimming in a shallow pool. Another had a woven doormat that looked straight from Pysgodd, the fir leaves green year-round. I soaked it all in, every last detail, searching for anything that helped me feel less lost.

Papa used to say sometimes people fall because there is something down there they need to find. I was falling and had been for a while. But maybe I'd find something in the dirt streets of Hiraeth that could connect me to myself, or to Papa, or perhaps to who my husband once was.

It was like trying to fish without a net as I grasped blindly at my surroundings, aching for any line back to Ronan. Had he stayed in any of these huts? Had he helped collect these seashells for windchimes during the summer solstice? Did he dress in the same linen pants and white shirts, perhaps with a signature red sash?

I was no closer to answers or to him when we stopped in front of a plain hut no bigger than the Dubryn shack. It was sturdy in its build, the bamboo straight and the straw roof tightly woven, but no charms or chimes painted the front. Nelle pushed open the unmarked door, ushering us into the warm single room. It was near empty, only a mat spread across the bamboo floor with a few lush blankets and a small stove, but there was something comforting in its simplicity. It was hot outside, the sun still high in the sky, but the room was dark, the clay shutters working remarkably well.

I hesitated in the doorway. It seemed cozy and warm, but I hated sleeping in cramped quarters, especially without Ronan by my side. It reminded me of the cramped, lifeless ceiling in Branwen Townhouse, and the traitor who put me there. I bit my lip, steadying myself before I started blubbering like a child again.

Nelle stepped past and fluffed the nearest pillow. "This is a guest hut, though we very rarely use it, so I'm sorry it's not quite finished. We can spruce it up a bit tomorrow. Still, I hope you find it cozy!"

"It's perfect," Vian answered, plopping onto the mat, sprawling out like a bird claiming its nest. After he was comfortable, his dark gaze found me. Tilting his head, he patted the space next to him. "Come on, Captain. Ronan will have my head if he finds out you didn't rest while you were in my charge."

Something unknotted in my core at the way he talked about Ronan like I'd see him again. Maybe he said it to make me feel better, or maybe the wind was whispering her secrets to him. Either way, I wanted him to be right with my whole soul, so much so I was willing to live in the blissfully cloudy waters of denial for one more night.

Taking the bait, I raised an eyebrow, settling onto the soft mat next to him. "Oh, I'm *your* charge now?"

Vian nodded once, an angular smile spreading across his features. "Yes."

"Alright, *Wynnaid*," I whispered, my own smile real. "I'll be good."

Nelle unfurled a blanket for us, the simple action reminding me of Reina again. "Genevieve and I will be here at nightfall to help you tidy up and get ready for the night."

"You sleep during the day?"

Her lips formed a tight line, and I knew I accidentally stumbled onto some sort of burr patch. "Some of us do, some don't. We take…shifts." She laughed dryly, darkness coloring her expression. After a moment, she blinked, the shadows dispersing as quickly as they came. "But you two both look like you need the rest."

Had my own exhaustion not already settled heavy on my shoulders, I might have pressed her for answers. But Vian was already curled on his side, hugging a pillow to his frame as if to further emphasize Nelle's point. We needed rest more than we needed clarity.

I sighed, relaxing back into the soft material beneath me. My entire body yearned for sleep, the wear of weeks at sea and the shipwreck etched deep into every muscle and bone. I barely found the energy to take my waterlogged boots off, kicking them until I finally managed to free myself. But my mind was heavy in a different way, one that I could not shuck off like a pair of shoes.

"I doubt I'll be able to sleep much. It's a lot to process," I said honestly, something in me unraveling in Nelle's tender presence.

Her hand found mine with a soft squeeze. "I can help with that if you'll let me."

I moved to pull away, but Vian's sleepy voice stopped me. "It's alright, Keira, it feels nice."

I nodded once, unsure of what he meant, but I didn't have the salt left to protest.

"Rest, little one." Nelle closed her eyes, and in an instant, a flood of calm washed over me. For a moment, it was like floating in the spring, the way the rest of the world quieted around me and my body felt light. My eyes, however, grew heavier. Like a stone, I sank into the deep, until all I could hear was a voice in the distance singing me to sleep.

19

Poisons and Placation

KEIRA

For the first time in three months, my sleep was dreamless. No nightmares, no whispering voices. Just the cold, dark embrace of a black sleep.

A gloved hand on my cheek brought me to waking. For a moment, I leaned into the touch, the part of me still trapped in the wasteland of the dreamworld aching to believe it was my husband's hand on my cheek.

The reasonable part knew it wasn't.

I blinked awake, and a young girl swam into my view. Despite my better part, my chest sank when indeed it was not Ronan sitting carefully at the edge of my mat.

I nudged Vian next to me, earning a low grunt.

"Good morning." The young girl nodded politely, her voice sweet as birdsong. No older than Tarran, she had wispy blonde hair nearly as light as Ronan's and round eyes just as brilliant blue. My stomach ached for home at the sight of her, and I couldn't help but wince. She seemed to take my disappointment personally, regret brimming in her sapphire stare. "Sorry to wake you."

"Morning?" I shot up, noticing the light pouring through the open cottage windows. My stomach sank as I remembered where I was, though I did my best to hide my devastation, forcing a smile at the girl as I noticed Nelle fussing with some linens on the other side of the hut.

"You slept through the night, dearies; we didn't want to wake you," Nelle said, tying her dark wall of hair back with a purple ribbon and smiling at Vian and I with a perfect row of white teeth. "But we thought you might like something to eat."

Vian sat up, rubbing a hand over his face and pushing his hair from his eyes. Sniffing himself, he grimaced. "Or perhaps a bath."

I didn't bother to smell myself, knowing full well he was absolutely right.

"I'm sure we can manage that," she laughed, the sound like bells, then planted her hands sternly on her hips. "But food first. You two look like you haven't had a good meal in weeks."

I wrapped my arms around my midsection, feeling suddenly small under her honeyed stare. I *hadn't* eaten well in weeks, and I could feel the harsh outline of my ribs beneath my sullied and smelly coat. On cue, Vian's stomach growled, drawing my attention. His protruding collar bones only confirmed the woman's assumption.

Lyr below, I'd been such an ass. This poor boy had starved himself on my account, nearly *died* at sea because of me, and I had done nothing to help him in return. I would have to talk to these women about finding him a safe passage to wherever he wanted to go. Even if I belonged on the island of the lost, he didn't. He belonged somewhere he could build a life. Not somewhere people ran from it.

"I'm Gennevieve, by the way," the younger woman peered from beneath her fringe-covered forehead, like a duckling through its fluffy down feathers. My trance broke as she offered me her hand, still covered by a midnight-blue glove. I took it, surprised at how vigorously she shook. "It's so nice to have new faces around."

"It gets boring when it's just us." Nelle winked and laughed again, and the sound eased the edge of my nerves, a wave of comfort washing over me like a spell. Hurriedly, she grabbed some neatly folded clothes and a small bucket of fresh water, handing them to Vian and I. "Get changed, breakfast is being served on the terrace. We can all make proper introductions after you look less skeletal."

Vian and I exchanged a quick look, but neither of us had any control over the situation or our hungry bellies. Without further hesitation, we peeled our sweat-and-salt-slick clothes from our ragged bodies, and after splashing ourselves down with the cold water, hurried into the fresh linens. They were identical to what all the women wore, minus any personal adornments: loose, but generously breathable, and I was grateful for anything that didn't smell like fish and arse. Vian's cream-colored tunic was longer, cut for a man's build, and it dwarfed him, long and lanky as he was. I didn't want to think about the last man that might have worn it, or how it would've hung so nicely on his frame, perhaps with a red belt, maybe even exposing the tip of his black tattoo…

Before I could punish myself by finishing that thought, Vian and I followed the two women out of the hut and into the early morning glow.

"You all eat together?" Vian asked as we followed Nelle through the cozy row of huts, walking the opposite way from which we came the night before.

"Every meal. For those who work at night, it's dinner, and for us early risers, it's breakfast." Gennevieve, almost as short as Reagan, bounced next to him as she tried to keep up with his long strides. "But food shared tastes sweeter."

My heart stopped in my chest as her words rang through me, the memory of a much deeper voice sharing the same sentiment summoning tears to my eyes.

"My Papa used to say the same thing," I blurted out, the anchor in my chest too heavy to bear alone. It was all too much. Gennevieve's resemblance to Ronan and to Reagan, the way Papa's advice rolled so sweetly off her tongue. It was a mirage, a reflection of all the things I held dear dangling in front of me, with the real thing still so far out of reach. My breath came short again, like walls pressing in around me, boxing me into the reality of how *stuck* I was.

Stuck and alone.

Nelle stopped for a moment to look at me over her shoulder, violet eyes cutting through the storm. "Your papa must have been a wise man."

An instant calm washed over me, my fingers unclenching and my lungs greedily sucking in air once more. The pain and panic both subsided, leaving only that delicious warmth that coated my whole body from my crown to my toes.

A small part of me thought to be wary as I eyed Nelle, the sensation unnatural. The dominant part of me didn't care. Whatever this island and its inhabitants were doing to me, I would be blissfully ignorant to it as long as I could dwell in this easy feeling just a little longer.

We continued through the encampment, and I avoided Vian's watchful stare. I wouldn't feel guilty for choosing the easier path, no matter what the wind whispered about me. Instead, I noted all the huts we passed, their cheery decorations and personal touches, trying to figure out if any belonged to the women I'd already met. A silly part wondered how many more I'd meet here and if they'd like me. If this were to be the place I finally succumbed to the festering spot on my shoulder, I hoped it would be friendly.

Then again, that only meant more goodbyes.

The smell hit when we rounded the last row of huts to a large, stone-laid patio. The small rocks varied in color, swirling in a pattern that looked like the lotus flowers we'd seen on the way in. My stomach growled with renewed vengeance as the scent drifted from the massive carved-bamboo table, large enough to sit a dozen people. On instinct, I imagined my whole crew sitting around it: Griffin lounging at the head, Saeth and Tarran bickering on either side of him, Rhett and Ronan laughing as Reagan passed breakfast around...

I bit my lip hard, focusing on the people in front of me, not the daydreamed phantoms of my family. I counted three heads already seated at the feast, each woman almost as appealing to look at as the teeming plates of exotic fruit, crumbling cheese, cured meats, and baked breads in front of them. At the sight of Marina, the nerves in my gut dissipated like ripples in a pool. Her crimson eyes sparkling in the morning light, she weaved strands of vines together. Next to her, two black-haired women I'd never seen before poured over a map, charcoal smeared over the taller one's left cheek. No one touched the food yet, but the three of them laughed and talked among themselves, a chorus of bright voices joining the island's birdsong. Siobhan and their leader Danura were still missing, and while I thought it strange, I'd learned from Papa not to question my blessings.

Three sets of eyes turned to us in perfect unison, conversation dying out as they sensed us.

Marina stood first, smile carving her rouged lips. "I forgot to mention it last night, but you're pretty enough to eat. No wonder Ronan couldn't wait to get home to bed you."

"I—" I stammered, my tongue turning to jelly in my mouth as my cheeks overheated. I was too embarrassed to let the casual mention of my husband register.

"Oh hush, let the poor girl sit down before you bombard her," Nelle ordered with a stern look at Marina. She ushered me to the table, and I said a silent prayer as I ducked around Marina and her blood-red mouth before she could devour me. Nelle sat and tucked me into the seat next to her. I settled in hesitantly, grateful when Marina plopped down directly across from me without a fuss. Gennevieve sat on my other side, sandwiching Vian between herself and Marina.

"These are our cartographers and hunters, Cassryn and Willow." Nelle introduced the two women I didn't know as she graciously piled food onto a plate for me. They were twins in appearance, their dark brown locks and olive complexions too similar to not be kin, their curls tamed back by matching ribbons, one black, the other white. But they were opposite in disposition.

"I'm Willow." The one in white, true to her namesake, was lofty and light as she spoke, gesturing vaguely to herself. "It's nice to meet you. Sorry my sister and I are a mess. We only just got off our shift, and we're eager to eat and get some rest." To her left, Cassryn only stared, face stony, before they dove back into a heated discussion about irrigation systems.

I tried not to let Cassryn's dismissal bother me, instead shoving the first bite of my own plate down my throat, casting all table manners aside. Auntie Vala might have died if she saw my lack of grace and etiquette. Nelle laughed as I stacked crumbly white cheese and a rich, brown bread in a pile nearly as large as my fist and downed it in one bite. Later, I'd apologize for being so rude, but first I had to quiet the grumbling beast in my gut.

The food was incredible, sweet fruit and rich cheese and flaky bread that sent my taste buds into bliss. Much like the rest of the island, everything was more—more flavorful, more satisfying. The more I filled my empty belly, the more my mind relaxed, diving further and further into the warm sunshine and pure rapture. The other women barely touched theirs, pushing it around on their plates, nibbling on the excess.

For a moment, I worried for the empty bellies back home. How meager were their breakfasts in comparison to this extravagance?

Still, I devoured my portion with a side of guilt as Marina leaned her head on her hand to look at me better. "Ronan told us all about you, but his stories didn't do you justice."

I swallowed the handful of deep blue berries I'd been munching on and wiped my mouth. This time, my husband's name did not induce vomiting or sobbing, much to my surprise. "He mentioned you too. Your stories. Thank you for helping him."

"Oh, it was our absolute pleasure." Marina's smile crinkled her eyes. "You'll have to fill us in on what that cad has been up to since."

"I said let the poor girl eat!" Nelle scolded with a laugh.

"Fine, fine." Marina rolled her eyes, waving Nelle off with a mischievous smirk that again reminded me of Griffin when he had a bad idea. If Finna and Griffin ever had a younger sibling, Marina could be her, the perfect balance of beautiful and brazen. With a flourish of her hair, she turned to Vian, who had an embarrassing amount of cheese smeared across his face. "You. Ronan never mentioned you. Start talking."

To his credit, Vian did not balk under her crimson gaze, wiping his face on his tattered sleeve before sitting straighter. "My name is Vian."

Marina leaned back against her chair, red lips only curling further. "Yes, I know, little *Tyawell*. Where are you from, Vian? My gift couldn't quite place you."

I stiffened, knowing what that word meant for him. But the Soul Wind shrugged, taking another bite from a bright red apple before talking again, mouth completely full. "The sky."

While I had grown used to the absurdity of his answer, it drew curious eyes from around the table. Pity squeezed my chest as I regarded my friend, knowing the truth of his origin. A bird with clipped wings, kept in a cage all his life to keep him from flying away.

If I were him, I'd lie, too.

"Huh." Gennevieve broke the awkward silence, cheery demeanor vanquishing the shadows that had crept across the early feast. "Well, that's a first."

"And you are from the salt." Vian's obsidian gaze narrowed, a challenge in his piercing stare with the odd declaration. A slave turned songbird, he would no longer silence himself.

I shot him a warning look. These women had been mostly kind to us, but I wasn't about to test what happened when their hospitality ran out. I had a bruise forming from Siobhan's staff, and

Marina's prowess as an interrogator did nothing to soothe my worry. Still, Vian's black eyes raked over every woman sitting, a secret swimming in that look, and my instincts prickled. What did the wind whisperer know that I didn't?

It must've been substantial, because five sets of gemstone eyes hardened at him. Even Nelle's back straightened in discomfort. The hair on the back of my neck stood straight with the sudden shift in the wind, a storm gathering on the terrace.

What did 'from the salt' even mean to garner such an uncomfortable, borderline-hostile response? As the women glared at Vian, I focused on them; they were like paintings, colorful and vibrant. Perfect pink cheeks, like peaches ready to be savored. Lush, seductive hair, some wild and some coiffed. And the mesmerizing eyes, each mined from the island's earth and polished into fine jewels. All tied up in pretty ribbons like gifts. Just like their exteriors, they had all been amiable, their witty banter almost rehearsed.

Papa used to tell Griffin and me about the frogs in Southern Hud. Vibrant and varied in hue, they were a sight to behold, he said. Only the most renowned magicka and scholars would breed them and use them for their poultices and spellwork.

He also said the most colorful ones were always the most poisonous.

Something deep within me suggested that perhaps these women and their colors were not meant to invite us in; perhaps they were a warning…or worse, a lure.

Instinctively, I stopped eating the food.

Someone cleared their throat behind us, snapping the tension like a dry twig. The woman responsible stood with her hands on her hips, and a chill ran down my spine. She was tall and imposing, black hair flecked with a few silver strands in stark contrast with green eyes almost as light as my own. A deep green sash wrapped around her forehead like a magick practitioner in Hud, every part of her visage just as intimidating. Another potentially poisonous frog, flaunting her marks.

Instead of striking, however, she curled an eyebrow at the coven of women. "Which one of you hags made it awkward? Here, let me in." She pulled up a chair next to Marina, staring me dead-on as she straddled it. She studied me for a moment like a jeweler valuing a sapphire. "So you're Cedric's kid. You've got his chin."

After all the mention of Ronan, I was truly surprised to hear my father's name tumble from her lips. My heart skipped a beat, the whole world tilting in and out of focus as new curiosity simmered in my core. Poison or not, I had fallen into her trap. "You were close to my father too?"

The woman nodded once, a wistful glimmer swimming in the depths of her eyes.

In all my grumbling and sulking, I'd forgotten Papa had spent time here, too. While I had my answers as to how he died, I still knew so little about how he'd lived. He was like mist on the morning sea, always present but so hard to grasp. I had spent so much of my life reaching out, desperate for even a handful of him, but it would slip through my fingers over and over again. But on this island, where time ticked slowly and daggers stayed fresh, I might be able to find something to tie me to the man behind the legend.

The very thought of that investigation sent a wave of fresh vitality through me.

"Cedric Branwen." Gennevieve batted her lashes the same way Marina did, dropping her voice to mimic her perfectly. "Five foot eleven, two hundred and twelve pounds, threat level seven, friendship level one million."

Marina spat out the cherry she was chewing, nearly choking on it. "Did Gennevieve just crack a joke?"

The laughter that erupted among the women was enough to clear the rest of the clouds Vian's comment had called forth. Gennevieve's cheeks flushed bright red, reminding me of Tarran, a laugh sputtering from my middle at the sight. It felt good to indulge in the laughter, to relish in the stomachache and sore ribs. The women were hiding something from me, but as I laughed, the part of me that cared floated away into the *Hiraethean* wind. If it meant finding out more about Papa, I was willing to walk right into their flowered trap and drink straight from the punchbowl.

"He was a good man, your father," the newcomer said as the laughter dissolved, and extended her hand across the table for me to shake. "I'm Laureli."

I froze, my laughter dying too. "That's my middle name."

Her sculpted eyebrow lifted. "So he kept his end of the bargain, then. Your Papa lost a bet. I'll tell you about it after Nelle fattens you up."

I watched as she bit into a pear, stunned silent by the little morsel of my father. Papa had mentioned the name was a friend's, though I'd never met anyone who used it before. "I—"

"Good morning, *Adolli*." Danura's voice cut through my question and silenced any other conversation as she approached the pavilion with brisk but graceful strides. White hair haloed in the sunlight, she was even more breathtaking than the day before. But now she wore the same linen pants as the rest of the group and a pearl blouse. Siobhan flanked her with a scowl on her face.

The calvary had arrived.

The women all stood, heads bowed. "Good morning, *Serenhi*," they greeted as a unified chorus, respect and admiration saturating their tone—all save Siobhan, whose eyes burned holes into my skull. I met her stare with my steel, a flicker of trouble dancing in my veins. If she wanted a rematch, I'd oblige. I wasn't the same half-starved, bound captive as yesterday.

Think tall, you'll be tall.

After another moment in silence, Danura took the seat at the head of the table, and the rest of the women relaxed back into their own chairs and previous conversations. Siobhan broke her stare as she took the seat to Danura's immediate right, but sat straight-backed, punctuating her rank.

Lap dog or guard dog, I didn't care. Siobhan could bark all she wanted. It was clear Danura held the leash.

The conversation picked up as plates were passed and food was dispersed, the newcomers getting their fill.

"You're late today, Sho." Marina flipped her hair over her shoulder, mischief incarnate. "Still recuperating from your tussle on the beach?"

Conversation screeched to a halt as the rest of the women braced for impact. Stormclouds gathered in Siobhan's expression, her muscled frame tensed to pounce. "Watch it, Mari."

Marina's wicked grin spread like wildfire, a retort on the tip of her tongue, but it extinguished at a sharp look from Danura. "Marina, we have guests. Some attempt at civilized conversation would be nice."

Marina folded her hands in her lap, servile once more. "Yes, *Serenhi*."

The rest of the women returned to their meal, quiet and polite beneath the rising sun. The captain in me was momentarily impressed by the breadth of Danura's authority; in a single command, the conflict was squashed, her crew docile. There was obvious respect among her ranks.

But there was something eerie about her presence. On the surface, she glimmered and glowed, the vitality and beauty of a star in her silver visage. But I'd spent enough time on a ship to know the difference between power taken and respect earned. The downcast eyes and slumped shoulders around the table suggested the admiration was accompanied by fear. There were fangs hidden in her moon-white smile. A dormant instinct registered her as what she was—a potential threat veiled in gossamer.

She turned her gaze toward me. "Keira, Vian. I take it you slept comfortably?"

"Very." I lifted my chin but made sure to adorn my best Mathonwy smirk. Danura wasn't the only snake swathed in silk.

She relaxed back in her seat, posture crafted with perfect, poised comfort. "If it suits you, then it might be best for you to sleep at night and find some work with our day shift."

"And miss all the fun at night?" Vian interjected, hands folded in his lap. Lyr below, what I wouldn't give for even a sliver of that boy's foolish confidence. But it was like watching a canary toy with a puma; he was quick, but it was only a manner of time until Danura picked his feathers from her fangs.

As expected, her gaze darkened, clouds marring her starlight features.

"You're not missing much, don't worry," Nelle laughed, but it was as shallow as a wade pool.

"We're fine with that arrangement," I answered before Vian became an after-breakfast snack. Whatever the women were hiding, it was easier to find out by playing the game rather than trying to change the rules. Papa always said it was better to build trust than suspicion. "What about work? I hope to help pull my weight if I'm going to stay here."

"You could come on the hunt with us tomorrow night." Willow perked up, dark hair bouncing with the action. She fiddled with her white ribbon, lost in a thought.

My curiosity stirred, stretching and yawning from its slumber deep inside me. Hunting reminded me of Pysgoddian springs with Papa, tracking the magnificent stags that could keep half a town fed for a week. I was only half the hunter as I was a sailor, but I couldn't help the intrigue that coated my voice. "The hunt?"

Willow nodded, eyes wide as a barn owl's. "We patrol the island every night, mapping any changes in the terrain, searching for anything that might have washed up. We could use someone who knows how to use a dagger, that way Cassryn and I can focus more on charting rather than—"

"She is not coming with us." Siobhan held up a fist, a commander signaling her troops to fall in. Willow closed her mouth, a frown tugging at her features, but did not protest. The other women shifted, the hierarchy clear once more.

The feral beast sleeping beneath the surface of my soul winked an eye open. If I was being honest, I had no desire to hunt.

This wasn't the cool, rocky majesty of the Pysgoddian evergreens, and Siobhan was graciously not my father. Hunting meant nothing without Papa. I hadn't been since he passed, and I hadn't missed it, either. What I missed was him, and I doubted crawling through the *Hiraethean* jungle trying not to get eaten by some monster would not fill the absence in my heart.

But for nothing other than the opportunity to ruffle Siobhan's feathers, I pressed on. "Why not?"

Cassryn rolled her eyes, the stone wolf coming to the lioness's side. "You know nothing of the island. You'd slow us down."

Now the *ceffyl* in my veins brayed, my curiosity and stubbornness fully awakened. I crossed my arms, hoping to accentuate what little mass I had left the way Griffin did. "Then maybe you shouldn't have blindfolded me on the way in."

Siobhan didn't need her bloodhound to bark for her this time. Her smirk was almost as sharp as her claws when she dragged her eyes over me once. "Right, we should've left you out there to fend for yourself."

"Siobhan." Danura drew her name out in a warning, yanking the leash again. Siobhan went silent, fist clenched around the silver fork in front of her plate. Danura turned to me, her smile less practiced this time as she picked a pomegranate from the table. "Please excuse her tone, but she does have a point. I'm sure you'd be fine to defend yourself, but the terrain does get dicey. The girls will find something else for you. I care more about your comfort, *Ariannad.*"

Ice ran down my spine. Any lingering thoughts of diplomacy rushed from my mind as the all-too-familiar name formed a pit in my middle.

Ariannad. The voices echoed from the beyond, a confirmation and a question.

My tone was only a hair short of hostile as I grabbed the table in front of me with white knuckles. "That name. Where did you hear it?"

Danura feigned innocence, porcelain face tilted to the side in a way that only stoked the fire in my veins. "Forgive me. It was a term of endearment your father used during his time here. I only thought—"

"That's a lie," I snarled. The mention of my father nearly sent me hurtling over the table to smack the lie straight from her mouth. "My father never called me that."

Danura's lips flattened into a thin line, her voice just as tight. "I shall refrain from using it then, if it makes you uncomfortable." It wasn't an answer, but the storm in my chest quieted. A momentary glimmer of kindness flashed across her unblemished face. "You've sacrificed much recently. I won't take your name, too."

A part of me wanted to demand answers, by force if needed, but I felt the stares of everyone at the table. I would not have made it to Danura even if I wanted to without her lemmings jumping in my path, and I had no war with the women who'd shown me kindness— Siobhan and Cassryn aside.

Whenever we went hunting in Pysgodd, Papa used to say patience was a sharper tool than any arrow ever made. Our accuracy and strength meant nothing if we weren't willing to wait for the right time to shoot. And though every instinct begged to know what that name meant, I did not have a clear shot. I would not jeopardize Vian's safety for my vanity. I didn't care what these women called me if it meant he had a way back to civilization when the time came.

Silence lingered like mist as Danura and I stared at each other, hunter and stag locked in the chase. Which of us was which, I couldn't decide.

It was Nelle who broke the quiet, her voice easing the edges of my nerves as it had this morning. "If you two are finished eating, I'll take you on a proper tour."

Like a wave erasing lines in the sand, my boiling rage dissipated into steam. In its absence, that same warmth from before wrapped me in a blanket of bliss.

This time, I knew it was unnatural. I was not as clever as my husband, but I'd been able to put two and two together before. Some of these women had gifts of their own, each individual to who they were. Marina's ability to interrogate a person on sight was clear after she made me vomit the truth on the beach yesterday...and this was Nelle's. She could take my rage and trade it for rapture with only a smile and a kind word.

It was unnatural, but I couldn't find it in me to care. I wanted to swim in the bliss, even if it was ignorant. A part of me was even jealous. I missed my own gifts, missed listening to the water instead of the darkness, missed the buzzing beneath my skin and the storms coursing through my veins.

I would find my answers, but it didn't seem so important now. All I wanted was to drift away in the easy feeling. Later, I'd figure out what arrows I still had in my quiver.

"What a splendid idea, Nelle." Danura nodded, lifting a hand to dismiss us. "You three may go."

Nelle stood dutifully, casting me a sorrowful glance before forcing her own smile and gesturing for Vian and me to follow. Warmth still lingering in my limbs, I obeyed, content to put the ugly anger and Danura's piercing gaze behind me.

Vian stared at me incredulously. It was an accusation, and I could read it plain as day on his face. I was supposed to be a captain, a leader. The Keira he met in the dungeons would never let someone else insult her, lie to her face, and then dismiss her.

I sank deeper into the buzzing coziness and avoided his eyes. The Keira he knew died in the shipwreck. This Keira burned for answers but no longer had the energy to fight for them. This Keira drank from the cup of simple pleasures, even if it was poisonous.

It wasn't until I was out of Danura's eyeline that Nelle's magic wore off and the ice crept up my spine once more. The dark spot throbbed with a bone-deep ache. I clenched my shoulder as pain shot through me, voices screaming in a furious chorus.

We're all the same, Ariannad.

20

Farmers and Friends

KEIRA

Nelle's tour flew by in a blur of colors, the whispering voices of both my subconscious and the island itself distracting me from her soothing presence. While this morning it had been paradise, *Hiraeth* was now a fever dream, every flower too bright, every noise too loud. A headache formed between my eyes, and I pinched the bridge of my nose to no avail. My shoulder throbbed relentlessly, and I tried not to think about what it meant. About how little time I had left.

Just as I tried not to think about what *Ariannad* meant. I'd never heard the name in any stories. Only those who knew of my connection to Lyr or the Dark God had ever used it, which meant Danura might be far more dangerous than she let on.

Ignoring that notion, I poured every ounce of my energy into listening to Nelle narrate, mostly to tune out the murmurings but also to get a better grip on how the Annwyn operated. Papa used to say the best way to chart a course was to first learn how to read the map. Until I decided if Danura was a friend or foe, the best I could do was at least understand how she ran her ship.

The housing compound was only a small part of the territory. Beyond the river and huts were finely cultivated fields, the rich soil and tepid air the perfect conditions for crops. They weren't the same dry, practical harvest found in Bachtref, but rows and rows of exotic fruit trees and bamboo forests stretching out deep into the island. There were cleared out sections for a small herd of sheep and goats to feed, and two larger huts that marked the edge of the territory before the wild of *Hiraeth* resumed. One served as a place to dry out leaves and branches for building supplies, the other a small slaughterhouse for whatever game the hunting party brought home.

Nelle casually informed us on how the women worked, and I absorbed every detail I could. There were only seven of them, but they split evenly into three teams, a few of them taking on extra leadership roles. Laureli oversaw the farming team, deciding which crops were best for food and medicinal purposes. To my surprise, Marina worked with her year-round, except for when the harvest came and it was all hands on deck. I'd never farmed a day in my life, but I imagined that dynamic duo made it far from boring.

Nelle worked as the head healer, but more proudly boasted that she and Gennevieve were in charge of homemaking, which involved everything from washing and sewing linens to cleaning and cooking. It was the job that kept all the daily activities running, the violet dove and little duck working around the clock to keep things in order. Nelle's soft spot for the girl had me missing my younger cousins.

Vian perked up as Nelle detailed the activities. "I could help with that. I've never had a home." He shrugged, but there was a hard edge in his words. "Might be fun to learn how to make one."

Nelle's whole frame melted into her smile. "We don't expect you to jump right in, but eventually, if a team calls to you, you are more than welcome to join. If you do, I'd be happy to make you both a token."

"Like the little accessories you all wear?" Vian gestured to the purple ribbon tying Nelle's dark waves out of her face.

"Aye. They are all personal, meant to represent a piece of the homes we came from." She toyed with hers absentmindedly before walking forward.

I considered asking for a blue sash to mimic my captain's coat before remembering I no longer deserved it. Captain Keira was dead and gone. I was nothing and no one now, and my clothes should reflect that.

We came to a large hut past the farmland, this one hidden among the overgrown trees and vines. "This is the command tower. Siobhan and Cassryn use it as a base, and it's where we have team meetings." Nelle bristled slightly, avoiding the obvious awkwardness between Siobhan and me before moving us forward without any pomp and circumstance. "Willow explained how that all works, and I doubt you'll join them after this morning."

Despite my spat with Siobhan, a forgotten hunger rumbled in my core. It reminded me of the way Papa used to track a course, not just following the stars, but listening to the way the wind and the current whispered to each other before he set a destination. It was a different beast entirely, this sea of trees and vines. A younger me would've jumped at the opportunity to explore her depths.

But I would not give Siobhan the satisfaction by admitting it. Nor would I follow her into some dark wilderness and make it easier for her to attack me.

As our tour concluded, Vian decided to follow Nelle to the homemakers and volunteer his services. Nelle offered to take me back to our hut first, but I declined. I did not want to be alone with my thoughts, not when they tended to take on voices of their own. The memory of the whispers echoed through my mind, sending a shiver down my spine.

No, I was not built to sit idle. Nor was I built for sewing and cooking, much to Auntie Vala's chagrin. But I needed to do *something*. I was not a captain anymore, but I would not spend however long I had left as a waste of air. So, if homemaking and hunting were both out of the question, perhaps it was time to try my hand at growing something instead of destroying it.

By the time I made it back to the farm fields, Marina and Laureli were already tending crops. In unison, they stopped to stare, wearing twin smirks.

"Mind if I join you?" I rolled back my sleeves as I approached, surveying the tools. They tilled the soil for something, this particular patch of land open and ready for use. The only farm I'd ever seen was on Bachtref, and there I more often stayed in the markets and taverns. This would be new, and a small part of me welcomed the novelty.

Laureli's slate eyes grazed over me. "We don't mind. I'm just surprised you joined us."

"The way Ronan painted you, you struck me as a hunter." Marina wiped the slight sheen from her brow and draped herself across the hand plow. "I expected you to put up more of a fight this morning. I didn't think the NightMare of the Four Seas would ever *farm.*"

A deep part of me sang at the old nickname, pride and sorrow swirling in my chest like a hurricane. Ronan had talked about me here, even when he was hurt and betrayed and angry. I wondered how many stories he'd told these women.

It made me miss him with such ferocity, I couldn't breathe for a moment. How many of his stories would I miss now? How many would I be in? How long until he found someone new to tell stories to? Or worse—how long until I was only a side character in his?

I dug my nails into my palm to stop myself from crying. I would not waste my tears here. I had chosen this path, for my sake and for his. I could not go back, only forward, until the Dark God finally ended my misery. Until then, I would do something useful, even if it meant burying the NightMare of the Four Seas and all her conquests beneath the fertile *Hiraethean* soil and letting someone new grow in her stead.

"I *was* a fighter." I surprised myself with my candor, but even if these women still had secrets, I had nothing left to gain by keeping mine. "But I've taken enough life. I'm going to try helping it grow instead for a bit."

Laureli's gaze swam with something akin to respect, solidifying my choice in a way I didn't know I needed. But it was Marina who spoke, mouth quirked to the side as she fiddled with a lock of her hair. "Based on my observations, your swordsmanship and tracking skills are definitely more attuned to the task of hunting. You're not going to be a very good farmer."

The laugh that bubbled from the depths of my sorrow was genuine. Had I had any pride left, I might have been offended, but I knew she was right. I was not built for dry land, and I wasn't raised to till and seed and plow. I was raised to strike and sail, to chart and rig and parry. I was a sailor and a fighter. But even if I was a fish out of water, I was going to find a way to keep swimming.

"So that's your gift, Marina?" I stuck a hand on my hip, my turn to observe and evaluate. "How does it work? Do you know everything about me at just a glance or is it subtler than that?"

Marina's eyes went wide, and she looked at the ground, suddenly very focused on the small patches of dirt that needed seeds. Laureli grinned like a Tannian hyena, handing me a small shovel as a peace offering. "I see you're getting used to our different brands of odd."

I took the small tool graciously. "Only if you're willing to accept the fact that I'm fairly useless."

"You're not useless, just lost." Laureli bent down to start digging another tiny hole, gesturing for me to join her. I crouched beside her, using the shovel to carve a twin hole in the mound of dirt next to her, watching her work. She continued as we went about our duty, "We all are a little lost here. Before, many of us had families and lives of our own. We have all been refugees at some point. You're not alone."

I didn't—couldn't—look up from my task without collapsing completely. "Does it get easier?"

"Yes. Over time. It helps to talk about it," Marina answered, bending next to me and offering a small smile before joining the ritual of digging.

It felt good to do something with my hands, even if the motion was foreign. Dig, scoop, repeat. Don't think about Ronan. Don't think about dying. Dig, scoop, repeat. The shovel was similar in weight to a dagger, with less focus on the wrist and more in the elbow as I pried the dirt from its lodging.

It took me a few moments to realize Marina was staring, expecting an answer. I shrugged, a new force behind my carving. "I've never been a talker."

Laureli stopped my shovel with hers, an eyebrow raised. "I thought you were trying something new."

Words balled and caught in my throat, a tangled web I didn't know how to unravel. "I don't know where to start."

"Why don't I start, then?" Marina sighed, sitting back and leaning into her hands. Laureli dropped her shovel and sat as well, straight-backed, motioning me to join her. I lowered myself, my legs already sore from crouching. Marina folded her hands in her lap, a storyteller waiting for her audiences' undivided attention. "I had a husband. We were happy. We were performers traveling with a troupe from Ir'de, and we loved it. I made us extra money by making matches for young women across the Deyrnas. It was paradise. I never wanted to leave."

She paused, her words hanging in the air like fruit on a vine, ready to be plucked. But I didn't know how to do this. I had always shown my feelings, expressing them in deeds instead of words. Even with Ronan, I still got tripped up when it came to what I wanted to say. Papa always said actions speak louder than words, so I let my actions be my battle cries. Ronan could talk for hours, and I was always happy to listen, but this unfiltered sharing with near-strangers was as foreign to me as *Hiraeth* itself.

"What happened?" I asked, discomfort rising as the silence thickened.

Marina's expression turned bitter. "He left."

"Oh." Shame cascaded down my spine. This was why I didn't talk. I shifted uncomfortably, avoiding her crimson stare.

"Left me for some Bachtreffian farmer girl. And it hurt like dying," she continued, voice free of any burden. A delicate hand rested on my knee, and when I finally found the courage to look back up at her, she was smiling. "But here is the happy part of the story. Now I have sisters, all with stories of their own. All with sacrifices they carry with them. Nelle had a husband and son, Gennevieve had six brothers and two sisters, Siobhan had a whole tribe back in Tan…but now, we have each other. And somehow, that's enough."

"I miss them," I said before I could think, my whole chest seizing under the weight of the words. Missing wasn't a strong enough word, the feeling more akin to losing a limb or a part of my soul. I wasn't complete anymore. Tears came streaking down my face, words tumbling out of me like they did on the beach. "My crew, my family…Ronan. I can't breathe without them."

"That will never stop." Marina offered a lopsided grin. "But it does get...less."

"Is that your gift talking?" I asked, wiping my face with the back on my hand.

She shook her head. "No, that's coming from a new friend."

The word *friend* reverberated through me like a song, chasing away the storm in my chest like the morning sunlight. Maybe, with a few friends, this wouldn't be so hard.

"You know what you need?" Marina sighed, standing up and brushing the dirt from her generous backside. "A ladies' night."

21

Campfires and Confessions

KEIRA

Nothing filled me with more dread than the idea of a ladies' night. Frankly, I'd rather Siobhan drag me through the jungle and feed me to whatever lions and bears and snakes waited in the underbrush.

My aversion lived in two chambers of my heart: one owned by the awkward, clumsy little girl who never learned to properly brush her hair and preferred cards with her sailor uncles over gossiping with her cousins, the other owned by the woman who would give anything for one more night with Finna and Saeth. The woman who didn't know if she could bear a night of stories and secrets without them.

The thought tangled in my stomach, swishing around with the fresh fish I'd eaten for lunch.

"Come on, it's not so bad," Vian soothed as we walked through the complex after finally scrubbing away our grime in a warm bath. His freshly-cleaned hair was tied back in a black ribbon—presumably from his afternoon with Gennevieve—that only accented his bright smile. "You look like you're going to hurl."

I rolled my eyes at the wind sprite of a boy. If only I could breeze through problems with the same charming ease as he did, perhaps I wouldn't feel the need to empty my guts onto the *Hiraethean* soil. Perhaps I wouldn't be in this mess in the first place.

I halted, guilt rooting my feet like the ground was made of quicksand. "I just...it feels wrong? To bond with them and spend time with them and maybe laugh and have fun when...when Ronan..." The rest of the sentence got stuck in my throat with all the other goodbyes I'd left unsaid.

Vian turned, tar-black eyes sparkling with fondness. "You're allowed to have a night for yourself." He inhaled slowly, a steadying breath deep enough to fill my lungs, too. "Breathe, *Ariannad.* You deserve that much."

In his voice, the name was a prayer that filled me with ease. True to his name, the Soul Wind blew through me, clearing out the dust and doubt as he bounced toward the clearing, a skip in his step. The warmth that bubbled up from my pit chased away the lingering, smoky guilt that still clouded my heart. The tether that tied us together tugged at my gut again, coaxing me to follow.

Perhaps he was right. If I could make space for the dark fairy in my life, I could clear some room for a few new female friends, too. Even if it meant enduring my hair brushed and braided.

My own steps felt lighter as I followed the little windsinger, his black ponytail bouncing behind him. By the time I caught up with him—my sides burning from the run and the laughter that stole the breath from my chest—he'd already made it to the clearing.

If I hadn't already been panting, the scene in front of me might have knocked the wind out of me.

It was straight from one of Ronan's fairytales. The women were already there, lounging on grass-woven beds and pillows made of some of the finest silk I'd ever seen. Nelle was, in fact, braiding Marina's long auburn hair, weaving a crimson ribbon through it to match her sash, both of them giggling. Willow sported a little wooden flute, playing a cheery tune that worked in perfect harmony with the soprano laughter. Gennevieve relaxed onto Laureli's lap as the older woman stroked her hair, clapping and humming along to the beat.

Cassryn, to my surprise, stoked an impressive bonfire, her face warmer as the flames licked the wood playfully. If even the stone wolf could melt and enjoy a ladies' night, so could I. Something sweet scented the air, my mouth watering at the burnt-sugar smell that fought against the florals of *Hiraeth*. Siobhan was absent, already off on her rounds, a blessing from whatever trickster god created this place.

This was not how I'd imagined the night. This was a gathering of nymphs and goddesses, ethereal in their grace and beauty and light.

Marina caught me before I could run away and never look back, her piercing ruby stare as hot as the bonfire's flames. She waved Nelle off, practically dancing across the clearing to Vian and me, hands planted on her hips. "What took you two so long?"

"Still getting acquainted with the island." I hoped the excuse didn't sound as pathetic out loud as it did in my head.

Gennevieve jolted up from Laureli's embrace and patted the ground next to her, blonde ringlets bouncing. "Come here, we have snacks!"

My heart swelled despite itself, the little duckling reminding me of home, of nights spent on the *Ceffyl* filled with the same laughter and music. Before I could think to feel guilt or regret, I crossed to her, plopping myself down on the cool dirt between her and Marina.

Gennevieve squealed with excitement, reaching for a silver plate of food and dragging it closer. She picked morsels off the plate—a small, thin crust of pastry that looked like it was coated in sugar, a thin piece of dark chocolate, and a charred white puff that looked like a burnt cloud—and handed them to me, the sticky substances coating my fingers.

"What is this?" I eyed her skeptically, pressing an indent into the soft white fluff. The same sugar and spice scent hit my nose, drool forming at the corner of my mouth.

"Delicious." Marina grinned, mischief sparkling in her eyes as she shoved the treat into my open mouth. "Don't ask, just eat."

The second the taste hit my tongue, I knew I had to be dreaming. The moan that escaped my throat should've embarrassed me, but I didn't care.

Marina wiped the chocolate from the corner of my mouth with her thumb before sucking the remnants of the confection off her finger. "I take it you like it, with that reaction. Ronan had a good reason to hurry home."

The blush that flooded my cheeks had to be redder than the ruby sash at her waist. Lyr below, how Ronan had survived this island, this *woman*, was beyond me.

Gennevieve smiled, passing more of the treats out, Vian eagerly sinking his teeth into one. Gennevieve watched him chew, the chocolate smudging on his lips. "Do you like them? I made it myself."

"You're magic," he praised her with his mouth full, nodding so quickly I thought he'd shake his hair off.

"Brigid's bust, do you taste as sweet as you look?" Marina teased with a flick to the boy's cheek before reaching into the bust of her tunic and producing a small silver flask. "If you two like that, you're going to love this."

Despite my better judgement, I took a deep swig when she handed it to me. There was no way I was going to survive this night without a little liquid courage. After all, Papa used to say every problem was better solved with a full belly and a mug of ale.

It was a struggle not to cough as the burning liquid seared my throat and lit a fire in my middle, stronger and hotter than the burning pyre. "That's strong."

"It does the trick," Willow giggled, stopping her playing as I handed her the flask, taking a swig of it herself and passing it to her sister. Cassryn's dreg was longer, rivaling one of Griffin's standard 'sips'.

"Enough corrupting the poor girl," Nelle admonished, but I didn't miss the grin that fought the corner of her lips, or the fact that she too took a deep swig, unflinching as the dragon's-breath liquor hit her lips.

"Here's a question for everyone." Marina ignored Nelle as she leaned back onto her pillow, accentuating her hourglass shape. "Which is the most satisfying; chocolate, booze, or sex?"

Nelle snorted, the liquor spewing from her nose, and Gennevieve blushed. I blinked, stunned silent, unsure if I wanted to laugh or plug Vian's ears before the nymph could continue.

"Chocolate." Willow didn't flinch, driving forward like an arrow. "No questions asked."

Gennevieve laughed, cheeks still red, as she passed her friend another bar of the dark sweet. "I like that answer."

Cassryn intercepted before her sister could take it, breaking off the tip of the decadence and popping it into her own mouth. "I don't know. Depends on who we're screwing, and if it's cheap liquor or the good stuff. Too many variables."

Willow swatted her, reminding me of Finna and Saeth for a moment. Sisters, one made of steel, the other silk, both strong in their own way. Finna might have asked a similar question one night, back when our greatest worries were which beverages and boys we fancied trying. I'd been barely fifteen, still basking in my 'first-kiss' glow, giggling in the haven of Branwen Townhouse....

"Ronan Mathonwy?" Saeth whispered in our fort of blankets, Ronan's very name making me blush harder than the flask of gin we'd swiped from Uncle Weylin. "A decent choice. Nice eyes, handsome. His cousin Rhett is prettier if you ask me. I like the rugged look." She flexed, imitating the budding muscles Rhett had displayed at River Mathonwy's birthday celebration. The three of us stifled our laughter before Vala heard us. If she burst through the door to Finna's room, we'd be dead.

Finna waved off Saeth's commentary, the queen taking her throne again. "Ronan looks like the type of man to kiss you with his whole soul." She waggled her sculpted brows at me, a twinkle in the jade of her eye. Her voice dipped low, drawing us closer in. "But if we are talking about someone with skills...have you seen how tall Ellian Llewellyn got this summer?"

The warm memory spread through my middle like ripples in a pond. Maybe Marina was right. Maybe I needed this reminder as much as I did this night.

Pulling me back from the edge of my mind, Marina wiggled a finger in my direction, still on the topic of simple pleasures. "Fine, let's say the booze was from the best, most expensive Ir'desian refinery…and the subject was someone of my stature." She caressed a hand down the length of her side, the action so potent, Vian turned away, face flaming. Marina smirked, delighted in her game. "What would you choose, Keira?"

I was glad I had nothing in my mouth, because I would've choked. Laureli, blunt as a battle axe, saved me before Marina could devour me whole. "Marina, are you going to tell a story tonight? Or just sit there trying to flirt with a married woman?"

"Ouch, someone's claws are out tonight!" Marina feigned hurt, resting her hand on her chest with a dramatic flick of the wrist. Then she stood, twirling once, the fire the only limelight she needed to begin her performance. "Fine, if my audience demands it. What story shall we have tonight?"

Willow tossed her flute, lounging against a deep purple pillow, the opening act ready to let the main stage debut. "I'm always partial to Gwynn," she offered, and it was all Marina needed to set the scene.

"Gwynn the hunter was known for his conquests around the world." Her voice dropped low as the storyteller took up her role, quiet settling over the audience. I watched, mesmerized, as she put even Ronan to shame with her ability to paint a picture with words. "He was so well known that soon, the King himself recognized his talent, and offered his daughter, Sinead, in marriage. Sinead and Gwynn met and fell deeply, madly in love, and ruled over the land with justice, as they were equals in every way."

My stomach clenched, the liquor sloshing around haplessly. I tried desperately not to think of my own blue-eyed equal.

Ronan looks like the type of man to kiss you with his whole soul.

"I love the romance." Gennevieve swooned, earning a laugh from the others. I couldn't bring myself to join in, not when only half of my soul rested in my body and the other half belonged to Ronan, wherever he was now. Did he mourn the life we could've had as I did? Did the very mention of my name make him physically ill?

"However, the Dark God soon heard of Gwynn's talents. In a jealous rage, he kidnapped Gwynn's bride and stole her away to the Otherworld," Marina said gravely, molding her fingers into claws as she talked of the Dark God.

A deep ache throbbed through my shoulder, almost as painful as the verbal punch to my gut. I blinked back the tears forming in my eyes—tears from the part of me that was my husband's wife, the part that the Dark God robbed me of.

Marina continued without notice, pitch rising with the climax. "Gwynn was lost without Sinead. He could not eat or sleep, could not focus on the hunt. So one day, weak and tired and lost, he wandered all the way to the Dark God's gate, begging for him to take him, too. The Dark God, greedy as ever, gave Gwynn a test: if he could defeat his hounds in a hunt, he would return Sinead to him, and they both could live among the mortals. But if he failed, Sinead's soul would be his forever, and Gwynn would wander the mortal realm for eternity."

"Telling stories again?" A voice startled us from beyond the treeline, ethereal and lofty as windchimes. Danura glided into the clearing like a ship across the water, white eyebrows raised.

"Good evening, *Serenhi.*" The women shifted uncomfortably as they bowed, some smoothing their hair out, Cassryn hiding the bronze flask underneath her tunic. I sat straighter, the hair on the back of my neck prickling, the Silver Sword's cutting glance finding its mark between my ribs.

"Go on, Marina." Danura broke into a smile, and they exhaled a collective breath. "Don't mind me."

Marina blinked, but dove into the tale once more, detailing the trials of Gwynn. In a few words, the women were bewitched once more, Gwynn's tribulations reeling them like fish on a hook. But I did not relax, the sip of whiskey sloshing in my gut as Danura swept across the clearing and lowered herself onto the pillow next to me. I stiffened, losing focus in Marina's intricate performance, bracing for Danura's cool indifference. I was surprised when she relaxed into a casual lean and popped a white confection in her mouth.

"Your father used to love this one," she mumbled as she chewed, nudging my side gently.

I stilled, the contact sending a shiver up my spine. But still, like a fish in a lonely pond, I bit the bait, the mention of my father stirring the insatiable curiosity in my chest. "He did?"

She did not look away from Marina's dance, but smiled, her freckled cheeks rosy in the firelight. "Mhmm. It was his favorite of Marina's love stories. He used to say love was more powerful than fate herself."

Nostalgia spread through my veins, warmer than the pyre in front of us. Papa's stories were never as rosy as Marina's, but I could always feel the love, the longing in every one. I imagined him sitting here, next to Danura, perhaps, his own cheeks warm from drinking and laughing, his eyes starry as Marina danced like the flames of the bonfire.

I hugged my knees to my chest, wishing I was holding him instead. "That sounds like him."

"You remind me of him. Brave, strong…" Danura hummed, staring through me. "He raised you well."

I swallowed the lump forming in my throat. I didn't feel brave or strong. I felt small. I'd run away from my family, from Ronan, to hide on the island of the lost and broken. But her approval woke a dormant desire deep in my core, the want of the wild little girl who used to follow her father around, mimicking the courage of his stride. The girl I was before I let the weight of my mark turned me into a coward.

"Tell me more about him," that little girl begged, desperate for any piece Danura might give me. "About his time here."

She watched me for a moment as she weighed her options—a dragon queen sitting on top of her horde, deciding how much of her treasure she was willing to give. After a moment that lasted a month, she exhaled, extending her peace offering. "He was young when he washed up. We all were, I suppose," she laughed to herself, her gaze swimming with the memories of a far-off time. "He'd been trying to secure deals for your family and got caught in a storm. We were good friends. He knew how to make the girls laugh, taught them everything he knew about the sea…"

A crack ran through my armor as she drifted off, caught up in the tide of whatever memory swam to the surface. I could picture it, too. Could picture Papa young and clean-shaven, the twinkle in his hazel eyes as he taught a starry-eyed little girl how to tie knots. Could picture him in the loose linen clothes, laughing with Danura and Laureli and whoever else was here. Marina and the other girls all seemed far too young, but Ronan had warned me about the island's time-altering magic. How many of these women had known my father as a young man? How many of them had he charmed with his easy, crinkly-eyed smile?

I was slammed with a wave of missing him, so powerful that had I not been sitting, I might've toppled over. I cleared the lump in my throat before speaking. "Thank you for keeping him safe. And for...for doing the same for us."

"No need to thank me, Keira." Danura's smile was soft, like clouds cast in starlight as she tucked a stray strand of hair behind my ear. "It's my pleasure."

The gesture wasn't meant to be alarming—in fact, it was dipped and soaked in affection—but it did not soothe me. It made the pit of my stomach tighten, a strange uncertainty mixing with the whiskey.

"Would you two like to talk through the whole story?" Marina whined, snapping me back to her tale. She bowed at the waist to Danura, a smirk flirting at the corner of her mouth. "Or can I continue?"

"I'm off anyway." Danura blinked and stood, brushing her dress off as she employed her favorite mask once more. "Enjoy your night, ladies."

She didn't look back at me as she fled, gossamer skirt trailing behind her. A shiver ran through me in her absence, as if she were nothing more than a phantom that passed by, a fragment of a fairytale too intangible to exist in this world for more than a few moments at a time.

"Anyway, so Gwynn fought back the hounds…" With an eye roll, Marina launched back into her tale, but I didn't hear a word as I stared after Danura, wondering what other secrets she hid behind the porcelain mask.

Marina's story intensified, finally spinning toward the bittersweet finale. But still, I barely registered any of it, only catching vague, melancholy lines about Sinead sacrificing herself to Arawn's dogs to save Gwynn, haunted instead by the ghost of Danura's presence.

We listened to two more stories I could barely focus on. The rest of the women seemed to enjoy them, their laughter crackling with the fire as the moon hoisted itself higher in the sky. It was Vian's voice that finally broke my trance as he hiccupped, "I'm sleepy."

I blinked, struggling to refocus as I took him in. He squinted at me in the flickering firelight, cheeks redder than Tarran's hair as he swayed. A slap-happy grin was smacked across his face and the empty flask somehow sat at his feet.

"No, you're drunk," I chuckled, the boy's lopsided smile enough to clear out the remnants of my discomfort. I offered him a hand and he took it, another hiccup shaking his frame. I hoisted his clumsy weight off the ground in a single tug. "Let's go, you cad."

Vian's arm securely looped around my shoulders, I turned to the rest of the audience, something bright spreading through my chest. The night had not chased away my demons, but it had let me escape them for a few moments. Even though they still waited in the shadows for me, I couldn't help but feel grateful toward the women who had provided momentary light. "Thank you, ladies."

The women mumbled warm goodbyes or similar groans of sleepiness, but one pair of eyes saw through my mask like it was made of the same thin material as Danura's dress.

"But it wasn't enough," Laureli murmured, her words somehow finding my ears alone. She stood, understanding pulling her mouth into a frown as she rubbed my arm gently.

It wasn't enough. A thousand "ladies' nights" would never be enough. Danura's story about Papa had only been the ledge of the deep, soul-crushing chasm of loneliness in my chest.

I was like Gwynn. Without my husband at my side, I'd always be lost, cursed to wander the stars alone, devoid of purpose. Without him, I was a compass spinning around without direction, no magnet to point me north.

"I just wish I knew that Ronan was alright," I admitted, the words shallow in comparison to the true depth of the ache in my core.

"You're lucky I owe your Papa a favor," Laureli whispered, the blue of her eye twinkling. "My hut, two nights from now, on the full moon. Make sure no one sees you. Come alone. I can help you see him."

22

Dragons and Distractions

RONAN

In a rare occurrence, Griffin was right. The trip to the spring did wonders for my body. After my soak, every muscle felt like it was dipped in bronze, fortified and made new.

Lyr, to his credit, was quiet, allowing me to wallow in peace. The rest of the crew were not so generous. The second I got back to Mathonwy Manor, they were on me, dragging me into Reina's kitchen and forcing me to sit through their sham of a war council meeting. I feigned interest, but my thoughts were unfocused. What did I care if the whole world went to shit? The person who might've cared had conveniently fucked off.

Ellian was persistent, something I hated to admit I admired. And even if we were far from friends, it was good to feel needed. Though I knew deep down I'd be as useless at war strategy as I was at sailing. I was not a fighter, or a captain, or a leader. I was an actor, playing whatever role kept me in the best light.

"I know what I heard, Griffin." His tone was sure, a true leader despite his apparent exhaustion. Though I'd never tell him, he was good at being a councilman, despite the hurdles Connor threw his way. He rubbed a tired hand over his face before repeating himself for a third time, irritation clear in the set of his scowl. "Orwellin scholars have been working on the poultice for ages. It kills crops. The first attack already happened in Bachtref. Ir'de and Pysgodd are next unless we warn them. They plan on starving people, and then when they become desperate and rise up, they're going to purge them."

My stomach clenched, empty though it was. The Deyrnas was flawed, and I didn't want to care for it. But starving masses and government-planned slaughter was enough to stir the dragon in my chest once more.

If only I knew what to do, I might be able to help. But I was useless. Who was I to stand against the entire High Council? What could I do to stop plague and war from marching across each island and dragging us all to the Otherworld?

I took another swig of my drink.

"Lyr's balls, it's just so *dark*." Griffin echoed my thoughts, hanging his head in his hands. Rhett rubbed his back gently, but his face was just as drawn. "Why do it? What is there to gain from killing everyone? There is no Council if there is no Deyrnas."

Ellian scoffed, an edge to his voice. "I don't know, but if we are going to stop this, we have to figure it out."

The table sat in silence, the weight of the responsibility hanging like an anvil ready to crush us beneath. Even Reagan was stony, chestnut eyes turned to hard mountain passes. I hated seeing her dragged into this; she deserved so much better. But I had apparently forfeited any say in her upbringing when I hid from her for two weeks, so I kept my mouth shut.

So did everyone else. We were all lost for words, for actions, for solutions. We were not the people who would solve this conflict. We were not Captains. We were the forgotten few, those not capable enough to do anything, but stupid enough to still care.

If Keira were with us, she'd have a plan. Or she would say exactly the right thing at the right time, inspiring one of us to find the missing piece.

The dragon stirred in my chest, enraged at her for leaving us behind, but also at myself for not being better. I hadn't deserved her in the first place. What would she think of me now, hiding and whining, letting her people starve and die when she trusted me to do the job? Keira would've fed the entire Deyrnas with her own supper first if it meant sticking it to Connor. And she would be ashamed of us now, sitting comfortably in Reina's kitchen, picking at our dinner like the rest of the world wasn't hungry.

"We need to keep people fed," I blurted out, not realizing I'd said it out loud until Ellian rolled his eyes at me.

"Yes, I know. We are working on it."

The beast in my chest growled at the impertinence in his tone, as if I had any pride left to protect. But the spark felt good. Like Keira was somehow watching me, whispering in my ear to 'figure it out, Mr. Mathonwy.'

"If you'll let me explain before biting my head off, *Councilman*...that's the first branch of this." I sat forward, trying to draw a map in my mind. "Connor is smart. People will not fight on an empty stomach. Feed them, and Connor will have to work harder to put us down."

Rhett looked at me, the heaviness falling from his broad shoulders as he straightened his back. "Good thing we know a couple of talented smugglers."

Griffin grinned at him, mischief brimming in his gaze. "We have two ships, and I could send some letters to old friends in Ir'de. If we can get half a dozen ships sailing...Ir'de has enough money and resources that even with the council meddling, they should be alright for a while if they are willing to share. Pysgodd, too. If we organized, it'd be easier."

Nods and grunts from around the table signaled agreement, life stirring itself back into the crew. But my brow still furrowed. It was easier said than done. How did Keira do it? How did she always manage to find the answer, even when fate and foe were both against her?

"Even if we do find a solid food source and start smuggling items, we won't stand a chance if Connor brings the full weight of the Deyrnasian guard on us." The words tasted like ash on my tongue, fire extinguished by reality once more. "If he catches wind of this, we'll be snubbed before we can even feed a single mouth."

"So let's not get caught." Tarran squared his shoulders, his boyish face lined with youthful determination and a newfound sadness. "That monster killed my father. Papa wasn't a good man, but he deserved better. The Deyrnas deserves better."

I offered a pitying smile, but it was shallow. I didn't have the heart to crush his spirit with the truth. His father had earned his fate a dozen times over, but as Keira once said, there was no use tarnishing a dead man's reputation. Tarran needed a hero to idolize. There were so few options left.

Saeth stayed silent, her lips pursed, so much more perceptive than her twin. There was no hiding the truth from a woman like her. Made of the same steel, she could sense it better than either of Griffin's swords ever could.

"We need a distraction." Reagan crossed her arms, pulling us back to the task at hand, dragon eyes narrowed. "Something shiny to pull Connor's focus while we set up some trade routes."

My attention snapped to my youngest cousin, another piece falling into place. The dragon in my core purred at the waning sliver of hope that stirred with her words.

"Like?" Ellian cocked his head, eyes lighter than they had been the entire conversation.

"Like a certain raven-haired outlaw." Reagan shrugged and folded her hands in her lap, a dealer at a cards table holding the ace. "For whatever reason, he needs Keira gone for this to work. That's why he framed her, right?"

Her name hurt worse than a gunshot to the gut. The flicker of warmth in my chest extinguished like a match in a hurricane. Of course, the only viable plan any of us could come up with was centered around Keira. Sometimes, it felt like my whole world revolved around Keira, like she was the sun and we were only planets in her solar system.

"Well, he succeeded, because she's gone." My voice was detached, but anger simmered underneath, at both Connor and myself for our equally-guilty parts in her disappearance. Fresh hurt welled in my littlest cousin's eyes at my tone, but I looked away before I could feel guilty for that, too.

"Aye, *we* know that." Saeth caught on first, her voice low and dangerous, like the way the tide pulled back from the shore before a tidal wave. In the lanternlight, the sharp lines of her face seemed even more severe. "But *he* doesn't. All he knows is that she escaped."

Something locked and unlocked within me, a missing part of myself slipping out of its cage and roaring to life.

Keira always said Saeth was the cleverest among us, but now, in the dimness of the warm kitchen, I saw her for what she truly was: ice and frost incarnate, sharp enough to slice and cold enough to burn. Saeth may have been born a Branwen, but she was a dragon through and through. Together, she and Reagan were going to reforge the world in ice and fire.

Griffin, blind as ever, groaned, "Do you want to start making sense, Saeth?"

"What if we made him believe Keira was still at large?" Reagan answered for her, a wicked grin spreading like wildfire across her features. "What if we could show her sailing all over the place, making noise wherever she went, loud enough to draw out Connor and make him act on his personal vendetta against her?"

Truth blazed through my core, hot as fire.

They were right.

"And do you have a magical way of producing our disposed Captain that we aren't aware of?" Griffin waved his hands at the girls dramatically. "If so, please let us know."

"We don't need Keira here," I said aloud as the tapestry of their plan revealed itself, clear as daybreak on the horizon. "We just need the story to spread." The story of Keira, the one I was still clinging to. The one I'd told Reagan over and over again on nights much like tonight, in this very kitchen. The story of a girl with the heart of the sea and eyes like stars, who could outsail Lyr himself.

"You want a fake," Rhett laughed incredulously as realization dawned on him, too.

"Aye." Saeth leaned back in her chair. "Outside of Porthladd, most people only have a vague idea of what she looks like. We need the legend, not the person right now."

The legend of the NightMare of the Four Seas, who could scare even the Dark God into submission. Who could drag her own good-for-nothing husband back from the Otherworld with her will and a spring alone.

It was brilliant. If we could fake it, even for a little while, Connor would come. He wouldn't depend on Leary or Locasta or anyone else to do his bidding, not after Keira escaped his clutches yet again.

"Uncle Cedric used to say a good story was worth a thousand men," Griffin mused, finally wrapping his head around it.

Reagan folded her arms. "Keira is worth a thousand and one."

"More." I swallowed down the ball of emotion in my throat, pride sparkling through me as I regarded the little dragon's bravery and cunning.

Keira was worth the world. And my youngest cousin was worth just as much. I had missed the moment, somewhere along the way, when she grew up. When she learned to out-think and out-maneuver a room full of trained adults, where she learned to speak her truth and not be stunted by someone else's shortcomings. Where she learned to spread her wings, the proud dragon she was, and take to the skies.

"What about when she comes back?" Tarran's brow furrowed, shoulders still slumped. "Will there just be two Keiras?"

Silence steeped the room.

His innocence almost made me believe, too. Made me want to dive into that fantasy like it was the spring, letting it weightlessly carry me away to a world where it was true.

She wasn't coming back. She was going to hide for as long as Connor was hunting her. Or longer, if she felt guilty enough about Weylin's death to blame herself. And with that mark on her shoulder…

I couldn't bear to finish the thought.

The muscle in Rhett's jaw clenched and unclenched as he cast me a furtive glance. "What if she doesn't? I know no one is saying it, but it could be."

"It's a good plan." I cleared the sorrow from my throat, shoving it down and focusing on what we could control instead. I spoke directly to Ellian, the default leader among us. "Reagan and Saeth are absolutely right. Connor has had it out for her from day one. If he thinks she's evaded him again, he'll hunt her himself this time."

Ellian weighed it, wringing his hands as he thought, before deciding. "It's a start. It'll buy us time."

"You all are missing a big point," Griffin interjected, tapping his fingers anxiously against the table. "Who is going to fake it? Reagan and Saeth are too young…sorry, Shrimpy."

He ruffled Reagan's hair, but she swatted him away, unamused. "Saeth could pass."

"Saeth is built like a twelve-year-old boy," Tarran snorted at his twin, then cringed at the arrowed looks both she and Ellian shot him.

"You're a prick, Tarran." Saeth crossed her arms over her flat frame self-consciously. Her voice was softer when she spoke again. "But he's right. Keira is young, but she has a presence. No one is going to believe that I'm the NightMare of the Four Seas."

I agreed, but for different reasons. Saeth had the presence, a young dragon coming into her own. But Keira was in her early twenties and had years of experience adding to the swagger of her walk. Saeth was too blunt, too sharp. As wild as Keira was, she was also a Captain. We needed someone with the same regal grace.

My heart sank as I realized how one-of-a-kind my wife truly was.

"I've always wondered how I'd look with dark hair," Reina said by way of an introduction as she swept back into the kitchen, sticking a hand to her hip. The smile on her face made it clear how long she'd been listening.

It took me a moment to process what she said. Saeth, as usual, caught on quicker. "That might actually work. No one really knows your face, not even in Porthladd. You're ten years older, but with the right cosmetics..."

The world froze. "Reina—"

She held up a hand to silence me, a queen commanding her subject. "No, Ronan." Head held high, she shifted her weight, mimicking Keira's stance almost perfectly as she addressed the room. "I'm tired of hiding. It's time to help."

23

Fortunes and Family

KEIRA

I was going to see Ronan.

It was the only thought in my brain as I lived through the motions for two full days after the bonfire night, tending the fields during the day, stopping only to eat and sleep when my body demanded it. It was an easy routine, and aside from Siobhan, the women had fully embraced me as one of theirs, an easy rapport building in a short span of time. Marina and Laureli taught me which crops worked best in the damp heat, while Nelle and Gennevieve cooked my favorites the second night, intent to make me feel as comfortable as possible. Even Cassryn stopped glaring at me over meals, her contempt dissolving into general disinterest.

Vian adjusted beautifully, and spent most of his time with Gennevieve, the little duck and the lark two birds of a feather. To my absolute joy, he even helped cook the feast, his orange chicken a near-rival to Reina's signature dish.

But with every joke and chuckle, every seed planted and meal shared, my mind drifted to what waited in Laureli's hut. What I left behind in Porthladd.

Finally, as the sun sank below the horizon on the second night, I snuck out of the quiet hut, the moonlight my only guide. She seemed larger tonight, brighter, as if she knew I needed her steady guidance to get through whatever the night brought. Laureli's hut wasn't very far from mine, only a few dozen paces. I just had to make sure Siobhan and her patrol weren't around to catch me.

Vian was hot on my heels, as usual, whispering against the quiet music of *Hiraethean* nightfall, "Keira, this isn't a good idea."

I did my best to tune out the worry in his tone, as I did the distant whispering of the island. The last conscious night I'd spent on *Hiraeth* was a nightmare. I needed tonight to be better, even if it was wishful thinking. "I need to know if he's alright, Vian. If you don't want to come, go back to the hut."

"There are a lot of scary things on this island," Vian hissed as he stumbled after me. If I was being honest, I was grateful for the company. Whatever the wind was whispering to him might prove useful if the women tried to lie again. The Soul Wind had a funny knack of blowing away the bullshit and revealing the truth. But if he stood in my way, I would leave him behind.

"I've seen them. I'm not afraid." My voice held a glimmer of the authority I used to hold as Captain. I was going to see Ronan. There wasn't a beast in the world scary enough to stop me, *Hiraethean* or not.

Vian huffed but stayed quiet until we rounded the corner and Laureli's hut came into view. Marked by deep green curtains that blocked out any light, the hut was dark, but a single column of smoke spiraling from the bamboo chimney confirmed that life stirred within. I knocked three times, as she'd instructed me.

"So, you came." Laureli opened the door and leaned casually in the frame, blocking our view of the inside as she gave Vian a cold stare. "I thought I said alone."

I pulled Vian closer, lifting my chin. "He goes where I go. If you want him to leave, I leave, too."

She paused, lips in a tight line as she weighed her options. I stood firm, fingers still wrapped tightly around Vian's wrist. Finally, with an eye roll, she pushed off the door, allowing us to step through and into the hut. "You're Cedric's kid, alright. Get inside before the watchdog sees you."

Pride bloomed in my core at the mention of my father. Being his kid was the greatest accomplishment of my lifetime. There was a swagger to my walk as I stepped inside.

The interior reminded me faintly of rich Ir'desian markets. Paper lanterns cast warm pools of amber light across the small space. Plush rugs and pillows were scattered around the main room, upholstered in deep gemstone-colored velvet more expensive than Madame Jessa's brothel. Lining the walls, crates made from deep stained wood with jeweled faces promised further mystery inside. From the ceiling, dried herbs and woven dream charms swayed in the breeze floating from the open windows, basking the air in a floral aroma. Silk tapestries decorated the walls, depicting creatures in iridescent metallic paints. On the largest one, a dozen or so sirens with fins of every color swam around a symbol that made my heart drop to my toes.

"You gave Ronan his tattoo." I stared incredulously at the symbol, etched in gold right in the middle of the tapestry.

"Nelle did, actually. Come sit." Laureli eased herself onto one of the plush pillows. Reluctantly, I tore my eyes from the intricate design and sat across from her, Vian nestling into my side. His back was straight with tension, but his face was a picture of calm. I wished I could say the same for myself. My nerves were tied in a knot deep in my gut, woven tighter than any of Laureli's silks.

Laureli closed her eyes, breathing deeply for a moment in the suspended silence. When she opened them, she reached for a nearby crate decorated in deep emerald jewels in the shape of a kraken.

Vian and I gasped in unison as she opened it, pulling out a glass orb the size of a melon. Swirling inside was a giant eye, larger than my head, an unnatural yellow iris peering back at us.

I nearly pissed myself when it *blinked.*

"You're a fortune-teller?" Vian leaned in, mouth agape, tension dissolving from his shoulders.

Laureli caressed the side of the orb like a pet, a soft expression melting the hard lines of her face. The eye swiveled to look up at her with what I could only call affection. "Aye. Before I came here, you could say I was the best in all of Hud. That's how you got that middle name of yours." She stared deep into the orb, a smile drawn across her features. "I saw that your Papa would raise a girl, and he swore on Lyr's ass he'd have a son."

Another bite of my father's past that I devoured whole. I couldn't imagine Papa with a boy. Had he wanted one? Was I meant to have a brother?

"Why'd you leave Hud?" I asked instead, swallowing down my questions about Papa, staring into the eye of the orb. I leaned closer to Vian, the Soul Wind brushing away the discomfort in my middle.

"I can't always see my own path." Laureli's gaze flicked up to me at the same time the orb's did, pain swimming in both their depths. "And I wasn't given much of a choice."

I swallowed the ball of emotion rising to my throat. I didn't know Laureli's story, but I did know her hurt. I had faced my share of choiceless choices, but there was a surprising sense of sisterhood that blossomed in my chest. Perhaps it was the curse of our namesake.

Laureli nodded, an unspoken moment passing between us as we shared the burden of those choices.

"So how does this work?" Vian tapped the glass, mesmerized, and the eye narrowed at him.

Laureli laughed, the heaviness of the moment forgotten to the island of the lost. "Touch here and think of him." She took my hands, placing them on either side of the orb. I didn't know what to expect but thank Lyr it didn't feel like an actual eyeball. It was warm to the touch, and it glowed where my skin made contact with the smooth glass. Laureli clasped her hands over mine, sealing them to the surface. "I'll do the rest."

For the first time since coming to the island, I didn't run from the memories of my husband. I shut my eyes, letting the tide of my thoughts carry me home. I thought of his insufferable smirk, the distinct shade of sapphire in his eyes. I thought of the way he sometimes snorted when he laughed, and the way he tucked his hands in his pockets when he was nervous. Or how he ran his hand through his hair when he was frustrated, or how those same hands weaved perfectly through mine whenever he held them...

Ronan looks like the type of man to kiss you with his whole soul.

"Open your eyes, girl." Laureli's voice dragged me back to the island, and I obeyed, blinking back the tears that threatened to spill over.

The orb had changed. The eye was gone, replaced by a picture clearer than a mirror...but it was not my reflection that stared back at me.

He sat in Reina's kitchen, leaning back in a chair with a drink in his hand. A stoic face, not a trace of my favorite smirk, but his skin was glowing, meaning he'd been to the spring recently. His disheveled blond hair masked his bright eyes, the curls at the back of his neck dusting the collar of his blue coat.

How long had it been for him? Days? Weeks? Was this the present moment, or had it already happened, a memory trapped in the kraken's eye? Body and soul, I ached at the sight of him. I wanted nothing more than to reach into the orb, to brush the hair from his eyes and hold him until my hands went numb.

"Ronan." His name was a prayer on my lips, foolish as it was. He couldn't hear or see me. But a silly, desperate part of me wanted him to know I was here. To know I still cared. To know I missed him more than anything.

As I spoke his name, the view widened, revealing the rest of my family sitting around the table with him.

"And the crew." Vian's voice caught in his throat.

Reagan sat to Ronan's immediate right, her curls in a messy ponytail, red tunic wrinkled and worn. She seemed harder, somehow, the harsh set of her mouth so different from when I'd last seen her. Griffin and Rhett were to Ronan's left, Griffin with his head in his hands, Rhett rubbing small circles across his broad back. Tarran and Saeth flanked none other than Ellian, all three looking as exhausted as I felt. Scraps of picked-at food sat in front of them, smaller than one of Reina's normal feasts, but hearty enough to keep them all healthy, it seemed.

"They look so tired," I voiced out loud, my heart breaking as I watched my family, the color drawn from their faces, the pride in their shoulders deflated.

Vian put a hand on my back. "Tired, but whole."

"Not whole," Laureli corrected, sympathy dripping from her gaze. "But safe. Surrounded by loved ones."

My tears fell freely, splattering across the orb like rain against cobblestone. I had abandoned them, which meant I had no right to tell them how to live anymore. I wasn't their Captain. But it ripped my heart from my chest to see them this way. I would've offered the same heart up on a platter to the Dark God himself if it meant just a moment with them. A moment to nudge Rhett's side after a well-timed joke, a moment to pinch Reagan's cheek to remind her she's still young, to smack Griffin over the head after a crude comment, to mess with Tarran's hair or tuck Saeth's behind her ear. One moment to hold Ronan close, to breathe in his citrus and sea-salt smell and commit it to memory. To tell them all to smile, to keep their chins up, to keep moving forward.

I'd suffer eternal damnation for a moment of that bliss.

But watching them, even down in the dumps as they were, it was close. I could sit here for hours, practicing how to read their lips, to read their bodies as they shifted on Reina's stools.

Papa used to say the most precious thing in the whole world was time. I'd wasted it before, like it was as easy to come by as fool's gold. Now, I'd sell my whole soul for a second's worth.

The hut door banged open, and as quickly as it came, the image in the glass disappeared, the eye blinking back in its place. It felt like being kicked in the face. I grasped at it, begging whatever god fed its magic to bring me my family back. It wasn't enough time. There was never enough time.

"What in *Serenhi's* name is going on here?" Nelle admonished from the doorway, a frown pulling the corners of her mouth as she planted a hand on her hip.

Laureli grabbed the crystal ball from my clutches, prying my fingers off and stuffing it back into its box. "You forget to knock, Nelle." She shot her friend a dark look as she slammed the lid, closing the gateway between me and my people with a final click of the lock.

I made no attempt to hide my desperation as I spun to Nelle. "Please, just a little longer. I needed to see him."

Nelle turned her face away from the lantern, casting her expression in shadows, but I caught the pity resting in the crook of her frown.

"Laureli." Her hands knotted in front of her, but her voice quivered. "We are under strict orders not to—"

"Not to what? To give a poor, lost soul some comfort?" Laureli cut her off venomously. "You sound like Siobhan."

If I wasn't so crestfallen, the candor in Laureli's tone would've impressed me.

Nelle snapped to look at her, violet eyes burning in the lamplight as if Laureli had slapped her. She bit her lip, deciding, then sighed, hands unwinding. "I'm sorry. Keira, I hope you got the answers you needed. But really, if you need anything in the future, please come talk to me first. I can petition Danura for you directly."

Her words were meant to comfort, her intention clear, but instead they fanned the flames in my veins. A fire had started in the empty clearing of my heart my family used to occupy, and in their absence, it was suddenly untamable.

I had sacrificed so much of myself to keep them safe. Like tearing off my limbs one by one, I'd conceded my home, my crew, my whole life. But this island would not take my spirit too.

It was an easy thought, to succumb to the darkness before it took me whole, to wait and waste and wallow in the sunshine until mine finally set. I'd been pretending since I got here that I deserved an easy end. Pretending that it no longer mattered if I fought, not when I had nothing left to fight for.

But I was not honoring those I'd left behind. If I wanted my crew to fight, to *live*, I had to lead by example, even if they couldn't see it. One day, when my time came, I'd ask Vian to find them, to see if they were alright in person.

What kind of stories would he tell of me? Would my end be worth telling?

"Am I in some kind of trouble?" I rose from my seat, the image of my family enough to help me craft my own mirage of strength. "It seems pretty unfair to me that I'm told to abide by rules no one will explain. I know enough snakes to know that omission is the same as lying. If you're not going to be transparent with us, what makes you think I'm going to trust you in return?"

Nelle's eyes welled with tears, but her voice was tender. "You're right." She smiled despite her quivering lip, the action as careful as someone holding a child. "I have to clear it with Danura, but it isn't fair to keep you in the dark. Not after all you've been through. You are a guest. It's time we treated you accordingly."

Slowly, she reached for my hand, and I let her take it. I knew Nelle did not mean me any harm. Her spirit was pure. I didn't need Lyr's gifts or Vian's whispering winds to know that.

But kind as she was, I would not back down. Not anymore.

"I'll talk to Danura myself." I gave her hand a gentle squeeze, but my voice was firm.

Laureli rubbed the back of her neck, shifting her weight. "Listen, girlie, I don't know—"

"That way you two don't get in trouble." I cut her off with a shrug. "It's clear there is a hierarchy here. She's the captain. And I respect your loyalty and fealty to her, and I don't want you upsetting your position to satiate my curiosity." I rolled back my shoulders, the action different without the weight of my captain's coat, but it fortified me anyway. *Think tall, and you'll be tall.* I had to act tall now, if only not to sully my crew's memory of me. "But if I'm truly a guest, there should be no reason why I can't petition her myself. Captain to Captain."

And for once, I almost believed it myself.

Nelle softened as she weighed my words, nodding once. An impish grin crossed Laureli's face. "See? Cedric's kid."

Stand-offs and Spots

KEIRA

There was a pep in my step as Nelle led me through the compound to Danura's cottage. I'd left Vian behind to play with Laureli's trinkets, and while I appreciated my friend's ceaseless support, there was something invigorating about marching on to finally grasp my destiny in my own hands again.

I had a purpose, a plan: get answers about who I was before my sun finally set. Find a way to connect with my father's past before it was too late. Do it with some dignity for the sake of those I was leaving behind.

Resting on the far edge of the compound, Danura's hut was larger than the others, easily distinguishable in the full light of the moon. Made of the same wood material but decorated in the bioluminescent flowers of the island, it was a beacon in the darkness much like the silver queen herself.

I was about to find out what her brightness was masking.

"Be good, please, Keira." Nelle's tone was stern, but I caught the way she kneaded her bottom lip between her teeth as she knocked on the heavy wooden door. Committed not to get my newest accomplice in trouble, I stayed quiet as we waited. I could be good, I just needed answers.

Quiet footsteps padded on the other side of the door, and I straightened my back, readying myself. *Captain to Captain.* I'd been negotiating all my life with less leverage and worse odds. If anything, *this* I could do right.

My false confidence collapsed when Siobhan threw the door open instead.

The warrior went rigid, fists at her side. Her lips parted as she tore her glare from me and set it on Nelle instead. "What is *she* doing here? She should be in her hut."

Suddenly a Pysgoddian wolf made flesh, Nelle tilted her elegant chin. "Shouldn't *you* be on patrol?"

My respect for the woman before me tripled as Siobhan floundered for a retort, fuming. I bit my cheek, fighting the urge to grin.

Before Siobhan could properly flay us both, Danura appeared behind her, silver eyes clouded with suspicion. She placed a delicate hand on Siobhan's shoulder, and while Siobhan's body remained taut, she stood back.

"Come in," Danura commanded, floating back into the small hut. Her gossamer dress swished around her ankles, and with a flourish, she sat on a highbacked silver chair against the room's back wall. Every movement of her body was effortless, but discomfort was clear across her stony face. She was not expecting guests—a slight advantage in my favor. "To what do we owe the pleasure?"

I took my time looking around the room, shoving my hands in the slim pockets of my trousers, relishing the impatient tapping of her fingers against the armrest. Her hut was not lived in, its bare interior merely a place of meeting. Another bamboo table occupied one end, little trinkets and tokens from all over the Deyrnas resting on it, but a thin layer of dust blanketed them. Unlike Laureli's room, there were no tapestries or pictures hanging from the walls. The only thing adorning the room was a small mirror on the opposite side of the table. It was a tactic to create distance, to make her seem scarce and needless.

I tilted my head. "Am I a prisoner?"

Nelle sighed, rubbing her eyes with the heel of her hand as I failed the only request she made of me. But I had no time for pleasantries. Lyr below, I had no time for much at all. Inevitability made me bold.

Danura blinked at me, lips pursing. "What?" She crossed and uncrossed her legs, hands gripping their rests tightly. With the tense movement, I thought to consider her physical capabilities. She was supple and soft, but that didn't mean she couldn't fight. She was in charge of the most strange and dangerous place in the world. That could not have been accomplished through kindness and sunshine alone.

This was a sham of a plan. I had no weapons, no reinforcements, and no idea what this woman was capable of. But like the fool I was, I doubled down. *Think tall, you'll be tall.*

"Am I a prisoner?" I repeated slowly, as if speaking to a child—or to Griffin. I shot Siobhan a look that could sour honey as I gestured to where she stood guard at the door. "Or am I under surveillance? Because it seems you've been keeping secrets from me."

Shadows crept across the starlight of Danura's expression. "Have I done something to offend you, my dear?"

"I'm not offended." I shrugged but did not drop her gaze. "I'm confused. And I'd love some clarification."

A sugar-coated smile broke across the smooth places on her face, baring a waning crescent moon of teeth. "We have nothing to clarify. We live simple lives here. I know you have had plenty of pain in your recent past, but not everyone has a hidden agenda." She clasped her heart, both pity and poison woven into the action.

I bit my tongue before I could tell her exactly where she could hide things. Papa used to say a Captain's composure was as necessary as their compass. If this woman really did know him like she said she did, she should've known I wouldn't be that easy to placate.

Cedric's kid.

Uncomfortable silence blanketed the night, the only sound the gentle brush of Nelle shifting her weight anxiously. Danura and I both stared, neither willing to give ground first. We were two stones, one of diamond and one of sapphire, neither designed to crumble.

Nelle broke first, voice soft. "*Serenhi,* perhaps we could—"

I held my hand to silence her, and she quieted. Something swelled in my chest as Danura's eyes darkened. Captains didn't like it much when their crew started following someone else's orders. I was not going to waste the opportunity. "Perhaps you could tell me the truth." I picked an invisible speck of dust from my fingernails. Danura's jaw remained tight, so I stepped forward, chin up and shoulders back like Papa taught me. "For starters, what does *Ariannad* mean?"

Danura waved it off like a pesky fly. "I told you, your father—"

"I asked what it means." I didn't give her the chance to finish the lie, my voice dangerously low. I would not stand for my father's name being dragged through the mud of this island. "I didn't ask where you claimed to have heard it."

To my surprise, Danura relaxed back into her chair to study me, but the clouds were gone. She regarded me simply, the traces of amusement dancing in the corners of her mouth.

"Silver wheel," she finally responded, and it sounded like the first honest thing she'd said since I met her. "Both precious and driven."

Silver Wheel. A glimmer of a memory swam to the surface, like a reflection in a spring.

Let me be the compass, Keira girl, and you can be my little silver wheel.

"Why?" My tongue was heavy as I tried to form the word, my father's ghostly voice still echoing down my spine.

Danura's gaze went cotton-soft. "You are very precious, Keira. To many people."

A chord resonated deep within me, something tangling and untangling as her words enveloped me in strange comfort. But I could not forget my purpose. I needed answers, not more riddles, pretty as they sounded.

I shoved the tender feeling back into its cage, donning my Captain's mantle once more. I would not be tricked into submission. "So why won't you tell me anything? What does 'from the salt' mean? And your gifts... I know Marina and Laureli and Nelle have them. Do they come from Lyr? Or another god?"

The openness in Danura's face disappeared faster than a drop of rain in the ocean. I watched as her porcelain turned marble, mouth pressed into a thin line. I'd struck too deep.

Despite the tropical balm of the night, her voice was icy enough to send shivers down my spine. "Keira, I don't know what you are looking for, but I don't have any answers to those ridiculous questions."

The words skewered me like a fish in shallow water, striking true.

What was I looking for? Answers? Answers to what? What did it matter to me or my crew if these women had gifts or not? What did I care for their secrets, outside the ones concerning Papa?

Sometimes we fall because there is something down there we are meant to find.

"I'm looking to belong." The admission surprised me as it burst out, an answer to a question I didn't know I was asking. "My whole life, I was the only one. The only one that could hear Lyr, the only one with any gifts or powers...but for whatever reason, we are the same." I hated the way the words tasted on my tongue, weak and vulnerable and lonely as they were, but it was the gods-honest truth. I looked at Danura with fresh eyes, not as a Captain negotiating a trade but as a sailor craving a crew. "I didn't choose to be here. I miss my home and my husband with every rotten part of me. But it feels like...I'm supposed to be. I'm running out of time, and I want to be part of something when my time comes. I don't want to face it alone."

My words hung precariously above us, heavier than clouds before a thunderstorm. The air had the same charge, my embarrassment and shame reddening my cheeks. I was aware of Siobhan glaring at my back, and Nelle's gentle hand coming to rest on my shoulder, but I didn't tear my eyes from Danura. Her face was impassive as she lounged in her chair, giving no indication if my realization had moved her. I waited, breath held, heart thundering in my chest. I had given up my ground, laid my cards flat on the table. The advantage was hers.

"Alright."

"Alright?" My pulse quickened, relief washing over me in waves.

"Yes, alright," she sighed, a crack in her composure as she rubbed her forehead. "I promise, *Ariannad,* if you can be a little more patient, you'll have your answers." She stood from her throne, skirts brushing the ground as she crossed to me. Up close, I could see the way the silver darkened ever-so-slightly in the center of her eyes. I couldn't help but lean in, my nails digging into my palms the only thing grounding me to my body. The corner of Danura's mouth turned downward. "But it will be easier to show you than tell you. Tomorrow morning, when everyone is at breakfast. But not yet."

"I think that's a great idea!" Nelle chimed in, her face alight.

I deflated like a sail without wind, but I tried to keep it from showing on my face. "Alright."

Yet. I could handle yet. Or, at least I hoped I could, a phantom pang in my shoulder reminding me I didn't have many *yets* left.

Danura's relief was evident in her thin laughter, the sound lighter than the bubbles in sparkling wine. "Hang in there, Keira dear." She reached out, patting me once on the shoulder.

I was not expecting the hiss of pain that escaped her lips as she made contact. She tore her hand away and clutched it to her chest, eyes wide with terror.

"*Serenhi!*" Siobhan was at her side in an instant, shoving me out of the way to inspect her master's hand.

"What in the Otherworld was that?" Danura seethed, ignoring Siobhan, eyes instead flicking back and forth between my shoulder and my face, accusations swimming in her silver stare.

"I—"

She didn't wait for a response, ripping back the shoulder of my tunic.

The black gore of my skin seemed to darken the entire room, a beacon of my shame. I shifted, smacking her hand away, but it was too late. She saw. Everyone did.

There was no more hiding. The sand in the hourglass had run out.

"Why didn't you tell me?" Danura stumbled back, tears lining her narrowed eyes.

"You're one to talk about honesty right now." I hastily covered myself again, hugging the tunic tighter to me. Rage bubbled beneath my skin, drowning the embarrassment.

Danura cursed under her breath, her whole body trembling. "Nelle, can you heal her?"

"No—not me. Not anymore," Nelle stuttered, horror and pity warring in her violet eyes. She held a shaky hand out, fingertips grazing the spot, now covered. She hid her mouth with her hand. "Oh, you poor thing."

Danura paced, staring at her injured hand like it might turn sentient and bite her. "This isn't natural."

"I know. It's a mark from Arawn," I growled, using the Dark God's name freely now—a dare in itself. I had nothing left to lose.

Danura halted at his name, a shudder shaking her frame. She turned to me again, fire burning in silver, a dagger in a forge. "I know. But it should've already cleared for *you*."

"Lyr's gift wasn't strong enough." The words were bitter on my tongue, like sand mixed with vinegar. How many sleepless nights had I fought off the demons of my mind with the same idea?

"Not his gift, girl," Danura hissed, still tenderly holding the hand that had touched the spot. Shaking her head, she stood straighter, nostrils flared. "Nelle, call the girls. It's time for the *Carthu.*"

Vipers and Vixens

RONAN

The brine-and-sweat scent of Sailor's Point always made me want to hurl. Even in the dark of night, our only light a few burning oil lamps, the smell brought back every bad memory I had of this place. The Eastern Docks were cleaner, less crowded. Still, we couldn't be choosy; we had to get out fast and quiet. I chewed an orange peel, trying to subdue the waves of nausea rolling through my gut.

At least, I told myself the nausea was a side effect of my surroundings. I didn't want to think of the alternative. I didn't have time to dwell on the shaking limbs or the deep-seated hunger eating at my insides.

I chewed my orange rind with renewed vigor and did my part to load the last of the supplies onto the *Ddraig* in the late-night fog while Reina and Reese joined us on the dock, about ready to take their crew and the *Ceffyl* straight to Hud.

"Well? How do I look?" Reina fiddled with her jet-black braid. The dye and painted freckles weren't perfect—a consequence of buying from Madame Neirida, the sea witch—but they would do. Reina's eyes were darker, and she didn't have the same muscle to fill out Keira's long blue captain's coat, but she had the lean of her stance perfectly, the cruel quirk of her lips. And with Cedric's compass sitting around her neck…

It pained me physically to part with it, but every actor needed a costume, and my sentimentality was not important anymore. Nothing was, save our task. I cleared my throat before I could fall down that thought-hole again. "Lovely as always, Auntie."

My father gripped my shoulders, an uncomfortable smile hanging awkwardly on his scarred face. "We'll make sure to cause a fuss wherever we stop. Don't worry boy, I've been practicing the story. I helped Keira escape while you played the victim—"

"I know, Pa, I made it up. I trust you." Lyr below, I appreciated the stumbling effort he'd made since I returned to Porthladd, but it could never erase the decade of distance between us.

He sighed, an unmistakable tinge of sadness in the honey of his eye, but he let go. What mattered now was keeping Reina safe during the coming storm, and he was a far better sailor and fighter than he was father.

"Lyr keep you both." I patted my Pa on the back before ducking in to press a quiet kiss on Reina's cheek. Distance and discomfort aside, they were here, helping me in ways I could never repay. "This is dangerous. Keira has plenty of enemies outside of Connor. Don't take risks, alright? Play it safe."

"Sometimes ye need to take a little risk." Reina's clay stare hardened. "I've spent enough time hiding to know. Keira did her part to protect me and mine, now it's my turn. If ye and my daughter can be brave, so can I."

I opened my mouth to offer another warning, but quieted when a pair of little listening ears approached.

"You look just like her, Mama." Reagan beamed as she wiggled between Reina and I, her eyes starry.

Reina melted, wrapping her daughter in a tight hug, and my father let loose an uncharacteristic smile. "Is yer ma yer hero yet, little dragon?"

Reagan buried her head into her mother's chest. "Always were."

Reina coughed, turning to me so Reagan wouldn't see the tear brimming in the corner of her eye. "Be good and listen to yer cousin, am I clear?"

I left them to say their goodbyes, not sure if I could bear the weight of them today. Tucking my hands in my pockets to keep them from shaking, I turned to the rest of my kin. Griffin took inventory, Tarran and Rhett already stowing things away on deck. It felt wrong to let Reese captain the *Ceffyl* without the real Keira, but she really was the fastest cutter in the Four Seas, even with a full cargo load, and I wasn't about to let my pride be my aunt's ruining. The *Ddraig* was better suited for cargo anyway, and if this plan worked, we would be hauling a lot of it. The first shipment would be to Pysgodd, a final stop before the waters froze, and we'd get as much meat as we could to take with us to Bachtref and the rest of the south.

"Ready?" Griffin raised an eyebrow at me as he counted the last of the supplies.

"Ready as a harlot on a Saturday night." I smirked, recounting the last boxes, if only to avoid his penetrating gaze.

Unfortunately for me, Griffin was far more perceptive than he let on, especially when he wasn't drunk. Which had been rarer lately, much to my chagrin. "Sure you don't want another soak before we go? It's been two weeks."

Two weeks of careful planning, of calling in every favor any of us were owed. Two weeks of gathering scraps from every corner we could find, making sure to leave enough behind for our own people. Two weeks of urgent letters written by lanternlight, two weeks of nearly sleepless nights. Fighting against tyranny, as it turned out, was a rather arduous task.

My body craved the spring, the very mention of it delivering another punch of the nausea to my middle. I knew he could see it on my face, the urges, the distraction as the hunger gnashed its teeth inside me. I also knew we were out of time. If we didn't leave before sunrise, Connor had the chance to stop us, and it wasn't a risk I was willing to take. My life wasn't worth forfeiting the crew's success.

"I'm sure. You might just have to be the Captain for this." I patted his arm, not bothering to wear my smile. I didn't have the energy for it.

"Maybe you should stay—"

"Don't even say it," I cut him off, extinguishing the concern in his gaze with the gravity of my tone. I was not going to be left behind. Even if it cost me everything.

Griffin opened his mouth again, brows furrowed, but the hazy outline of two other figures at the end of the dock shipwrecked our conversation in the shallows.

"Miss us?" Saeth wore Ellian on her arm as they approached, fire dancing in the ice queen's gaze. Her cropped hair was skewed and her tunic was buttoned crookedly, a sign of *exactly* what made the pair late.

At least someone was happy, though I doubted the Councilman shared his bedfellow's excitement. His face was drawn, the circles under his eyes darker than when I'd last seen him. Either Saeth was the true animal in this pair, or he was just as nervous as I was for the upcoming voyage.

A petty part of me was glad I wasn't the only one who hadn't gotten any sleep.

"We were waiting for you." Griffin rolled his eyes at Saeth's grin.

"We stayed too long at my house, I'm sorry. I had to make sure my Pa was safe." Ellian untangled himself from Saeth's iron grip, adjusting his fur coat, a performer ready to take on the role of Councilman once more. "My final warning letters went out this morning to all of the Councilmembers across the Deyrnas. Some will be on our side. Others…"

"Others won't hesitate to come after you and your kin," I finished for him, the only courtesy I'd offer him today. In truth, he'd been more helpful than anyone, his business connections and status the only reason we had a leg to stand on. And he was making sacrifices too, risking his position and his life for uncertainty for the Deyrnas. The Llewellyn name had weight and authority, and he's offered it up on a silver platter for the sake of truth and justice. But I couldn't get rid of the ash in my mouth every time I tried to thank him for it.

"All hands on deck." Griffin gave the order, wasting no more time. His voice was sure, but I watched his fingers twitch at his sides, his coat not stitched for a Captain. "Rhett, Saeth, in the rigging. Ellian, you have the sharpest eyes, so you'll be in the crow's nest. Reagan, Tarran…"

"Belowdecks, we know," Reagan whined, pushing Tarran up the gangplank with a full lipped pout.

Griffin crossed his arms. "I was going to say you can untie the mooring."

"It's going to be a pleasure to sail with you, old man." A wicked grin carved the little dragon's face, deadlier and sharper than anything I'd ever mustered, before she dragged Tarran onto the ship.

Lyr below, where she got it from, I didn't know. And frankly, I was not in any rush to find out.

"I'm not that old." Griffin shook his head, a laugh falling from him as he ushered Saeth and Ellian onto the ship. But before he climbed the gangway, he looked over his shoulder, eyes traveling past me to the silhouetted crest of Dubryn Hill poking out in night. "Last call, Ronan."

Before I could tell him to shove off and move on before my self-control crumbled, another pair of hooded figures darkened the end of the dock.

"On your toes, Cousin," I whispered to the Swordsinger, suddenly very glad for the gaudy swords at his back. Griffin leapt down to the dock next to me, fingers twitching toward Truth's sheath.

"Don't you dare shake one of those sticks at me." The first figure dropped her hood, candied acid in her tone.

Every muscle in my body tensed, something primal and vicious surging through my veins as Finna Branwen sauntered down the dock, Councilman Leary a dog at her heels. I thought of the thousand ways I wanted to eviscerate her, hundreds of insults fighting for first prize on my tongue. In the month since the wedding, I had imagined this moment even in the blackness of my nightmares. I tasted blood as I bit back the words intended to slice her apart. This woman who had told my wife she was inferior so many times, she started believing it; this parasite that would trade her family for a cage disguised as a false throne.

Griffin's jaw dropped and he took a stumbling step toward his traitor sister. "Finna? Lyr's ass——"

I held an arm out to stop him, first stinging insult cocked and ready to fire. "What do you want now? Come to sentence another cousin to death?"

"Save your venom for someone who cares, blondie." Finna rolled her eyes, but I saw the flicker of a grimace she fought to hide. "I'm here to help."

The lie was honey on her tongue, sweet and decadent. I wanted to believe her, wanted to devour the treat she dangled in front of me and pretend it was sugar instead of shit. But I knew this charade like I knew my own name. She'd performed well the night of Keira's sentencing too, her ugly tears and shouts at the wedding a pretty display for the entire town that would not hesitate to cast her out if they thought her disloyal. It was the perfect ruse: get Keira out of the way for Connor without losing the favor of the people.

Her crest was not a snake, but a fox, and Finna Branwen-Yorath was the Queen of Vixens.

"I don't recall asking for your assistance." I struggled to hide the bitterness in my cold tone, hands in my pockets only to stop myself from wringing her pale neck.

Leary scoffed, folding his arms. "You idiots will want to hear her out."

The leash Griffin had on his anger finally snapped as he drew Truth from her sheath. His patience toward his sister was boundless as the sea, but Leary had earned none such courtesy. "You vile shitstain—"

Leary stumbled back, drawing his own dagger as he fell into a ready stance.

"Shut up, Griffin." Finna swatted his sword away like a fly and nodded once to Leary, her pet rolling over at her command and sheathing his own weapon. Griffin looked to me, red in his eyes, waiting for permission to skewer the man, but I shook my head. We didn't have time for bloodshed, and a dead Councilman would severely impede our departure.

With a sigh, Griffin lowered his blade, the god of war still peeking over his shoulder, but the immediate danger gone. I focused every ounce of hatred and anger I had in my body on Finna. "Put your pretty mouth to some use and start talking or leave."

She matched my reproach with her own, disgust resting in her downturned lips, but to my surprise something real simmered in her envy-green eyes. "Listen, I was wrong, alright? Things have been..." She swallowed, throat bobbing for dramatic effect. "...*different* than I imagined. Connor is always with Morwyn Locasta, and they keep whispering about a ritual..."

The image of Locasta and Yorath ritualistically plotting a plague filled my mouth with bitterness, but I didn't let it show. Instead, I donned my favorite smirk, the one that still fit like an old coat, relishing in any discomfort the princess might have suffered at her own hand. "What, is sleeping with leeches not to your liking?"

"Watch it. We are here as a courtesy." Leary's voice dipped low with the warning, and my grin widened.

"We?" Griffin sneered, crossing his tree-trunk arms across his broad chest. He didn't need Truth or Triumph—he was a war made man, and he wouldn't let the wolverine pup begging for Finna's scraps forget it.

"The councilman has been very helpful," Finna spat at her brother, but her gaze softened, her hand drifting to her belly absentmindedly. Her brow furrowed, accentuating new wrinkles I hadn't noticed before. "I don't think I can do much to help here. Connor is shutting me out; he doesn't trust me, not after the scene I made for Keira. But I did find this." She reached in her cloak pocket, producing a folded piece of paper and holding it out for me to take.

"What is this?"

"Trade routes." A smug smile slithered onto her face. "Sleeping with leeches has its perks if you can tolerate the awkward sucking."

Griffin snatched the paper from her hands, unfolding it with eager, clumsy fingers. "How did you—?"

"Oh, please. As if I couldn't tell mama was hiding something. I knew you'd all run away again, but this time, perhaps you'll be a little prepared." Finna stuck a hand to her hip, daring me to look with a glare.

Against my better judgment, the sliver of hope I'd been saving for a rainy day took over as I glanced at the paper. The familiar map of the Four Seas was decorated with tiny red lines, all labeled in great detail. It was a perfect guide, highlighting not only the strengths of the Council's routes and their trading partners, but the weaknesses, too. A good sailor could see the holes clear as day, the neglect in Ir'de and Pysgodd especially, the only two islands rich enough to sustain themselves even without the Council.

It was foolhardy. Perfect.

It was also a trap. No matter how badly I wanted or prayed for an easy way out of all this, I would not get it.

"I expected better from you, honestly. The lack of subtlety is beneath you, Finna." I tore the mockery from Griffin, throwing it on the ground next to her and pressing it under my boot. I took a menacing step toward her. "Do you really think we're that stupid? You expect us to believe that *you*, of all people, would do something selfless for the family you've betrayed time and time again for your own self-interest? We may be fools, but we aren't that dense. I guess you'll need to find a better way to earn Connor's trust back."

Finna stiffened, mask shattering, uncharacteristic rawness shining through the cracks. She reached down to gingerly pick up the sullied paper, hands shaking not with fear or guilt, but rage. When she looked at me again, her jade eyes were redder than Griffin's, burning with a volcanic mix of fury and sincerity. "I have put my life on the line for this information. But you're right. It's not for you, not for Griffin, or Keira, or any of you. This is for me. For my son. He deserves better than all of this." With a tilt of her chin, she masked her fire once more, trapping it beneath layers of marble and lace. But I could still see it simmering in her eyes, a queen sitting on a throne of ash and stone, as she shoved the map into her brother's hand. "Take it, Griffin. It's your choice whether or not to use it. But don't come crying to me when everyone is still hungry because your pride got in the way."

I exhaled sharply, ready to tear the map and Finna to shreds, when a voice in my mind halted me.

Truth.

Lyr's command was simple, but it turned my limbs to stone.

It couldn't be true. It was *Finna.* She was the one to lure Keira here, she practically signed my wife's conviction notice herself using her crocodile tears as ink.

Take it.

As much as I wanted to tell the sunken god to go drown, and as much as I wanted to beg him to take Finna along with him, something sputtered in my chest, alive and demanding to be felt.

Hope. Somehow, the seed I'd kept under lock and key had broken free and taken root, blossoming with a few lines on a map and a word from a faceless god.

"What's your stake in this?" I turned to Leary, searching desperately for anything that might squash the growing, burning sensation that made my heart race.

I didn't miss how he looked first to Finna, stars in his eyes, before steeling his expression once more. "I'm a sailor, not a slaver. Even I have lines I won't cross."

"Yet you'll still cozy up to the master's side at night like a good dog." The insult lacked the usual venom, my fangs retracting.

Leary, sniffing out my wavering resolve, cracked a smile. "Right, and I'll lead him in the exact opposite direction of wherever you're going, like a *smart* dog."

With that, I was a goner, shot down and sunk. My mind raced as I struggled to swallow down the thousands of objections that instinctively rose to my lips. It was a good plan. Let Finna and Leary cover our tracks while we always stayed two steps ahead of Connor. Run supplies to people and deplete the Council of theirs, striking their sources and repurposing them to the hungry.

Lyr below, if this was real, if the sunken god was right about Finna's sincerity, if it was not just a fever dream or a poorly veiled trap…

It was not just enough to help us survive. It was enough to win a war.

"I have to go. This is the best I can do." Finna grimaced as dawn purpled the sky, drawing me back to reality. She pulled her hood back over her head, not bothering with any heartfelt goodbyes to her brother. But she hesitated, gnawing at her bottom lip before addressing me with one last smoldering scowl. "*When* you find Keira, tell her Agatha's cards don't lie. And tell her anyone who touches my family will have me to answer to."

26

Rituals and Revelations

KEIRA

My hands shook despite the hut's cozy warmth, the look on Danura's face still haunting me. Around me, the women bustled, bees in a hive as they prepared me for what was to come. Nelle's expert hands tugged at my hair while Gennevieve washed me in honey-scented soaps, dressing me in the finest blue gossamer gown I'd ever seen. Hanging precariously off my shoulders, it was nearly translucent, the color of the ocean at dusk and just as shimmery, the fabric caressing my skin as tenderly as a wave.

But I was not prepared, no matter what dress they stuffed me in. No amount of silk or soap could hide or wipe away the inky blemish on my shoulder as it crept toward my elbow.

"Hand me the lavender," Nelle ordered Gennevieve as she wrangled my hair into intricate braids, weaving the flowers through them tighter than a sailor's knot. Griffin would be impressed.

"You just look so lovely in blue!" Gennevieve clapped, hands in fine turquoise gloves today, her round eyes like little moons as she watched Nelle work. A giggle rose from her, full and bright as she swished the skirts of her own sea-glass gown, tan skin glowing against it. "We match!"

I smiled back, charmed by her effortless joy, but it didn't meet my eyes. "Why do I feel like you're preparing me for a sacrifice?"

Nelle laughed, the sound like bells, as a final tug pulled my hair. She twirled to face me, her deep purple gown spinning like petals around her, an orchid ready to bloom. She patted my cheek with lavender-scented hands, but I caught her as she eyed my shoulder with thinly veiled remorse.

"The *Carthu* is one of our most sacred practices." She busied herself fastening thick silver bracelets around my wrists, purposefully averting her gaze from the spot. "It's a ceremony of truth and sacrifice, yes, but in a good way. We let go of the hurts that burden us and allow ourselves to heal, to show our true forms."

A lump knotted in my throat, the charm evaporating. The truth of my form was just as hideous as the spot on my shoulder. I'd always been a monster, a kin-killer, a curse hiding behind a worn blue coat; that wouldn't change just because I wore a spider-silk gown and some bracelets.

Finishing with the clasps, Nelle backed away, admiring her handiwork. The bracelets suddenly felt as heavy as the truth that chased me all the way here, pretty silver shackles fit for a queen.

"I promise I'm not hiding anything else." It wasn't a lie—the mark was proof enough of my inner hideousness, a physical manifestation of the black spots that blemished my soul.

"Hiding and holding are different, deary." Nelle frowned, fisting the sheer fabric of her shift as she forced herself to look at my mark. "We all have scars here, just not all of them as visible as yours. You're going to be just fine, Keira."

At her words, the buzz of power washed over me, warm and bright as sunrise. The hazy deliciousness of Nelle's power was easy to get lost in, but I anchored myself to the floor, shrugging the sensation off like an old coat and narrowing my eyes at my violet-eyed accomplice. "I like that trick of yours."

Gennevieve furrowed her brows, linking her arm through Nelle's and pulling the older woman close to her side. "It's not a trick, it's a gift."

"Do you have one?" I cocked my head, focusing on where her slender fingers, still covered with the gloves, wrapped around Nelle's arm.

Her light dimmed, and I instantly regretted the question. "Depends on who you ask. I have one, but it's not as nice as Nelle's."

The older woman frowned, opening her mouth to protest, but Gennevieve shook her head. As a show of faith, or respect, she backed away from Nelle, removing a single glove with extreme care. Biting her lip, she reached toward me with the gloved hand, snatching one of the flowers from my braid, and placed it in her exposed palm. Like an egg in a frying pan, the flower sizzled and burned, then wilted completely. Color drained from it, evaporating into the air, leaving only a dried, empty husk where moments ago, fresh petals bloomed.

Before I could speak, Gennevieve brushed off her hand, removing any trace of the act. She fumbled to put her glove back on, tiny tears budding in her eyes. Nelle rubbed gentle circles on her back.

"Some gifts look like curses." Gennevieve grimaced, tucking her hands behind her.

A ripple of discomfort shot up my arm, my own curse reminding me it was still there, waiting to drain me of life like the crumpled flower carcass on the floor.

Hiding was different than holding. Maybe I wasn't the only silk-wrapped snake on this island. Maybe I wasn't the only *Melthith*. But the girl in front of me did not deserve hers, a gentle soul charged with the burden of destruction.

A small, forgotten part of me begged to be unleashed, the same girl that used to know how to turn tides and make her curses her strengths.

"I think you're a warrior." I took her hand. "My crew could use a gift like yours."

Gennevieve's eyes brightened enough to clear even the Dark God's shadows.

The door burst open, scattering the light once again, and Marina sauntered through the door. "Are you ladies still fawning over her? Brigid's balls, Keira, you look stunning." She planted a hand to her hip as she looked me over, her red gossamer dress hugging her like a vine clinging to a tree. Her full lips wrinkled into a frown as her gaze stopped at my shoulder. "Minus that ugly thing."

Nelle smacked her arm. "You don't always have to be so blunt, Marina."

"The truth will set you free," Marina snickered, gesturing grandly toward the door. "Let's go, ladies, we have a whole-ass *Carthu* to get through."

I sucked in a deep breath before walking out into the night. The moon was at her apex, her giant silver eye glaring down at me, and I lifted my chin and rolled back my shoulders. I was a *Melthith* and a wretch. The moon, the stars, the gods could all judge me from their lofty perches if they wanted to. But I would not hide any longer.

There was a purpose to my every step as I followed my new friends towards the river in the center of the compound. Marina wove her arm through mine, and while I'd never admit it, it was nice to have a companion next to me as we made our way into the ceremony.

The others were already there, all waist-deep in the river, gossamer skirts billowing around them like lilies in a pond. Willow, in a pretty pink dress so light it was almost white, laughed as she splashed her sister, the sound doing wonders for the nerves tangled like fishnet in my gut. Cassryn, unbothered, swayed gracefully next to her, black skirt fanning around her like an Ir'desian dancer at her own private ball. Nelle and Gennevieve, now giddy, ran to join them, skipping toward the water with golden laughter.

I didn't recognize Siobhan at first where she spoke with Laureli. Her hair braided intricately in a twisted bun, she wore a warm, sunset-orange gown that softened her usually hard frame in a way I didn't imagine possible, the warrior suddenly a princess before me. The scowl that crossed her face as soon as she saw me, however, was most definitely Siobhan.

No more hiding. I painted on my best Mathonwy smirk in return.

"Does she ever smile?" I whispered to Marina, squeezing her arm tighter for support.

"Siobhan?" Marina's brow furrowed, her usual swagger subdued, a frown tugging at the corner of her full lips. "I'm sure it's been strange with you two, especially with Ronan, but—"

I froze, halting us both as I tugged her arm. "What do you mean, with Ronan?"

Marina sucked in her bottom lip, taking a tentative step away from me before looking back at Siobhan with wide eyes. "If it makes you feel better, he ended it as soon as she wanted more than friendship."

I barely registered her words, ice running down my spine despite the balm of the night.

I met Siobhan during a very lonely time on the island…

My husband's voice floated back into my memory, searing every inch of me like a fish in a skillet. This was the woman who had him when I couldn't. This beautiful, powerful creature that hated me for putting him in her path in the first place. Something dark simmered in my core, primal and possessive, as I imagined her bronze hands on my husband's flesh, her lips on his throat...

Part of me wanted to cut those hands off and slap her with them. A younger, less-cursed version of me would've done exactly that. Would've marched over to her and hit her so hard, she would've forgotten his name. My husband had been vulnerable and lonely, so I couldn't blame him, no matter how badly it stung to know I hadn't been his first. But to know that this woman had *feelings* for him, had wanted more than his body…

Hands fisted at my sides, I bit back the acid, shoving it down my throat with all the petty, jealous words I wanted to hurl at her. "Well, neither of us can have him anymore."

She could hate me all she wanted. Ronan wasn't here, and he wasn't hers, or mine, or anyone's. He had his own life to live now. And I had bigger fish to fry—namely the Dark God that still infested my shoulder like a parasite.

The wind shifted, and Vian's voice cut through my rage like a hot knife.

"Keira!" he shouted, running up to me, a boxy smile slapped across his face. He was absolutely ethereal, a dark fairy from a storybook. In his long, iridescent black tunic, the material draped delicately over his slender frame, there was no doubt he was god-touched. A crown of blue and purple luminant flowers swept back his ebony waves, accentuating the shadows of his high cheekbones. *Wynnaid* indeed; he was the night sky incarnate, my brother in all ways but blood. He raked his pitch-black eyes over me with similar approval. "You look divine."

I couldn't help myself as I tackled him in a vise-tight hug, nearly toppling us both over. "Remind me not to leave without my good luck charm again, *Wynnaid?*" I whispered into his hair, breathing in his summer-breeze scent.

This wraith of a boy had saved my life. Saved me from the cell in Porthladd, but saved me before that, too, in his own cell in Orwellin. Saved me from making a choice I would've regretted forever. Saved me from the black spot on my shoulder in a different way, not letting me sacrifice my morals to end my own misery. And he'd dragged me to the end of the world to save my miserable rump yet again, and I'd never even thanked him for it.

You need me, too. His words from the day in the dungeon rang through me like a bell. No matter what this ceremony brought tonight, no matter how hard or scary it was, I would do it for him, if only to pay the life debt I owed.

His thin arms wrapped tighter around me, a laugh rumbling in his chest. "The wind smiles on you tonight, Captain."

"Welcome, *Adolli,*" Danura boomed across the clearing, wading into the river herself, silver skirts fanning out behind her. I stiffened at her arrival, scanning her hand for injuries. Whatever happened between us was beyond strange, and the memory of the hatred in her eyes as she touched me still burned through me. But this woman seemed entirely unfazed, happy even, as she moved through the water with the grace and fluidity of a nymph. Her hand bore no mark, no evidence of our encounter.

"Thank you, *Serenhi,*" the women answered in unison, Nelle gesturing for Vian and I to join them in the current. I gripped Vian's hand, and together we walked to the river, ready for it to cleanse us of this nightmare. The water was warm, even without the sun's gentle embrace, and I wanted to float away in it. If this ceremony was about truth and forgiveness, this river was the perfect place to drown our secrets. Our pasts. I imagined it whispering to me, not like the ocean once had, but in sweet giggles and babbles. Any worries I had were carried away by my new, cascading friend.

The women formed a semicircle in the wide bank, Nelle to my immediate left, Vian at my right, hand still in mine. Danura stood in the center, arms raised to the heavens. "The *Carthu* is a rite of passage for all who seek to belong to the Annwyn." Her eyes closed as she tilted her face upward, letting the moonlight smile on her. "To be born anew, we must shed the burdens of the past."

The women around us bowed their heads, foreheads nearly kissing the river's tender face. "From water and salt we come, to water and salt we go."

I followed, sucking in a breath as I greeted the river, my own reflection staring back at me. I'd never worshipped in a Temple before, my prayers offered to the gods on my own terms. But there was something immediately captivating about the ritual, the connection stirring up a long-forgotten part of me.

Danura scooped water into her hands, pouring it down her front so her dress clung to her, defining her shape in an amorous caress. "Let the waters of new life wash over you, cleaning the filth of pain and sorrow and healing the wounds of loss and shame."

The women repeated the action, sheer dresses now translucent as they washed themselves in the water. I looked to Vian, expecting a blush on his fair skin, but he only smiled before pouring water down himself, his own clothes embracing his lithe frame. I copied the action, something freeing inside of me, a knot untying. I used to skinny dip on nights like this, the feel of the euphoric water against my bare skin a small victory in itself. I was part of the water, a collection of droplets feeding into a larger pool, our energy one and the same.

A hum rose from the women, a chorus of a sweet melody I'd never heard before. Marina stepped forward, joining hands with Danura in the center, pride in the arch of her back. Danura nodded once to her, and as their fingers interlocked, they rested their foreheads together.

"Who is first?" Danura whispered, but it somehow carried over the humming like a prayer on the wind's back. "Keira?"

The other women all looked at me, kind but expectant expressions written across their faces, Laureli even winking. All except for Siobhan, who still regarded me with the utmost contempt in her furrowed brows.

I froze, discomfort prickling beneath my skin. I wasn't ready. The water suddenly felt cold, and the mark on my shoulder throbbed, waves of pain shooting down my arm. I gripped Vian's hand again, my anchor against this current.

"I'll go," Siobhan announced, and when no one objected, my worry subsided. She trudged to the center, chin high. With an easy movement despite the damp, heavy fabric, she slipped from her gown, her bronze-cut form on full display. But her chin didn't fall, nor did her gaze, as she stood brave and bare before the congregation. The humming intensified, now a chant of strange, ancient words, the women all swaying and swishing to its heartbeat. It was both dizzying and electrifying, the perfect synchronicity enveloping the small circle like the eye of a hurricane.

A sliver of a smile lifting the sharp corner of her lips, Siobhan reached for Marina's free hand.

The second they made contact, she began to speak-sing, the words hurried and frantic, but clear. "My mother sold me to slavers when she found out I wasn't a *faoladh*. I was a warrior, their very best. I was supposed to be their queen, and they reduced me to nothing. The men they sold me to abused me, they *raped* me, and left me for dead." Her whole frame shook, but her eyes stayed upward, fire brighter than the sun blazing in them. Her song became an anthem, louder and more deliberate. "Now, I am reborn. I will never be weak again. No one will ever touch me without my consent again. I was a slave. Now, I'm a weapon."

And in a flash of blinding orange light, Siobhan collapsed into the water, the river dragging her under.

I screamed, the sound tearing from my throat as I rushed to her, sloshing through the water with abandon. No one else moved, no one else dove to save her, their tempest song growing louder and louder to drown out my cries.

Panic wrapped its fingers around my throat, squeezing tight. She had to be drowning, no bubbles or splashing signaling her life.

Until Siobhan crested, leaping through the air in a graceful arc, her great citrine *tail* snapping behind her.

Sirens and Secrets

KEIRA

My mind warred with my eyes.

Siobhan's tail was like a tropical fish's, her scales glittering like gemstones. Gills carved dark chasms in her ribcage, and her eyes seemed brighter, *wider*, as they drank in the dark. She smiled at me, revealing a row of jagged teeth made to tear and devour. She was both beautiful and deadly. Water and salt. Salvation and ruin in one.

A harsh laugh escaped me as I sank further into the water. "You're *sirens*?"

"*Haleni.*" Vian fished me from where I stood in the river, my mouth agape like a decked cod, a knowing smirk on his lips. "Salt-born."

"Not what you were expecting, hmm?" Nelle's violet eyes danced as she held her hand out. Tentatively, I took it, letting her guide me back to the circle. Her touch sent a familiar glow of tranquility through me, and this time I gobbled it down greedily, desperate for comfort.

They were sirens.

The pieces all fell into place. Their strange, unexplainable gifts, their secrecy, their sisterhood…

As if she could read my mind, Siobhan swam up to Danura, her sharp fangs exposed. A kind smile on the Silver Sword's face, she extended her free arm to the citrine siren, her pale flesh reflective in the moonlight.

I almost lost my lunch when Siobhan sank her glittering teeth into the flesh just beneath the crux of her master's elbow and *drank*. If it weren't for Nelle's quiet power sweeping through me, I might have screamed again.

"Don't worry, Keira, it doesn't hurt her."

Siobhan pulled back, lips stained bright red, beaming up at Danura like a goddess. The woman smiled back, fondly stroking the side of Siobhan's face, bright blood running freely down her forearm.

The humming resumed as if nothing happened, Siobhan wiping her face as she joined the circle again, Danura and Marina still in their embrace, the ceremony kicking up once again. The *Carthu* had only just begun.

A breathless laugh floated from me, dizzy and giddy—from the revelations or Nelle's gift, I didn't know. I was a *Melthith* among sirens, one demon of the deep sharing her heart with seven others cut from the same cursed fabric.

A part of me felt a tinge of fear at these creatures with gilded claws, the villains of every sailor's story. They could rip me to shreds or drink me dry if they wanted to. But a much larger part of me welcomed it. We were the same. Ruination and destruction. Beauty and power. *Duweni.* Godsborn demons with the ability to flatten any truth that threatened to cripple us.

The next siren swaggered forward. Laureli. Without shame or hesitation, she ripped the gown from her body and grabbed Marina's hand.

Her song was a war cry, tempestuous and raw. "I was the greatest seer in all of Hud. I was a warning bell, proud and strong. But I was stolen from my home by pirates that wanted to use me for my gifts. They stowed me belowdecks, letting me in rot the dark and damp, using me for my eyes but never allowing me to see. Now my gifts are uncompromisable."

She let free a violent howl and plunged herself into the depths, emerging again remade, coated in emerald scales from her navel down.

One by one, they swam forward, their songs adding to the storm, the frenzy. Some were wild and riotous, others bittersweet and painful, but they were all heard, all echoed by the circle. And as the light broke the darkness each time, we all sang for them, sang *with* them, sharing both their hurt and their triumph as one. And one by one, they sipped from Danura's wound like it was the fountain of life.

"We were mapmakers, traveling the world, unearthing the secrets." Cassryn and Willow were next, an eerie unison to their twin tale. They held each other close, their voices low but carrying over the water like morning mist. "But we lost ourselves along the way. We pay the price of our mistake and lead others to safety."

"I was my father's favorite daughter. I lived for my brothers and sisters, working the land with them, sowing life into the soil day in and day out. But Papa was a mean drunk, and he'd beat the life out of us every night when the sun set. I took it to protect my family, my brothers and sisters, but one night it went too far." Gennevieve sobbed into Marina's arms, clad only in her gloves. But there was power in her pain, the little duck transformed into a swan in the river. "Now, no one can hurt me. No one can bruise or beat me. Now I am death's dark hand."

I didn't remember when I joined in, when my voice became the loudest and proudest. But I sang myself raw, letting the water fuel me and the current carry me. My throat turned to fire, but I didn't care. I belted the loudest for Nelle as she made her stand in the water.

"All I ever wanted was to bring people healing, but my life was taken from me by people that only know hate. I was the greatest healer in all of Pysgodd." Her song was a lullaby, the calm in the eye of the hurricane. "My medicines were priceless, refined from the finest materials in the Deyrnas. I saved hundreds of lives, but I could not save the ones that mattered most. My son and my husband were killed for greed, and I bear their marks. I bear the survivor's guilt. I do my part now taking care of my sisters as I should've cared for them."

When she emerged again, her beautiful amethyst fins reflecting the moonlight, my tears broke free, the storm in my soul releasing.

Vian swam forward, tearing me from the moment, the hair of my neck prickling with worry. But there was no trace of fear on his expression, his jaw set and his coal black eyes burning. He took Marina's outstretched hand, the baritone of his voice sustained and amplified by the wind, like he was a whole chorus unto himself. "I was raised a slave, and now a runaway." He stripped, the black clothes discarded into the river, revealing countless jagged scars across his chest and back. Some were fresher—red and angry, like they still remembered the lash. Others were deep-set and aged, now permanent reminders of the years he'd lived with them.

My breath stole from my chest. What had they done to him in Orwellin? Gods above and below, what had this boy endured? Deep within me, a different storm stirred, vicious and angry, a tidal wave begging to be unleashed.

Vian did not hide. Running a wide hand across his mutilated chest, a smile brighter than sunlight on the horizon broke across his face. "But I am *Duweni*. I am a son of the wind and sky. I am *more*. One day I will be their reckoning. One day, I will walk hand in hand with liberation and I will set the world free from the darkness I was caged in."

There was no physical transformation, no flash of light, no drinking of blood, but Vian was changed. The slope of his shoulders shifted, the tilt of his chin more pronounced. Not a slave turned songbird—a phoenix rising from the ashes. Night made man, spreading his death-black wings, ready to take the whole sky in their span.

The song came to a stop, eyes turning to me, waiting.

"Keira?" Danura's voice was hoarse, though I hadn't heard her sing. "Will you join us?"

"I—" Agony slithered down my arm at the thought, slow and tortuous, though I wasn't entirely sure it was physical. "I'm not going to drink your blood."

"Keira, it's time to let go of your pain. Your guilt." Nelle's calm hugged me close, her words melting my final wall.

Vian reached for me, long fingers wrapping around my wrists, my savior pulling me to safe shores once more. "It's time, *Ariannad*. It's your turn."

The singing began again, as soft and subtle as the tide shifting. Swallowing down the last of my fear, I shifted to Marina.

No more hiding. No more running. It was time to face my fate.

Before I could convince myself not to, I slipped off my dress and clutched Marina's hand. "I left my crew and husband behind, and it hurts." The first wave tore from my mouth without melody or rhythm. "I miss them. I miss my Papa. I'm not enough on my own."

I broke down, falling to my knees in the water, Marina's hand my only lifeline. Darkness burned through me, my arm screaming in pain. Sobs tore from my throat unabashedly, and my throat closed around them.

I missed them. I missed them all.

I couldn't do this alone.

I couldn't do this.

"Dig deeper, *Ariannad*." Vian's hand came to rest on my back, a cool breeze licking the sweat from my neck, his strength seeping into me.

I was not alone.

I was never alone.

I pushed past the agony, past the darkness battling in my chest. My song was rough, unbalanced, but I sang it anyway, Marina's hand in mine and Vian's touch on my back mooring me to the melody. "My uncles are dead because of me. Because of my bad decisions, my poor judgement calls. I killed Lochlan, and I almost killed Ronan. I wasn't strong enough to save any of them. I'm not strong enough to save anyone. People only get hurt because of me." I let it all out, spat and vomited it into the river. The river didn't judge. It just accepted and cleansed, letting me empty myself of the pain, the guilt. Of every mistake that followed me, every missed step, every rotten word said in anger. Every ghost that haunted me, Papa's bloody corpse, Aidan's, Lochlan's... Amilee and Toivo's... Weylin's. Ronan's...

The river washed away every rotten part of me that I'd been holding inside, everything I'd let fester and spread like the sickness on my arm. Save one final thought, one final admission.

My grip around Marina's hand tightened as I parted with the final piece of what I owed the Dark God. "I deserve to die instead. I deserve this."

I drew a ragged breath, my whole body shaking at the effort, my sobs running dry.

"You deserve the world, *Ariannad*." Danura sank lower into the water, facing me now. Taking my face in her smooth hands, she kissed my forehead once, tears in her eyes. "You are strong and capable and beautiful."

"Strong, capable, beautiful." The chorus joined in, the harmony rattling through me. Fresh tears started as their words struck my exposed, raw core.

Danura kissed my head again, lips soft as a butterfly's wing. "You are precious and driven. You are the silver wheel, steering the course through deep waters, a guiding light to all who are lost."

"Precious and driven," the sirens echoed again, louder now.

"Let it go." Danura's final kiss delivered an abundance of fresh energy blazing over me and inside me. "Time to move forward, *Ariannad*."

And when she pushed me fully into the river's embrace, when I sank into the salt, the light that exploded from my core was entirely mine. The whole island bathed in it, brighter than every star I'd ever counted on Papa's deck.

I was darkness. I was rotten and wicked. I was a monster. I was destruction.

But I was also light. It was a small part of me, but it was mine. It was the moon, glowing overhead, an uproarious protest against the encroaching night, a beacon to the lost and the damned.

When I emerged again, the mark on my shoulder was no bigger than a bullethole.

My soaked dress back on, I sat with my knees to my chest on the bank of the river, toes in the coarse, pink sand as I tried to process what happened.

What *had* happened under the water?

I remembered the light—the burning, blazing light. But it did not turn me into a siren. It did not give me fangs or scales or claws or bloodlust. It gave me something much, much deadlier.

I felt it, unlocked deep within me, the glowing, flickering, twisting thing. It was storm and stone, both wild and fixed. It was foreign, new and undefined, primordial and unformed, waiting to be forged.

But it was also me. It was mine.

I'd been lost for so long, I forgot what it felt like. But in the river, I found something. Something I didn't even know I'd lost.

Sometimes we fall because there is something down there we need to find.

The women—*the sirens*—danced and swam and sang still, their song now a jig, a celebration of the *Carthu* well done. Some staggered off, their duties calling them, but nearly half stayed, joy bright on their expressions. Part of me ached to join them, ached to dance and sing until I dropped, my body feeling lighter than it had in months. The spot on my shoulder was so much smaller now, and while I could still feel it, still sense the lecherous sap on my energy, it was less. Muted.

Part of me didn't know how to dance anymore. Where did I start? Stripped of my burdens, what would be left to fuel my steps?

Gennevieve broke from the sirens, swimming up to me with the sweetest of smiles on her young face. She rested her arms against the river's bank, turquoise tail wagging behind her like puppy, blonde fringe stuck to her forehead. "You doing alright, Keira?"

"Aye." I hugged my knees tighter to me, forcing a smile. "I just need some space...it's been a long night."

"Sorry to trouble you." A frown creased her forehead. "I know the tails are a lot, and the blood thing...but we get a bad reputation. We're cursed, not cruel. Usually, we only drink animal blood, and none of us have ever lured anyone to their death, as far as I know—"

I laughed, the sound sparkling from that glowing place in my core, halting her with a gentle hand on her elbow. "No, Genni, you're never any trouble. It's a lot to process, but you all saved me. I know who you are on the inside, no matter how many fish parts you have or what you like to eat. Thank you for checking on me."

Murky waters cleared from her eyes, the river carrying away any of the shame that still rested on the girl's shoulders. Even with her razor-sharp teeth, her smile was luminous. "You know, Danura might be able to help. She should be just beyond the clearing." There was a deep knowing in her stare, eyes of a girl who'd seen far more than she should've at her age but decided with quiet strength to grin despite it. She winked before joining the revelry once more, calling out over her shoulder, "Stay close to the treeline. Things get spooky at night."

I sat in the sand a moment longer, contemplating my options, not necessarily wanting to face anything that spooked a siren. But Danura's touch still lingered, the strange energy that flowed between us still fresh at my fingertips. She was the only one that hadn't shifted, but perhaps she was something more than a siren. Perhaps Genni was right. Perhaps another conversation would quell the last harsh edges of doubt still gnawing at me.

Small victories, Keira girl. What do you want, and how do you get it?

I wanted to know how she healed my mark, or mostly healed it, anyway. I wanted to know if it meant I had a future outside of this island. I wanted to know what the thing inside me was, and if it was here to stay. I wanted to know what Danura was, if not the siren queen.

But more than anything, I wanted someone to hold my hand, kiss my forehead, and tell me it was going to be alright again.

I stood. No more overthinking. No more hiding. Following Gennevieve's advice, I stuck to the trees, not looking to run into any of the little *neid* anywhere, or worse.

Two dozen paces west of the river, I heard them before I saw them.

"*Serenhi*, please." Nelle's voice, laced with an uncharacteristic panic, pierced the balmy night. "She has to know, this is just cruel."

I halted, ducking behind the nearest tree. Legs sturdy beneath me, I crawled on the mossy ground, cursing the damp fabric of my dress. Careful not to rustle any leaves, I shifted until I spotted them.

In a smaller clearing, framed by tall, dark trees, Danura stood with her back to Marina, Laureli, and Nelle, all in their human forms again, her jaw clenched tightly. The moon cast shadows through the dense leaves, but it was bright enough to see by, and I didn't need a spyglass to note the anguish written across the sirens' faces.

My heart thundered in my chest, so loud it was a miracle they didn't hear it. I kept my breathing quiet.

"She's one of us now, she has a right." Marina shook, tears staining her face.

Dread pooled in my core, her words sinking like stones. What did I deserve to know? *So much for no more hiding.*

"You don't think I know that? She has *always* been one of us." Danura spun on her, a snarl escaping her lips. "But she's not safe going back."

"And neither is he if she doesn't!" Marina did not balk, fists at her sides in bold defiance. "He was one of ours, too."

"Still is." Nelle lifted her chin, stepping closer to Marina, two sentries dutifully manning their posts.

Danura reached out, pity dripping from her frown, but Marina recoiled, lip quivering. Danura sighed, clasping her hands in front of her. "You know I'm fond of the boy, but he forfeited our protection the day he left."

He. The boy.

Ronan.

My Ronan.

My hand flew to my mouth to keep myself from crying out. It took every ounce of my self-control not to collapse where I was, or attack and demand answers.

"She has the right to make the same decision." Laureli's voice was quiet, but she stood tall, leaning forward into her height. *Think tall, and you'll be tall.* I wondered if Papa had learned that from her, too.

"I said, enough," Danura seethed, raising her hand to strike, but Nelle stepped in her path, and Danura caught herself.

I was surprised by the fire in Nelle's stare, her violet eyes suddenly reminding me of Esme—a hurricane made flesh. "*Serenhi,* there is a war going on, and if we don't tell her, that boy will be swept away with it, along with the whole Deyrnas."

My chest swelled and seized, battling itself. The kinship toward these women, who spoke for me and Ronan both, burned brighter than starlight. But my rage was stronger, *deeper,* as her words pierced my flesh, arrows raining down into my softest parts.

War in the Deyrnas. And Ronan, *my* Ronan....

"So? Let them all rot. What good have any of them done for you?" Danura's voice was ice, slicing through me with the precision of one of Griffin's swords. "You know their wickedness firsthand. I feel sorry for the boy, I do, but my mind is made up."

It was not me that moved, not consciously. Captained by the smoldering, scorching thing inside, I trudged forward. But I relished the movement, savored every step.

I was going to tear her apart. And then, when I was done, I was going to save my husband from whatever grim fate the sirens were trying to protect him from.

"Tell me everything." My voice was not recognizable. For months, it had been weak, quivering, soft. Not anymore. Now, I was something stronger.

Danura's already-pale face went ghost-white as I stepped into the pool of moonlight. She waved the sirens off, Laureli shooting her a glare before leading the crying Marina away. They both offered me sad smiles as they left, defeat resting heavy on their shoulders. Only Nelle hesitated, shifting her weight uncomfortably, eyes downcast.

Danura smoothed her dress, painting on a pretty grin. "*Ariannad.*"

The white-hot flame deep in my core ignited again, the name a call to war. I was not her silver wheel, a precious tool to be used and puppeteered. I was my father's daughter, with the stars in my eyes and the wind in my sails. I was my husband's wife, with a viper's smile and a dragon's heart. I was my crew's Captain, made of sea and blood and sky and salt.

I would not forget again.

"No. My name is Keira. Keira Branwen-Mathonwy." I kept my expression as cold and hard as marble, but the tumultuous, ravenous thing still swirled and blistered beneath the surface. My next command had the authority of the whole sea behind it. "Nelle, tell me everything."

Nelle was hurried, desperate, clasping my hand in hers. "There is a war. Laureli had a vision—"

"Silence, Nelle." Danura's voice rose, a wave about to break, her eyes wide with fear.

Nelle did not pause, did not heed her call, defiance in the delicate tilt of her chin. A dove turned hawk. "Ronan and your crew are headed straight for trouble. He's going to need you, otherwise he's gone."

Gone.

My heart stopped and started, the contents of my dinner threatening to reappear. I staggered back, limbs heavy as cannonballs.

Lyr below, I had abandoned him. I left him behind, knowing there were slaves in the Deyrnas, knowing people were starving. Knowing it was the perfect recipe for disaster. Yet I was so selfish and foolish, I couldn't see past the mark on my shoulder. Couldn't see past my own guilt and grief, blurring my vision and deafening my ears.

I was no longer powerless, no longer afraid of the Dark God, or Connor, or myself. I was no longer afraid of death. Death would be afraid of *me*.

"I'm leaving." It wasn't a question. Finding my sealegs beneath me, I stormed off into the trees.

A hand around my wrist halted me, Danura rooting me to my spot. "No, you are not."

I shook her off, the force inside me sizzling at her touch. I would not be chained. I would not be shackled. I ripped her silver bracelets from my wrists and threw them to the ground, stomping them into the bare earth. "I thought I was a guest, not a prisoner. Now I'm going to go and save my husband, whether you like it or not."

Hurt flashed across Danura's features, bleeding into an entitled sneer. "You and your friend will not make it off this island alive without my help. I thought you cared for Vian. Will you condemn him too? What good are you to anyone dead?"

The mention of Vian twisted my insides. The thought of leaving him behind cut deep, the wrongness of it shrieking in the back of my mind. But I could not ask him to risk his life for me again. Not to go back to the people that would chain him and cage him, the people who had scarred him and tortured him, mind and body. Still,

I kept my expression flat, my mask impenetrable. "I do not fear death. Let him come for me. Vian can stay here if he wants."

A scoff behind us both had me spinning, my heels digging into the warm dirt. Vian stood at the clearing's edge with his arms crossed, his form flirting with a shadow, already dressed and packed.

"I'm coming, too." He slinked forward, adjusting the canvas bag on his shoulder, my favorite boxy smile sparkling against the blackness. He threaded his fingers through mine. "We are the same. We stick together, *Ariannad. Duweni.*"

As much as I'd grown to hate the names whispered to me in the shade of my own mind, hearing them on Vian's lips renewed me.

Silver wheel. Godsborn. Soul Wind. Same. Together, we would sail to whatever fresh hell waited for us. Together, we would save our little family, and anyone else that needed us.

Gratitude surged through me, warmer than sunlight. I wouldn't ask him, I couldn't. But I would not deny his help, either, if he was offering it willingly. I squeezed his hand, trying to pour every ounce of my boundless appreciation into the place where we connected. "Should've known you were listening. Thank you, *Wynnaid.*"

Hand in hand, we walked away, ready to leave Danura and this forsaken island at our backs. The sirens could have their *Carthu.* My truth was beyond these trees. My home.

My husband.

"*Ariannad,* stop. *Now.*" Fear rose in Danura's quivering voice, ugly and possessive.

I didn't look back when I answered her. No going back. Only moving on. Only letting go. "You're not my Captain or my queen. I do not answer to you."

Her voice was a lethal low, a rumble before thunder, but it carried. "No, I am your *mother.*"

I halted in my tracks, stalling Vian. Slowly, I turned to look at her. She stood still, silver eyes—*my eyes*—afire, eagerness and distress warring in her expression.

The word echoed, intensifying the swirl in my chest.

Mother.

"What?"

She took four long, lithe steps to me, tucking a strand of midnight hair behind my ear. It burned where she touched, but I was too frozen to flinch. She swallowed, throat bobbing, before she continued, "Your father, when he was here...he and I shared something beautiful. And you were born, and I loved you so much. But your Papa took you, said it was safer to raise you with your own kind..." Tears streamed freely down her ivory cheeks, accentuating the constellation of light freckles. My freckles. She took my face in her hands, holding me like I was both priceless and fragile.

My heart stopped and started again. No one knew my mother, only that Papa loved her well. She was lost to my history, no more potent or real than a ghost. "You're lying."

The Queen of the Lost looked at me with sad eyes. I'd seen the look before, but as an outsider. I'd see it on Reina as she waved goodbye to Reagan, on Vala as she straightened Griffin's coat. "No, *Ariannad*. I'm not lying. Not anymore."

Something—perhaps the orphaned, lonesome child that still lived deep down—threatened to break under the weight of her gaze. "Come with me then," I choked out, my head spinning as I tried to hang on to my last threads of strengths. "Help me save him."

"I can't." Hurt strangled her voice, face twisting in agony. "*Ariannad*, listen to me. Look what you've been subjected to out there. I have waited for you to come home to me for twenty-one years. I'm not letting you run away again to go get killed."

For a moment, I let myself imagine. I imagined being on Papa's ship, Danura's kind, cunning eyes watching me as I climbed the mast. I imagined her teaching me to braid my hair or kissing my knee when I scraped it. I imagined her on Traeth Beach, calling me and Ronan home for supper, her windchime voice carrying over the sandy shore. I imagined her laughing with Vala while making berry bread or scolding me for sneaking out with Griffin.

I imagined her holding me close when Papa died, her tears mixing with mine. Imagined her there on my wedding day, tying me into a dress she bought for me instead of Finna's hand-me-down. Imagined her toe-to-toe with Connor, her power and grace cutting down his backstabbing plays with brutal efficiency.

But they were not memories. They were nothing more than the daydreams of a lonely girl, one I'd left behind long ago.

I had no time for fantasies. My real family was waiting.

"I don't need a mother. I need my husband."

Vian did not protest as I dragged him into the thicket of Hiraeth.

28

Ancestors and Allies

KEIRA

Voices screamed inside my head as the dark forms of the *Hiraethean* jungle whirled past us, though they were not the ones I'd grown accustomed to.

Mother. Ariannad.

Danura's voice echoed within me, my head aching as I pushed forward, Vian in tow. Perhaps if I ran far enough, I could forget this awful place, forget the woman with silver eyes and a dagger tongue. Forget the small, broken part of me that craved her affection like the attention-starved little girl I was.

The part of me that loved my husband was louder, as were Nelle and Marina's words.

He's going to need you.

There was nothing else but that as I cut through the thicket, stumbling blindly beneath the moon's meager glow. If it weren't for Vian's hand in mine, I would've started running, not caring if I fell into a ditch or ran into a tree. I needed to find the shore and something buoyant enough to float. That was my only task.

"Keira, we should slow down." Vian's voice was low, a quiver stuck in his throat. "There are things out here—"

"I don't think we have time. They aren't just going to let us leave." I silenced him, swallowing down my own fear. I didn't care what might be slithering along the ground in *Hiraeth*. It was just another reason to put the whole Lyr-forsaken place half a sea behind us.

As we pushed past a particularly stubborn vine, we nearly ran into the most odious creature I knew on the island, her fangs bared and her staff pointed at my throat again.

"Stop right there." Siobhan smacked me hard across the face with the base of the staff. Stinging pain rocked me from my spot, rage boiling in my core as I stumbled back.

"Siobhan, that wasn't the plan!" Nelle scolded as she slipped out of the nearest shadow. Like she was approaching a wounded animal, she stepped towards me carefully, hand extended. I stiffened, knowing her delicate features were a mask for a creature just as deadly as Siobhan, but I did not flinch as she touched me. With a single graze of her elegant fingers, the pain evaporated into thin air.

"Thanks," I muttered, eyes still trained on Siobhan and her staff of doom.

A smug grin crawled over the predator's features. "Danura is right. You won't make it out of here alive on your own."

I clenched my fists at my sides, trying to keep my breathing even. As much as I wanted to wring her neck, to test the glowing heat in my core and see if it had its own set of fangs, I did not have time for Siobhan and her pettiness. My husband needed me, preferably uninjured. "Listen, fish-for-brains, I get why you don't like me, but if you ever actually cared for Ronan, you'll let me go to him now."

Nelle winced at the insult, but Siobhan didn't so much as blink. After a moment, her staff lowered, her stony eyes giving way to something wild. "I know." The corner of her mouth tilted upward, her grin untamed. "We're coming."

Perhaps the island had truly made me insane...or she smacked me too hard. "What?"

Vian's brow furrowed as he stepped instinctively closer to my side. "Then why did you hit her?"

Siobhan's grin dropped like it was heavy. "You deserved it for leaving him alone in the first place." She weighed her staff, tossing it between both hands like she was debating on smacking me with it again. I braced for impact, but none came, a rueful sigh in its place. "But you're going to need warriors and weapons. I happen to be both."

I studied her for a moment, the fire in her gaze, the square cut of her chin. She was determined, that was clear, and useful. As much as I hated it to admit it, she was a weapon carved from pain, forged in hatred, and sharpened by experience. But I didn't know if I could trust her not to put those skills to the test and drown me the second we were on the water.

"You hate me." It was not a question, but her response would be the only test I could afford to administer. I had wasted too much time already. My Ronan was waiting.

"Aye. I hate you." There was nothing fanciful adorning her voice, only the cutting edge of a blade, the truth both clean and painful. "But I love him more."

Her words poured dog piss in an exposed wound, but I tried not to let it show. I loved him more, too. More was enough to endure whatever fresh hell it would be to sail with Siobhan. More was enough to endure death itself if that's what it took to save him.

I looked to Nelle, noticing the oversized sack she carried with surprising ease in one hand. "You too?"

The woman's smile flickered like a candle on a stormy night as she worried her lip between her teeth. "Laureli's vision...you'll need a healer. But I wanted to come, too. I made a vow to watch over the people I care about, and Ronan is one of them."

The cavernous pit in my stomach doubled, not wanting to know why we might need a healer handy, but my heart swelled at her kindness, too. At their loyalty to Ronan. Loyalty that had not wavered even when I did.

I needed these women by my side. Ronan needed them, too.

I looked to Vian for any indication of his displeasure, but he only shrugged, leaving the choice in my hands. My eyes flicked back to Siobhan as I gripped Vian's hand tighter, letting his steady warmth ease any lingering doubt. Perhaps I was a fool, perhaps she would lead me right back to Danura—*my mother*—and cage me on this island of wonders and horrors. But I had to believe that Ronan had true friends sleeping among the sirens. "Lead the way, then."

Siobhan steeled her gaze, slipping into her familiar role as she scanned the trees around us. No one knew this jungle like she did. She belonged to it. I waited as she calculated, sweaty palm gripping Vian's. "We're getting close to the shore. We'll have to make a raft or something, since you two can't shift—"

A cracked twig nearby silenced her, and the hairs on the back of my neck stood straighter. In unison, we took a ready stance, pressing our backs together. I craned for any further sound, but I was greeted only by the thunderous beat of my own pulse.

"What was that?" Vian hissed, folded tightly to Nelle's side. The siren's fangs flashed, a dove trained among tigers.

"Hush." Siobhan's voice was lower than the morning tide, her muscled back radiating heat through mine. Another crack due east and much, much closer had us both whirling toward it, Siobhan's staff at the ready.

I heard him before I saw him. Heard the deep, ancient voice slither into the very depths of my being.
Duweni.

When his dripping form appeared in the clearing, sunken eyes and inky skin bleeding into the onyx of the night, I was the only one who didn't shriek. Recognition was instantaneous, hitting me like a staff across the face.

"Get back, all of you." Siobhan was the first to react, swinging her staff with unparalleled force, missing the *ceffyl* by mere inches as it bucked out of the way. When the horse reared, razor sharp teeth bared, Siobhan raised her staff to strike again.

"No! Don't hurt him!" I caught the weapon as she brought it down, blocking her path and setting my back to the *ceffyl*. She opened her mouth to protest, but her words were stolen from her, eyes wider than moons as the *ceffyl* nudged my back with his nose.

I turned, meeting my companion's abyss-black eyes. "Hey there, Dewy."

I could almost hear my husband in my mind as I greeted our old friend. *"Great, let's give the murderous water horse a pet name."*

The horse huffed, nostrils flaring as he breathed me in, but stayed still, no sign of aggression in his powerful form.

"Dewy?" Nelle's voice quivered, throat bobbing as she shimmied ever so slightly behind Siobhan and her still-readied staff.

"He's my friend." I ignored them both, stroking the creature's damp mane, letting the seaweed-like hair slip through my fingers. The animal whinnied and nipped at the end of my braid, no more frightening than a well-trained steed. An unexpected laugh tumbled from me, light amidst the damp, suffocating humidity of the *Hiraethean* wilderness.

"*Duweni.*" Vian's laugh was brighter than a fresh star in the night sky. Fearless, he strode up to the *ceffyl*, patting his rump firmly. Twice. "I like him."

Nelle and Siobhan looked as if they were seconds from giving birth to a pair of sea-cows. I swear to Lyr I could hear the horse's dark chuckle in the back of my mind, like waves lapping against a rocky shore.

Follow, Ariannad, he commanded, my guide once more.

Last time, he'd led me not to what I wanted, but to what I needed even more. I said a silent prayer to Lyr that he had not abandoned me completely, that this was a messenger sent to right my course, a silver wheel in need of steering.

"He wants us to follow. Let's go." Vian surprised me as he translated for Nelle and Siobhan, winking once my way so fast I almost missed it. *Duweni* indeed.

Without any hesitation, the *ceffyl* brayed and stalked off into the night, a chipper Vian on his heels. The sirens and I followed dutifully, Siobhan still choking her staff with a white-knuckled grip.

We wove rapidly through the foliage, the sound of the sea crashing against the shore growing louder and louder the farther we traveled. My heart echoed its call, thundering wildly in my chest. Each beat seemed to sing his name, over and over like a war chant— *Ro-nan, Ro-nan, Ro-nan*—as I marched through the bioluminescent nightmare after Dewy. But I didn't care. I didn't care when my dress snagged, or when thorns and twigs pricked me hard enough to draw blood. I wanted to be out, to find a raft, and to go home.

To my Ronan. My husband.

Even if it meant diving headfirst into a war I knew little about.

It was three hundred paces or so when Dewy came to a decisive halt. The underfoot was sandy, and as we brushed past the last few trees, the shoreline greeted us with its horizon-wide smile. And resting in the shallows of the small beach, kissed by the moon's light, a small, single-masted schooner. Carved from ebony, she was in perfect health, floating gracefully in the shallow tide. A few mended sails, and we'd be on the high seas before sunup. I squinted against the darkness, making out the white letters on the side.

Awelymor. Sea breeze.

My heart started and stopped.

A fine ship, ours for the taking. Just big enough for a crew of four, and fast enough to outrun whatever *Hiraeth* sent after us when Danura realized I'd unintentionally kidnapped two of her favorite subjects.

It should've been named *Salvation.*

"This is better than a raft." Vian ran clumsily across the sand to the *Awelymor*, arms open wide and smile wider as he splashed into the water. "I don't know whose it is, but it is mine now! The Sea Breeze…it suits me."

"I don't know—" Siobhan stammered, staggering toward the small craft. Wading into the water, she poked it with her staff, making sure it wasn't a mirage intended to trick her. "I do rounds every night, and I've never seen—"

Nelle laughed, unbridled and free as she joined Siobhan, her skirts billowing around her. "Let's not look the gift horse in the mouth, shall we?"

"Thank you, Dewy." I planted a kiss on the *ceffyl's* cheek, tears brimming in my eyes. Again, this creature had come to my aid in the darkest hour, a gift from the gods themselves.

The horse licked my cheek with a wet, slimy tongue, and I swatted him away, wiping my face with my shirt.

Until the world stops turning. He did not bid me any other farewell before disappearing into the midnight mist.

"Well, Captain." Vian's grin was wicked as he boarded the ship, standing on the bow like a figurehead, ready to pierce the horizon with his will alone. "Let's set sail."

I sucked in a steadying breath, swallowing down my dizzying excitement and fear as they jumbled up inside me, tighter than sailor's knots.

Later, I'd unravel them. Later, I'd worry about the strange new buzzing in my deepest parts, and the bullethole-sized curse it battled. Later, I'd consider the women I was leaving behind, and the one who dared title herself *Mother*.

All I cared about now was saving my husband from the fate I'd forsaken him to. My Ronan.

I dove into the water, unafraid and unwavering.

Strategies and Snares

RONAN

Mornings in Bachtref were always too bright. The sunlight streaming through the open window of the Golden Sickle Inn blinded me, and it wasn't even eight in the morning. I covered my eyes, the headache throbbing between them.

It's just the sun, I lied to myself.

And perhaps the fact that I'd been up all night bickering with Ellian about our next move, the blacksmith denser than the iron anvils he hammered against.

"Keep up, we've been over this." I rubbed my temples, ignoring the bone-deep hunger that sloshed around in my stomach. *I'm just tired. Just the sun.* With a sigh, I scanned Finna's map again, highlighting the faint red line that tracked from Orwellin straight to Ir'de. The land of silks and scents was the artery of Connor and Locasta's operation, their only source of food. Without it, Orwellin was just a hunk of marble floating in the ocean. "Pysgodd isn't enough. We need to monopolize Ir'de if we're going to have any chance at feeding people. They've been fair trading with us, but they are still trading with them, too. It's time to choose a side."

Ellian leaned back in his chair, running a hand through his haphazard curls. "I know. I'm a Councilman, Ronan. I sign the contracts."

The ugly, ravenous beast in my chest bristled, readying for a chance to bear his fangs. "Without reading them, if I remember correctly." It was a cheap shot, dredging up the history we both wanted to bury, but the rotten part of me took it anyway, rolling my sleeves back. I was already too warm, too tired to keep my composure, my mask slipping and the rage and hunger swimming to the surface. "It's a shame I never got to work with you before my divorce."

Ellian grimaced, but the insult glanced off him like he was made of the same steel he wielded. "We have the Pysgoddian council on our side. Now that the ice is thawing, it'll be easier—"

"I know, Councilwoman Tommins sent me a letter as well." I waved Ellian off. The old Councilwoman had been a drinking buddy of Cedric's, one I met on our very first trip to Pysgodd. Like the snowy mountains of her home island, she was as formidable as she was cold, and would not yield easily to corruption. When Ellian sent his first round of letters—the ones that cast him as an outlaw, the ones that detailed Connor and Locasta's treachery for the world to see—she was the first to toss in her support. But even with Pysgodd defecting from the High Council, we were still outnumbered and outpaced. I stared again at the jagged outline of Ir'de on the map in front of me. "But we need to start moving things soon. Our recent haul was better than most, but unless we can get Ir'desians to deal with us at a lower rate, we won't have anything left to trade in a week."

"I'll write to Councilman Travers again." Ellian grumbled the Ir'desian councilmember's name as he pulled a fresh piece of parchment from underneath a pile of other hastily-written correspondences—some far less friendly than others—from councilmembers and merchants across the Deyrnas.

We'd had a skirmish or two with some guards, but this was what war really looked like: tired faces, ink scratched against parchment, two friends bickering as the morning light blinded them. Councilmembers bartering lives in exchange for coin. People bartering loyalty for scraps of bread. Sailors bartering sleep for precious time.

It had only been a month since we left Porthladd, but it felt like a lifetime.

"Remind Travers no one else will buy all of his spices if we're all dead, aye?" I stood, stuffing my hands in my pockets. I needed to be out of the sunlit nightmare, somewhere dark and cold where I didn't have to think about greedy Councilmen and cold war strategies and how *exhausted* I was.

Ellian nodded, his protest dying with the last breath of his own energy, fatigue steering us both to calmer waters. "I'll write Agatha again too, see if she knows anyone in Ir'de with influence. I think she has a cousin there."

"Captain?" Griffin peered through the doorway, red hair a tangled mess, white tunic unbuttoned and disheveled as if he'd just woken from a restful sleep. My envy was a hissing pit of snakes in my gut, my limbs groaning, desperate for anything soft to pass out on. Griffin grimaced as he took me in, confirming my suspicion; I looked just as bad as I felt. "Sorry to interrupt, but Reina and Reese are here."

Out of time yet again. I bit my cheek to stop myself from cursing my own father to the Dark God's keep for being early. This was a good thing, really; the more sunlight we had to unload our ship, the more mouths we could feed. More bodies converted to the cause. More soldiers in our growing army.

Fewer pawns for Connor to manipulate.

"Let's go feed people." I painted on a brave face, knowing it was thinner than a butterfly's wing. "Ellian, come with us. They need to start trusting your face, too."

Ellian rolled his eyes, sheathing his quill like a sword. "Aye, Your Highness."

"Clever." My skin prickled, the mockery of my new title releasing a wave of nausea through me. I didn't want to be Captain or King. I didn't want to be in charge. I wanted my wife back. I wanted my family safe. I wanted to rutting sleep or to soak in the Lyr-forsaken spring.

But I was the Serpent Prince now. I had no room or need for rest. I was born to deceive and raised to snake through life unnoticed until my venom was already pulsing through my enemy's veins.

The Deyrnas needed a symbol of hope. They needed Keira, or her alternate, to make them believe in something better—a tomorrow worth surviving for. And they needed me slithering in the background, silently killing off the opposition one letter or deal or bribe at a time.

I slinked out of the room without another glance. There was no looking back, not anymore. There was nothing left to salvage of the world we'd left behind. Only forward. Only the future. Or there would be nothing of that, either.

Griffin straightened his tunic as we descended the inn's creaky steps. At least one of us would look rested and healthy. Self-consciously, I stood straighter, hoping it would help as we stepped out of the warm, fragrant inn and into the harsh, unforgiving light of morning. My shoulders sank again as the day greeted me, even more debilitating than I'd let myself imagine.

The line of the hungry led all the way to the docks, hundreds of them, mostly skin and bones. Hundreds of sunken, ashen faces stared at us like royalty as we passed, some even bowing as we made our way to where the *Ddraig* and the *Ceffyl* waited. Others hid beneath heavy cloaks, too ashamed to even show their faces.

Lyr's ass, had all of Bachtref lined up?

Dread and regret sat heavy in my core, my legs slower with the burden of every body I counted on the way. The *Ddraig* was full, our last haul from Pysgodd generous, but not enough to feed the hordes.

Still, at the edge of the dock, my aunt stood in front of the stockpile, midnight hair woven in tight plaits as she helped Reese and Rhett distribute the goods to the waiting masses, the blue Captain's coat sitting proudly on her squared shoulders. I swallowed hard, the image slamming into my chest with the weight of an anvil. It was worse than the hunger, the exhaustion, worse than any scrape or scratch or gunshot I'd ever endured.

"These should last you a while," the imposter Keira said with a wicked grin that matched my wife's so perfectly even I had to squint to catch the trickery.

Reina taught me everything I knew about pretending. The White Snake was a true actress, taking on whatever colors the world painted her in. And like a real snake, she could twist and manipulate herself to fit whatever shape the audience called for.

Today, they called for a savior. So desperate they'd take an actor in a costume instead.

A frail woman took her meager rations—two loaves of stale bread, a small sack of cured meat, and a hide of fur to help trade for more—with tears in her eyes, charmed entirely by my aunt's performance. "Thank you, *Rydha*. Thank you. You're so generous."

Rydha. The liberator. They'd been whispering it in quiet corners of the world like this since the day she freed Vian and the others from their cages. Over the last month, it had crescendoed into a battle cry sung at the front lines of every raid and revolt.

Reina, the genius, with a word and a shoulder salute, had turned Keira into a symbol—the face of a revolution.

My aunt stroked the woman's cheek gently, wiping away a tear, her mask slipping for only a fraction of a moment. "Stay strong."

The woman moved on, shuffling away so the next tear-filled townie could crawl forward, an island of once-proud farmers reduced to beggars. Rhett stood at the front of the line, scowling at them all like a statue, light eyes darkened with suspicion. "Stay in line, please.

We'll make sure you all leave with something." His words were kind, but held a threatening edge, his massive frame only adding to the bluntness of it. The few Bachtreffians closest to him shrank, giving him a wider berth as they scuffled past.

"When did you become a warden?" I mumbled through a toothy smile as I took my place next to my cousin, waving to the onlooking townsfolk to help ease the tension.

"When did you become a prick?" He glared at me, but uncrossed his arms, a shallow attempt at a smile snaking onto his face.

"I was born this way." I shrugged, tucking my hands into my pockets and sauntering over to the stockpile, my own performance necessary in Reina's facade.

"Good of you to join us, Mr. Mathonwy." My aunt cocked her head to the side, evaluating me with one sweeping look as she passed out another ration.

"Need any help, Re—*Rydha.*" I caught myself a moment too late, my tired tongue nearly toppling the entire trap with my aunt's name.

"Start handing things out, you insufferable cad," Reina chuckled brightly so the eavesdropping crowd could hear. She dressed herself in another of Keira's dagger-tipped smirks, but it didn't quite match this time, a hidden warning swimming in her brown eyes—the only features that were truly still *hers.*

Get it together, they screamed. *There is too much at stake.*

For the first time in my life, I decided to keep my mouth shut as I passed out a ration to the next bleeding heart on the line.

We fell into step with each other as the morning stretched into full day, a well-choreographed dance. Ellian, Reese and I did our jig alongside the figurehead, our smiles as rehearsed as they were fake.

"Griffin, Tarran, start unloading the next crates from the deck," Reina commanded with easy authority, like she really was the cousin-made-captain who spent her childhood bossing these boys around.

"Aye, Captain *Keira*," Tarran awkwardly emphasized her name as he saluted, the lie practically written across his rosy face. Griffin nudged him toward the stockpile with an eyeroll. Hopefully, the ray of tactless sunshine would be less conspicuous behind the scenes, better as a quiet stagehand.

Next to them, Reagan frowned as she scoured over a piece of parchment. She and Saeth had been keeping inventory, a role she'd taken with a surprising and admirable seriousness. But her tiny scowl meant nothing good.

"We're on our last ten crates, Captain," she addressed her mother with sad eyes.

Reina ruffled Reagan's hair with the same sisterly affection Keira would, but I didn't miss how her chin fell a fraction. "Good work, little dragon."

I chewed the inside of my cheek, staring out over the unshrinking line. Ten crates left. Ten. To feed hundreds.

As the crates emptied, as our shoulders sagged in exhaustion, the desperate people of Bachtref still lined up, willing to starve in the line with the small sliver of hope feeding their souls, rather than starve alone.

Turning them away would've been heartbreaking. But we didn't get the chance.

It was half past three when the first two guards, clad in Orwellin black, spotted us. The first—somehow even taller than Griffin—stood only three dozen paces away when he shouted to us, drawing our attention and ending our show. "Oi! You lot!"

"Shit. That's not good." Griffin dropped the crate he was carrying, hand twitching at his side. Truth and Triumph whispering in his ear, he shot a worried look to Ellian. "Councilman?"

"Shit is right." Ellian narrowed his eyes, the shifter bristling like a wolf with raised haunches. "Who sent them?"

The guards walked up to us, hands already wrapped around the hilts of their longswords.

"Good afternoon, gentlemen." I strolled forward, ready to play my part, standing in front of Reina. Ellian stood tight to my side, donning his orderly mask as we covered my aunt.

"What are you doing?" the guard grumbled, Orwellin dialect jumbling the inherently stupid question.

Around us, townsfolk shifted and shrank, worry darkening their already-shadowed features. I shrugged once. I wouldn't let these hooded idiots derail what we worked so hard for. Not with so many watching, waiting for the *Rydha* and her snake husband to set them free from their desperation. "Handing out some leftovers. Our ship isn't big enough to carry them all home, you see——"

The second, smaller guard cut me off. "You need a permit for that."

I cocked a smirk, ready to strike back. "If we were selling them, we would need one." I picked an invisible speck of dust from the short man's uniform, my patience wearing thinner than Ir'desian silk. "But there is no transaction. We're simply giving things away."

Ellian stepped forward, smoothing out the guards' ruffled feathers with his best councilman's grin. Only I saw the snarling wolf beneath. "For example, Officer, we have this case of whiskey from Councilwoman Agatha Amos's legendary tavern that we can't bring with us...perhaps you could take it off our hands?"

The smaller guard paused, considering Ellian's bribe like the spineless lemming he was. A pregnant moment passed, victory so close, so easily won with just a case of whiskey and Ellian's effortless charm...

"Her. She's the one on the posters." The tall one smacked his companion's shoulder, pointing behind us to Reina, realization lacing his voice. "And you——"

Fuck.

Finer than the sand on Traeth beach, victory slipped through our fingers, the *Rydha's* signature too recognizable even when forged.

"Who?" Ellian cocked his head to the side like a dog listening for a whistle, simultaneously stepping to block the guard's view of Reina, but it was too late.

"Don't play dumb with me, you little shitstain." The taller guard cracked Ellian across the face, knocking him back like the man's hand was made of hammers. Ellian gripped his face, stanching the blood dribbling from his lip, but he had no time to recover before the chaos descended.

"They're here! The fugitives!" The second guard cried out, and all order collapsed around us. From the crowd, the sound of dozens of swords being unsheathed pierced the quiet, guards throwing off Bachtreffian cloaks to reveal obsidian uniforms beneath.

"It's an ambush!" Rhett was the first of us to draw his sword, the Red Fang ready to riot. The crowd panicked, frenzied screams filling the air, commoners running for their lives. Some of the bolder onlookers snagged what they could, rushing the stockpile of goods as the guards corralled us, their focus on me and my crew.

On Reina, dressed as Keira, posing as the most dangerous woman in the Deyrnas.

But my Aunt was not the NightMare of the Four Seas. She was not the *Rydha*, born with sword in hand, ready to strike. Her only real weapons were her wits, and those would do nothing to protect her from the guards charging us.

I would not forgive myself if they succeeded.

"Let's go!" I cried above the noise, adrenaline propelling me forward. I grabbed my aunt's shoulders and pushed her toward my father, whipping out my pistol and dagger. "Reese, get her out of here!"

I had failed to protect my real wife. I would not fail to protect her alternate.

The tall guard took aim at me, sword crashing like an anvil against my dagger, knocking the tiny blade from my hand. I cursed under my breath, rolling away his next blow, clutching my pistol. I didn't want to fire, didn't want to turn a swordfight into a shootout, but I wouldn't have a choice if his next blow was any closer.

Ellian came to my aid, his talented sword nearly as lethal as his teeth. Like the blacksmith and *blaidd* he was, he toppled the guard over with his first brutish swing, a smile carving his face. The guard struggled to meet his blow, arms shaking against the weight of Ellian's mass. I scrambled to my own dagger, thanking my furry friend for the time he bought.

But some beasts were small. Captain Cedric always said snakes didn't need to be big to be venomous.

I missed the motion as the second, shorter guard dove into the fray, sinking his sword into Ellian's powerful thigh. The councilman howled as he dropped to his knees, blood pouring from the wound. The tall guard raised his sword again, a hunter ready to kill.

I pulled the trigger.

A fresh chorus of screams erupted as the guard fell, my bullet striking true, drawing the attention of half a dozen of his hooded companions. The crowd swarmed, reason and caution devolving as people ran for their lives, the guards tangled in the mass panic.

"Shit," I cursed, hauling Ellian to standing. The blacksmith winced, sagging against me, trousers already redder than my coat. His eyes rolled back, face blanching. I smacked his cheek, perhaps a little harder than I should've. "Come on, Councilman, stay with me."

Ellian's eyes fluttered open, and I loosed a breath. But we were not out of the dark yet. No, this was only the beginning. And if we didn't start using our heads soon, it would be a swift march to our end.

This was what war looked like. Letters and lost nights, yes. But also innocents panicking and being cut down as the guards fought to capture us. A friend's blood trickling onto a stone street, mixing with the fallen foe's. I swallowed back the fear lining my throat, the dragon devouring it and replacing it with the fire I needed to survive this.

I scanned the mayhem, desperate for any sign of the rest of my crew. Rhett was hacking away at guards, already carving a path for Reese and Reina. Tarran and Saeth herded Reagan away, headed to the ship, not needing a direct order to know it was time to signal our retreat. Only the Swordsinger looked back, his twin blades slicing through anybody that stepped in his path, his sights set on us.

"To the ship?" he hollered as he finally cut through, red eyes filled with sorrow.

Today, we lost. Bachtref lost. The Deyrnas lost.

"To the ship," I growled, sharing Ellian's weight with my ginger cousin-in-law.

As we hobbled to the gangplank, averting our eyes from the madness and bloodshed around us, the revelry turned riot, I made my solemn vow to any and all gods listening.

We would not lose again. This was war.

And Connor Yorath would pay with his life.

✧✦30

Tempests and Tattoos

KEIRA

The *Awelymor* was a fine vessel, well-stocked and well-crafted in every way. It was hard to believe that it was not made for us. Nelle appointed herself to take stock of the supplies, and we were far better equipped for the return journey than Vian and I were on our way here. We had five full weeks of rations, warmer clothes, and plenty of hammocks to rest in. The ship was too small to carry any heavy artillery, but I was pleasantly surprised to see the weapons room decently stocked with daggers, swords, and pistols. I took my time arming myself, feeling more and more like the old Keira with every piece of metal I strapped to my body. Amongst the riches, I found a small opal-hilted dagger the color of moonlight on the sea that I claimed for myself and an obsidian bow for Vian. He accepted it and the quiver of black-feathered arrows with stars in his eyes that rivaled the heavens, sending a fresh wave of appreciation through me. Whoever this ship actually belonged to had impeccable taste. I almost felt bad to have stranded them on *Hiraeth.*

Almost. Not enough.

Ronan needed me. And I needed to get off that island.

Sailing felt like euphoria. I didn't know if it was because I'd been away from the sea too long, or if it was the destination—my Ronan, my true home—that called out to me, but I felt renewed. Reborn. Like the person I'd become in the warm waters of the *Carthu* and the person I had always been finally met and melded, two halves made whole.

It made it easier that I had a decent crew. Siobhan and Nelle were far more seaworthy than I expected, easily following my commands as we cast off into the vast blue. Nelle was not a warrior, but she had her sealegs and was clever with her knots, her precision surgical. Siobhan was a multi-purpose tool, her brute strength and unparalleled grace useful in every role I gave her. Perhaps the security that she could never drown made her bold, but I didn't care as long as it made her effective. Not that I liked her, but after the first three days of sailing, I prayed to Lyr in sheer gratitude for her existence. Gods above and below, watching her work, a small part of me understood *exactly* what had attracted Ronan to her. There was no task she couldn't handle, and she accepted each new challenge with a feral grin and a twinkle in her eye.

That was until the fourth day at sea, when the storm came.

I assumed that two sirens and a wind-whisperer wouldn't be too rattled by some rain and a few—albeit strong—gusts of wind. I was wrong. The *Awelymor* was well-built, but she was small, and each wave that crashed into us threatened to knock us all from the deck, the rain pounding the black wood an added misery. We rocked like babies in a violent cradle, each of us trying to hang on and carve a course despite the cold, unrelenting rain.

"Gwynn's blades, can't you do anything about this weather?" Siobhan burst out from where she'd been hiding belowdecks, wrapped in a fur blanket. Nelle shivered beside her, sideways rain plastering her dark hair to her face in unruly lines. They'd held out for as long as they could, but this type of storm was hard for even experienced sailors to weather.

For Nelle's sake, I suppressed the urge to roll my eyes, fighting the frustration bubbling just beneath my skin. "I can't. Not anymore." I gripped the helm with renewed strength, squinting against the rain. "Vian?"

An uncharacteristic pout sat on the boy's lips as he climbed down from the rigging, careful not to slip. "The wind isn't listening. Says it's not her storm."

Siobhan stomped up to me, yanking the wheel into her own hands. "Can't, or won't?"

"What?"

"You heard me!" A grimace contoured her features. "Can't, can't, can't. Such a victim, Keira. What Ronan saw in you…"

A beast deep inside me roared to life, my blood hot in my veins. I had my opal dagger at her throat faster than a lightning strike. I kept my voice low, venom dripping from my fangs. "Keep his name out of your mouth if you want to keep your tongue."

Siobhan's actual fangs protruded, fingernails turning to long, webbed talons as she tapped the edge of my blade. "Oh, and you'll take it from me?" she sneered, cocking her head to the side to give me better access to her throat. It was a challenge not to slice it. "With that toothpick?"

"Will you two stop it?" Nelle huffed, stepping between us and whacking my dagger away, a turbulent storm in her violet gaze. "This is miserable enough without your squabbling."

Vian raised an eyebrow at me, muttering before excusing himself to the warm cabin, "The wind agrees."

A wave of guilt wracked through me. A tiny part knew I deserved their reproach, knew arguing with a grumpy Siobhan was pointless. But still, it stung, my failure chasing me again even when I thought I'd drowned it in the river back in *Hiraeth.* I was back in my element, a Captain at the helm, and yet I was still helpless. Useless.

I turned my back on Siobhan, stalking to the single mast to tie something before I could tie my hands around her neck. "I'm sorry I am not a siren and that my gifts were taken from me," I mumbled to the rain and whatever selfish, damned gods were listening.

Siobhan missed nothing, her siren ears more acute than I'd hoped. She carried on after me, tone coated in condescension that reminded me uncannily of Finna. "Pshh, is that what they told you? Or is that what you tell yourself so you don't have to deal with it?"

Her words struck an open wound, lodging neatly between my ribs. My heart dropped to my gut, splashing as it made impact.

An odious part of me knew she was right. I hadn't dealt with it. I had gotten so used to running, I forgot what it felt like to stand and fight for something.

Well. If she wanted a fight, she'd have one.

"Watch it." I spun on her, standing to my full height. This was a stolen ship, but it was mine now, and I was Captain. For a moment, a flicker of something familiar rose like a cresting wave deep within me, an answer to the rage blistering in my core. I let it seep into my skin, hot as starlight and untamed as a *ceffyl* when I squared my stance. "It's a good thing you have a tail, because I'm one second away from throwing you overboard."

"Another empty threat from an empty little girl!" She stepped close enough that I could smell the sand-and-sea scent of her. She glared at me, citrine eyes glowing as her anger built like the storm around us. "I think maybe if you stopped pitying yourself for three minutes, you'd realize no one could ever take your power from you, and you'd start being useful."

"I am not pitying myself!" My threadbare hold on my temper broke, a dam bursting in my chest.

"Yes, you are!" She exploded as well, shoving me back with a hard push to the shoulders, a wolf howling at the sky in protest.

For a moment, we stared at each other in stunned silence, our breaths heavy. Fury still whirled in my chest, but it lacked oxygen, a fire strangled out. The truth sat heavy in my gut, guilt and self-pity the anchors weighing me down far too long. I was drowning, and even though I'd left some of it behind, if I didn't let go of the rest, it would sink me.

Siobhan inhaled sharply, shattering the uncomfortable pause. Her fangs retracted, exhaustion taking anger's place. "Look, I get it, alright? I know what someone in pain looks like. I've hurt enough people, and I've been there myself. But you'd better start dealing with yours if you're going to save Ronan. Your power can't be taken. It was yours first. You're Danura's *daughter*, for Gwynn's sake." She looked at me, something wistful and envious burning in them like coals despite the damp air. "You control your own fate."

She didn't wait for my response before she marched to the portside rail and dove into the deep, citrine tail trailing behind her.

I didn't feel any more at ease with her gone. The pit of my stomach clenched, the truth of her words colder than the rain that still blasted us.

Being Danura's daughter meant nothing to me. She had shown me kindness, but she was a coward hiding behind the trees and traps of *Hiraeth*, content to let the rest of the world rot while she flourished. A trait, I realized, I'd inherited. I'd been running for far too long. I left Ronan, hiding behind a scar on my shoulder and my fear, blaming it all on Lyr for abandoning me.

He had not. *I* was the one who abandoned her loved ones. I was the one content to let war brew over a fight I started and was too afraid to finish.

But Danura's yellow-bellied blood did not run alone in my veins. I was my father's daughter, too. My father, who stood for honor and duty, even if it meant sacrificing himself. My father, who was just a man, who didn't need any gifts to be powerful. My father, who stayed and fought for good until his last breath.

My father, who told me I was born to rule the sea and stars, that my fate was mine to command, if only I had the bravery and drive to take the silver wheel in my own hands.

Something rumbled within me, in the part that was Cedric. The part that had been too long forsaken. I didn't know if anything still existed of Lyr's gift, or whatever else dwelled beneath the surface, the hot, aching, buzzing thing I'd encountered in the bright light of the *Carthu*. But I would find out, and I would make it mine. Not for Danura, or Siobhan, or anyone else, but for my father's legacy, and for the one I had yet to make for Ronan and me.

As if sensing my will, the rain eased its assault, only a few daring droplets still falling from the grey clouds overhead.

Nelle cleared her throat, her hand on my shoulder a lifeline back to the schooner's rain-soaked deck. An apology rested in her delicate grin. "You'll have to excuse her, she'll feel better after a hunt—"

"No, she's right." I clasped her hand, so close to the mark I'd let control me for too long. "I don't like it, but she's right."

Nelle's expression shifted like the tide, unexpected mischief twitching in the corner of her upturned lips. Her hand slid down my arm, firmly grasping my right hand instead. "May I?"

I nodded once, eager to see what the dove hid beneath her feathers. Needing no further prodding, she closed her eyes, long, wet lashes kissing her cheeks as she scrunched her brow. When she pressed my hand between her palms, I felt the now-familiar tingle of her power, the sweet comfort that smelled like jasmine and herbs, floral and fragrant.

I was not expecting the sharp sting of pain that flashed across the back of my hand in strange lines. I tore from her grasp with a muttered curse, and my breath caught in my chest as I inspected my hand.

Where there had only been white flesh, there was now black ink in intentional, elegant lines, finer than the best artists in Ir'de could manage. I blinked as the image became clear: a crescent moon, done with the same intersecting lines and swirls of Ronan's tattoo. Inside its frame, a ship wheel with nine spokes, and at its center, the four cardinal points of a compass, all drawn with the same swirling, ornate design.

Tears welled as I traced it with my finger. It did not smudge. It was a part of me, perhaps the most beautiful, important part. "How—?"

Nelle shrugged. "Perk of my gift."

I stared at the marking again, admiring her handiwork, a vain part of me keenly aware of how nicely it would look next to Ronan's tattoo. "Does it do anything? Like Ronan's?"

"It's not enchanted, no." Nelle leaned against the mast, a glimmer in her eye that reminded me so much of Papa's, I thought she might have conjured him then and there. "You don't need any of my magic. But it *is* a reminder of who you are. No one can tell the sea to submit, but even the tides follow the moon's command. And yet, no one could ever try to control all of you, not even the Dark God. You're not the tide, you're the moon. You are strong enough on your own."

Gratitude sat heavy on my tongue, gagging me. So because I had no words to express the depth of my appreciation for her, I simply wrapped her in a tight hug as I tried to stop the tears from soaking her further.

"Land!" Siobhan's voice broke us apart as we both turned to see her climbing back over the side of the ship. She staggered onto the deck, pointing starboard. "I see land!"

My gaze followed to where she led it, to a small mass perched on the clearing horizon. The rain had stopped altogether, sharpening its image.

"Any idea where we are?" Nelle's voice was tighter than a knot as she looked to me.

I could've made it out even in the rain, the brightly painted buildings of the hilltop city recognizable to any sailor that ever wanted to make a coin or two.

Aehnad City. The bustling hub of the land of silks and scents. And by some miracle, the easiest place to hide from the council outside of *Hiraeth* itself.

If Ronan wasn't in Porthladd, there was a very good chance he'd be here, reaping the bounty of the island while hiding in its shadows.

"Ir'de."

PART

3

Starborn

31

Accords and Apparitions

RONAN

The incensed interior of Madame Katrin's brothel smelled of sex and poor decisions, even in the back room used strictly for business. Though the furnishings were luxurious, all velvet and silk upholstered, the cushions begging its visitors to relax and stay a while, I shifted uncomfortably where I sat at the head of the oak table. But I kept my mask secure, a smirk hanging nonchalantly on my expression. Katrin expected the Serpent Prince. It was my job to deliver.

The lowlight made the contract hard to read, but it was there. Madame Katrin was making good on her word. In exchange for any furs we could get our hands on and some anti-itch salves we managed to snag back in Hud, her workers would work as spies for us, providing the valuable insight we still needed for the next phase of the plan.

That is, if there was a plan. Some mornings, I felt sure of my choices. We'd managed to keep Porthladd and Bachtref afloat with minimal injury thanks to Finna's map, and Ellian's letters had given us the advantage over Connor. Now, Pysgodd and Ir'de had dethroned their High Councilors, breaking off from the Deyrnas entirely—which would've been terrible for them both, to be excluded from trade and markets, had it not been for our little smuggling ring. Our fleet had seven ships now, Councilman Leary and the *Madyn* joining our ranks entirely after the Bachtref food riots, bringing some friends with him. It cut Connor's resources in half while doubling ours. And by some miracle, we hadn't been caught yet, Reina and Reese always two steps ahead of wherever Connor chased them, the perfect decoy.

But there were still slaves in Orwellin. And an army of guards and Tannian assassins—who'd been well-bribed—defending the High Council. And Connor still ran Porthladd, even from afar, the sanctions tighter than ever.

We couldn't outrun them forever. Eventually, we'd have to stand and fight.

A deep pang of hunger rattled through my empty core, a shiver running down my spine. That was if I *could* stand; I'd forgotten how long it'd been since I'd seen Porthladd last. I'd made a quick stop to the spring during our last haul, when Reina had Connor circling Hud for her. Had it been four weeks? Or five?

I didn't want to dwell on what that meant.

We needed allies. Powerful ones. But where to find them was another question entirely.

Luckily, there were still plenty of councilmembers who still dared journey to Ir'de for their more *exotic* goods and services. Madame Katrin's establishment being the most famous place for such riches.

I looked up from the accord to where the woman sat across from me, meeting her dark gaze. Hair nearly as black as Keira's fell in meticulous curls around her heart-shaped face, her full lips in a permanent pout that oozed sensuality and danger second only to Marina. If I didn't know any better, I would've guessed she was a siren, too.

In a way, she was. Every good businesswoman I'd ever met had hidden claws and fangs that could rival any of the Annwyn's. A powerful ally indeed. I signed my name to the page, hoping whatever information she had was worth the additional trip for Pysgoddian fur.

I leaned back in my seat, watching carefully as Katrin examined the page with slender, dexterous fingers and hungry eyes.

"Start talking, Katrin dear," I purred, hating the way I caressed her name. It was always harder to keep up the act when I was this exhausted. How many nights had it been since I slept well? I'd stopped counting after three last time.

Still, a satisfied smirk carved the marble of her face. "There was another fight in Orwellin. Councilman Renfrid has always been a talker, and my girl Ivette, poor thing, had to hear about it all last evening. Apparently, a rogue guard freed more slaves, and they killed a minor councilman. The rest of the guards put them down, but people are fired up just hearing about it."

The dragon in my chest winked awake at the news. If the rebellion was growing, even in Orwellin, maybe we stood a chance. I'd have to tell Ellian as soon as I could. I hoped the councilman who died wasn't one of his friends, but chances were that if he was from Orwellin, he was the enemy.

One less bastard standing in our way.

If only I could thank the rogue guard personally. Hopefully, Drystan was among his men, and not the one delivering the beatings. I'd hate to have to end him when the time came.

Katrin tapped her painted nails on the stained oak to get my attention, leaning so far forward her bosom threatened to spill out of the thin, flowing dress that barely covered her to begin with. Her voice dropped into a husky haze when she spoke again, eyeing me like a prize. "You've started quite a commotion, Captain Mathonwy."

The title brought the taste of acid to my lips. Captain Mathonwy was my wife, or less often, my father. I'd never quite fill it, no matter how well-painted my mask was. I grimaced, looking to the doorway—so close, but so far. "We didn't start it."

"I meant it as a compliment. Thank you all for what you're doing." She let loose a breathy laugh, but her expression shifted, storm clouds rolling over the sea. "I have a cousin in Bachtref. She sent me a letter not too long ago saying just how much they owe you. She was there the day of the riot. Your crew is the only reason anyone on that island is still alive."

I winced again, thinking of the gaunt cheeks and sunken eyes on the island that still haunted my nightmares every time I laid to rest. We'd been back and forth half a dozen times, and still it wasn't enough. It might never be.

I wasn't enough. Even after all this time.

I chewed the inside of my cheek, gnawing at already-raw flesh. Somehow, I would have to be. For my wife's memory.

I said a silent prayer to Lyr for Councilman Renfrid's loose trousers and looser lips. Knowing the situation in Orwellin helped immensely, as did the ability to blackmail Renfrid whenever we needed more. I'd never met the old bastard personally, but I'd have to introduce myself soon enough.

"Thank you for your discretion." I slapped a few extra coins on the table to reiterate just how grateful I was in her language before standing to go. Careful not to drop my facade, I flashed a rotten smirk her way, relaxing into the doorway for emphasis. "I hope this partnership continues to be fruitful."

"It's part of the job." Katrin shrugged, but her stare was wolfish. Slowly, deliberately, she clapped her hand to her left shoulder. "Tell the *Rydha* she will always be welcomed here."

If only the *Rydha* were here. If only Keira could come back, make it all better.

I shoved my hands deep into my pockets, steadying myself. We hadn't seen nor heard from her in months. Not even a whisper on the wind, not a single sign or signal. The last droplets of my hope were all but dry.

If only the people knew they were following a martyr who hadn't even lived to see their cause.

I excused myself from the back room without another word before the thought could crush me entirely. Griffin—who was supposed to be guarding the door—was flirting with a saucy redhead girl with breasts the size of his head, his shirt already untied. Brushing past him, I made a beeline for the door, desperate to be out of the cloud of incense and sorrow.

I'd let Rhett deal with his own messes today. I didn't have the energy.

Mumbling a goodbye, Griffin scrambled after me.

Ellian was waiting out front, resting on the clay wall like a shrubbery, the Councilman still too proud to sully his reputation by actually entering the brothel. Then again, perhaps he was just well trained; he and Saeth hadn't been spending much time together these days, but old habits died hard. When he saw us, he straightened the lightweight green wrap he wore, still not used to Ir'desian fashion.

"Any last stops for today, Captain?" He rubbed the sweat beading on his forehead, Nef's eye sweltering as she stared down at us. It was still morning, and yet already springtime in the Southern Isles was oppressively hot.

I adjusted my own tunic, the light blue fabric clinging to me while I surveyed the already busy street, the hubbub of the market waiting for no one. I was sweaty and dizzy just *thinking* about being among the crowd, elbowing my way through packed bodies and loud merchants. The dragon in my core whined like a kicked dog at the thought. "Let's go back to the inn, grab some chow with the rest of the crew, and get some rest. We sail at dawn."

"I might need to buy some new clothes first." Ellian scratched at his chest like a mutt with fleas, looking at a nearby stall with desperate eyes. "I can't stand this flowy shit."

"Fine," I sighed, no energy to argue in this heat. "You have ten minutes, princey-poo. We'll wait here."

Ellian clapped me on the back before limping toward the nearby tents and stalls, still favoring his injured leg after the ambush in Bachtref and disappeared into the chaos of it.

Griffin slid down the earthy wall, drooping like a wilted flower. He still managed to raise an eyebrow at me. "It would've been much nicer to wait inside. Ivette was rather charming."

"Can you think with your head and not your cock for *five minutes*?" I snapped, another wave of dizziness hitting me, my skin crawling in the inferno. As a boy, I used to love to bask in the sun's embrace until my skin felt tight and my eyelids heavy. Now I couldn't stand it for more than three minutes. To think I once abhorred the cold climes of the North.

Even without his swords on his back, the Swordsinger saw through me. He hopped to his feet with the agility of a cat, narrowing his eyes. "We should go to Porthladd. It's been a while."

I ran a tired hand through my damp hair, desperate to have it off my face. I'd let it get too long, some strands reaching my jaw. "We left them enough last trip to keep everyone fed for a little while longer."

Griffin crossed his arms, giving me a look that screamed *bullshit*. "No, I mean it's been a while since you soaked."

I froze like a Pysgoddian river in winter.

It had been long. Too long. And I'd be lying to myself to say that my body's recent weakness wasn't a direct result of the cravings that kept me up well into the night. But luckily, I was an excellent liar. I tucked my hands back into my pockets. "Pysgodd tomorrow. Katrin took the last of our furs, so we'll need to replenish, and perhaps restock on cured meat if we can afford it."

"Ronan," my cousin protested, brow furrowed as he scanned my profile, not pleased with whatever he saw. "Please don't be stubborn, yeah? You look—"

"Enough, Griffin, I'm fine." I was not about to risk the crew's safety for a rutting bath. If Finna's letters were right, Connor would be back by now. Plus, her notes had been fewer and farther between, with more jaded side notes about Locasta's presence in Porthladd. If we went home now, we might run into two very powerful, very *angry* enemies.

We hadn't come this far to turn back.

For a moment, it looked like he was about to disagree once more, but then his jaw went slack, color draining from his face.

"Ronan?" Behind me, a different voice broke over my name. One I'd heard in my dreams every night since I was ten.

Ice ran down my spine, hair standing in its wake. My mouth dry, I turned to the voice, legs already numb beneath me.

It was like she was real this time. Lyr below, she looked radiant, the warm glow of the morning sun baking her cool skin in gold. Her nest of unruly hair was braided back for once, the form of her cut in a loose-fitting white tunic that hinted at her subtle curves. Silver eyes clashed against her dark lashes like an eclipse, sparkling even as she squinted at me.

A weapon made woman. A goddess made flesh.

It was a cruel, wicked trick. I'd been seeing her apparition in my daydreams more and more, when the hunger was worst, when the cravings made me shake and vomit and sweat. When I needed her most, she'd come to me, serene and severe at once, but never like this. Never so real.

Griffin gasped out a question for the phantom in front of me. "Keira? Lyr below, is that really you?"

A smile brighter than every star in the sky broke across her face, tears forming rivers across her freckled cheeks. Her eyes did not leave mine as she stumbled forward once. Twice. "Ronan."

The air stole from my chest. Something escaped my mouth, a mix between a breath and a sob as it all came crashing into me.

She wasn't a ghost. She was *here*.

"You came back." I choked on my own voice, frozen to where I stood, afraid to move a muscle. Like if I moved, I'd shatter the illusion and she'd evaporate. "Where—?"

"*Hiraeth.*" She stepped closer again, tentative, but close enough now that if I just reached out, if I could just move my arm, I'd be brushing my fingers against her cheek, I'd feel the velvet of her skin, the heat of her pulse...

"What happened—?"

"Ronan, I'm so sorry." Keira cut me off, tears that could drown me pouring from her. Before I could react, she leaped into my embrace with force that made me sway. But as my arms found their way around her waist, as they felt the laugh that escaped her, the whole world righted. The whole world was here, in my grasp, sniffling into the crook of my neck, holding me so tightly I could barely breathe.

She came back.

I'd never let her go again. I didn't need air or food or water or sunlight or the spring. The rest of the world faded away, less than an afterthought. I just needed this. Needed her. Needed the unwashed scent of her hair, the tangible weight of her body against mine.

Another muffled sob lost itself in my shoulder. "I missed you so much, but I thought I was doing the right thing—"

"It's alright. I know. I thought you were..." I rubbed small circles across her back, needing to touch her, each stroke a reminder that she was real and here. And *alive*. "I missed you so much, Mrs. Mathonwy."

With the gentleness of a doe, she pushed back from me. A chill rattled through me, the loss of contact unbearable even in the suffocating Ir'desian sun. But darkness gathered like stormclouds in her expression. "Ronan, I had to come back, there's a war—"

"We know all about the war, Keira. Who do you think's been fighting it?" Griffin groaned, grabbing his cousin's shoulders and turning her toward him, away from me. He patted her down, checking for injuries, raising an eyebrow as he noticed some fresh, black ink scarred on the back of her hand. When he too decided she was real, he crushed her to his chest. "What in the Otherworld have you been doing for the last three and a half months?"

My heart raced in my chest, deafening the details of what they were saying. Griffin was *holding* her. *I* had held her.

She came *home*.

"Three—" Keira reared back, her face white as a ghost. Moonstone eyes flicked to me, brimming with a cocktail of fear and confusion. "No, it can't be, I was only gone two weeks, maybe three—"

I cursed under my breath as my mind floundered to catch up, reality crashing back around me. Of course. She'd been in *Hiraeth*. It had probably only felt like days for her, and if she'd met the Annwyn, they would've kept their secret from her for as long as they could. "Give us a minute, Griffin. Go find Ellian."

"Aye, Captain." Griffin didn't need his sword to tell how serious my command was. He ruffled his cousin's hair once, beaming like a cat with a canary in its teeth. "I'm glad you're back."

Keira smiled, too, but it didn't reach her eyes as she watched Griffin practically skip toward the markets of the silk city.

The world swayed again, the heat rising in tendrils from the stone streets only mimicking the heat prickling in my palms.

My wife was here. She was seemingly unharmed, by some miracle, and if anything, she looked better than when I'd last seen her. Her skin had color to it again, her hair silky and eyes bright. Her shirt covered her shoulder, but I could see the crest of her collarbone, and where the black had once been inching nearer and nearer to her throat, there was none.

Lyr below, did she find a cure? If she'd been in *Hiraeth*, she must've met Nelle. My pulse was fire in my veins, my inner dragon roaring in triumph at the very thought. "Do you know? What the women are?"

Keira nodded, expression distant, part of her perhaps left behind on the island of lost things. I knew the sensation all too well. "Yes. Nelle and Siobhan came back with Vian and me. We came to warn you and help you."

I raised an eyebrow but didn't question it. Nelle and Siobhan were the last two sirens I'd ever expect to stray from Danura's side, her two most loyal subjects. Then again, my wife was made of miracles, and not even loyalty could defy the force of fate named Keira Branwen-Mathonwy.

I tucked a strand of hair behind her ear, one that had fallen into her eyes when Griffin messed with it. The touch sent a jolt of lightning burning up my arm, hot and *addicting*. Every single point of contact made me weak in the knees, made my heart beat faster and my cheeks flush red. I forgot how dizzy and euphoric it felt to love her from up close. But the shame wedging its way into my heart sobered me, dragging me down from my high. "Things are worse than before you left. I'm sorry, Keira girl. We let you down."

Her warm hand cupped the side of my face. "You've done so well. I see it, Ronan. I hear them whispering your name in the streets." She raised an eyebrow playfully. "That's how I found you, my Serpent Prince. Now it's my job to keep you safe."

Ellian's booming voice shattered the intimacy of the moment. "Keira! Thank Lyr you're alive!" He dropped his sacks of goods, staggering to her like an ox and lifting her in a too-tight hug. It was a punch to the gut, but Keira's laugh was enough to battle away the ugly, jealous beast inside me. Ellian finally put her down, thwacking Griffin on the arm so hard it echoed. "Griffin, you owe me money."

Keira glared at her cousin, hands on her hips and weight shifting in a way that meant business. "You bet against me?"

Griffin rubbed the sore spot on his arm but grinned anyway. "I wanted to lose. I missed you, Shrimpy."

Somehow, it was like she never left. She slid so easily back into her role, a chameleon blending in with her surroundings like they'd been painted for her alone. As soon as we got back to the inn, Reagan and Saeth would pounce on her, too, glad to have a real Captain back in their midst. It was a true gift, the stuff that legends were made of. Reina had done well in her charade, but nothing could ever come close to Keira's presence.

Where I fit into it all, I didn't know. She seemed happy to see me, yes. Lyr's ass, I was more than happy to see her. But she didn't come back because she loved me or couldn't live without me. She didn't come because every morning, it was harder and harder to breathe without me.

She came back to warn me, to protect me. As if I was still something fragile that needed saving. Not someone she could rely on.

Right on cue, a vicious, stabbing jolt of hunger shot right through my middle, so harsh I doubled over, a man reduced to half once more. Keira turned her attention back to me, confusion and panic blending as she knelt beside me.

"Ronan? Are you alright?" She reached up, feeling my forehead with the back of her hand. The touch sent another wave of the same adrenaline through me, but this time, it was overwhelming and nauseating. Everything blurred into the torrid haze.

And when the world went black, all I could hear was my wife's cry as I dissolved into it.

32

Triumphs and Transformations

KEIRA

I was too late.

Ronan—my bright, beautiful, brave husband, who had worked so hard, who kept my family and the entire Deyrnas safe when I abandoned them—collapsed, crumpling to the ground.

I fell to my knees beside him, fear seizing my limbs and clawing its way up my chest. "Ronan, wake up." I shook his shoulders, his name tearing from my throat. "Ronan!"

"Shit." Griffin scrambled to Ronan's other side, feeling for a pulse at the side of his neck. I didn't need to check to feel how weak it was; I could feel him slipping from me already, the tether that tied us together stretching farther and farther.

No. *No.* Not again.

"How long has he been away from the spring?" I glared at Griffin and Ellian, rage and sheer panic pulsing through me with wicked speed.

Griffin's mouth flattened into a thin line. "Fuck, Keira, I told him."

"Griffin, *how long*?" I snarled, brushing Ronan's long blond locks from his face. He was so pale, dark circles under his eyes, a pasty sheen of sweat on his brow. It had been too long.

"Four, five weeks? Maybe a little longer?" Ellian answered, his voice strung as tightly as a bowstring, wringing his hands.

Griffin rocked back on his heels, guilt greying his expression as he tangled his hands in his hair. "Keira, you don't understand, things are rough—"

"I don't rutting care, Griffin!" Five weeks. Over a *month* away from the spring. Esme's warning echoed through me, a punch of nausea wracking through my gut.

Remember, don't let Ronan stray for too long, he won't look as peachy if he does. He has to keep coming back.

I had to do something. Anything. I had to save him. I couldn't bear the alternative, not when I just got him back, not when I just found him again…

But I was useless. I had nothing. The spring was half a world away, and I had no gift, no power over death. I stroked my husband's face, my tears splashing against his clammy cheeks. "No. Ronan, my love, stay with me, *please*. Not again."

"Keira!" Vian's voice pulled me from the edge of devastation as he ran down the street toward us, Nelle and Siobhan hot on his heels.

A fountain of hope burst open in my chest, washing away the panic when I saw her—our healer. This is why we were here. Why *she* was here. Her very presence was medicinal, her goodness and light enough to fight back even the darkest spots. We weren't too late.

We couldn't be.

"Move out of my way." Nelle pushed past the other two, settling next to Ronan at Griffin's side.

"Who the hell are you?" Griffin shot a protective arm over Ronan, a wildcat snarling at a young dove.

"I'm not the one who let him get this bad, that's for sure," Nelle shot back, shoving Griffin's arm out of the way with surprising ease.

"It's fine, Griffin, they are friends," Vian said quickly, wedging between them. He looked at me, fighting the doubt that lingered in the corners of his grin. "We're here, Keira. It's okay. The wind says so."

My grasp on Ronan's hand was tighter than any knot I'd ever tied. I couldn't let go. I wouldn't. "Help him, please."

Nelle nodded once, no longer a siren or a friend, but simply a healer. She placed her hands directly on his chest, face screwed up in concentration, eyes squeezed shut. After a moment, she looked to me, her face no less grim than it had been a second ago. "Let's get him inside, out of this heat. Now."

My stomach did another somersault, a fresh wave of sobs catching in my throat, but I nodded, gesturing for Griffin and the others to help. Carefully, we lifted him, Griffin and Ellian maintaining most of his weight, Siobhan at his feet, while I cradled his precious head. My hands shaking, I tried not to think about last time. Tried not to remember the much longer trek up *Dubryn* Hill with Esme. Tried not to remember the cost.

He was still breathing. He was feverishly hot, hotter than the sun. Not the still, cold balm of death. It would be different. It had to be.

We banged through the door of the brothel we'd be standing in front of. A scantily clad woman in silk that could rival Marina's beauty watched with her jaw on the floor.

"*Rydha?* Oh—Ronan!" she stammered, recognizing my husband's unconscious form far faster than I was comfortable with. "Quickly, this way!" She hurried us to a nearby room, throwing back a curtain and ushering us into a comfortable little nook with a lush bed in the middle. We lowered Ronan onto it, Nelle working to rip his shirt off with surgical precision.

"Leave us," she commanded, a Captain at the helm, and the brothel mistress obeyed without protest, closing the curtain behind her. Nelle's violet eyes simmered with determination before she screwed them shut again, pressing her palms to the mark over his chest—her careful artistry that had saved him from my wrath all those months ago. I begged Lyr that it would be enough to save him again. Griffin, Ellian, and Vian all waited at the foot of the bed, watching the healer work, hopeful, expectant looks on their faces, all whispering prayers that drifted alongside mine.

Eyes flying open, Nelle cursed under her breath with language fouler than any sailor I'd ever heard, earning a shocked blink from Griffin and Ellian. "He's burning up, the fever is spreading. He's been away from the spring too long...the power is overheating him."

A storm brewed in my middle, violent and begging to be released all over the floor. "Can you heal him?" My voice quivered as I waited for an answer, for the *yes* that would save me from the precipice of my grief.

"I'm trying." Nelle chewed her bottom lip as she passed her hands over Ronan's temples. "But he wasn't built for this gift like you were, Keira. He's not a...he's not strong enough."

The storm roared, seeking vengeance upon mortality itself. Ronan was strong enough. He had to be. Because I was not strong enough to say goodbye, not now. Never again.

Ronan drew a shuddering breath, the sound tearing me limb from limb like a starved wolf. We needed to act. We were running out of time.

"He *is* strong enough!" I howled, gripping his hand and pressing it to my cheek. I shut my eyes, willing my life into his through the place where we touched. If he wasn't strong enough, I would be for us both. "Ronan, please, hang on."

Siobhan stepped forward, pearly tears budding in her eyes. "Maybe Keira can—"

Nelle shot her a look that could stop death in its tracks. "No, it's too risky, she doesn't know how to use it yet." The healer shook her head, waving Siobhan off before dipping a scrap of cloth in the basin next to the bed and wringing it out over my husband. "We just need to pray his fever breaks. Siobhan, get the ginger and basil from my sack…"

The rising storm shuddered and stopped altogether, along with my heart, as Siobhan moved to fetch Nelle's herbs. I halted Nelle's hand before she could reach for them.

"Use what?" I loosened my grip on her arm, but my gaze held steady. Pleading. "Please, I'll do anything. Use *what?*"

Nelle hesitated for a moment. "There are consequences."

"I don't care. Please, I need to save him."

Nelle slowly pulled her arm back, not looking away as she judged. Decided. My husband's fate was in her hands now, and I trusted her. But I would give anything, pay any cost to be something other than useless. I came to save Ronan, not wait for someone else to do it.

After a moment that felt like an eternity, she let go of the breath she held. "Fine. Listen very carefully to me, Keira." She turned, gripping my shoulders and pulling me back to standing. Violet eyes met mine, hardened by focus and grit that reinforced mine. "You're Danura's daughter, whether you like it or not. And if she can turn us into what *we* are…"

My mouth went dry as I put the pieces together. The moment in the river, the moment of pure light and fire… "I can make him a siren?" The question was barely more than a whisper, like if I said it too loud, it wouldn't come true.

Nelle nodded gravely. Once.

"A *what?*" Griffin bellowed, stomping over to me, pushing Nelle out of the way. There were daggers in his stare, sharpened by his guilt, his nostrils flaring like an angry bull. "Keira, who in Lyr's name are these women? We need to get him back to Porthladd as fast as possible, we are wasting time!"

He started toward the bed, but before I could smack him for being an idiot, Siobhan was in front of me, shoving him hard, her fanged teeth bared. "Do yourself a favor and shut up before I choke you with your own curls."

Griffin fumed, eyes red with rage, but Ellian hauled him to the door. "Griffin, let's go make sure Madame Katrin keeps the patrons away."

I watched my cousin go, realizing how little I recognized the fearful, wrathful creature that possessed him. Not that I could judge. My absence had changed him, had changed them all, and that was my burden to bear, the guilt resting like the whole world on my shoulders. A piece of my heart shattered, fragmenting into more tiny shards than there were stars in the sky.

But maybe I could make things better now. I could save my husband and perhaps the rest of them, too, if only I were brave enough to try.

I looked at the tattoo on the back of my hand, at the reminder of the insurmountable, inexhaustible power of the moon. *Of me.* "Nelle, tell me how."

"Keira, if you do this…" Nelle bore the warning with a heavy tone, sweet sadness in her eyes. "There are consequences. The blood...he'll have to drink it to maintain his power. Food doesn't nourish us. Animal blood will do, but it's not the same as...well, human. And he won't age. Not normally, at least. For the ritual to work, he technically has to die first, just for a moment. He surrenders his body for a new one."

My heart shuddered at the very thought. "Does it always work? Will he come back?"

Nelle did not answer for a moment, breath held. Then, "I've seen it fail. Twice. It takes energy from your side too, and if you're too tired...it could kill you both. But I've also seen it work for every one of the women on the island, myself included. And if it does work, he won't need your spring."

"It doesn't matter," I answered before fear could stall my pulse. The longer I waited trapped in my own doubt, the worse our luck would be. I didn't care if Ronan drank blood, or piss for that matter, or if he stayed young while I grew old and grey. He just needed to *live*. So I would take my chances with the Dark God. "Tell me how."

Nelle rolled her shoulders back, chin tilted upward, a warrior in her own way. She was the queen of smoke and whispered prayers, but she knew how to wield the kind of fire that was hot enough to purify. "Water. We need as much as we can get."

"There's a tub through here." Vian jumped to the task, urgency in his step as he followed whatever Nef-sent trail the wind whispered his way, pointing through another silk curtain in the rear of the room. He forced a familiar, square grin, one that did little to untangle the knots in my middle, but I appreciated anyway. "Makes sense, with what they *do* here."

"Let's move him." Nelle gestured to Ronan with her chin, already looping his arm around her neck. I took his other side, my breath catching in a ball in my throat when he twitched, his own breathing shallow and sporadic. We dragged him carefully to the back room, where a deep, stone bath cut into the floor, cool, clear water swirling in its embrace. It was large enough for six people or so to stand waist deep, depending on how intimately they were spaced out.

My throat constricted, terror sucking the air from my lungs and squeezing tightly. The last time I'd dragged him into the water, the last time he was hurt...

"Breathe, Keira." Nelle's voice was soft, and the honeyed warmth of her power slid over me like a soft blanket, smoothing out the raw edges of my panic. Her eyes trapping mine, we lowered Ronan into the water, Siobhan and Vian helping as we waded in.

We propped him up against the stony ledge, his head rolling to the left, blond curls matted to his forehead with sweat. His cheeks were flushed red, but the skin around his eyes had started to bruise like the power was beating him from the inside, begging to escape.

I bit back the sob that came rushing up, trapping it behind my teeth. I was going to save him. No matter what.

Nelle stroked my cheek softly, forcing my gaze back to hers. "I'm going to hold your hand again, giving you my energy, alright?" she said, interlocking her fingers with mine. Together, we took a steadying breath, her dizzying warmth flowing through the space we connected. She smiled for my benefit, but her voice was rushed, urgent. "The other hand stays on Ronan, no matter what."

I nodded, pressing my tattooed hand over Ronan's heart. Praise and thanks to every god that ever lived, it still beat, fast and faint underneath my fingertips.

"Siobhan will stand with us, and Vian too...might as well get as many *Duweni* as we can." Nelle conducted the others, each placing their hands on my shoulders, their presence steeling my resolve. Nelle continued, hurried but clear, "Only you can focus to where the power sleeps for you. For Danura, she always feels it in her forehead, in her temples. That's why she stands head to head with Marina during the *Carthu*. But for you it might be different. Close your eyes, it'll help."

Begrudged to stop looking at Ronan, I closed my eyes, focusing not on the flickering pulse beneath my fingertips, but inward. Into the dark, small spaces of myself I'd been afraid of for so long.

Inward, deeper than I'd ever gone before. To the thing I met for a moment in the river, the primordial piece of creation I had taken with me when my soul escaped the void and entered the world. With Ronan's presence strengthening me, and Nelle's guiding me, I kept digging, deeper and deeper, until there was nothing else below.

It was there. *I was there.* Storm and stone, twisting and crashing. Light and dark, tugging and gnashing. Destruction and Creation. Death and Life.

"My stomach," I voiced aloud.

Nelle's free hand rested on my lower abdomen with cool, delicate fingers. "You're doing so well," she breathed, her voice so, so far away. Down here, in the abyss of myself, I could barely hear her. But still, like light sparkling on the surface of the water, she spoke, navigating me back. "Now, don't focus on bringing him back or saving his life, it's too vague. Just focus on what you want for him, for his future. Focus on changing it instead. Focus on offering this body as a sacrifice for the new. A creature that doesn't age, that's not affected by time. A creature that can shift and adapt, that doesn't need air, that is connected to the water even from far away, that can handle the gift Lyr's spring gave him."

I inhaled deeply, letting the feeling expand and grow and take root. I thought of Ronan's body, harder than the rocky shore that stood unmovable even when the sea crashed into it. Thought of his heart, beating faster than any wind could ever catch, strong and true. Thought of him diving deeper into the sea, into the darkness, the light in his eyes bright enough to warm even the blackest, coldest abyss.

Heat and pressure built in my pit, burning and stinging. In a violent chorus, the small spot on my shoulder hissed and sneered, a wave of blinding pain flashing down the length of my arm. I bit back the urge to scream. I wouldn't just withstand it. I would make it mine.

Biting into it, into the pain and darkness and stone, I devoured it whole, sucking every last drop down. I was my father's daughter—and my mother's. I was sea and sky and moon in one. I was the tide, controlling my own fate. I was a silver wheel, forged of metal and earth in light and fire, created to steer my own course. To steer Ronan's, if that's what it took.

I would make him not just a siren, but more. He'd be a man, with the breadth to hold not just the spring, but the sea itself in his arms. I would make my husband a god. One no mortal inconvenience like time or distance or weakness could threaten ever again.

"Nef's breath, she's doing it."

Vian's reverent voice was the only warning before the light exploded from me, brighter than the sun. It knocked us all back into the now-scalding water, splashing as we scrambled to find our footing.

I opened my eyes, coming back to the surface, back to myself. The taste of ash and sick filled my mouth, my limbs shaking and weak beneath me…

But when I saw Ronan's golden tail twitch out of the water, my strength was restored.

33

Wishes and Worshipers

RONAN

In the darkness, a voice floated from above the waves, softer than the mist that hugged the shore.

"Ronan?" the mist asked, her voice so familiar, so close and warm... "Are you awake?"

I was not awake. I did not exist. I was only a thought, wading in the dark, warm in-between…

No, I was alive. Reborn. I let myself float toward the sound, an anchor pulled up through the heavy drift of the current. Blinking, my eyes fluttered open, expecting the bright sunlight on the sea.

I met instead with her face, even more luminous.

Keira burst into a smile, a sun pulling me into her orbit. "You're back." Her hand caressed my cheek, sending a shiver down my spine.

"What happened?" I sat straighter, shaking off the deep grogginess that fogged my head, realizing only now I was in a sunken tub, the water sloshing awkwardly over my naked form. Keira was still dressed, her clothes soaked, but the shoulder of her shirt was singed off, revealing the black spot on her shoulder, no bigger than an apple. I stretched my legs, which were somehow impossibly sore, like I'd been running for miles without water or rest.

An uncomfortable cough sounded behind me, announcing my audience. I jolted to cover myself, spinning to the sound.

Ellian and Vian stood in the doorway, the former with an awkward, fake smile on his dark features, the latter dripping wet and looking like a crow after a rainstorm.

"Good to see you're okay, *Dynaur.*" Vian smiled eagerly, spewing nonsense as if nothing was different between us, like he hadn't been gone with my wife for months. "If you all will excuse me, I'm off to find Griffin." He breezed out of the room without further ceremony, caught in whatever wind called him.

In his wake, another form slinked into the room. Orange eyes like sunsets cast in bronze, a familiar mane of hair that reminded me of summer and regret. "Siobhan?"

Slowly, like I was drying off the pieces of rain-soaked parchment, things fell into place. Keira had come back...she'd brought the sirens with her...passing out on the street, the sweltering heat. Panicked screams and hushed whispers. Then hands on my face, my chest. Hunger that could eat me from the inside. Water cold enough to burn, flashes of light.

Then darkness. Nothing. Vast, frozen emptiness.

The feeling of being ripped apart and sewn back together. Every limb sore, but remade. Gold mined from the molten core of the earth. Rebuilt from scratch.

Lyr below, what had these witches done to me?

"You look like a shipwreck." Sho crossed her arms over her chest, right side of her mouth twitching upward.

No, not a shipwreck. I was sore, and tired, yes, but I was not wrecked. I was something built new from the scraps and debris. Something...stronger.

Siobhan shifted her weight, casting her gaze downward. Still, after all this time, she was such an enigma. So powerful, so fierce, but so unsure of where she fit. My laugh was real. "You look like a fish out of water, old friend."

"You two know each other?" Ellian raised a brow, narrowed gaze flicking between us in a way that made me keenly aware of the fact that I was indeed naked, and standing in the same room as my wife, her former suitor, and my previous bedfellow.

If I hadn't already made a show of it before, now might have been a good time to play dead.

"Intimately," Keira nudged my hip in the water, a look that could scare a shark on her face. So she remembered, then. And still she brought Siobhan with her. To save me. To save the Deyrnas.

Blame it on whatever I'd endured, but my legs shook underneath me.

"Well, I'm Ellian Llewellyn." He took two long strides toward Siobhan, unaware of the tension, his hand extended, a lamb walking right into the tiger's den. "Councilman, actually."

Siobhan snorted, eyeing him like her next meal. "Is that supposed to impress me?"

To my surprise and relief, Nelle burst through the curtain with a steaming bowl of something that made my stomach rumble, pushing Ellian out of the way. "Enough standing and chatting," she admonished, setting the bowl down on a table so she could properly secure her hands to her hips. "These two need to eat and rest, so everyone but Ronan and Keira can make the rest of their introductions *outside*."

At the very thought, my stomach growled, more ferocious than any creature I'd ever met on *Hiraeth*. I was sure I'd eaten breakfast this morning, and yet whatever fish stew was wafting from the fragrant pot was enough to make me salivate.

"Let me take you ladies shopping. It seems like you didn't have much time to pack." Ellian straightened his clothes, flashing a grin at Siobhan, who rolled her eyes.

"That would be lovely, Councilman." Nelle patted his shoulder twice, shooting Siobhan a look to escort him out. Dutiful as ever, she smacked on a scowl and dragged Ellian from the room to go play cat and dog elsewhere.

Nelle sighed, suppressing a chuckle, then turned to me, expression warm. She carried the bowl of stew carefully, setting it on the stone edge of the tub for easy access. "You're feeling alright?" She pressed the back of her hand to my forehead, scanning my face with violet intensity.

I breathed in deeply, the stew scent already placating my aches and pains. Too hungry to resist, I took a spoonful, nearly moaning as flavor erupted in my mouth. White fish and ginger, with a kick of hot peppers—and something rich I couldn't name. Everything tasted sharper, like I was experiencing it in color for the first time after a world of grey. After a meal this fine, I reckoned I'd be good as new.

As usual, the healer had worked her magic. Gratitude swelled in my chest. I knew what it meant for her to be here, to have left *Hiraeth* behind for Keira. To have left the rest of her sisters. "Aye. Thank you, Nelle. For everything."

Nelle jerked her head toward Keira with a conspirator's wink. "Keira did the hard work." She stood, beelining for the curtain, blush coloring her cheeks. "I'll give you two some privacy."

Fish stew flopped in my middle. For the first time in three months, I was truly alone with Keira. In a Lyr-damned brothel bathhouse, no less.

I'd been avoiding this, whether I acknowledged it or not. Avoiding meeting her gaze head on, avoiding the pity I knew would be waiting. Avoiding the moment where the rest of the chaos faded away, and it was just us again, left with all the things we'd done and left unsaid.

I didn't know If I was ready for all of that, so like the true coward I was, I went for something easier to swallow before she could rip open wounds that hadn't closed yet.

"Will you tell me what's happening?" I looked at her through my lashes, wearing nothing but my favorite smile. "For starters, why am I naked?"

My flirtations bounced off her well-honed armor like rain on a rooftop. She stared at her hands, tracing the black ink on the back of the right one. "You fainted. It's been too long since the spring." Steel eyes flicked up to me, angry tears welling in their depths. "Esme warned you, Ronan. How could you be so reckless?"

Her words stung worse than a snake bite, clamping down around my throat. "You left. I didn't have many choices." My voice was shallow, and I hated it. Her breath hitched, and I instantly wanted to take it back, to swallow the words down and let them disappear. She left, but I was the one who hadn't heeded the warning. I was callous and cocky, thinking I could outrun my problems by chasing after someone else's.

The silence between us was a vast chasm. It stretched on for moments that felt like days, so long I didn't know how to begin to cross it.

"I'm sorry." Hurt laced her tone as she sank further into the bath and onto one of the stone seats. A harsh laugh broke from her, melting with her tears. "I thought I lost you again. I was just scared."

My whole chest ached, the serpent of my guilt squeezing around me. I waded to her, desperate to touch her, to comfort her until the tears were dry. But I didn't. I couldn't bring myself to it, not yet. "Keira, how did Nelle save me?"

"She—" Keira stopped, eyes trained on me. She exhaled, and I watched her slip back into her mental Captain's coat. To protect her or me, I didn't know. "We—*I* turned you into a siren."

A pause. Then another.

She did not laugh. It wasn't a joke.

My legs twitched, as if remembering the punchline when I didn't.

I pictured the sirens in *Hiraeth*, their bloodstained mouths, their scaled tails and sharp claws, the gills along their ribcages, the jagged teeth and dragon eyes…

The hidden taste of the fish stew suddenly had a name, one that made my gut churn. *Blood.* "How?"

Keira reached for my hand, tentatively, as if she was afraid she'd break me if she moved too fast. Our fingers entwined, the warmth of her palm heating mine. "Turns out, Danura is my mother. Lyr isn't the only one who gave me a gift."

Another pause. Still no humor dancing in her eyes, no upward twitch of her lips. She was serious.

It wasn't funny, but I laughed anyway. It bubbled up from me until my shoulders shook with the force of it, my ribs aching with the effort to breathe.

Danura was Keira's *mother*. It made perfect sense, in a way, the physical resemblance close enough aside from the hair. But the undeniable grace and power, the regal air and untamed spirit...that was uncanny. Whatever creature Danura was, Keira was made of the same starstuff.

And now, she had her very own siren at her command. Like mother, like daughter.

Welcome, Duweni.

Lyr whispered in my head, a deep cackle reverberating through me. I rolled my eyes but could feel the kinship in his voice.

Keira's brow knotted with worry, but I pressed a quick kiss to her forehead, smoothing out the lines. "All this time, I thought it was Lyr that led me to you...but maybe he had some help. Fate is a tricky bitch."

So was Danura. She'd known all along and hadn't told me.

Keira shifted closer, sending ripples across the bath's surface. "I'm sorry I didn't ask you first, but I was so scared. I just got you back, I couldn't—" Frenzied words tumbled from her lips, but I barely heard them as I stared at her, fully realizing the glorious creature before me. The creature with the power to make and remake. Beautiful and chaotic as a storm, but as giving and generous as the earth itself. I tucked a strand of her wet hair behind her ear, the contact sending a shiver up my spine.

She had saved me. A more foolish version of myself might have resented her for it. But I couldn't, not anymore. Not when I'd spent night after night praying for any miracle that would bring her back. Not when I would've chosen the same for her. I no longer cared if I was a siren or a squirrel, I was happy to follow her leading.

"Your mark. It's smaller." I let my gaze travel to the curve of her shoulder, to the obsidian-against-moonstone color. "Danura?"

"Sort of. A little bit of me, maybe, too." She smiled, something unknotting in her. But the expression shifted as easily as the tide, a new tangle forming in the line. "Are you angry? That you're—"

"No, I'm not angry, Keira." I silenced her with my finger to her lips. I would not let her eviscerate herself with guilt for a decision I would've made myself. For a decision I would've made for her, too, if I had the opportunity. We'd been trapped in this cycle for so long, each of us falling on our swords to save the other. With Aidan, with the spring, in Orwellin...we'd made this choice before, over and over again. But I hoped neither of us would ever have to make it again. "I'm just tired. I'm tired of being the damsel in distress, waiting for you to sail home and rescue me. But maybe now I can actually help. Sirens are pretty durable, from what I've gleaned."

"There are...side effects." She looked down, throat bobbing. "You have to drink blood to stay alive, and you won't age normally. You'll probably outlive me by triple, and that's if I live a long and healthy life. Which is unlikely, given who I am."

I cupped her face in my hand, my whole world resting in my palm. "I don't care. I just want to be useful for you."

She leaned into my touch, mumbling into the tingling place we connected, "Do you feel any different?"

"Yes. In a good way," I admitted absentmindedly, savoring the silken skin of her lip, tracing its bow shape with my thumb. It had been so long since I'd touched her, since I felt the corporeal proof of her breathing next to me. And everything was heightened, like lightning bottled in the tip of my finger, the sensation so simple but overwhelming. I pulled back before I could let myself become intoxicated by it. "It's like I felt after the spring, but more. So much more. And like it belongs to me now."

"I meant—" She swam closer, lips parted and eyes hazy. "Do you still feel the same way about us?"

This time she had to be joking.

"Keira, I have missed you more every single day since you left. Like missing a vital organ," I laughed, stroking her face with the back of my hand. She was so warm, so soft, it was hard to focus on anything other than the feel of her, the pink shade of her lips. "So, no, I don't feel the same. I feel even luckier that you're here. And I won't let you go again, even if you go wrinkly and grey first."

And so she could feel just how desperately I missed her, I brought my lips to hers. The kiss was slow, deliberate, like we were meeting each other for the first time all over again. She was velvet and silk, and I was acutely aware of every inhale, every subtle shift as she angled herself to me, deepening the contact. Unmistakable heat riled in my basest parts, demanding and needy as her lips parted, allowing me to explore further.

Lyr below, I missed her. My hands knotted in her raven hair, pulling her closer, the places we touched alight like wildfire.

She extinguished the flame as she pushed against my chest, separating us. In an instant, I was starving for her touch. "Ronan, Nelle said you should rest."

The beast in my chest roared to life, no longer a dragon, but a *sarffymor* raging with primal need. In one swift motion, I hooked my arms beneath her, lifting her from the water and sitting her on the ledge of the bath. Her eyes widened in surprise, and I didn't care as I knocked the bowl of stew over, red contents spilling onto the stone.

Our gazes locked, I caressed her shoulder, pushing her burned, ruined shirt further off her frame. She didn't stop me, only stared with desire blazing in her eyes as I gripped the shirt and tore it from her completely, the soaked fabric giving way.

"I am not fragile anymore. You don't need to take care of me." My voice was low, my mouth dry with the thought of every part of her I wanted to touch, to *taste*. To worship. "Let me take care of you."

This time, the kiss was needy, fervent. It was a reparation for every kiss we'd missed in the last three months, every moment we'd pined for the other's embrace. I swallowed the moans as they tumbled from her lips, each one feeding the creature roaring with triumph inside me.

But it wasn't enough. I needed more. Needed all of her. I kissed down her throat, leaving marks as I went, sucking the soft flesh gently between my teeth.

"Such a wicked mouth," she muttered huskily, biting back another string of moans.

I was undone, my skin tight and hot even in the cool water. I didn't want just a taste. I wanted a *feast*.

Drawing her up with one hand, I yanked down her trousers with the other. Gathering my intentions, she shimmied out of them, casting them away. I let myself take a full moment to soak in every curve and edge of her, each line drawn by the gods themselves. She was a vision. A goddess.

Reverently, I placed my hands on either side of her thighs, kneading the supple, muscled flesh while kissing her throat once more, earning another string of unintelligible moans.

When I was satisfied, I gently pushed her back onto the stone and spread her legs wide.

"Ronan——" She leaned up on her forearms to protest, but as I sank my mouth onto her sex, she fell back, hips bucking into me. "Ah, *shit*."

I let my wicked tongue work, every curse and minute shift of her hips and quivering breath adding to my pleasure as much as hers. I savored the task, savored *her*, sweet and begging to be worshiped.

To be adored. My own half-forgotten pleasure throbbed, aching to bury myself in her softest parts. She tangled her fingers in my hair, pulling tightly. A shudder ran down my spine as I stared up at her from her center, halting my ministrations.

"I need you." It was a command and a plea, her dark pupils boring into my middle.

The leash I had on the creature broke as I lifted myself out of the water, muscles relishing in the soreness, hovering over her. I kissed her cheek, her throat, her chest, before lowering myself slowly. Carefully, watching every twitch of her lips, I sheathed myself inside her heat.

It wasn't long before we were panting, each thrust bringing us both dangerously close to the edge, her symphony of cries crescendoing. Everything was blissfully hot and tight, my skin coated in the fire and ecstasy of her.

As she sang the final note, my release snapped, coursing through me like a breaking wave. We moved as one, the goddess and her devotee, the moon controlling the tide.

"Stay with me this time, please," I murmured into her hair as I collapsed at her side, the euphoria still buzzing in my veins.

"Forever." She wrapped herself around me, her breath steadying. "I'll be with you forever."

It was the sweetest lie I'd ever heard.

34

Crews and Comrades

KEIRA

Among all the miracles I'd experienced, this was the greatest. Ronan still loved me. Still wanted me.

And Lyr below, he was *alive*.

Maybe the miracle would one day become another curse, when I started to slump and sag and he was still the beautiful, ethereal creature before me. Maybe he'd decide he'd rather live his long life with someone whose time wasn't marked by a black death spot. When that moment came, I'd let him go; but for now, he was wholly and truly mine.

I couldn't keep my eyes off him. His hair was lighter now, each curl touched with gold, a crown fit for a king. The sapphire of his eyes shone brighter in the faded glow of evening, azure lanterns shimmering on their own. He seemed taller, *stronger*, the breezy red tunic we'd stolen from Madame Katrin's hugging the impressive cut of him. I'd already sampled his power in our bathtime rendezvous, and my heat rose at the memory. I chased that thought from my mind before it could land me in trouble.

Still, it was a struggle to contain my joy as we made our way to the Ir'desian inn, hand in hand, every fiber of my being singing.

No matter what the tide brought us next, we'd have this momentary miracle, and that was enough.

But as we passed the clay-and-stone buildings, warm and brown baked in the setting sun, my eyes caught glimpses of dark blue smudges of paint. On doors, marked on the backs of canvas tents, decorating market stalls and signs…

Blue *ceffyl dwrs* with red eyes.

They stared us down as we finally approached the heavy wooden door of the tavern, a little building called *The Spiced Pig*. Ronan opened it with a smile, eyeing the particularly large *ceffyl* painted on its face. The smell of spiced wine and roasted meat wafted toward me, so decadent it made my stomach grumble. But the sound that greeted me was even more satisfying, feeding my hungry soul.

"Tarran, please stop staring at those peaches like you want to screw them, will you?" Saeth's anvil-blunt tone carried over the sound of other patrons mumbling and finishing their evening meals.

Tarran's answering whine filled my chest with unnamable happiness. "I wasn't!"

Drawn to the noise, I stepped further into the inn's tender embrace, rounding the corner to see where my crew sat, perched and lounging across a wide oak table with far too many goblets of ale for the time of day. Saeth had skewered the peach with her dagger, waving it in Tarran's face, while Griffin watched. On the other side, Reagan, wearing a red Ir'desian wrap dress that made her look far too grown up, braided Vian's long hair, the boy's ears flushing the same scarlet as her dress. Siobhan and Nelle had already made it back, sitting among them like they'd been there the whole time, a very flustered Ellian and Rhett trying to rein in the chaos.

My breath stuck in my chest, halted by the tears budding in the corners of my eyes. My family, whole and real, laughing and drinking and teasing. I stood and watched, mesmerized, like a kid looking through a baker's window at all the sweet things I craved but could not have.

"You absolutely were, Tarran. There is drool on your chin." Reagan smirked as she tied a knot at the end of one of Vian's miniature braids, still too entranced in her work to notice Ronan and I standing in the doorway, gaping at them.

Griffin chuckled, stealing the peach off the end of Saeth's dagger and sinking his teeth into it. "Don't tease the poor lad in front of the ladies," he sneered with a full mouth, juice running down the sides of his chin. "It's not his fault he's still a massive virg—"

"I swear to Lyr, I'm going to buy you all muzzles." Rhett slammed his mug down, kneading his brow with a fist. "Feral pups. It's a nightmare to look after you all."

Ronan rubbed circles across my back, his touch anchoring me to my body. But still I felt like a spectator, not a participant, unable to cross the threshold from audience to performer and join the play. Frozen to my spot, I could only watch.

Nelle's warm laughter filled the room as she nudged Siobhan's side, the two of them already melting into the picture of my family. "We know that feeling all too well, don't we?"

"Don't listen to him. You're only two years older than me, muscles." Saeth licked the blunt edge of her blade clean of fruit juice, eyes trained on Rhett. "I'd like to see you *try* to muzzle me."

Vian, his dark hair a crown of braids atop his head, looped his long arm around Reagan's shoulders, the girl blushing at the touch. He leaned down to fake a whisper in her ear, a mocking hand in front of his face. "Saeth would win."

Saeth sat back in her chair, a smug smile creeping over her features. "I'm so glad you're back, Vian."

Ronan cleared his throat, strode up to the table with his snake's smile and bobbed his head at me. "Someone else is back, you oblivious fools."

I held my smile as carefully as one would hold a child, the feeling both foreign and unpracticed as I waved to my crew. They followed my husband's gesture, the banter fizzling out quickly like the afterlight of a flare.

"Captain." Rhett stood first, nearly knocking over his chair. "So good to see—"

"Out of my way, you oversized oaf." Reagan pushed past her cousin, running toward me, almost tripping over her flowy wrap. Before I could react, she crushed me in a hug, slender arms twining around my waist, head burrowed into my chest. After a moment, as I remembered how, I held her back, breathing in her rose-and-rainstorm scent, planting a kiss on the top of her head. She squeezed me tighter. "I knew you'd be back. I *knew* it."

My heart threatened to burst, full to the brim. Perhaps her will alone had brought me back, had delivered the small victories I needed to guide me home. To where I belonged.

"Thank you for not giving up on me, little dragon." I did my best to mask the quiver in my voice.

"You know, she wasn't the only one." Tarran pouted as he joined the hug, encompassing us both in his long arms. Lyr's arse, he'd gotten tall, the lankiness in his limbs falling away to reveal a lean undercoat. It had been three months, but Tarran was on the verge of manhood. Still, the sun in his smile was all boy. "I said from the beginning you were coming back."

"We missed you." Saeth sauntered over, swatting her twin away so she could press a quick kiss to my cheek. "All of us."

Missed me…like I'd gone on a holiday. Not like I'd left them behind to deal with my mess. Not like I'd ran off to the island of the lost, prepared to die without ever seeing them again.

Papa used to say the word 'guilty' was only meant to be used before 'pleasure'. Still, I couldn't help the way it sloshed in my gut like rum on an empty stomach, waiting to take its revenge.

I cleared my throat, focusing instead on the bright ball of joy that blossomed in my chest. Today was a small victory, a reunion I'd never thought I'd see, and one that deserved celebration. This time, my smile was not entirely fake. "Well, I'm back, and I brought some friends." Gently separating myself from Reagan's cobra hold, I motioned to the sirens sitting casually at the table, nursing mugs. "I take it you all have met?"

"Reagan has been a very generous hostess." Siobhan shrugged, turning so I could see the intricate braids that decorated the underside of her curls. Next to her, Ellian laughed heartily, revealing a single tiny plait in his tangled hair, too.

Nelle grinned. "Your family is lovely, *Ariannad.*"

Reagan nudged my side, her smile faltering around the edges. "Are you staying this time?"

The wind was ripped from my sails. She had believed in me, and yet this girl with a dragon's heart could not trust me. Not after I left her once, not a word of goodbye, nor with anything to protect her from the harsh truths of the world.

I would not repeat my mistakes.

"Yes," I promised, both to her and myself. "If you're all running from Connor, I'm not going to let you do it on your own. We might as well run together this time."

I looked to my family, old and new, the starlight in my middle burning with determination. I would not abandon them again. Connor Yorath would have his war. He could bring plague and death to my door, and I would meet him with my dagger sharp and my spirits high. I was not afraid, not anymore.

For the innocents lost, for my father, for the whole Deyrnas. For the precious band of misfits who sat at the table. For the people that drove me to my destination, the captains to my wheel.

Connor could have his war. And I would have his heart on a platter.

"Let's set some of Connor's plans on fire while we're at it."

"Better yet." Saeth clapped me on the shoulder, her eyes scorching with the same rage that lit my fuse. "Let's burn it all to the ground."

"Alright you nutjob arsonists, is it my turn yet?" Rhett ruffled Saeth's hair, the suggestion of a smile on his stony features. Sticking her tongue out, Saeth linked arms with Reagan, leading her back to the table.

I narrowed my eyes at Rhett, the hair on my neck upright. "Your turn for what?"

"Come here," he said, and to my complete and utter shock, he lifted me into a bear hug, spinning me around like I weighed nothing before plopping me back down onto unsteady legs. "It's been murder dealing with Griffin without you here to keep him sane."

"I can still hear!" My cousin sprang up from his seat, finally joining us in the fray. He'd been quiet, which was stranger than a raven without feathers, but it seemed no level of moodiness could stop him from a retort.

"You were meant to!" Rhett winked at me as if this were somehow my idea before swaggering back to the table, joining in the chatter that had struck up again.

Griffin and I regarded each other in silence for a moment. He was my cousin by blood, but my brother in spirit. Since we were children, it had always been us against the world. Yet I'd left him behind to fend for himself, left the whole world resting on his shoulders alone. Ronan might have been the interim head of the family, but Griffin was the shoulders, just as he'd always been for me. He was the pillar the rest of them stood on, carrying the load when it became too burdensome.

I didn't know which I owed him first, a 'thank you' or a 'sorry'.

"I didn't mean to bite your head off before. The sirens are lovely." He quirked an eyebrow at me, a question in our unspoken language. *Are we alright?*

I could only manage a nod, neither 'sorry' or 'thank you' finding voice. "You were protecting him, in your own way. I can't fault you. You stepped up when I couldn't." My voice was thick as I tried to convey both emotions. "My Pa would've been proud of you."

His throat bobbed. "Welcome home, Shrimpy."

He took my hand, steering me to the table where my family waited. I nestled into the empty chair between Ronan and Saeth, right in the middle of a fresh argument—right where I belonged.

Saeth draped herself half across the table, mischief brewing in her eyes. "So what's this I heard about you having gills now, Ronan?"

He blinked, stammering, "That's—"

"Vian already told us, don't even try to lie." Reagan crossed her arms, silencing her eldest cousin, as was her right.

Ronan quickly regained his composure, dropping an arm around my shoulders, Mathonwy grin cocked and ready to fire. "And you believed him?"

Reagan opened her mouth to protest, but Siobhan beat her to it, interjecting even though she'd been talking to Ellian and Nelle a moment before. "It's true. I saw it myself." She waggled an accusatory finger at him, her expression wild as she fed into the tale. Reagan snickered, her feathers puffed up with pride.

Ronan's cheeks reddened, but his mask never faltered. He was the picture of cool indifference, apathy his cloak and dagger, the only indication of his embarrassment the way he shifted ever-so-slightly toward me like I was his shield.

Unfortunately for him, I was in the mood to be a sword.

"Gold is your color, Ronan." I jabbed him lightly in the side, whispering loudly enough that Reagan and Saeth could hear. The girls dissolved into a fit of giggles. Ronan shot me a dark glare, but it was shallow, his lips fighting to hold back a laugh of his own.

"*Dynaur.*" Vian perked up, tilting his head at an angle I'd come to know meant trouble. "Golden boy."

Tarran flicked the wind-whisperer's cheek, fondness brimming in his gaze. "Man, I forgot how odd you are."

"Can you make me a siren next, Keira?" Reagan squealed, stretching her legs out across Vian's lap, her heels stuck together, mimicking a fin. I froze, imagining Reagan with fangs, sinking her teeth into some poor sailor. But both Nelle and Siobhan snorted, two more victims of the tiny tyrant's campaign for total domination. "I want my tail to be red! Or, ooh, maybe a bright pink…"

"Never mind the tail, Rea." Saeth cut her off with arrow-point efficiency, her hazel eyes fixed on me. "Look at Keira's ink!"

I stiffened, the urge to hide my hand heating my skin, but it was too late. Every eye at the table turned to me to study the ink I now wore as a crest. In the lanternlight, the black was even starker, the moon, wheel, and compass all intertwined in an intricate dance on my skin. It was art, and it was mine. And if any of my cousins thought to tease me for it, I'd have their tongue.

"Lyr's tits, you got a tattoo?" Griffin yanked my hand, examining the mark with his jaw on the floor. "In *Hiraeth?*"

I shrugged, wishing my mask was as well practiced as my husband's. "Nelle gave it to me on the way back."

Heads whipped around faster than hurricane winds, attention now diverted to the healer. Nelle crossed her legs, leaning further back in her chair, a proud grin dancing on her features. "If you're good," she said with a quick wink to Griffin that had the Swordsinger blushing, "I'll think about giving you one too."

Not to be outdone, my cousin smoothed a hand over his head of curls, a preening bird. "I already have the family crest on my left arse cheek, but I *did* just say to Rhett that I think it needs a twin."

Everyone but Rhett erupted into raucous laughter, Tarran snorting his ale through his nose.

"I need another drink," Rhett sighed heavily, whipping his coat of Tarran's spewage. "I'm at my wits end."

Ellian whacked his back, a knowing twinkle in his eye. "I'm surprised you have any wits left. None of us had very many in the first place."

Gods above and below, I missed this. The bickering, the shallow insults. The giggles over a few mugs of ale, the moments of rest in a world of chaos. I tried to etch the precious pictures into my mind, to carve them into the warm clay of this place and keep them on the shelves where I could take them out and dust them off whenever I needed a reminder. Reagan's mess of curls, the way Vian smiled at her with a glimmer in his black eyes. Rhett's well-practiced scowl, and the way it softened whenever he made eye contact with Griffin. Saeth's teasing jabs at Tarran, and the gentle way she'd tuck his curls behind his ears like a doting mother hen. Ellian's booming laugh that made heads turn, Siobhan's fanged grin, Nelle's sneaky winks....

The way Ronan sat taller as he watched, pride radiating from every gilded fiber of his being. The way the sight of him stole my breath and stopped my heart and would until my very last day.

This was what we were fighting to keep. This was what Connor threatened to destroy with his greed and tyranny. But he couldn't take it away, not really. He couldn't buy or steal the loyalty, the love. It would conquer all.

Something crashed behind us, jarring me from the moment. A man in a plain cap and grey longcoat—Porthladdian, by the cut of it—stumbled inside, knocking over a pitcher in his frenzy. The patrons fell silent, my crew included, as the intruder shattered the inn's carefully crafted comfort.

"Keira? Keira Mathonwy?" he called out, and I froze, dread pooling in my gut. The voice was familiar, one I couldn't quite place, but to hear my name...

Griffin figured it out before I did, his skin blanching. "Papa?"

Donnall spun to us, tearing the cap from his cropped mane of ginger-and-salt curls, locking eyes with his son. His were red and puffy, the dark circles beneath them heavy with truths I didn't want to hear.

It had been months since I'd seen him. The last time I heard my name on his lips, he'd cursed me, blaming me for his brother's murder. The last time his eyes met mine, they had hurled accusations that cut like daggers.

Kin-killer.

"Griffin!" Relief relaxed Donnall's shoulders as he staggered toward us. He stopped when he saw me, and this time, fresh tears lined his eyes. "Keira. Oh, thank Lyr yer here, too. I'm sorry, but I need ye..." He broke down entirely, sobs wracking his burly, sturdy frame. He gripped his son's shoulders and shook him slightly. "Griffin, my boy. They have yer mama. They're going to hang her."

35

Losses and Loyalties

RONAN

When I was a boy, my mother taught me to play chess. People called my father the snake, and rightfully so—he earned it, a thief and a cheat by nature and a liar by choice. But no one ever suspected Eleri Mathonwy of deception. No one saw the cunning underneath the kindness of her crystal-blue gaze.

I did. I knew she was a snake draped in flowers, fragrant and beautiful, but just as calculating as the rest of us. She would lie in the greenery like a garden snake, hiding amidst the beauty, ready to strike.

Mama's favorite rule of chess was to lose wisely.

Lose only what you can afford to. Lure your opponent in, let them take your pawns, your castles, your bishops. Those, you can live without. But never let them have your Queen. And when they are close enough, let her strike.

The cramped bedroom of *The Spiced Pig* was even smaller now, the air sucked out by the weight of Donnall's message. The old sailor perched at the edge of the bed Griffin and Rhett shared, his head hanging in his hands, his son's hand precariously on his back. Ellian and Keira sat in chairs facing him, born negotiators ready to hear his plea and strike an accord. I clung to the clay wall like a shadow, content to watch, not trusting myself to be kind. My serpent's tongue was already forked and ready to spew venom at the man who would lead us home to our ruin.

Not that I blamed him. I would forsake my own name, my own *blood* for my wife's sake, too.

Never let them have your Queen.

"How did you find us?" Ellian's tone was soft, but it had a sharp edge, the blacksmith in him striking the steel while it was hot.

Donnall lifted his head, the red in his eyes even more pronounced by the few lanterns that scattered the room. "I have my ways...the symbols everyone is paintin' on the doors makes it easier."

"Tell us what happened." Gentleness coated Keira's voice. It belonged to a niece, not a Captain. I crossed my arms tighter, if only to stop the beast in my chest from bursting out and tearing Donnall to bits.

We'd all been tricked and duped by Connor enough times. We'd given him pawns and bishops and rooks; he'd chased us from our home, threatened our lives, and hunted us across the Deyrnas. But Donnall should've protected his wife himself, should've gotten off the barstool at the *Raven* and helped her. Instead, while Vala worked tirelessly to feed Porthladd, he'd wasted the last six months mourning the dead brother that landed us all in this mess in the first place. Now he wanted *my wife* to come save him from his own incompetence.

I felt for Vala. She was a true Branwen, loyal to her core, proud and brave in the face of danger. But she knew the risks of staying behind. She knew, and she chose to stay despite them, for Finna and for Porthladd.

Lose wisely.

"Vala...she's been selling the goods ye've been bringing... Lyr below, I didn't even know, I've been such a self-absorbed prick." Donnall's words echoed my thoughts, and I almost scoffed. But the tears lining his eyes gave me pause, tugging at the strings of my heart I thought I'd steeled over. "But Connor caught her. Charged her with high treason fer dealing with fugitives and enemies of the Council."

Ellian pinched his nose, looking gravely back to me. "And with me and Leary gone, Agatha is alone against him."

"They sentenced my Vala to death." Another full-bodied sob shook from Donnall. "We only have three days left. I found you just in time."

"Lyr's balls." Griffin stood, pacing like a caged animal. I understood how he felt; we were all caged by this. By Connor. "What is Finna saying?"

I was wrong to assume Donnall's face couldn't look more pained. When his daughter's name struck him, he paled further. "No one has seen her fer weeks. She's been holed up in that estate, sayin' she needs rest with the baby on the way." He looked to Keira, ugly tears streaming down his face, and fell to his knees at her feet. "I didn't know where else to go. But you can't let him hurt them. *Please*, Keira."

Something territorial and protective roared to life in my chest. I stuffed my hands in my pockets, slinking out of the shadows toward the old man. There was real fear in his eyes, and grief, and pain...but it wasn't my problem. He'd forfeited his right to my kinship the day he spat in my wife's face in front of Aidan's funeral pyre. He had chosen to be a pawn in Connor's game instead of a knight in ours. So I would be the villain in his eyes, donning my Mathonwy snake mask, if it meant I could save Keira from further heartache. And even if she hated me for it, there were worse things than her scorn.

Her death, namely.

Never let them have your Queen.

"I don't know what you expect us to do about it," I scoffed, my smirk fitting like my favorite coat. "Just waltz right in, hand ourselves over to Connor? You know how heavily guarded he has things."

I braced for it, but Keira's glare still stung my weaker parts, slicing through me like the new dagger she wore at her hip. Griffin halted in his tracks, flexing his jaw, eyes burning. Rhett, Lyr bless him, placed a hand on his arm before the Swordsinger could react further, but even his icy eyes clouded with suspicion, a frown tugging at his mouth.

My smirk creased deeper. They'd all have to hit me harder than that if they wanted to make a dent. I would take their blows, would sacrifice every pawn I had with a wicked grin if it kept them from dying.

I turned my personal brand of pity and contempt back on my main target. Donnall's lip quivered, the mighty man reduced to a cowardly boy before me. "I don't know. I just thought…ye've all managed to stay alive and land a few good hits on him too." He scowled at me, fresh tears bursting free. "She's too innocent to die."

Griffin gripped his father's shoulders, expression tight as a hanging rope. "We aren't going to let her die, Papa. We'll think of something."

"Keira girl, I'm so sorry I didn't believe you. Aidan was my brother, but…I've been an arse." Donnall stood, taking Keira's hands in his, his sobs now shaking both of them. "But I need our family, our crew. You're the only ones who can stop Connor."

"Go get some rest, Donnall," Keira sighed, squeezing his hands back. "We'll figure it out in the morning."

He nodded, broken and bent, stumbling out the door, presumably to drown his sorrow at the bar. My stomach coiled as I shut the door behind him, wishing I could shut him out of my wife's life entirely.

I took a steadying breath that did nothing for the molten rage in the pit of my stomach.

"What do we do now?" Rhett sighed first, plopping onto the bed Donnall had occupied a moment before.

Griffin's eyes burned with betrayal. "You say that like we have a choice. We can't leave her to die! Rhett, she's my *mother*."

"I know the feeling, Griffin. I've already lost my Pa to this war." Rhett's voice was tight as he dredged Roland's name from the depths.

Another pawn in place of the Queen. My uncle had done his duty, saving Reagan and Griffin and everyone else in this room with his sacrifice.

Griffin, trapped in his fear, took up the task of wearing down the floorboards with his pacing once more. "I'm worried no one's seen Finna, either."

With a step, I blocked his path, my own worry gnawing at my nerves. Fire met steel as our gazes locked. "What if it's all a lie? What if your Ma is asleep in her bed, dreaming of berry bread, and Connor bribed Donnall to draw us out? Maybe he's tired of playing games. He knows you'll react like this, so he's baiting you. Us."

I might as well have shat on his mother's corpse with the look Griffin gave me. A part of me knew to be ashamed, knew if my own mother were here, she would have smacked me across the head for abandoning my kin.

But shame was for the living. I would deal with my own guilty conscience later. Now *I* was the snake, shedding the dead parts of my skin to survive.

"Of course it's a trap." Keira's sharp voice cut through the tension, a Queen striking mercilessly. She floated between Griffin and me, placing her tattooed hand over my chest. "But that doesn't mean we shouldn't try, Ronan. Donnall is right, Vala is too good for it to end like this. She is my family, and she's been fighting for us this whole time. If it was Reina—"

"It *has* been Reina." I cut her off, shooting the truth at her like a well-aimed bullet. "How do you think we've managed to keep ahead of Connor? My aunt has been risking her life impersonating you for months."

Keira winced, my bullet hitting its mark. She blinked twice as it registered, then looked to Griffin. Still steaming, the Swordsinger nodded once. "Aye. Madame Reina has been our ace."

I spoke softer this time, though it did nothing to distill the venom of the words. "Vala knew the risks of staying behind. It was her choice to be closer to Finna."

Keira's throat bobbed as she found her voice again. "That changes nothing. If Reina and Vala are willing to risk themselves for us, I'm willing to return that kindness."

Lightning struck in my middle, branding me with fresh fear as her silver eyes searched mine. Eyes that I would lose if I let her run into Connor's trap.

Eyes that had already steeled over with determination. A mind made up.

"The choice is yours, Captain," Rhett cut in, loyalty squaring his shoulders—a knight coming to his Queen's aid.

"No, it's ours." I kept my voice low despite the desperation and despair crashing like thunder inside me. "Keira, you haven't been here. You haven't been playing this chess match with Connor for months. He's trying to get us to give up our winning move. We've worked too hard to lose now."

Griffin's rage erupted as he shoved me, sending me flying back. "How dare you, you—!"

"He's right, Griffin." Keira silenced him like a mere boy in the presence of a goddess. But her words contradicted her slumped stance, the little girl peeking out from behind the coat of the Captain. "I can't pretend I'm the best person to make this choice. You have been fighting this, you're the ones who have been tracking his moves and dodging his attacks…"

"Precisely." I brushed off my shirt, desperately clinging to my mask. If she was faltering, I had to strike while the opening was there.

But I was too late.

When I was a boy, my mother always beat me at chess. Now Keira made her final move, setting the match.

"Let's put it to vote, then," she commanded, the battle fought and lost, my King surrendering to her Queen. "The whole crew."

Checkmate.

36

Sails and Swims

KEIRA

The yays had it, eight to three.

The decision was not as fast as I thought it might be. When Ronan voiced his opposition, my crew listened, loyal to his natural authority. Ellian of all people ardently supported his campaign, the former Councilman a shrewd businessman before he was a *blaidd*. No matter how much he cared for Vala, Porthladd and the Deyrnas mattered more.

His emerald eyes filled with tears, he was the first to stand with Ronan. "None of us are more important than this war. If we go back, we forsake three months of hard work and thousands of other lives."

The part of me that lived by my Father's commandments couldn't blame him. Couldn't blame Siobhan either as she followed suit, her loyalty to Ronan equal parts uncomfortable and admirable. She was a warrior, unafraid of battle, but the best commanders knew when to signal retreat.

It didn't matter in the end. It only took a word from Griffin, and the votes were cast. Eight to three.

Still, my crew was fair. Even when given the option to stay behind, no one batted an eye when I asked them to join me on yet another hopeless, luckless quest. The risk was clear; there was a significant chance we'd all be hanging with Vala in three days' time. But if we didn't try to save her, she'd die for sure.

We set sail for Porthladd at dawn.

For home. For Vala.

Ronan barely said a word as we boarded the *Ddraig*, his mask glued on as a semi-permanent fixture. It stung like sea-salt in an open wound, but I didn't let myself fall into the trap of licking it clean. My crew needed a Captain, and I had bigger choices to make. We needed speed, not cargo, if we were going to save Vala, and the *Ddraig* was not built with the grace of the *Ceffyl*. She was a freighter, sturdy and sure as the dragon she was named for. But the *Awelymor* was not large enough to hold the twelve of us, meaning we had to leave her behind in the Ir'desian port. Hopefully, her true owner would somehow stumble upon her one day. Unfortunately, it also meant forsaking most of the goods Ronan and the crew had worked so hard to secure for the last few months, taking only the necessities with us to lighten the *Ddraig's* load.

It was an incentive to survive. The Deyrnas needed this to be a return trip.

After we shoved off—no more cargo to unload, ready to set sail with enough momentum to still reach Porthladd on time—I mustered the courage to deal with the extra weight of my brooding husband.

I found Ronan on the portside rail around noon, his nose buried in a book as he lounged precariously on the edge. He looked like he'd jumped right out of whatever story he was engrossed in, a faerie too beautiful for us mere mortals to look at directly, like the sun blazing above as the crew busied themselves.

I wished I could let him drift off into whatever happy ending the pages held. But reality chased us on swift sails, and fate waited for no one.

Small victories, Keira girl. What do you want, and how do you get it?

There were larger victories I couldn't guarantee anymore. I couldn't promise my crew safety. I couldn't secure my family's happiness. But I could try to make things right with my husband. If this was to be our last sail before misery and agony descended once more, I would make it count.

"When I was a little girl, I used to climb up the *Ceffyl's* mizzenmast and jump from the top beam without warning," I said by way of hello, gripping the rail's smooth wood tightly, praying the *Ddraig* might lend me her sturdiness. "My father used to call me his little heathen. Said I was the fiercest thing on dry land."

Hesitantly, blue eyes flicked to me, the boy with a prince's heart already entranced by the story unfolding. "You've always been too brave for your own good."

"Not too brave." I shook my head, laughing at the memory as it flooded my mind. "Too trusting. I jumped because I knew Papa would be there every time to catch me. I never doubted him, because he taught me that's what it meant to be a family."

Ronan was quiet, his eyes glazed over as he stared at the sky, drifting to a faraway memory. I wanted to follow him to whatever daydream he created, but I couldn't. I'd been daydreaming for too long. It was my turn to be the consistent one who'd catch whoever jumped.

"Donnall came to us because he trusted us. Because that's what family does." I leaned onto the rail beside him. "I think I've been running for too long. And if I keep running, I'm never going to catch my breath. This has to end."

Ronan shut the book with a pronounced smack and sat up. "Running has kept us alive."

His look struck me like a lightning bolt, hot and penetrating. I was not used to the new ferocity of his actions, the intensity of his every look, the preternatural grace of his movements. He was a manmade god, or close to it. But I didn't need the storm within, I needed his humanity.

I needed my husband.

"It's kept us alive, aye. But what are we living for?" I kept my gaze on the horizon, on the faint line where the sky and the sea met despite their differences. Perhaps we could come to such an accord—the vast, unyielding sea and the limitless, uncatchable sky. I looked to him with as much love and gentleness I could. "If the people we love die, if the people who are close to us get caught in our wake, what's the point? You've been painting me as the face of this revolution...but what are we revolting for?" I reached for his hand, lacing my fingers in his, savoring the sweet heat of his skin. "This time, I'm ready to fight. And if that costs me my life, so be it. It's better to die with honor than live as a coward."

Ronan pulled his hand back, his disinterest a thin veil for the world of fear that lived in the ocean of his eyes. "I think we've both stared death in the face one too many times. Let someone else take a turn."

I swallowed down the hurt that strangled me. A few harsh words and dirty looks couldn't come between us. Nothing could. Not even death.

I would not fear the Dark God, not anymore. I would make him fear me. Like Airid, I would cut down anyone in my path, so when the Dark God finally greeted me face to face, he'd be the one who wanted to run.

"We call ourselves the liberators." I steeled my voice, meeting my husband's gaze directly. "*Rydha*, right? I think we can manage to save one woman."

Ronan was still, carved from marble. "And I will choose to save you every time."

In one swift motion, he hopped off the rail and dove into the deep blue, gold tail splashing behind him.

A stone dropped through me, heavy enough to sink the whole ship if I let it. *So much for less cargo.* If this was a small victory, I was nervous to see what failure looked like.

The rest of the afternoon was marked with similar luck. The crew was busy and having so many hands meant far less work for everyone aboard, a nice change of pace for most. Every sailor was more amiable the less needed they were. I just hadn't realized how little they all needed *me*.

Siobhan followed Ronan into the sea, the two of them swimming circles around the ship in a game that made my heart twist with my gut. But if he needed his space, I'd give it to him, Reina's wise words echoing through me. He didn't need my bullheaded persistence right now. He needed a swim and a think, and if Siobhan could help, I had to bite my tongue and thank her for it.

Nelle and Reagan didn't quite need me either, the two busy braiding both hair and ropes, taking their jobs in the rigging just as seriously as their new self-appointed duties as 'crew beautification' experts. After they gave me a long, twisted plait, they banished me from their salon and welcomed Vian, their next customer. Saeth and Tarran sparred for most of the afternoon, the former winning more matches than I'd expect. But Ellian was there to give them both pointers, the blacksmith's eye keen and his blade sharp. Based on how utterly bored Saeth looked, they'd been training hard the last few months, the instruction now child's play. Donnall, Lyr bless him, worked like a horse, swabbing the deck like a fresh sailor, outpacing even Rhett as the two of them took it upon themselves to get the *Ddraig* into tip-top shape.

"Good work, Deckhand Branwen," I called, hoping the simple compliment could help sew together the divide between us. His apology had felt sincere, molding together broken pieces of my heart I'd left unattended.

Donnall smiled back, but his eyes stayed on the ground. "Aye, Captain. It's the least I can do." He climbed back into the rigging without another word.

I couldn't blame him. Lyr knew I wouldn't be very chatty either if my spouse was locked in a cell somewhere.

Still, it left me with very little to do but sit and watch, a Captain turned passenger. Desperate for something to tie, to scrub, *to fix*, I found my truest friend in the crow's nest, his flaming red hair like a torch.

"Griffin?"

"Aye, Captain?" He peered over the edge, alert and ready.

The storm in my chest stalled, his presence calming the raging winds into gentle summer breezes. My voice sounded less like a child and more like a Captain as I called back to him, "Chart the course slightly to the east. I want to run into Reina and Reese up the coast of Bachtref, give Reagan and Saeth to them for safekeeping."

Griffin swung down easily, rope burning through his hands as he landed on the deck in front of me. "No, Saeth is coming. We need her in case there are tight spaces. She's the skinniest." He crossed his arms, assessing the crew with none of his signature mischief. "We'll have Tarran and Reagan man the ship, have it ready to fly if we need to."

I scrunched my nose, discomfort prickling under my skin. Usually when Griffin disobeyed an order, it was with a wink and a smirk, or a vulgar gesture that warranted a laugh. But the cold set of his eyes did nothing to suggest any prank. I cleared my throat of annoyance before pushing the order again. "We should still head off Reina, make sure—"

"Not happening. We need her to keep up the ruse more than ever." Griffin crossed to the helm and gripped the wheel with sure hands, adjusting it slightly westward. Finally, he cracked a grin, but it held no humor or devilry. Only pity. "If Connor thinks you're still in Bachtref, that's the only advantage we have. Sorry, Shrimpy, you're just going to have to trust me on this one."

A knot formed in my stomach, but I did my best to smile despite it. Perhaps I wasn't the only Branwen with their arms outstretched, waiting to catch any family that decided to take the leap of faith. Perhaps that's what being a good Captain meant—having the faith that my crew could land on their own two feet.

The thought should've relieved me. It didn't.

"Aye." I nodded to my cousin, hoping that my painted smile was enough to convince us both.

"Good, you're getting better!" Siobhan's voice sounded on the portside, pulling my attention away from the helm. The siren hoisted herself over the rail with ease, wearing nothing but slim bands of fabric over her most intimate parts. She beamed as she reached a clawed hand out, hauling Ronan up with her. He climbed over, every exposed muscle of his lean body flexing with the action. Lyr below, the sight of him knocked the wind from my sails, the water clinging to him and the flimsy swatch of cloth around his hips doing nothing to hide the sheer beauty of his stone-cut form.

But the fire in my core lit for a different reason as the two of them collapsed onto the deck, chests rising and falling in breathless laughs over a joke I must have missed.

"The shift is easier now." Ronan propped himself up and shook out his hair like a wet dog, his golden mop of fur glistening in the sunset, his returning smile just as bright. "Let's go again?"

Jealousy rolled through my gut, bitter on my tongue as I watched my husband smile at the siren. There was none of the malice or fear that he saved for me on his face. Lyr's ass, the worry had entirely erased itself, leaving only the sunkissed boy who used to smile for me and me alone.

It took all my strength to swallow down the ugly, envious little monster before walking up to him. "Can we talk?"

Ronan's smile fell. "Give us a minute, Sho."

Siobhan offered a pitying glance my way before leaping into the waves, shifting midair. Never in my life did I desire a tail, but here I was, wishing I could jump overboard and swim all the way back home.

Stone blocked out the sun in Ronan's expression again. "I'm training, Keira."

Any hope I had sputtered and flickered, like a bucket of ice water dousing a flame. "Ronan—"

He ran frustrated fingers through his hair, tugging the knots from the wet strands. "I'm not angry at you. What you said before…you're right. I'm tired of running, too. I'm not like you, Keira girl. I ran because I didn't think I had what it took to fight this." Some of the ice melted as he stood, breathing me in. My mouth went dry as he tucked a strand of hair behind my ear, the touch sending a jolt of lighting down my spine. "But if we are doing this, I want to be ready. I have a weapon now, and I'm going to use it to protect you, Mrs. Mathonwy."

A kiss pressed against my cheek, then he was gone again, the sea swallowing him whole. I wished it would swallow the festering, shallow feeling squirming inside me like worms in rot. I leaned against the rail, a dizzying wave of nausea hitting me. A long-forgotten pain in my shoulder throbbed, distant but irritating, the sensation like pins and needles under my skin.

When had I become a passenger in my own story? When had the tide shifted to where I was drifting aimlessly, letting the current pass me by?

Saeth jumped up onto the rail, straddling it like a horse. "Everything alright, Captain?"

I mumbled under my breath, "Am I Captain?"

She shot me a look that could bend steel. "Yes. We're all just adjusting." Rocking back, she glanced to where Ellian leaned over the starboard rail, watching Siobhan and Ronan swim, shouting encouragement. "Some more than others. Is it just me, or are there far too many shifters on this boat?"

"Couldn't have said it better myself." My laugh was dry. I owed Siobhan a debt I'd never be able to repay, but I'd be a liar if I said I hadn't imagined seven different applications for orange siren scales today alone.

Ellian shifted into his wolf form, and with another splash, the massive black beast plunged into the warm waters after them as if someone had yelled 'fetch'.

Saeth's eyes rolled so far back into her skull, all I saw was white. "Lyr's tits, what is it with the men on this ship? Is it the *tail*?"

"Are you and Ellian—?"

Saeth shrugged, cutting me off before I had to voice the question, her lips pursed. For a moment, a hint of sadness swam in the jade pools of her eyes, but it froze over faster than it came. "I think I'm over that. He's too…"

"Intense?" I offered the only word I had to describe the handsome, larger-than-life councilman-blacksmith-violinist-*shifter*.

"No, *docile*." The corner of her mouth tugged up in a sinister grin, the sparkle in her eyes like sunlight on a frozen lake. "I want someone who can keep up."

"Good luck finding one." This time, my laugh was real, and Saeth joined in until both our shoulders shook.

The same girlish laughter from a distant memory rippled through me like a tiny drop of water in a great pond. There were so many nights, ones I'd taken for granted, when Saeth, Finna, and I had done just this. Had giggled and gushed, had shared tales of conquest and jealousy. Finna always had the best advice on how to make a man blush, and Saeth would think up the best insults for the other snobbish brats who would mock me at the market. We would've been unstoppable, the three of us, had we not stumbled over our own skirts in petty attempts to outdo each other.

Maybe, when we saved Finna, there would still be a chance for us to try better. Three queens to rule the Deyrnas together.

"You know, Ronan's just trying to keep up with you," Saeth said when we caught our breath, the last laugh fizzling out as the sun made its final dip into the sea. She didn't force a smile, but there was less of a cutting edge to her truth, like a blade wrapped in silk. "The last few months…he didn't handle it well at first. But then he picked himself and the rest of us up because he wanted to prove himself your equal. Prove that he was worthy enough to be your match. Let him try for once."

I looked to the twilight-bruised sky, where the stars peeked out from their resting places, yawning into the night. I prayed to each one of them that Saeth was right.

My stomach knotted like the tight, uneasy feeling I'd get before diving off a high cliff or jumping from the highest beam of the mast. That moment before a fall, where all the what-ifs would race through my head, my muscles clenched and braced for impact. But for Ronan, I had to jump anyway. Had to hold my arms out wide and let myself go, knowing he'd be there to catch me.

My favorite voice coaxed me from sleep that night, a warm hand stroking the side of my face. "Wake up, Mrs. Mathonwy."

I blinked awake, eyes struggling to adjust in the sleepy lowlight of the single lantern in our cabin. I'd been dreaming, visions of frozen wastelands and dark eyes and little girls with black hair running in incoherent circles in my mind's eye. But when my husband's face, clear and real, came into focus, the golden rays of his form cleared away the lingering chill.

"Ronan?" I rubbed my eyes, scanning my surroundings. It was still night, the lantern burning bright, the inky sky pouring through the small, round window. Ronan perched at the edge of our bed, watching me intently. "Is everything okay?"

A rare, unfiltered smile, beautiful enough to stop my heart. It carried all the apologies we left unsaid. "It's warm outside."

I raised an eyebrow at him. "And?"

He stood, offering a hand accompanied by my favorite wicked grin. "Fancy a dip?"

Girlish excitement flickered in my middle as I realized his intention. *Skinny dipping.*

I took his hand without hesitation, the last shadowy fingers of the nightmare relinquishing their hold as my husband's heat and light enveloped me. My heart raced with joy I'd hadn't properly felt in weeks. Shuffling out of the bed, I followed his long strides out of the cabin and onto the *Ddraig's* deck.

The night air was balmy, springtime lacing every breath with warmth and possibility. I came alive when it hit my skin, soaking me in the same buzzing energy. The moon hung above, thin and curved, her playful crescent grin egging us on.

Come play.

It had been so long since I felt like this. So long since I'd felt free. I didn't know if it was the moonlight or the breeze, or my husband's bright eyes, but something unchained within me. Like the part that was Captain, the part preparing for the coming war, the part with responsibilities and worries stayed behind in bed, letting the girl who only loved the sea and her husband out for one last night of bliss.

Ronan must have felt it too, his smile bright, gold hair falling in his face as he tore his shirt from his chest. My mouth went dry as I took him in, that sculpted form even more delicious in the soft white hue of the witching hour.

"I can't believe we are doing this," I whispered, a shiver of excitement running down my spine despite the warmth. A part of me knew it was selfish and foolish, a temporary respite from the inevitable. But I needed it. Selfish and stupid, I needed this moment to drift in the ocean with my ridiculously handsome husband.

Reading my mind like a map, Ronan stepped closer, flicking the collar of my tunic. His voice dipped lower than the tide, just as commanding. "No commenting, Mrs. Mathonwy. Just strip."

Heat flooded me, a forgotten desire budding in my tightening middle. I'd missed this man, this wicked-tongued snake, and the golden heart he hid underneath. I toyed with the buttons of my tunic, rising to his unspoken challenge. "Are you flirting with me, Mr. Mathonwy?"

Heavy lidded eyes bore holes into my soul, the Serpent Prince in his prime tonight. "Are you complaining?"

Gooseflesh prickled across my skin as his voice caressed me like the sea air. It felt so good, so *easy* to slip back into these lighter, younger versions of ourselves. The Sea Snake and the NightMare of the Four Seas, sparring together like we had been since we were little. I quirked an eyebrow as I slipped my tunic from my shoulders, unflinching when my exposed flesh tasted the tepid night. "I am complaining, actually. You're looking at me like you're going to devour me whole."

"I just might." Fangs flashed as he ran a hungry tongue over them, watching me peel my trousers off. He reached out, brushing his knuckles over my skin, gaze drinking me in with greed. "I do have the equipment for it now."

No, we were not the same young lovers who used to spar and flirt and skinny dip together. Now we were more. The Siren Song and the Silver Wheel, creatures who had been broken and bruised and had come back from the precipice stronger.

But maybe we didn't need to forsake who we used to be to give life to who we needed to be. Maybe tonight, they both lived in the liminal moment, carried by the sea and witnessed by the moon.

"Insufferable cad," I purred before leaping over the rail—an invitation to *come play*. I didn't wait to see if my husband followed. I knew he would.

I hit the cold seawater with a smack, relishing in the delicious mix of fear and freedom that accompanied it. I let the vast, unending sea swallow me whole, swallow my pains and my worries. Swallow the mark on my shoulder, the past I was desperate to forget and drown. Swallow the road ahead, darker still, the heaviness it promised. For a brief flicker of a moment, it was just the moon, the ocean, and me, three primordial beings simply existing in careful harmony, my breath held and suspended as I floated in the nothingness.

Another moment, and something fast and bright shot through the water, grabbing my middle and dragging me upward.

"What do you think?" Ronan's fanged smile was feral as we crested the surface, his long arms caging me to him. I could feel the webbed claws as they tickled the small of my back. Silken, cold scales brushed my abdomen, new and strange, but welcome. They were proof of all he'd survived, proof that we would survive whatever came next. Sapphire eyes searched mine as he held me close. "Still afraid of swimming?"

It was a loaded question, one that called forth the demons and darkness I wanted to forget tonight. I wrapped my arms around him, toying with the wet strands of golden curls plastered to the back of his neck. "I'm not afraid of anything when I'm with you."

A deep chuckle rumbled through him, the storm in his eyes clearing. "This reminds me of our first kiss."

Perhaps we were both waxing sentimental tonight. I played along, fondly remembering our first awkward, toothy kiss in the turrets of Mathonwy Manor. "At your cousin River's party?"

He pressed his lips to the base of my throat, the touch as light as the sparkling wine we'd sipped that night. "No, our first real kiss, as husband and wife. In the spring."

His words slammed into me with the force of a tidal wave. It felt like a lifetime ago, lived by different people. Two idealistic fools who bore no resemblance to the careworn, hardened pessimists we were now. I missed them both terribly. Missed being his wife first and a Captain second. I swallowed hard, tears springing to my eyes.

I'm not there yet.

Yet. I can handle yet.

That was the night we became one. That kiss, pretending we were strangers in the easy warmth of Lyr's pool, that temporary moment of bliss before the storm. Before the consequences of our actions came to call. Before the world crumbled around us.

I'd forgiven him that night, whether I admitted it or not. Even though we'd had our share of frustration and desperation since, the thing we made in that moment had stayed strong, never snapping even when it frayed.

I buried my face in his chest, holding on tight to that lifeline. In so many ways, I'd failed him. I left him, abandoning him to wait alone for that *yet* to come. "I'm sorry I haven't been a good wife to you. You deserve better, something easier."

Ronan pulled back, his claws scraping ever-so-slightly along my waist, sapphire eyes soft as the water that lapped against us. "If I wanted easier, I would've married someone who doesn't hit as hard as you."

The part of me that was Branwen—the part made of salt and steel and stubborn resistance—awakened, ready to spar with my favorite partner. "Siobhan hits even harder than I do, if that's what you're into."

Ronan floated back, cocking his head to the side like the arrogant, wicked snake he was. "Are you jealous?"

"A little," I admitted with a shrug. My tone was teasing, but my words had sharp edges of doubt and envy and guilt that had been slicing me from the inside out this whole voyage. "I mean, she's a siren, you're a siren...she knows how to put you first and not drag you into a hopeless quest to try and save her aunt..."

"It's not hopeless." Ronan swam closer again, a single claw tucking a wet strand of hair behind my ear. He looked at me with starry eyes, like they held every sailor's whispered prayers in their depths. "We have you. I'm a siren, but you're something even greater. You're irreplaceable. Trust me, we tried."

I choked back the ball of gratitude that lodged in my throat.

This was my husband's real gift. Not the claws or fangs, or the pretty new tail. But the ability to cure my ills with a simple turn of phrase. The spellwork of his carefully woven stories, the ones that rebuilt me from the inside out. And that wasn't something anyone bestowed on him. That was entirely his, the golden core of his soul that he shared with me.

If I was irreplaceable, Ronan Mathonwy was incomparable. No one would ever match him, this story made man.

Taming you would be like taming the sea.

Capturing Ronan would be like harvesting the stars. Nothing could ever be as bright and vast.

"Thank you." This time, it was me who pulled him close, desperate for the feel of him against me. "For...for stepping up, for coming with me, for making me laugh tonight...for being my equal."

His gaze shot to me, eyebrows flying up. My heart skipped a beat as his frame melted closer, wrapping me tighter to his scaly side. "Thank *you*." He kissed the top of my head, the whole world righting itself. "For always being there to remind me of who I am."

"Aye, Mr. Mathonwy." I breathed in the citrus and sea of him, stronger since he shifted. "Rotten and wicked, you're mine."

And I was fully, completely, eternally his.

After two full days at sea, with full sails and the wind on our side, Porthladd's docks finally came into view. For the first time in my life, the sight was not welcome. This was no longer our home, not anymore. It was a place of corruption and pain, of all the vengeance we were owed and all the justice we had been denied.

Still, in my deepest, darkest parts, a flame flickered. It was small but bright, strong despite the howling winds of doubt that threatened to extinguish it. It had been flickering for some time now, growing a little every day, fed by nights spent skinny dipping and afternoons spent laughing. Fed by the hopes and dreams of my crew, my family.

Burn it all to the ground, it whispered to me in the dead of night. *Rebuild it better.*

Destruction and creation. Dark and light. Fate and fortune.

We would save Vala and Finna, we'd get them far away where we could keep them safe. Then, when everything I loved was off the gods-forsaken island, when all that was left was just Connor and his guards and his deception...I'd set it all on fire.

From the ash, like a phoenix, we'd start over.

The merriment that had been tangible in the days before dissolved into the sea, the reality of what we were about to face sitting heavy in our guts. No one laughed or braided hair, no one sang shanties or swam or sunbathed in the crow's nest. My crew was lethally quiet, preparing for their roles, coming to terms with the risk of failure.

The night before Vala was to be hanged, we knew it was time. We could not guarantee safety, but no matter what happened, we would free Vala—or die with our own freedom and honor intact. No more running.

Papa always said nothing worth having came free.

Swords and daggers strapped to our bodies, eyes forward, we anchored at the dock, ready to pay whatever price fate demanded of us tonight. All that was left were goodbyes we hoped and prayed really meant 'see you later'.

"Tarran, Reagan, be good for Nelle." I ruffled my cousin's orange mop of curls, standing on my tip-toes to reach. He smiled, but it didn't reach his eyes. Those were glassy with tears he was too stubborn to shed.

"Aye, Captain." He saluted me, wrapping an arm around Reagan and Nelle each. "I'll protect them."

Crossing my hand over my chest, I returned his salute, heart swelling with pride before I turned to my siren sister, her violet eyes like lightning in a summer heat storm. "Thank you for staying." I hugged her tightly, so grateful for this warrior of light and goodness keeping my most precious cargo safe.

Nelle's slender arms wrapped around my waist, her honey voice mumbling into my hair, "I'm a healer, not a fighter. Get back in mostly one piece, and I'll be here to help." Just as warm as her embrace, her power enveloped me, the sugary-sweet calmness dissolving on my skin and sinking deep into my core. I exhaled, relishing in the temporary rapture, one last moment of pretending before reality came to chase away the sun.

I squeezed tighter, not ready to let go. "If we aren't back by sunup, you take the ship and run," I whispered so only she could hear. "Get to Bachtref, find Reina and Reese."

I ripped myself from her arms before I could lose myself entirely to the escape and was instantly sobered by little dragon eyes fighting tears.

"Be safe, Captain," Reagan sniffled, jaw set and chin up.

I stroked her cheek, fighting to wear a brave mask for her. "What, no witty retort?"

"Come back safely." She smacked my hand away, a forced grin snaking its way onto her face. "I'll have one ready for you then."

The rest bid each other farewell, Siobhan and Nelle sharing a stiff embrace, Rhett and Griffin teasing Tarran one last time for good measure, Reagan even pressing a chaste kiss to Vian's bright-red cheek. The Soul Wind had insisted on coming, his trick with the dungeon guards last time an ace up our sleeve.

Gratitude surged through me as I stood tall next to my equal, watching our crew. Our family, some connected by the blood in our veins, others tied by the blood that had been spilled. Last night, Ronan and I had let ourselves drift away in the sea, let it remind us of who we were. But today, this was the reminder we needed. Not who we were, but who fought at our side—and who we were fighting for.

And before we could forget again, my husband and I set off down the gangway, crew at our backs, ready to wage war for our family.

37

Dungeons and Darkness

KEIRA

The night was quiet, Porthladd's streets haunted by the silence. The moon was barely in the sky, her white eye still only winking above the rooftops. On a normal night like this, with the warm late-spring air and crisp sea scent, the streets would've been flooded with sailors enjoying an evening stroll in eager anticipation of whatever the night might bring. But the townsfolk were nowhere to be seen, the cobblestone streets empty, the windows shuttered, the streetlamps dark. Every few streets, we'd hear the signature, rhythmic clinking of armor as a few guards patrolled, their obsidian uniforms bleeding into the night. Every time they neared, we held our breath and flattened ourselves against a wall until they passed.

We knew it was too easy. Still, we clung to our hope like shadows in corners, desperately weaving our way from Sailor's Point to the town square.

"She's in the dungeon," Donnall whispered as we approached the council building, hiding behind the Baine's Bank across the street.

I peered up at the brick-and-stone-faced structure that once caged me—that still did, in a way. My body had escaped the cold, damp dungeon, but I left something behind. I left the part of me that was Porthladdian, tied to this land, to my family.

Vala wasn't the only person I'd be freeing tonight. One way or another, I would be rid of Connor's tyranny, and I'd finally free myself from the cage he helped me build.

"That old thing?" Vian snickered in the dark, the light somehow avoiding his presence. "Piece of cake."

I smiled at my accomplice in the sliver of moonlight, deep appreciation coating my nerves in iron. "The guards won't be."

"Leave them to us." Griffin cracked his knuckles, drawing Truth and Triumph with a feral smirk. "I'm going to enjoy this."

I let my cousin's fire light mine, the flames scorching through me with renewed purpose. I scanned my crew one last time, their dark figures deadly, their blades like shadowy teeth in the mist of night. Ronan was not the only one among them who had transformed into a weapon. Siobhan was born a warrior, but next to her Saeth looked like she was cut from the same steel. Rhett and Ellian flanked her, twin mountains of stone. Griffin always had an 'I can kill you with a look' air to him, but life hardened him, his grin sharpened from a dagger point to a scythe's lethal edge. Even Vian, who was still a boy in so many ways, looked like he belonged to the darkness—like the night sky was painted in his image, not the other way around.

Through every challenge, they had been here at my side, unblinking in the face of danger, unwavering in the presence of doubt. Even when I wasn't strong enough to fight my own fate, they were riotous and defiant, *daring* the gods and the stars to try and stop them.

If I failed tonight, they would not. They hadn't yet.

Saeth called Ronan my equal, but she was wrong. These monsters and devils were all my superiors and my saviors, Ronan the captain among them.

"Rhett, Ellian, and Saeth." My voice was stronger now as I inched around the bank, sharpening my view of the target. "Find

Finna, get her out. Drag her by that head of hair if you have to. Meet us on the ship."

Rhett nodded eagerly as Saeth drew her dagger. She'd named it *Wenwyn Dant*, the Poison Tooth, and I knew it would be earning its title tonight. Only Ellian paused, a question burning in his emerald eyes, the shifter smelling my bullshit with his wolf's senses.

I swallowed the lump in my throat, squeezing his hand once. "Sunup, get Nelle and the kids to safety."

"I made my mother a promise to keep you safe." His voice rumbled deep in his chest. "I'm sorry I couldn't keep it."

The blacksmith, sturdy as the steel he forged, disappeared into the night without further protest, Saeth tight on his heels.

"Lyr keep you." Griffin gripped Rhett's face before he could follow, the Swordsinger shedding his armor in a rare display of vulnerability as he planted a firm kiss on the blond's lips. The contact lasted only a moment, short and sincere, but it made me blush nonetheless as I looked to the ground.

Rhett blinked twice as Griffin pulled away. Pride puffed his chest as a smile lit his features. "I love you, too, Griffin Branwen."

Griffin's wistful stare followed the blond as he jogged after Ellian and Saeth.

My heart clenched, wishing for my cousin's sake that the words didn't sound so much like goodbye. When this was all over, if we managed to survive, Griffin and Rhett deserved their own ship and any other happiness I could afford them. I'd sacrifice my own if that was the price.

"The wind says it's time," Vian announced, neck craned like a hawk about to dive in for a kill.

Later I'd worry about the cost, about what I owed my family. Now I needed different parts, parts that commanded the sea and stars, parts that called *sarffymors* from the depths and could restitch torn flesh. Parts I had salvaged in the warm waters of *Hiraeth*. Parts I'd only just discovered.

"How many?" Ronan's fangs descended, long talons protruding from his fingers as he too called on his monstrous parts. Rotten and wicked, we were created for each other, two demons ready to devour their prey.

"Four bodies, exterior. On the roof." Siobhan sniffed the air, her own jagged teeth peeking out from behind her lips. "Three interior. But the scent of one is…strange."

I inhaled sharply, not wanting to know what *strange* meant, the spot on my shoulder aching in response.

"Wanna make a wager?" Griffin twirled Truth in his hand, the metal glinting in the moonlight matching the twinkle of mischief in his eye. "First one to four kills wins?"

Siobhan readied her staff and clicked her tongue. "You're on."

"We'll carve a path, you four get to Ma." Griffin clapped his father's broad shoulder and darted around the building, war churning on swift currents. Siobhan moved to the opposite side, the two of them twin blades ready to cut down the enemy. Ronan, Donnall, Vian and I waited for their signal with bated breath, muscles tensed and hearts pounding with anticipation.

In less than a moment, chaos reigned.

A crash from the rooftop of the council building, followed by the signature clinking of steel.

"What the——?" A guard roared, but his voice cut off abruptly. I watched him fall through the air, his body splattering onto the ground with a sickening *crack*.

"Now!" Griffin cried from the flat-topped roof, perched like a gargoyle manning his post.

We sprinted for the front door, legs pounding the cobblestone in sure, even meters. Something in me spurred to life again as adrenaline pulsed through me, like starlight and lightning in my veins—my father's little heathen finding an untamed thrill. We skidded to a halt at the massive wooden barrier, Ronan quickly pulling the picks from their permanent residence in his coat sleeve.

"I'll cut around the back," Donnall growled as Ronan fumbled to pick the lock of the main entrance, his hands twitching impatiently.

"Alright. Be careful." I nodded, sending the old sailor around the corner just as the lock clicked open.

Ronan tucked his picks away, my favorite smirk decorating his features. "Still got it."

"Insufferable cad." I winked at him before swinging it open, wild hope driving me forward as I barreled into the marble foyer, my dagger and cutlass both at the ready.

The wide interior was dark, a single oil lamp flickering in the corner of the oblong room, casting long shadows across the wooden pews. At the head, the four empty mahogany chairs of the council's dais somehow appeared larger and more intimidating, like dark sentinels.

The fifth chair—Connor's throne—was occupied. A sole guard stretched across it, his massive legs dangling over an arm irreverently...until he caught sight of us and scrambled to his feet, sword drawn.

"Sound the alarm!" As he sang his warning, recognition settled over me, cold and burning like water in my lungs. This was the guard who tortured me, who nearly broke me the last time we met face-to-face.

Leaping across the pews with ease, I brought my blade down on him, sweet satisfaction pooling in my core as my steel met his. Quickly, I spun on him, jabbing again at his side. He dodged narrowly, nearly losing his footing, but he managed to parry, his sword swinging with the weight of an anchor as I met it again.

"Miss me?" I gnashed my teeth at him, a *blaidd* ready to tear him to shreds.

"Rotten bitch!" he snarled as he lunged, trying to wrap his thick arms around my torso. I spun out of the way just in time, landing a firm kick to his ribs as he stumbled to regain his balance. Lyr below, it felt good to test my strength and steel, to feel the salt in my veins and the fury of a *sarffymor* in my heart again. This was who I was born to be, this weapon sheathed in flesh, this storm caged by bone bars.

But I didn't have time to play with my meal, not with Vala rotting somewhere below us and my cousin waging war on the roof. I bit my lip as I brought my sword back down with the force of a hurricane, ready to strike—

A gunshot pierced the air, and the guard folded down at my feet. His blood stained the marble floor, crimson stark against ivory even in the flickering light.

"Never give them the chance to shoot first." Ronan's eyes were colder than a Pysgoddian mountaintop as he tucked the obsidian pistol back into its holster at his hip.

A chill ran down my spine in a strange mix of fear and appreciation as I lowered my sword, gaping at my husband. Rotten and wicked indeed.

This time, I'll protect you.

I surveyed the room again, stepping over the man's corpse. Still no sign of Donnall, which made the hairs on my neck stand at attention. But we had no time to wait for the old man, no time at all to waste if we were going to find Vala and get her out of here.

"This way!" Vian scurried around a corner, frantically waving us over. Ronan and I shared a single look before chasing after him. He led us through two doors and down a flight of stone steps, his pace faster than the winds that whispered to him. The air chilled as we descended, damp and suffocating, my neck prickling with cold sweat after sprinting down the first two flights. At the bottom of the second, the narrow corridor opened up into a room that instantly filled my stomach with dread. The chill settled in my bones, the horror of my own stay here swimming into my mind's eye. But more potently, my instincts pricked with concern. There were no guards in the dungeon, only the stench of rot and mold. It stung my nose as I squinted against the dark, searching for any signs of life.

"Auntie Vala?" My voice reverberated against the damp stone in a ghostly echo. "Auntie, are you in here?"

"Keira?" Donnall's booming voice called from deeper within. He must have beat us to her. Heart pounding, I ran to him, to the last cell in the cramped, icy chamber, Ronan and Vian flanking me.

Donnall stood outside it, tears streaming down his face as he stepped aside. Relief and despair battled in my gut, emotions catching in my throat when I saw her: Vala, lying on the stone floor, clutching the bars for support as she struggled to lift her head. Underneath a curtain of matted hair, a deep purple bruise marred her left eye, her day dress torn and sullied to shreds.

Fury flashed through me hotter than sunfire. I would end Connor for what he did to her, to the grandmother of his Lyr-forsaken *child*.

As her stare found mine, her face went ghost white, her panicked, shrill voice rising from her hoarse, overused throat. "Oh gods, no! No, it's a trap!"

There was no time to react before another body moved from the shadow in the corner of the cell, his long, skeletal fingers reaching out and yanking Vala by her hair to standing.

"Hello, Mrs. Mathonwy." Connor smiled, gaunt cheeks as hollow and soulless as his eyes. "You're certainly a hard woman to hunt."

38

Traitors and Tyrants

KEIRA

"Thank you again, Mr. Branwen, for your aid. The Deyrnas is in your debt," Connor sneered at Donnall, tossing him a purse of coins, the contents rattling like bones. Donnall blanched, eyes downcast, as he caught the blood money and stuffed it into his pocket.

My stomach clenched as the truth settled heavy in it. I'd met this pain before, but it stung fresh every time, Donnall's betrayal another bullet through my shoulder.

This wasn't just Connor's trap. This was Donnall's. My uncle— made betrayer. Another Branwen wearing a serpent's crest.

Kin-killer.

Something fractured within me, shattering the last ties I had to the Branwen name. My rage was quiet, melting the splintered debris of my shipwrecked family into something deadly. Something sharp and hot and ready to burn.

"What did you do?" I asked aloud, my voice sounding miles away.

"I'm so sorry, Keira. They were going to kill my girls." His voice quivered, the mountain of a man trembling before me. Ronan surged toward him, but Vian caught his arm, holding him back before he could slice my uncle in two.

The look that Vala gave him was darker than the spot on my shoulder. "Spineless coward," she spat, earning another tug at her hair from Connor.

Pain flashed across Donnall's face, nose screwed up and eyes full of tears. He turned back to Yorath, to the puppet master—away from all of us. Another member of my kin lost forever. There would be no salvaging the broken, shattered pieces of this family, not anymore.

I should've felt loss, grief. Instead, all there was inside me was fury.

Ice wrapped itself around my heart as I struggled to maintain my composure. My feet pulled me forward, white-hot rage pulsing through me with every beat of my heart. I was fire and ice, destruction and creation, and I was going to rip Connor Yorath's head from his shoulders with my own hands. "Let Vala go, Connor, or I swear I will—"

"You'll what?" He yanked Vala's hair again, drawing a frail whimper from my aunt. I stopped as the sound tore through me like a freshly sharpened dagger. Connor snickered, digging his claws deeper into her skull. "Have your cousin up on the roof finish me? Too late."

A whistle, and at least a dozen more guards appeared from the back doorway, surrounding us. In their midst, a bound and gagged Griffin thrashed and kicked. Alone.

The room spun as defeat slammed my senses. Where was Siobhan? Had the guards bested them? Had she survived? My cousin's eyes found mine, regret and fear brimming in the red of them.

Griffin was many things. Afraid was not normally one of them.

Something snapped in my core, a dam bursting, something visceral and violent breaking free. "Don't you touch him!" I lunged, the first guard catching me before I could tear the ropes from Griffin's wrists myself. Swift as the wind, I brought my knee to his groin, the tall man doubling over as I wriggled free. I had to get to Griffin, had to get us out—

The click of a bullet sliding into its chamber halted me. I spun to the sound, to where my husband's gun was just barely out of its holster, un-cocked.

Connor snarled as he held the silver pistol—*Weylin's gun*—to Vala's temple. "Take another step, Mrs. Mathonwy, and your auntie dies."

The silver glinted even in the dark of the cell, just as it had the night my uncle used it. A phantom pain shot down my arm, the black spot on my shoulder throbbing as like called to like.

"Good girl," Connor hissed, eyes flicking between Ronan and me. "Drop your weapon, Mr. Mathonwy."

The muscle in Ronan's jaw flickered, his hand still on his pistol. He breathed once. Twice. Calculating. Could he shoot Connor before he could hurt us? Yes. But not before Connor killed Vala. Not before the Dark God's weapon dragged another Branwen to the Otherworld.

Never give them the chance to shoot first.

"Do it," Vala whispered. Tears lined her eyes, but her smile was bright. "Just save my daughter."

An exhale, and my husband threw his pistol to the ground. A guard quickly retrieved it, tucking it into his uniform.

Connor's grin was darker than the shadows. "Good choice, boy."

"Please," Donnall whined, wringing his hands, thick voice breaking over the single, desperate syllable. "I did what you asked. Let Finna and Vala go—"

A shot rang out.

Donnall fell. Blood pooled around him, the mark on his forehead matching his brother's as he stared at us with lifeless eyes.

The world stopped turning.

"I'm glad to be rid of that bothersome wretch," Connor sighed, staring at the body, his lips curled with disgust. As if he had swatted a fly, not shot my uncle in cold blood.

Bile rose to my throat. The last of my father's brothers dead. The Branwen clan finished. The thousand shattered parts of me cried in unison for the legacy lost, for the man Donnall had been before...

And Griffin erupted.

He thrashed backward, headbutting the guard holding him, strangled, muffled cries muted by his gag. He spit it out, a curse fresh on his lips. "You fucking scum, I'll kill you!"

He surged toward Connor, eyes blazing. Two more guards seized him, struggling as the Swordsinger bucked and kicked, feral and unhinged as they gagged him again. Vala screamed in terror, throaty and raw, mother and son in harmony.

They both silenced when Connor pressed the gun back to Vala's head.

My blood ran cold, heart stopping altogether. Vala's eyes were wide with fear and agony, her bottom lip quivering. For a moment, the whole room was suspended in stillness, the only sounds Griffin's labored breathing and Vala's whimpering.

Guilt ensnared my heart. My uncle had made his bed with Connor, but Vala's pain mimicked mine. Every muscle in my body protested, the starfire in my veins begging me to spring forward, to save her, to do *something*. Instinctively, Ronan and Vian both stepped closer to me, ready to follow, to strike at my command. But Donnall's body...my uncle's body, unmoving, red blood staining the stone floor...was enough to freeze hell over.

I would not be responsible for making Griffin an orphan tonight.

We'd been outplayed. We knew this was a trap and we blazed forward anyway, our blind hope the final nails in my family's collective coffin. It had only ever been a matter of time.

I inhaled sharply, the hair on the back of my neck peaked. My voice dropped into a growl, the beast in my chest howling, ready to set fire to the man in front of me. "What do you want, Connor?"

Heeled footsteps behind us, a sharp drumbeat against the cold stone.

Tonight, death wore a dress. Black silk—an affront to the dungeon grunge, like she was headed to a ball, not an execution. I gagged as it brushed through the pool of blood pouring from my uncle's corpse. The material hugged her skeletal frame, dipping low across her chest, revealing a death-black spot above her breast.

A *Melthith* spot. Arawn's mark. As if the Dark God himself had walked through the door, the voices whispered from the shadows, gleeful as their mistress paraded closer.

We're all the same when we're dead.

The triumphant smile she wore was even more sinister.

"It's not what *we* want, Keira dear. It's what He wants," Morwyn Locasta purred as she swept through the dungeon, bringing the breeze of her roses-and-rot scent with her. She floated next to Yorath, his face lighting up in a way that made my stomach roll. Gingerly, she reached through the bars of the cell and caressed the side of his face. "Good boy, Connor my dear."

"Yes, Mistress." He leaned into her touch, frenzied rapture in his beady eyes. Locasta stroked his cheek again as one would a pet, Vala shrinking away from the pair as much as she could.

A new storm kicked up in my chest, tempestuous and terrible, as the pieces fell into place. As the veil of my ignorance was ripped from my eyes, revealing the true fester and rot of the woman before me.

No, this was not Connor's trap. Connor was a puppet, like me and Ronan. Like my family, like all of Porthladd. Morwyn Locasta was the true, diabolical heir to the throne of corruption that presided over the entire Deyrnas.

"You have us where you want us." My husband's voice was icy enough to burn. He angled himself in front of me, his talons sharpening. "I assume it's not just to stare, Councilwoman."

Locasta looked him over once, as if noticing him for the first time. Eyes narrowed and lips pursed, she regarded him with shallow indifference. "We want nothing of you, Mr. Mathonwy, not anymore. Though I see you have some new appendages that might be rather useful." She twirled a matchstick finger at his talons, an eyebrow raised. Something shifted when she saw Vian behind him, disinterest transforming into something ravenous. "You're one of mine, aren't you?" She tilted her head, stepping closer as she sniffed the air. "Yes. I'd remember that smell anywhere."

"I belong to no one." Vian stood taller, eyes somehow sparkling in the dark, like stars across the sky. "But I'm glad you remember my face. One day, it'll be the last one you ever see."

Locasta rolled her eyes, waving him off like a pesky fruit fly before turning her obsidian stare to me. "No matter. We only want Keira."

Ronan's fists clenched and unclenched at his sides, his frame tensed for a fight. "Over my dead body."

The visceral, real image of his corpse flashed through my head, painful as the day it happened. The black sludge from his stomach, the sickly pallor of his skin, the empty, cavernous silence of his heartbeat. Panic finally worked its way past my defenses, digging its fangs into my jugular and biting down hard. Still, my husband stood tall in front of me, unafraid, his proud chin tilted up at Locasta with nothing but boldfaced defiance.

And I will choose to save you every time.

He made his promise on the ship. If it came to a fight, if it came to one of us sacrificing ourselves, he would lay down his life for mine. Again and again, like the sun setting to honor the moon, he would extinguish his own flame every evening just to see mine shine for a brief, fiery moment.

I will choose to save you every time.

Not if I chose first. Like Vala had tried to, her courage fortifying mine.

"Name your terms." I stepped in front of him, arms raised in surrender. As the words tumbled from my mouth, sweet relief pooled in my stomach. No more running. No more fighting. Donnall would be the last sacrifice to the Dark God's ravenous appetite. Vala would not die tonight. Nor would Ronan, or Griffin, or Vian, or any of the people I called family.

There was victory in surrender.

"Let my family go, and you can do what you will with me."

"Keira—" Ronan protested, his long fingers clasped around my arm, but I shrugged him off. I ignored the way Griffin whined against his gag, ignored Vian's sharp intake of breath. My eyes trained on Locasta, on the surprise in the lift of her brows, on the impenetrable blackness of the spot on her chest.

"Oh no, my sweet." She stepped closer, the smell of syrupy decomposition making my eyes water. Dark eyes raked over me, predatory and hungry. "We'll do nothing to you. He wants you unblemished."

I shot a dagger-edged look at Connor. "Who?"

"Do you really need to ask?" Locasta chuckled, leaning in so her breath tickled my ear. "You've heard his whispers, haven't you?"

We're all the same when we're dead, Keira girl.

One voice carried above all, colder than a Pysgoddian winter and darker than a crow's wing. Sick rose up my throat as the realization struck.

Locasta smiled wider. A finger trailed down the side of my face, and at her touch, my spot sang with fresh, blistering pain. I doubled over, a cry tearing from my lips as I smacked her away. Connor laughed, breathy and hysterical, Vala sobbing in his grip. The Councilwoman joined in, her cackle shrill. With fire burning in her eyes, she reached out faster than an adder and tore back my coat, exposing the black spot of flesh beneath.

"What happened here?" Locasta's brow furrowed, laughter dying in the stagnant air. She spun on Connor, darkness simmering in her gaze. "I thought you said she was ready."

Connor's face blanched, the blood rushing from him.

"She was!" he stammered, fear prickling in his gaze. He loosened his grip on Vala's shoulders, pleading with his keeper, eyes wide. "I promise, Mistress, I saw it myself, she—"

"Now!" Vala yelled, elbowing Connor hard in the gut. With a cough, he doubled over, Weylin's gun clattering to the floor.

Chaos burst out in a fraction of a breath.

Griffin moved first, slipping his bonds and punching the guard to his right across the face. Ronan followed faster than lightning, drawing his sword to fend off the other guards while Griffin scrambled to his mother, yanking the cell door open. Instinct taking over, I barreled into Locasta, knocking her to the ground. We smacked the stone hard, my bad shoulder hitting first. I winced, but despite the sharp ache, I rolled on top of her, bearing down. The storm in my center swirled with vengeance as my fist connected with her face. Fresh blood spurted where my knuckles sliced her cheekbone, but she grinned, tucking her heels underneath her and bucking her hips to throw me off with surprising strength. Rolling, my shoulder singing in pain, I kicked her hard in the head as I skittered away.

The woman's head lolled to the side for a moment. Crouching, I surveyed my crew as my pulse deafened me. Ronan was managing the guards, a typhoon of talons and teeth, faster than I'd ever seen him move before. Griffin had Vala's arm over his shoulder, the two of them limping, but standing. Connor still squirmed on the floor, new bruises forming over his eyes.

But my stomach sank when I couldn't find Vian, the songbird vanished entirely. Ice ran down my spine, but before I could call for him, Locasta sat up, black eyes filled with unending rage.

"Enough!" she cried, and some unseen wave catapulted me back onto the ground. A crack splintered my ribs, squeezing, its stabbing pain blinding me. The wind rushed from my lungs as I gasped for air.

Then the world went entirely black.

Not the black of a restful sleep, or the black of silken hair. It was suffocating, total blackness. The blackness of despair. The blackness of death itself. It closed around us, tendrils of the obsidian smoke tying themselves around my limbs, every point of contact agony, like thousands of hot nails stabbing and blistering beneath my skin. Someone else screamed at the same time I did, and Griffin cursed.

I tried to pull away, but the ghostly ropes tightened, one snaking its way around my neck. I gasped for air, the noose tightening and searing every place it touched. As I struggled, the ropes slammed me to the ground.

Pain so intense I saw stars. My head spun as I tried to move, but the ghostly hands scratched and pulled as if I was being burned from the inside, as if they were going to drag me to the Otherworld through the stone floor.

Slowly, the impenetrable blackness dissolved, the phantom fingers still suspending us.

"You think you're so clever. I'm going to enjoy breaking you." Locasta stood over me, fingers curling around the smoke, whites of her eyes completely back. She leaned in, and the smoke's hold tightened around my throat. I clawed at the phantom fingers to no avail, squirming underneath her like a worm. "Keira, my dear, dear girl, this won't do. We need to dress you in something blacker."

As if she summoned it, something dark and dreadful rolled in my gut, an answer to her call.

"Don't listen to them, Shrimpy." Griffin spat a clump of blood on the floor, a crimson-stained smile breaking across his face. Struggling against the phantom chains, he flipped her a vulgar gesture. "Come on, you crazy bitch, you want to have some fun? *I'm* the life of the party."

Before Locasta could devour my cousin whole, light burst through the room, hotter and brighter than any star. I squeezed my eyes shut, blinded. Footsteps—many of them—echoed in the chamber. Then a smack, and Locasta shrieked.

"Actually, I think I am." A familiar, seductive voice quipped as the light faded around her curvy silhouette.

I blinked twice, unable to believe my eyes as Marina halted before me, a hand on her hip and a red-lipped smirk on her face.

Next to her Siobhan had her staff at Locasta's throat, her teeth bared in a feral smile. "I hope you don't mind that I brought some friends."

And behind them, surrounding the guards, were Vian, Madame Neirida, and the four other sirens of Hiraeth.

39

Sisters and Sacrifices

KEIRA

The sirens came. Laureli, Gennevieve, Marina. Willow and Cassryn.

My friends. My sisters. *They came.*

The starfire in my veins roared to life again, beating back the ugly, coiling darkness Locasta's spellwork fostered. *Hiraeth* was the island of the lost, but on it, I had found something inexhaustible and brilliant. Something wholly mine and yet shared.

A sisterhood. A power.

Morwyn Locasta was no match.

Marina, Gennevieve, and Laureli stood at the front, teeth sharp and talons ready. Dressed in sleek, body-tight armor made of metallic, ivory scales, they were damnation incarnate. Neirida too wore the strange armor, her own fangs revealed and ready to devour.

She was one of them.

"Did you miss us?" Gennevieve broke into a sunbeam smile, her razor-sharp teeth glinting in the lowlight. Tonight, she wore no gloves, a creature of ruin ready to be unleashed. She growled at the guards, three of whom flinched away.

"Of course they did." Marina flipped her hair over her shoulder and threw a mischief-soaked wink to Ronan. "Hey handsome, nice to see you again."

He dipped his head. "A sight for sore eyes, as always."

"Are they—Lyr's ass, sirens?" Vala croaked, eyes wide as she tucked herself into Griffin's side.

A frenzied, whirlwind laugh bubbled from my chest. Sirens. Demons. Creatures of death and calamity.

My sisters.

"Haleni witches," Locasta spat, the dark tendrils in the room stirring to life again as she stared down Siobhan's staff with nothing but malice. "You do not frighten me."

Siobhan cracked her neck with a deep, rumbling chuckle. "We should."

Dark and light crashed together as she lunged for the wraith. Violence doused the room again as the two beasts snarled and snapped at each other, Siobhan with her staff, Locasta with deadly fingers of smoke.

"Guards!" Connor shouted, crawling out from the cell and running for the stairs, abandoning his mistress with one last longing glance. "Stop them!"

Instinct surged within me, my dagger drawn as Siobhan distracted Locasta. Heart thundering in my ears, beating with faith and gratitude for my tribe, I attacked the nearest guard. His steel met mine, the first note in our ode to mutual destruction. My sisters took to arms with me, the defiant cries of talons and teeth against metal ringing through the air. The song crescendoed, each strike met and parried like a drumbeat, each grunt and cry of pain harmony.

Between blows, I scanned the darkness for my crew. Ronan and Griffin were twin blades in their own right, facing four guards with light-footed ease. Vian held Vala safely in the corner, away from the fray. Cassryn and Willow moved in perfect synchronicity, the cartographers mapping out the plan of attack. Cassryn, second in command to Siobhan, was taking on two large guards herself, her speed unparalleled as she climbed onto the one's shoulders, dragging him down. Willow wove between several more, landing small, precise cuts, while Neirida picked off the stragglers. To my left, Gennevieve had a guard on the ground writhing in agony as she disintegrated his entire leg into a pile of ash. The sight was almost enough to make me scream.

Some gifts looked like curses. Hers was both.

Siobhan and Locasta were still locked in their tussle, shadow and sunshine mixing as they wrestled. They were all one body, all one organism breathing and moving and striking together. Like the *Carthu*, when we shared one heart and soul, we were all connected— a single sword crafted for bloodshed.

"How did you get here?" I cried over the music to my comrades, ducking a blow from the guard. Crouching, I swept his feet from under him, the satisfying smack of him hitting the ground feeding the dark, hungry beast in my breast. A single strike of my dagger silenced his song forever.

"We left right after you did. Did you think I wouldn't see you sneaking off?" Laureli grinned mischievously as she shoved the guard she was sparring backward with impossible strength. She met my gaze, stepping over the dead guard at my feet to clap me on the shoulder. "Your mother sent us. She says she's so proud of the woman you've become, but don't forget who you are deep inside."

The world halted.

My mother. The same woman who would've let Ronan die sent her most precious allies—every last one of them—to help me.

Don't forget who you are deep inside.

This was not the time or the place for self-reflection. It didn't matter whose daughter I was if my family bled out on the floor in front of me.

But as if it heard Laureli, the bright, ancient thing inside me perked its ears up, rustling awake. The piece of me that could make men sirens. That could change the course of death and make it one of life. The Silver Wheel, forged from starstuff and captained by the tide.

I wondered if it was just a tool, or if it could be a weapon, too.

"Enough of this sappy shit," Marina whined as she felled the foe in front of her. "You get your family safe, we'll catch up."

She was right. Ronan and Griffin only had two guards left among them, but there were still more, and who knew how many waiting beyond the walls to attack. Connor had escaped, and we still had to catch up with the others, find Finna, and get back to the ship.

But I couldn't help but glance back to Siobhan, her dark skin entangled with Locasta's silky flesh.

"You are my family, too." My voice was thick in my throat, the words catching as I grabbed Marina's hand.

"Yes, but we have much sharper teeth." She squeezed my hand one last time before shooing me away. "Now go!"

The scarlet siren dove back into the fight, a wild grin on her bloodred lips. I would not waste her effort. This would not be the last time I saw them. Fate was a tricky mistress, but I knew deep in my bones that our threads were still woven together.

Adrenaline pounding through me, I leaped over the guards, dodging the debris and clashing swords around us. My sisters held steady, carving a path to get me out of these dungeons, back to my family. Ronan's eyes met mine as I ran across the chasm, something snapping taut between us, a rope pulling me back to shore. With a swift jab, he ended his fight just as I made it to him and Griffin. Vian, sensing our imminent surrender, hoisted Vala to standing, acting as a crutch. But Griffin swooped in, lifting his mother in his arms like she weighed nothing more than a feather. "Are you alright, Mama?"

Vala's tearstained cheeks lifted, warmth chasing away the shadows as she regarded her youngest son. "I'm fine. I'm tougher than I look."

"Let's find the others and run." I herded my crew up the back stairway. Ronan went first, taking them two at a time, claws and pistol at the ready like a creature crafted of thunderstorms and gunpowder, unafraid of whatever danger lay ahead.

I didn't know what god gifted me Ronan, but they would be my patron tonight.

Griffin bore Vala up the winding stone steps, Vian and I taking the flanks. None of us looked back or spoke of what we left behind. We kept our gazes forward, the purpose clear despite heavy hearts.

Save Finna and Vala. Get to the ship, where Reagan and Tarran waited. Let the sirens choose their own path, even if it meant leaving them behind, too.

I whispered silent prayers with every step. To Lyr, that his sea demons would prevail, the tide in their favor. To Gwynn, the hunter god, that their weapons would be sharp enough. To Cerridwen, that whatever magic flowed through their veins would be enough to extinguish Locasta's curses. To Nef, that the winds would carry our sails fast.

To the Dark God himself, I prayed that he prepared himself for the universe of pain I would bring to his doorstep if any of my family fell to his keep.

We burst from the dungeons, stumbling into the back alleyway. There were several more bodies, all in black uniforms, their faces mauled by sharp, jagged lines. Two were nothing but piles of ash and rot, Gennevieve's handiwork. A shudder ran through me. If this is what the sirens could do on land, I didn't want to know how deadly they'd be under the waves.

Maybe they didn't need my prayers. They were the answer to them.

We ran down the street as fast as we could, Griffin slowed by Vala's weight. As usual, the Swordsinger had taken his lumps, cuts and bruises decorating his arms and face. But he didn't say a word of complaint, only trudged on, uneven steps matching ours.

We were halfway to Sailor's Point when we saw them. Halfway home. So close, but so far.

"Is that—?" Ronan spotted them first, his siren's eyes like spyglasses even in the shade of night.

I barely recognized my eldest living cousin, and not because it was too dark. She wore a white nightdress, the thin fabric catching in the breeze like a ghost's raiment. There was blood on the hem, but not a worrying amount, not nearly as much as the splatter on Saeth's blue tunic. Her belly was slightly rounder than I'd last seen at the wedding three months ago, the little miracle inside her finally taking form. But her face was gaunt, the glow dimmed by heavy bags under her eyes. Her hair was limp and matted to her forehead, auburn turned burnt and dull. Saeth supported her by the elbows, an equally drawn expression on her face.

"Keira!" Finna gasped as her gaze found mine across the cobblestone street, relief sagging her shoulders. "Thank Lyr, Keira, you found Mama!"

I'd never heard my name sound so sacred, especially not from someone with such a forked tongue. Yet it healed something in me I didn't know was broken.

"Finna!" Vala cried out for her daughter, her tone matching the warmth of a thousand suns. Victory howled in my chest, a wolf raising its riotous bellow into the night. Finna was worse for wear, but she was alive. We were not unscathed; there were scars she'd carry forever, Griffin and Vala too, but we were alive to deal with them and watch them heal.

That was no small matter. It was everything.

I ran to hug my cousins, wrapping them in a crushing hug. They were both sharp as daggers in my arms, but I didn't care. Bony and edged and vicious as they were, they were mine. And I wouldn't let them go again, no matter what trouble fate had planned for us. I would protect them both until my dying breath.

Finna was stiff at first, but after an exhale, sank further into my arms, burying her delicate face in my hair. Even at her worst, she smelled like raspberry soap. I laughed into her curls, blinking back traitorous tears. Only she would smell like a summer harvest after being held captive by Connor and his minions.

"Where are Rhett and Ellian?" Griffin asked, voice darker than death, shooting the inflated bubble of hope in my chest with a pistol.

Saeth pulled back from my embrace as the anvil sank to my toes, panic lifting in its place. Her face darkened, thin lips pressed into a line. "Rhett got caught by a guard. There is something *wrong* about them, they're so strong…" She rubbed the back of her neck, looking anywhere but Griffin's face. My heart thundered louder than cannonfire as she inhaled, steeling herself before she continued, "He won, but the guard cut his eye. It was pretty bad. Ellian ran him to Nelle. Finna insisted on finding you all first."

Bile rose to my throat, but I bit it back for Griffin's sake, cursing under my breath—a silent vow to whatever god would make the shifter the fastest and Nelle's hands the steadiest. Rhett was a fighter. I'd seen him take on Tannian assassins with a spear in his thigh. If anyone could survive, it was him.

He had to.

Griffin's throat bobbed, his face blank. "Is he—?"

"He'll be fine, Griffin." Finna floated to her brother, the queen of grace and gunfire taking up her crown once more. She stroked his face with the most gentleness I'd ever seen but stopped abruptly. Jade eyes narrowed on his stained hands, on Vala's sullied rags. When she spoke again, her voice was stone. "Whose blood?"

Griffin paled further, eyes watering as he choked out the words that would destroy his sister entirely. "Papa's. Sorry, Finn. He's gone."

A shuddering breath. Then another.

"No." Finna stumbled backward, nearly tripping over her nightdress. Her eyes darted between us, hands fisting her hair. "No! I thought we had time, no!"

I reached out, my heart breaking as the silk queen unraveled. I knew her grief like my own heart, knew the pain of losing a father, knew the crushing weight of betrayal. And I would hold her hand through every painful second of it if she'd let me. But we had to get to safety first, before any more of us joined Donnall and Papa in the Otherworld. "Finna, it'll be alright, let's get to the ship—"

"No, it's not alright!" Her tears streamed freely, ugly and unbridled as she put together whatever dark picture was forming in her mind. "You don't understand! If Connor has the blood of a betrayer now, he only needs the innocent—" She shut her mouth, eyes widening, a hand flying to her stomach. Then she collapsed to her knees, the stones cutting them open, sobs overtaking her completely. "Oh gods, *what have I done*? This is all my fault."

"Finna, what are you talking about?" Saeth knelt in front of her, scanning her face for lunacy. I offered her a hand—later, we'd deal with our grief, with what we had to let go. Lyr's ass, I'd throw a whole *Carthu* for her if I could. But now we had to run, had to get off this gods-forsaken island.

Save Finna and Vala. Get to the ship, where Reagan and Tarran waited. Make sure Rhett was alive. I was still a Captain. I had to act like it. "Listen, I know you've been through—"

"You have *no* idea what I've endured." Her voice shook as she did, the tremors like earthquakes. Ghosts danced in her eyes, ones I hoped I'd never meet. "The things they are doing...the things they *did* to me... Morwyn Locasta is a demon. She wants my...and now..."

I grabbed her jagged, too-thin shoulders, tugging her gently back to the place of the living, away from whatever phantoms chased her. "Then tell me. Tell me when we are *safe*, alright?"

She shook me off, voice rising in panic. "No, listen to me for once in your life, Keira Branwen!" She wiped her tears with the back of her delicate hand and grabbed my face, forcing me to meet her gaze, to acknowledge the pit of despair and fear frozen there. "The things she plans for me...for *Owen*...it's *nothing* compared to what they want from you. It's the Branwen curse, and they've already started the ritual. I should've known during the wedding, Keira. I should've stopped it then. The blood of the betrayer is the first step, then the stolen soul of an innocent...the heart of a god... You can't let them finish. You have to run and never look back, no matter what. Do you hear me? It doesn't matter who they have locked up or what they threaten you with. You take the crew and you run as fast as those skinny legs will take you."

"What *curse*, Finna?" Fear rumbled and twisted in my core as I tugged her upward. Her words made no sense. Nothing made sense except for the unending dread pooling in my gut. Finna was poise and delicacy and fire. She was caustic wit and silken stares. She was not spiraling fear and bruised faith. But I would see her through this. I would be by her side as she rebuilt and remade and raised her son in whatever version of better came next. "Let's just go, alright? Whatever they did to you, we can fix it. I'm not leaving you behind this time."

"I have been selfish my whole life. And I'm sorry that it kept me from seeing you." Tears silently slid down her cheeks, but something sparkled in her eyes, bright enough to vanquish the phantoms. Gently, she took my hand, reaching out to Saeth with the other. Her perfect, effortless smile spread across her face. "I've always wanted a little sister to fuss over and corrupt. I should've realized I had two of them."

To both of our surprise, she pulled us into a tight hug, slim arms snaking around our waists. I met her embrace, emotions tangled into an indiscernible ball in my chest as I willed all my strength into her. She had always been my role model, whether I wanted to admit it or not. Her beauty and poise, yes, but her ferocious spirit and unparalleled intelligence, too. The way she bowed for no one. The way she could inspire loyalty with a smirk and a flip of her hair.

We would do better. We would survive, if we could just get to the damn ship, and we would start fresh—me and my sisters in every way but parentage.

"I love you too, Finna." Saeth looked at me over Finna's other shoulder, worry creasing her brow. "But we're wasting time. There will be more guards."

"No." Finna whispered into my hair before she pushed away, fingers trailing against my side. "This ends here, with me. It's my mistake. I should've listened. But I won't let him hurt you, and I won't let her take my baby's innocence and turn him into a monster."

I hadn't felt her take my dagger. Hadn't seen the sleight of hand. The trickery from the queen of foxes had been too quick.

When she plunged the blade into her stomach, all the way to its obsidian hilt, I felt it. Felt it like it was my gut she sliced open. Like it was my blood pouring onto the cobblestone.

"No!" Time stood still as Saeth screamed in horror, piercing the night. Piercing my heart like a dagger. She cradled Finna's lower stomach, the gash staining her hands red.

Griffin rushed to her other side, stanching the wound with his broad palm, rage and panic fighting for dominance in his expression, crimson eyes the same color as Finna's dress while his whole world bled out before him. "Finn, what did you *do?*"

"Finna! The baby—no!" Vala collapsed, too broken to crawl to her daughter, her screams inhuman.

"Run." Finna smiled at her brother, her teeth a darker scarlet than her hair as she spat blood onto the street. "Go, please."

Frozen, I watched in horror as Finna pushed Saeth away with the last of her strength, into Vian's arms. Pain in my own knees as Finna collapsed to the ground; pain in my own chest as she choked on a cough. She dug the dagger deeper, past the point of no return. My gut convulsed it as she clutched her middle, as the life inside her sputtered out, as the future died in the pool of blood.

Her son. My *nephew*.

Something snapped inside me, something hot and bright and vicious. I would not sit idly by and watch. I was no longer useless, no longer just a witness to my own demise. I had something in me now that could make and unmake. That had remade my husband out of stone and starstuff. That could defy death and fate with a riotous burst of light and life.

I dropped to my knees in front of her, my hand on the gaping void in her stomach. It didn't matter if the guards were coming. I would end anyone who got close to us. I would make time stop, if only to save her. To save *them*.

"Keira, no, stop," Finna groaned, halting my wrist. "Please. There is no hiding from Locasta. She sees everything. If we don't die, she'll turn us into something worse than death. I won't let my baby be a curse."

I swatted her away. "Not if I make you something she can't touch."

I shut my eyes and looked inward, blurring out Vala's screams and Finna's protests. Shutting out the feel of my cousin's blood on my hands and the cold night begging me to run. Inward, to the hot, blistering place inside me. To the primordial chaos waiting in the depths of my soul.

Finna would be the Queen of Sirens. She would be made of scales and silk, soft and deadly at the same time. Her son would be born of stone and steel, too, a Branwen, not a Yorath. A miracle, not a curse.

Something shuddered and burned inside of me, scorching my veins as it rumbled up from the depths.

"Keira, please." Griffin's voice broke over my name. "Save her, please."

It was the only reassurance I needed. Pain shot through my arms, my palms, but I bit down. My arms shook with the effort, the burning nearly unbearable, but I wouldn't stop, not until she was whole—

"Keira, stop!" Saeth's voice pierced the veil, shrill and frantic. "You're hurting her!"

My eyes flew open, and the burning stopped. Finna's were rolled in the back of her head, only the whites visible. Her whole body convulsed like lightning coursed through her. Across her stomach, scorch marks appeared like tiger stripes.

Then she stopped moving.

"What did you do?" Griffin snarled, daggers in his eyes, holding his hysterical mother back. The boy, not the Swordsinger, sobbed for his sister. "Finna, wake up! Please."

Panic seized my chest. *No.* Why hadn't it worked? What did I do wrong?

Nelle's warning flashed through my mind, too late. Even Danura had failed.

If you're exhausted or the body can't handle the change…

No. I shook Finna's shoulders. I would not let her die. Not on my watch, by my hands. "Finna, please, come back!"

Fox eyes fluttered open, and relief flooded my core. She was alive. I hadn't killed her. Perhaps it wasn't too late to save her.

She shuddered, focusing for a moment, looking past me to my husband. Shaky, she sat up on her elbows, one last burst of strength. "Ronan, get them out of here." Then, the final tilt of her chin, the ultimate defiant action of the woman made of fire and silk. "Tell Connor I'll be waiting for him in hell."

I felt it too when she stopped breathing. Felt the air rush from my lungs. Felt the life drain from my limbs, the hope extinguish in my heart as hers stopped beating.

"Come on, Keira girl, we don't have time. She's gone," someone—Ronan—said as he dragged me back.

I didn't feel it. I didn't feel his arm around my middle, didn't feel him squeezing tighter as I thrashed. Didn't feel my throat go sore as I howled her name over and over.

"I'm sorry, I'm so sorry," a voice—*my voice*—said somewhere far away, a little girl's final word to her dying sister. An auntie's prayer to the life that never lived.

40

Duels and Doubles

RONAN

My wife screaming in my arms, I ran to the *Ddraig* as fast as my legs would carry me. I held her steady even as she kicked and shrieked, Griffin and Vian behind me dragging Saeth and Vala. The three of them screamed, their banshee mourning cry signaling our position to any of the foes Finna had died to protect us from.

Ronan, get them out of here.

The serpent-tongued redhead and I were never friends. But she had given her life to protect the precious, vicious cargo in my arms. To protect our family, in spite of her own growing one. I would uphold her dying wish even if my wife hated me for it. Even if I hated myself.

"No, please, Ronan, Finna, the *baby*," Keira sobbed, finally slumping against me, her voice raw and strained. "I messed up. We have to go back, we can take her to Nelle. It's not too late…"

"She's gone, Keira. They're gone." I hugged her closer, then lowered her to her feet. Another sob wracked through her as she pressed into my chest. Never had Keira seemed so small, so delicate. My wife was made of storm and starfire, but the trembling creature in my arms held none of that.

I didn't blame her. Life was so fragile. So fast. The image of Finna bleeding out, convulsing as my wife's gift burned her from the inside out, still fresh in my mind, was the only reminder I needed.

I let Keira go, though it physically pained me. We had to move. Had to keep pushing, even if our legs were lead and our hearts were stone. Silver eyes met mine, bloodshot and stained red from the tears flooding them. "Let's make sure it wasn't for nothing."

"Keep going." Vian caught up to us, still towing Saeth behind him, her whole frame rattling as she mumbled to herself, staring back up the road—proof that even the hardest, coldest ice could fracture. Vian's eyes narrowed, the only one of us still looking to what came next. "We have trouble."

Dread slid down my spine. I remembered the last warning from the wind whisperer that went unheeded, the panic and pain on his face during the wedding—the night that could have changed everything had we only listened and gotten Keira out of there on time. Maybe gotten Finna out, too. Maybe saved her son from whatever Connor had planned.

Our foolishness—*my foolishness*—knew no bounds. And Connor and Locasta and whatever darkness employed them had been feeding off it ever since, like vultures from a carcass.

"What's wrong?" I froze my heart over once more, focused only on whatever I could sink my fangs into.

"There are more guards, the wind—" Vian shut his eyes, face screwed up in concentration. "We have to get to the ship. Connor and his men are there."

Keira's gaze found mine, our panic a taut thread between us. We said their names together, the same fear swimming in both our heads, "Tarran and Reagan."

The air was thin as we sprinted to the docks, ignoring townsfolk who peeked their heads out of their shutters to spy on us, ignoring their gasps. This town could rot for all I cared, the cowards and cheaters it sheltered not worthy of a second glance. Every sharp impact of my boots against the stone was a war drum driving me forward. The storm swirled in my chest, lightning cracking overhead like an answer to the white-hot heat pulsing through my veins. Perhaps I'd be the hurricane that would sweep this whole rotten town away, my wrath ancient and violent if something were to happen to my cousin.

I could not lose the last piece of innocence holding me to my sanity. I could not lose Reagan. Neither could my family, not after all they'd already sacrificed tonight. I ran a tongue over my fangs, proof of my new, primal strength. I had been given a gift, my wife's magic fortifying my body. Still, it did nothing to vanquish the demons living in my mind, the ones that screamed we were too late as we finally approached the *Ddraig*.

My stomach sank to my toes. Like a swarm of bees, nearly three dozen black uniforms rushed the deck of my family's ship, ready to jab the vulnerable aboard. I did not wait for the others to catch up with me as I bounded up the gangway in long leaps and threw two guards off, shoving them into the shallows and pushing past them onto the deck.

The deck was already bathed in chaos. Thunder clapped overhead, echoing the clang of metal on metal, the war cry of bodies hitting the ground. Surrounded, Rhett, Tarran, and fur-formed Ellian stood in the center of the circle, protecting Reagan and Nelle as they huddled together, Nelle's fangs unleashed. They fought with ragged breaths, drenched in sweat.

"Tarran, to your left!" Rhett bellowed as a guard charged, Tarran meeting his steel with desperate strength. Rhett wielded two swords at once as he fought off the horde, a scrap of fabric over his left eye dark with blood. Ellian snapped and snarled, tearing into the arms of any fool who got close enough. I joined the fray, throwing myself at a guard that was about to sink his sword into Ellian's flank and slicing his throat open with a quick swipe of my talons, his body falling at my feet.

"Took you long enough." Rhett rolled his single eye at me, grunting as he slashed through another guard.

"I'm here now." I drew my blade, ready to cut a path from here to *Hiraeth* itself if that's what it took to end this madness. "Belowdecks *now*, Reagan." She nodded, the fire in her eyes doused by fear, quickly scurrying to the door, Nelle at her side.

The guards were everywhere. Fueled by a bloodlust that went deeper than whatever coin they'd earn, they charged at us with purpose, droves of them, over and over. Devotees, ready to fall on their sword with a smile, ready to eviscerate anyone who dared defy the Dark God. Perhaps they were his puppets too, bodies possessed by the same dark greed that fueled Connor.

Rhett and I fell into a rhythm together, dancing along to the sound of war. Step, parry, dodge. Breathe. Check for my crew. Stab, slice, bite. Breathe again. Behind us, the others clambered onto the deck, Keira leading the charge, her sword finally drawn. Her face was cold. Gone was the quivering, broken creature who watched her cousin die, but there was no life in her gaze as she stared down the hive of soldiers.

She was stone. She was the moon, both bright and lifeless. She was steel. A weapon without a soul.

And Lyr below did I love her.

The last voice any of us ever wanted to hear coughed once before speaking, his slimy form appearing behind the helm. "Ahh, Mrs. Mathonwy, you made it!"

Connor clapped his hands together and the ship halted. In eerie synchronicity, the guards ceased their assault, swarming into formation in front of the helm with swords still pointed at us, ready to strike at his command.

Devotees at a dark priest's altar.

My crew paused, taking the moment to catch our wind. The formation was tight, but we could take them. My eyes flicked to Keira, to my Captain. To where stone melted into lava, molten and furious.

"You rutting *bastard*." Her rage was direct as an arrow and twice as sharp. She stormed up the stairs to the upper deck, practically vibrating with fury. Efficient and precise, she sliced mercilessly through the two guards who dared move against her. "You killed her! You killed your own wife and son! I will make you bleed and cry and scream for every fucking second you spent with her."

Like a spell had fallen over the deck, the guards all froze as my wife charged the Councilman. Their shoulders went slack, arms dropping to their sides—puppets without strings.

I tried to move, to take advantage of the stillness, but my limbs were motionless beneath me, heavier than steel. I watched the crew, all stuck with me, the panic surging in their eyes. I struggled against the nameless enchantment, but nothing helped. Bitter fear rose up my throat, so thick I choked on it.

We could only watch. Witness. Only Keira and Connor were free from the curse.

"What—?" Connor stumbled back at Keira's advance, snarling and sniveling, a worm in man's clothes. "That useless *bitch*."

"Say it again, I dare you." Keira caught him by the collar, her hands so tight around his black robes they practically glowed with her white-knuckled grip.

Connor yelped, terror in his eyes, the rest of us frozen in equal parts disbelief and fear. My wife shoved him back against the mast so hard it *cracked*. Sweat brewed at the top of his brow, the heat of Keira's glow too warm to withstand. My instincts prickled, a voice screaming inside me I didn't understand. Something was wrong. The knot in my core knew it, the whole ship knew it, but none of us could move, paralyzed by fear and witchcraft working together.

I opened my mouth to call to her, to reach her when my feet could not, but my voice sputtered and died in my chest, a phantom gag suffocating my tongue.

"You spineless piece of shit," Keira snarled at Connor, a *blaidd* ready to sink her fangs in. She shoved him again, the massive beam of the *Ddraig's* foremast groaning as Connor winced. Hazy tendrils of black smoke swirled around Keira's fists, dark and deadly, as her reason succumbed to hatred. "I swear you will rot in the Otherworld even if I have to drag you there myself."

At the very mention of the Dark God's domain, my stomach clenched hard, like I'd swallowed a dagger. The world spun nauseatingly, like time and space only existed as an anchor to this one moment. Keira's other hand clenched around Connor's throat, a tiger with a canary in its maw, the frail man writhing in her grasp like the weasel he was. His eyes rolled in the back of his head as his head lolled to the side, consciousness slipping from him.

His life was hers to take. In a breath, she could end this insanity, could end the pain and torment. A messenger of death, she could send his soul to where it belonged, rotting in the Dark God's favorite cell.

I wanted her to do it. I wanted her to take what she deserved, to silence the man for good. I wanted her to throw his corpse overboard so he could be a meal for the bottom feeders.

And yet.

Wrong, wrong, wrong. Every fiber of my being revolted, all the light in my veins shriveling away from the scene in front of me.

And that's when I saw it. Along her shoulder, her neck, her face....

Black veins. Spiraling, swirling as they extended their lethal reach, the Dark God staking his claim to her left side.

Say something, the familiar, ethereal voice commanded, the sunken god's desperate plea.

Save her, Lyr panicked, but he sounded so far away, like he was submerged in the deep beneath us. Like he, too, was caught in the net of whatever spell ensnared us.

Save her, or the Dark God will win her.

"Keira, your mark!" I forced the words past my lips, past the stone that had lodged itself in my throat.

Keira's head snapped my way. Like the moon eclipsed, her eyes were the same inky shade as her hair.

"What the—?" Tarran stuttered, taking a stumbling step back, his trance broken.

Keira blinked once. Twice. Light chased away the blackness, the silver and steel restored. My wife restored. Her eyes found mine, panic swimming where only darkness had existed a moment before. She dropped Connor, staring at her hand like it was foreign to her, the unconscious man crumpling like a piece of parchment at her feet.

In the same moment, the leash ensnaring us all snapped. Griffin drew first, wielding Truth and Triumph like he was born to. The guards scrambled to action once more, the swarm buzzing again, their havoc unchained as they protected their master's comatose form with a wall of bodies. Somehow, there were more now, multiplying as they surrounded us. Every muscle in my body ached to unleash the beast within, to tear them all apart.

"Ronan!" Keira shrieked as a guard drew his sword again to my left. I twirled faster than an Ir'desian dancer, dodging his initial blow. Swooping beneath his arm, I slashed the vulnerable, exposed patch of flesh at the pit of his arm with my talons. The man cried out and dropped his sword as his arm went slack, the deep gash spewing blood all over my face. The human part of me gagged at the heat of it, the iron taste. The siren part…

Sweeter than any of Reina's desserts. Richer than Bachtreffian butter. Bolder than one of Agatha's best kegs of whiskey.

Staggering back, I wiped it from my eyes, my tongue, wishing I could wipe it from my memory, too. Wishing I could shove the craving back into the abyss.

I didn't see the second guard coming. He barreled into me, knocking the wind from my ribs as he tackled me to the deck. A cough tore through me, stabbing pain in my side, my lungs on fire as the force collapsed them. I couldn't catch my breath as his fist connected with my face, the searing ache throbbing across my jawbone. I slashed blindly, missing his mass entirely, the weight of his knee instead coming down again right to the same rib.

A sickening crack. Stars danced in front of my eyes. I rolled to my side, flinching as another lightning bolt of pain flashed through me.

No, flashed *around* me, hot and bright. In a second, the guard's weight was gone and someone screaming.

Keira stood a foot away, her arm outstretched, palm still glowing white. Across her face, the black lines now mixed with white, the war in her veins a mirror to the one on the ship deck. And on his back, the guard lay dead, his face *melted* off.

Never before had Keira frightened me, but the moment our eyes met, all I could feel was sheer, unadulterated terror toward the corporeal curse I called my wife. The meager contents of my stomach stained the deck before I could bite them back, the smell of charred flesh and bile the backdrop for the grisly scene.

"You alright?" Keira rushed to me, patting me down for injuries.

I couldn't help it—I flinched away from her, from the darkness clawing at her face. Hurt flashed across her expression, her hand drawing back like I'd burned her. Like she was afraid she'd burn me.

A millennium passed in the single second my wife and I sat there, gazes locked, trust severed, with the apologies we'd never have the chance to say trapped behind our teeth.

"Need some help?" A voice pulled us from the moment, rooting us back into the reality of our impending doom. I swallowed down my shame and regret as I pushed to my feet, pain already subsiding like it never existed in the first place. Siren magic had its perks.

Siobhan was bruised badly, her cheek purple and swollen, and the cut over her right eye looked deep; still, her jagged smile was sharp as ever. I counted five women behind her, all in various states of disarray, but all breathing. All alive. And all ready to jump back into the fight.

I didn't know if Danura was gods-blessed, but everything and everyone she touched was. These women would never know the fathomless depth of my gratitude and awe for them. Words were never enough to express it.

"Took you long enough," I said instead, a sly, familiar smirk finding its way onto my face.

"Cerridwen's tits, do I need to do all the work here?" Marina rolled her eyes as she tore into a nearby guard, shifting midair and plunging them both into the deep. The other women followed behind her, taking their posts, fighting back the guards and spilling blood as they were designed to do.

"Locasta?" Keira's face was marble as she surveyed the sirens for injuries amidst the disarray.

"Don't know." Siobhan's mouth pressed into a firm line, a tinge of fear paling her warm skin. "After a while she just disappeared into a cloud of that gods-awful black stuff."

My heart shuddered, the beast in my chest beaten to submission at the mere mention of those ghostly, black hands. The same tendrils that veiled my wife moments before. Same ones that fought to blacken her skin and her soul.

"Let's just get these assholes off my ship." I drew my sword, ready to push the form Keira crafted for me to the limits. If Locasta's darkness was intent on damning my wife, I would fight for the light. I would fight for the good in her until my fins fell off, or until there was nothing left—whichever came first.

The guards did not falter, did not give up their assault. Even as we tore them limb from limb, our steel and claws felling them one by one, they attacked again, both shouting and whispering prayers for the Dark God's mercy.

But we would not falter either. Tarran and Rhett and Ellian, their exhaustion total and their bodies spent, still raised their swords again and again. Vian and the sirens, their gifts depleting and their power shrinking away, still barred their teeth, over and over. Saeth and Griffin, hearts heavy and limbs shaking, still sliced and cut and turned their grief into blades. Keira, despite the darkness that clung to her like ivy, lit them all ablaze, the white light from her fingertips enough to halt fate itself in its tracks.

Still, it was not enough.

Still, the guards came. Dozens.

Still, we fought, determined to do so until our dying breaths.

A small, pitiful part of me, the one that had laid in bed sulking while my wife left, the part that hid away in *Hiraeth* in the first place, begged me to flee. To save myself. The stronger part of me knew that if I did, if I faltered for even a second, I'd regret it for the rest of existence itself, long after the Otherworld called me.

So I danced, on and on. Step, parry, dodge. Breathe. Check for my crew. Stab, slice, bite. Breathe again. Try not to look at all the blood. Over and over.

Then, a single word with the power to break me.

"Sails!" Tarran roared triumphantly over the pandemonium from his place near the rigging. "Keira, you won't believe it!"

My head swiveled to where the sunny boy pointed, to the ship I knew almost as well as my own. On the starboard side, her glorious white sails stark against the black horizon, the fastest cutter in the four seas was within spitting distance.

The *Ceffyl Dwr.*

My heart leapt from my chest, beating faster than a hummingbird's wings, the taste of salvation washing away the sick and iron on my tongue. Perhaps the goddess of fate did smile on us after all, good fortune delivered right on time. Victory swelled in my chest and tears lined my eyes, a fool's celebration.

My mother used to warn me the match was never over until someone called checkmate. Still, it was so close within reach, I could almost touch it. So close.

So far.

Reina and Reese stood on the rail of the *Ceffyl,* their crew behind them, ready to board, all wearing the *Rydha's* mark. Ropes swung as our saviors descended onto the ship, cutting through the hive of unnaturally determined guards, cutlasses poised to strike.

"Die, ye scum!" My father exclaimed as he thrust his sword through a soldier's eye, raining rust-colored blood onto the deck as he withdrew and the guard toppled to the ground. A rotten grin slithered onto his scarred face, the king of cobras reinstated in his floating kingdom. "Miss us?"

For the first time in my life, I was entirely grateful for my father's existence. "Pa! How on earth did you two know where to find us?"

He cleaned his blade on his sleeve, darkening the signature red. "Ye won't believe this, but I followed a *sarffymor*. Nearly shat myself when I laid eyes on the beastie."

The image of Keira's massive, black-scaled companion brought a new wave of dread to my gut, but I thanked her and the sunken god that sent her nonetheless as I sounded the retreat. "Everyone, to the *Ceffyl!*"

"Where's Reagan?" Reina, hair still dark and coat still blue, scanned the fight just as the woman she impersonated would, desperate for a glimpse of a chestnut curl or dragon-toothed smile.

My gratitude for the White Snake, even in her ebony disguise, was more than I could bear. "Belowdecks with Nelle and Vala, she's safe. I'll get her, you just get everyone on the—"

"Mama?"

So close.

So far.

Somehow, the tiny voice floated over the roar of battle. I twisted to where she stood on the upper deck, looking over the railing, standing on her toes so she could get a glimpse. There was no fear in the dragon's eyes, only the purest love as she saw her mama for the first time in months.

A cannonball sank through me. Reina's face paled and her eyes widened.

"Get down here right now, young lady!" Reina cried, rushing toward her, black hair and blue coat flying behind her like a flag.

Like a target.

In the uproar and upheaval, in the frenzy and furor, no one thought to watch if Connor was still unconscious behind his wall of minions.

The guards moved in unison. He sat up, silver pistol shaking in his hand, aim trained to shoot Keira.

Not Keira. Her imposter. The woman who could craft a legend with nothing more than a borrowed compass and an old coat. The woman who had done her duty so admirably, even those closest to her had to look twice. The woman made of the secrets and stories told around a kitchen table, her only weapon her warmth. The woman who ran right toward him, arms outstretched toward her daughter—not a concern for herself, only for her baby girl.

"Safe journey, Captain Mathonwy," Connor croaked with a wide grin.

He pulled the trigger.

Pale skin and midnight hair dropped to the deck. Blood darker red than my family's crest pooled across the boards, stark against the brilliant blue of her coat.

"Reagan." Blood trickled from her lips as she dragged herself forward. Once. Eyes on her target. On her daughter.

Then they closed as she collapsed.

No movement, not even the rise and fall of her chest. No life.

"*No!*" My father's scream shattered the last fragile piece of hope I had left.

41

Debts and Death

KEIRA

Death had a *smell.*

It smelled of fear and regret. Of opportunities missed and moments lost. Of the hateful words I couldn't take back and the ones I'd left unsaid.

Death smelled like the wretched, festering black spot on my shoulder, a reminder of not only the souls I'd sent to the Dark God, but the guarantee that part of me was already his, and would always be.

Today it smelled like rust and blood. Like a young girl's tears as she cried for her mother. Like the saltwater and stillness of Reina's unmoving form.

"Mama, please, no!" Tears stained Reagan's face as Reina's dark pool of blood stained her hands. Still, the little dragon shook her with all her might, as if, if she gripped her tightly enough, she could anchor her mother's soul to this world. Reese was already at her side, a brother turned mourner—just like Griffin and Donnall and Weylin. Just like the rest of my family.

The world shuddered to a halt. My heart threatened to stop with it, the ache of beating too terrible to withstand. I was only paces away, and yet the distance between me and the truth was an insurmountable chasm.

The deck went quiet, the fighting ceased as we all warred with our grief and disbelief. The only sound was the little girl's lonely sobs, wracking through her tiny frame with unjust force. "Mama, no. Come back."

Papa once said fate was a tricky mistress, one that always had an answer and never needed a reason. I believed it once; believed that some answers we had to accept blindly. Believed fate had a plan for us all, whether it made sense to us or not.

But for the first time in my life, I didn't agree with my father.

There was no sense to this answer, no greater plan. Finna, the baby, Reina...this was pure cruelty. Fate was a dark, senseless thing. Darker than the black crawling up my arm, clouding my vision and numbing my mind. There was no more light left in the world, the magic at my fingertips a poor imitation of it.

And it was *my fault*. I had him. I could've killed him. But I'd let the Dark God win; I'd let my hate veil my vision, let his hand guide my course. I'd thrown away my reason and agency for a moment of anger.

It was all my fault.

"Reina!" Ronan tripped up the steps to the upper deck, skidding onto his knees next to his fallen aunt. There were tears in his sapphire eyes, grief and rage snarling and snapping for dominance. Tears I had put there. Tears I had done nothing to save him from.

"What—?" Connor's face darkened as he realized his error. As he looked at me from behind his guards, standing at the bottom of the stairs, breathing and entirely unharmed. Bewildered fury flashed across the sunken planes of his cheeks as he raised a quivering finger, pointing at me like a ghost. "No! How are you—I shot you!"

Guilt slammed into my middle like a ship crashing in the shallows, my breath running ragged. All I could do was stare at her limp body, a poor substitute for my own.

The bullet was supposed to have been mine. *I* should be dead. Not Reina. Not Finna.

Me.

"You monster!" Reagan let loose a throaty scream, the little dragon roaring at the worm. "I'll end you for this!" And before Reese or Ronan could whirl around to grab her, before the rest of the crew could remember their limbs beneath them, she charged, her ruby-hilted dagger drawn and ready.

"Reagan, no!" The light in the deepest part of my core came to life, scorching heat running down my legs, propelling me forward. I took the steps two at a time, moving faster than a whisper on the wind, but still it wasn't enough.

Connor was not a strong man, but Reagan was blind in her rage. She ducked under the guard protecting Connor and knocked the silver pistol from his hand, sending it flying across the deck, but as she twirled to jab her dagger in his side, she missed her mark. Connor dodged to the right as Reagan tumbled forward, dropping the dagger at his feet. I was only inches away when he scooped her up and pressed the blade to her throat.

"Everyone, stay calm," Connor barked at my crew, armed and furious, as the sharp end of the gold and steel dagger pointed at the most precious cargo this ship had ever carried, "or the girl dies with me. Let's drop our weapons. I only want Keira."

"Rotten prick," Reagan gritted through a clenched jaw, wriggling against his hold. "I'll drag you with me!" With a grimace, Connor pressed deeper, small, crimson droplets coating the tip of the dagger.

"Reagan, careful," I warned, my voice lethally low.

Deep in my core, another key unlocked. Not like before, when I had Connor unconscious, my fingers wrapped around his throat. Not the cold, unseeing rage, not the darkness that begged me to kill him. No, this time the burning fire rose to my hands, the same way it did when the guard attacked Ronan. Dark and light swirling together in a hurricane, I was disaster embodied. I held fate in my palms, ready to unleash the blistering, festering destruction.

Still, all I could see was the blade against my youngest cousin's throat. My kindred spirit. And the fear was enough to steady even my insatiable desire for Connor's head.

"Stand down," I called to my crew as I dropped my cutlass, letting it clatter to the deck, panic clawing up my throat. "I'm yours, Connor. Let the girl go."

Weapons hit the floor, no one hesitating, surrender already flying its white flag in our hearts. I held my breath, looking for the small victory, for anything I could latch onto to save her. But there was nothing. No one. No solution that didn't leave the most precious little girl dead on the ground next to her mother, her corpse adding to the death-scent.

None except one.

There was victory in surrender. Perhaps there would be adventure in death, too.

But Connor smiled, not yet satiated with his stolen victory. Holding Reagan tighter, he leaned forward to whisper into her mane of unkempt curls, a cat playing with its food. "How does it feel, little one? To admire the woman both your parents died for?"

It would've hurt less if he shot me through the heart with Weylin's pistol. I forced myself not to look at Reina's body, forced myself to ignore the bile rising in my throat at the thought.

Reina, warm and bright, extinguished forever. Reina, who had forgiven me for what I did to Lochlan, even though I didn't deserve it. Lochlan, the first victim of my own vengeance.

Instead, I focused on the fatherless little girl who stared at me with wide chestnut eyes. The girl with a dragon heart that knew mine, the kindred spirit hidden in a den of snakes.

The lost child I'd made an orphan.

"My father died in a..." Confusion furrowed Reagan's brow, and I watched the doubt creep in, watched her shoulder slacken ever-so-slightly.

"Connor, just give her back." I took a coward's step forward, my shame a noose tightening around my neck.

He rambled on, a chuckle reverberating deep in his chest, "A shipwreck, was it? Ronan's ship, so I've heard the story go."

Reagan's glassy-eyed stare begged me to lie. Begged me to tell her it wasn't true. "Keira?"

Ice ran down my spine, the hair at the back of my neck standing upright. I tried to form the words, to tell her it was a mistake, to justify what I'd done. What my grief made me do. But they died on my tongue faster than snowflakes in summer, just as intangible. My shoulder ached, the nightmares of Lochlan's drowned, swollen face swimming back to the surface of my mind, just as visceral as Reina's cooling corpse right in front of me.

I was a monster. A cursed *Melthith* long before the Dark God's spot ate away at me. I'd always been an agent of his darkness, murdering and massacring for him, saving him from dirtying his hands. How many had I alone sent to his keep? How many had died in my wake?

Lochlan. Aidan. Weylin. Donnall. Finna. Baby Owen. Reina. Others whose name I never bothered to learn as I stabbed and drowned them.

The world tilted, Reagan's tiny form blurring against the backdrop of all the atrocities I'd committed. "Reagan, it wasn't…I—"

Her brown eyes narrowed and hardened like clay, like the final piece of kindling added to my well-earned pyre. "I *trusted* you."

She looked away, shutting the door between us for good.

I felt the moment the darkness won. Felt it crawl up my arm and into my heart, finally strangling the last piece I'd held onto for so long. Whatever primordial, ancient light I'd wielded flickered out like it no longer belonged to me. Like it too was disgusted by me, monstrous and wicked as I was.

There was no going back. No redemption.

And yet, I'd never felt so light. Like the glassy surface of the spring, my choice was suddenly clear.

There was no small victory, no salvation. Not for me, anyway. But I could trade my wicked, black soul for Reagan's without any hesitation, nothing left to tie me to the world of the light and the living.

I looked to the one person I needed most, to the cousin who carried me on his back when we were little. To the Captain who would carry my crew home after.

Griffin's eyes were bloodshot as they met mine, his rage and pain clear as mine. His hatred and readiness were my mirror. My brother didn't need words to understand my signal, the silent command carrying through the thread that tied us together as kin. *Take care of them.*

The Swordsinger did not protest. He nodded once. *Do it for Finna and Owen.*

"Let her go, Connor." My voice sounded as empty and weightless as I felt. I raised my hands, finally free of the shackles I'd earned the day my father died. "I surrender."

"Keira, no!" Ronan's plea threatened to break me. But Connor beamed, smug and righteous.

"Take her."

As the two guards moved to grab me, the frenzy unleashed again. It was like I was watching it from afar, floating above it like in a dream, as my crew did exactly as planned. Griffin followed the order like I knew he would, picking his swords up, hacking down three guards who surrounded him. Saeth finished them off with a dagger she pulled from her bust. Rhett and Tarran were yelling something, their fists connecting with faces, while Ellian howled behind them. The sirens, all shifting in unison, attacked, talons at the ready. Vian ran to me—*no, to Reagan*—swift as a shadow, the Soul Wind to the rescue. Victory roared in my chest as he twisted Reagan from Connor's embrace, slicing his own palm on the blade as he swirled like a tornado.

It was the only distraction I needed. It was quick, the cool metal singing as I pressed it to my skin, like calling to like as the curses met. I tucked it in my coat, so fast the guards didn't see it before I jumped in front of Vian and Reagan, as they grabbed my arms, dragging me toward Connor's hungry stare. Reagan crashed onto the wood, yelping as her hands and knees scraped hard, but she'd heal. She'd live.

Connor's gaze was laced with fury as he pointed the blade beneath my chin. But it was a mere inconvenience. I already won.

"No, don't you touch her!" Ronan bellowed as he tore through guard after guard to get to me, sapphire eyes ablaze. A god of destruction himself, rotten and wicked. And mine. "Keira! Keira, no…remember what Finna said!"

I allowed myself one last long look at him, tuning out the clatter and the chaos. I had never deserved him. Gold hair like sunshine, a smile that could make you feel just as warm and loved. Eyes bluer than the sea, a wit just as impetuous and deadly. The crooked slant of his nose, the gentle roughness of his hands, the determined set of his chin….

Rotten and wicked and perfect.

No one would ever deserve him. And yet he loved me, had shared his world with me, had let me pretend like I was good enough to stay by his side.

Later, I would mourn the life we might have lived together. There was no time now. If I lingered any longer, my will would shatter easier than glass.

"Ronan Francis Mathonwy, loving you was my single good deed, and I will love you until the world stops turning." I held back my tears, offering a smile I hoped conveyed the fathomless depth of my love for him. Maybe in a different world, in a different life, it would've been enough. "I'll wait for you in the Otherworld."

I heard him screaming, but I blocked it out, tearing my eyes away before I could change my mind, before I lost the strength to do what came next.

The guard that held my left arm might have expected me to reach for Connor, for the dagger. He didn't think to stop me from reaching the silver pistol in my coat pocket.

I fired it straight into Connor's heart, my debt to the Dark God finally paid.

Shock and surprise as red stained his dark tunic. It bloomed like a rose, the fairest one I'd ever seen. Black eyes met mine, rage simmering in their depths. Defiance. Cockroaches didn't die easily. Not without company.

As he fell to his knees, his dagger slid across my neck.

My path was set by a small dagger and a slit throat. My fate would be sealed by it, too.

"No! Keira!" My husband cried as he sprinted to me, but I was already a world away. I gasped for air, pain searing through my mark and across my throat, burning and dizzying. The guards dropped me as my legs gave out, but I didn't feel my body as I hit the deck. All I could feel was the hot liquid pooling in my gullet, choking and gagging me as the pain blackened my vision. My hands flew to my throat, hot blood—*my blood*— coating them in gore.

I heard my name, over and over again, sung from the voices of my loved ones. Rhett's pained baritone. Tarran's tight tenor. Saeth's shrill soprano. Music that warmed the final part of my soul that was mine. Music to die by.

Connor and I stared at each other as we both bled out, the world around us darkening as the tethers holding our souls to their bodily cages frayed and snapped.

"I'm not afraid of death. My master will welcome me with open arms," he coughed, clutching his chest, grinning with crimson teeth. "But you used the gun. Your soul is his now. Let's go home, Mrs. Mathonwy."

In one last defiant gesture, he grabbed my hand.

The music stopped.

A cloud of blackness swallowed us both whole as he dragged us to the Dark God's throne room.

42

Gifts and Gods

RONAN

It was dawn by the time my crew came for me. Nef's yellow eye had just peeked above the horizon, bathing the gory aftermath in garish, judgmental gold. The guards all collapsed when Connor died, mere dolls, unseeing and motionless without the enchantment that animated them. Ellian and Tarran had taken the task of dumping their bodies into the harbor, not bothering to say any mourning prayers. I hadn't left my spot, the pitch-black mark among the many red that painted the *Ddraig's* deck, like an inkblot on a piece of parchment. Knees to my chest, the cold brass compass resting heavy against my skin, I simply waited.

And waited. As midnight bled into dawn once more.

Like if I waited long enough, she'd come back, just as suddenly as she disappeared, in a flash of light and heat. Or perhaps I'd find her again on some sunny Ir'desian afternoon. Perhaps she'd walk through the markets like she walked out of a storybook, moonlight sparkling in her eyes.

"Ronan, they're gone," Griffin said by way of greeting, voice tight and hoarse from the tears he'd shed with the rest of the crew.

He looked haggard, the pyres he built waiting to be burned, the physical manifestation of our collective grief.

Two pyres.

One, robed in purple, lavender, foxglove, and baby's breath covering every visible inch. When the sirens had volunteered to gather Finna's body, Vala spent the entire night weaving the flowers together, working until her fingers bled. The other was decorated in every white silk we'd managed to keep aboard from Ir'de, accompanied by pink and red rose petals all the way from the Manor. The sirens returned with full baskets of the fragrant flowers, a piece of Reina's castle to send with her to the Otherworld.

Two pyres. Two funerals fit for queens, and for the little prince one carried.

One pyre was missing. We didn't have a body to burn.

"No, she's not gone." My voice was distant, unrecognizable.

Creatures like Keira Branwen-Mathonwy did not just wink out of existence, consumed by a cloud of smoke and disappeared forever. No, she was still alive somewhere. Still breathing. Still fighting.

"Ronan." My name was pitying on Ellian's tongue. The *blaidd* rested a hand on my shoulder, his fur replaced with a simple white mourning coat. "It's time to light the pyres. Please. Sitting here won't bring her back."

Two pyres, not three. Only two deaths I would mourn today. *I'll wait for you in the Otherworld.*

Ellian was right. Sitting and waiting in front of a lifeless mark would do nothing for my wife. I'd lost her once before, and worse, I lost myself to the waiting. I'd whined and drank and sulked; then I ran, avoiding the guilt and grief like I'd been hired to. I would not make the same mistake twice.

This time, it would be different. This time, I'd follow her through the dark and cold. All the way to Otherworld, if that's what it took.

I stood, the compass warm to the touch, a lifeline to my lost wife. Its face stared up at me, like Cedric Branwen himself was watching, the careful inscription daring me to believe.

All that are lost shall be found.

Perhaps whatever magic Captain Cedric bestowed on this trinket could lead me to her.

"We are going after her," I announced to the sea of sullen faces and sagged shoulders that made up my crew of mourners. "We say our prayers, then we set sail."

The crew stared back blankly, as if I insulted them by spitting on their graves.

Not theirs. Keira's.

"To where?" Saeth scoffed, her eyes red and puffy. Raw tears sprang to her eyes, her lip trembling as she fought to keep them from falling. "She's gone, Ronan. We have no idea how to track her. They're all rutting *gone*."

I floundered for an answer, but a quiet voice behind me beat me to it. "She's with Arawn."

My head swiveled to where Nelle stood next to the pyres, lightning-hot anger bubbling up within me at the very whisper of the Dark God's name. I held the compass tighter, letting it turn me to the same hard metal. "No, she's not dead. She's just lost. She doesn't *feel* dead."

"Because she's not." Nelle delicately placed rose petals on Reina's pyre, one gentle queen's homage to another. But when her gaze met mine, there was no softness. Only violet gemstone, hard and impenetrable, sharp enough to cut yourself on. "She *can't* die."

Not dead. Alive.

Alive and waiting. Alive and maybe hurting. Alive and scared.

"What does that mean, hmm?" Griffin crossed his arms, dwarfing her as he stood in her face. "Why would you say something like that. Do you see the state he's in?"

Nelle opened her mouth to protest, but Siobhan stepped between them, baring her teeth. "That slimeball weasel of a creature who took her could never *dream* of killing Keira," she snarled, voice sure and straight as the staff she carried. I was surprised at the respect and reverence that coated my wife's name on her tongue. "Only a god can kill a god."

Some still say the gods walk among us.

My heart dropped down my throat to my toes. I gaped at her, the words taking a moment to register. Brilliant, glorious hope filled my lungs as I breathed in, the realization like water after a drought. The beast in my heart stirred, called by its master.

"What?" Saeth perked up, tears drying, the same foolish hope blossoming in her eyes. "Keira's gift? I thought the mark—"

Nelle shook her head. "Not a gift…her power. It has always been hers. She is her own source."

"*Duweni,*" Vian hummed from a shadow, his form bleeding into it. "It means *godsborn*. She is a goddess, just as her mother before her. *Ariannad.*"

The name rattled through me like windchimes, melodious and alluring, and I realized I knew the story. Danura, the light-bringer herself, had told it once on the island, her magic enchanting me as she wove her web.

Ariannad. Goddess of the silver wheel. The guide to all who were lost, the master of fate herself.

Keira had always been more. I had worshipped her as divine from the moment I first saw her, standing on the deck of her father's ship, raven hair carried by the wind, wild grin carved into her face. She had stared down the sea like it was hers to tame, a girl of eight ready to hold it all in her arms.

I imagined that same unbridled girl trapped in the Dark God's clutches, and feral rage pooled in my gut once more.

I was not the teller of this story. I was merely an actor, a pawn in the goddess of life's cruel, wicked game. But I would play my part, and I would save my wife even if it killed me.

"Where would Arawn keep her?" My voice was low, the dragon in my gut roaring and flapping its mighty wings.

"The only place that's safe. Right by his side," Nelle said simply, confirming my fear. "The Otherworld."

I'll wait for you in the Otherworld.

My wife's last words were not a goodbye. They were a request.

Come find me. Save me.

The path started to clear before me, the puzzle pieces falling into place. Connor's treachery, Locasta's tyranny...Arawn wanted her. He wanted her badly enough to destroy the whole Deyrnas for her. I shuddered as I thought what he might do to her now that she was his.

No, not his. No one's. She belonged entirely to herself. No amount of darkness could ever extinguish her riotous light.

And I would fight the Dark God himself to see my wife shine again.

"No!" Laureli burst forth from below deck, falling over her long green skirt. Her knees hit the ground, and she hung her head in her hands, a creature of death bowing before the sobs took over. "Oh, *Serenhi's* breath, no!"

"What's wrong?" Nelle rushed to her, kneeling next to her, rubbing her back. "What did you see?"

"We have to get her, we have to go now!" Laureli dragged her hands from her face, expression distraught despite the soft warmth of Nelle's calming power. She crawled toward me, body convulsing as her eyes turned pure white again, the next vision wracking through her. "No, we have to get them *both*."

Another stone fell in my gut, heavy enough to drag me all the way to the sunken god's keep. "Both?"

"No, no no no," Laureli muttered, sniffling, savage tears raining onto the wood. "Ronan, I'm so sorry—"

"What did you see?" I knelt before her, panic surging, the dragon roaring and raging, desperate to break free.

"The ritual, the Branwen curse...he's going to use her for it. Soul of the innocent...your daughter." Laureli spat the words onto the deck, the ice in her eyes echoing the frozen parts of my heart. "Keira is pregnant."

END BOOK TWO

Sister of the Stars

☙ Pronunciation Guide ☙

Adolli ⤳ (ah-dOH-lEE)

Annwyn ⤳ (ahn-wEEn)

Arawn ⤳ (ah-RAH-wihn)

Ariannad ⤳ (ah-REE-AH-nihd)

Awelymor ⤳ (ah-wEHl-EE-mawr)

Bachtref ⤳ (bAHk-trehf)

Blaidd ⤳ (blAY-iht)

Carthu ⤳ (kAWR-thOOH)

Ceffyl Dwr ⤳ (kEHf-eel dweer)

Clogwynn ⤳ (klAWg-ween)

Ddraig ⤳ (trAY-ihg)

Deyrnas ⤳ (dAY-er- nahs)

Dubryn ⤳ (dOOH-breen)

Duweni ⤳ (dOOH-wehn-ee)

Dynaur ⤳ (dEE-nawhr)

Faoladh ⤳ (fohl-AHd-uh)

Hiraeth ⤳ (hih-RAYth)

Hud ⤳ (hOOHd)

Ir'de ⤳ (EEr-uh-day)

Lechyd Da ⤳ (lEHtch-ee-dAH)

Lyr ⤳ (lEEr)

Madyn ⤳ (mAH-dEEn)

Melthith ⤳ (mEHl-thEEth)

Neid ⤳ (nEE-ihd).

Orwellin ⤳ (awr-wEHl-ihn)

Porthladd ⤳ (pAWrth-laht)

Pysgodd ⤳ (pEEs-gawt)

Rydha ⤳ (rEEd-hah)

Sarffymor ⤳ (sahr-FEE-mawr)

Serenhi ⤳ (seh-rehn-hEE)

Tan ⤳ (tAHn)

Tyawell ⤳ (tEE-ah-wehl)

Tysor ⤳ (tEE-sawr)

Wynnaid ⤳ (wEE-nAY-ihd)

ACKNOWLEDGEMENTS

This is always the hardest page to write. Not because I'm not grateful, but the opposite: I am so overwhelmed with sheer gratitude, I could fill an entire book with thank you notes. Much like Keira, I live and breathe for my crew, without whom this would be impossible.

To Renee, my editor and dear friend; thank you for believing in me and this book, even when I didn't. For reminding me my worth is not measured by my work, but for also inspiring me to make my work the best it can be. I'm honored to chase after stars with you.

To Cassidy, my critique partner and angst queen; thank you for every moment of laughter, lamentation, and advice. For the TikToks that made me want to keep writing through the hardest parts of this, and for the tweaks that changed the fate of this story for the better. There is no one I'd rather have a hot cup of readers' tears with.

To Dani, my critique partner and soul sister; thank you for your healing presence in my life. For explaining how torches work, and for lighting my heart with your praise and friendship. Much like the characters you inspire, I would be nowhere without your gentle pushes and expert diagnosis.

To Katie M, my developmental editor; thank you for your enthusiasm and encouragement. For the zoom calls that helped me re-chart the course when I lost the way, and for the memes and messages that reminded me why I write.

To Camilla, my proofreader; thank you for polishing this mess into something presentable, and for your friendship. I'm so glad I got to finally work with you in a professional setting.

To Fran, my incredible cover designer: Once again, you worked your magic, and I am so in awe of your talent and professionalism. Thank you for making book two just as stunning as her older sister.

To my beta team, Maddie, Cass, Chiara, Katie M., Katie C., Sania, Z, Ashley, Jen, Chelsea, Sydney, Sara, Lauren, Celia, Jess, and Kat; thank you for the incredible feedback and help. This round of editing shaped the story the most, and I am bewildered by your dedication and creativity. Thank you all for working so efficiently and for the honesty, enthusiasm, and candor that truly gave this story its voice.

To my street team: your enthusiasm and creativity is unmatched! Marketing is a daunting task for an introvert like me, but you all made the experience both enjoyable and efficient!

To my insta tribe: there are too many of you to name, but I am forever in debt to you all. The love for Daughter of the Deep has truly helped me survive the chaos that was 2020, and the continued excitement and genuine support is a force of nature. I'm so proud to be an indie author thanks to all of you.

To my sisters, Jenn and Jess; for inspiring so much of this tale. For the plethora of childhood memories that make me nostalgic and fuel my creativity. For being my built-in best friends.

To my parents; thank you for fostering my daydreams and celebrating my weirdness. I'm proud of the person I am because of you both.

To Armand, my best friend and the love of my life; I'm honored to share my small victories with you. Thank you for letting me live out my own love story, and for being the best thing to ever happen to me. You are my home.

To the Daughter of the Deep fans; thank you for the art, the videos, the cosplays, the posts, and the incorrect quotes that make me smile on my hardest days. For loving my characters and helping me fall in love with storytelling all over again.

And finally, to you, dear reader: thank you for coming back for more and reading until the end. This book challenged me and changed me, and I hope it changed something for you, too. Thank you for your time, your indulgence, and your imagination. I hope you'll sail with me in the third book.

ABOUT THE AUTHOR

Growing up on the east coast in small-town New Jersey, Lina spent her early days playing pretend and making up stories for her friends and family. Little did they know, that pastime would soon turn into a lifelong passion for storytelling in all of its forms. While she's a marriage and family therapist by profession, she's a writer at heart. When she's not scribbling ideas about fictional worlds into the margins of her notebooks, Lina spends her time reading anything she can get her hands on, driving her fiancé crazy with her wild daydreams, and snuggling her adorable pups.

9 781734 826548